Poolbeg Press and the Radisson SAS Hotel & Spa

Offer **YOU** ar a

luxurious **tw**

Radisson SAS Hotel & Spa, Galway.

The perfect break for those requiring total rejuvenation, relaxing and luxury!

This amazing prize consists of the fabulous **Level 5 "Drift Away" Spa Break** which includes two nights accommodation for two people sharing in one of the luxurious Level 5 executive rooms at the Radisson SAS Hotel & Spa, Galway. At Spirit One Spa, each guest shall enjoy a Mini Facial, Cleopatra Bath, Therapeutic Swedish Full Body Massage and unlimited use of the Thermal Suite and Leisure facilities.

To win this fantastic prize all you have to do is answer this question:

What is the name of Lisa's new baby?

Answer: _____

Name: _____

Contact number: _____

Address: _____

Email: _____

Send this page in an envelope to: *More to Life* competition, Poolbeg Press, 123 Grange Hill, Baldoyle, Dublin 13.

Also by Sharon Mulrooney

Daddy's Girl
Matthew, meet Matthew

More to Life

More to Life

Sharon Mulrooney

POOLBEG

Published 2006
by Poolbeg Press Ltd
123 Grange Hill, Baldoyle
Dublin 13, Ireland
E-mail: poolbeg@poolbeg.com

© Sharon Mulrooney 2006

13579108642

A catalogue record for this book is available from the British Library.

ISBN 1-84223-195-2

Typeset by Patricia Hope in Palatino 10/13.5
Printed by Litografia Rosés S.A. Spain

www.poolbeg.com

About the author

Sharon Mulrooney was born and educated in Galway, and moved to London in 1987, where she has had a successful career in Human Resources, and more recently, in writing. This is her third book to be published. Sharon is married to Colin, and has two children, Conor and Aoife.

Acknowledgements

Thanks to Izi who has shared the journey to forty which inspired this book, in more ways than one! Thanks to all the people who have passed the big four zero hurdle and told me the journey is worse than the arrival.

Thanks to my family — the one I live with every day, and the one that spawned me –, for their unquestioning support in my pursuit of literary dreams!

As ever, thanks you to Ros Edwards, my agent, for her enthusiasm and encouragement, and to Paula Campbell at Poolbeg for her confident direction.

This book is dedicated to Mom and Dad —
always encouraging and supportive,
and often inspirational.

Chapter One

The rain lashed against the windscreen of the rented car, and Alison leaned forward, struggling to see the next twist that the strangely cambered road might take. On both sides of the smooth black tarmacadam there was a deep boggy ditch, and for miles she could see nothing but bleak stony hillocks, broken occasionally by a stunted windblown tree. She couldn't go any faster than twenty miles an hour, terrified that she would end up in the ditch, with no prospect of rescue. She thought she could see the outline of a road sign looming out of the twilight, and she slowed down even more as she approached, seeking the reassurance that she was at least heading in the right direction. It was a huge sign, worthy of a motorway, but as she got closer she realised it was useless: a declaration that the road she was travelling on from Knock Airport had been funded by the EU – the only thing missing from the circle of blue stars was the head of the Madonna. Very apt considering

Knock's status as a shrine blessed by suᴄʰ
She sighed in exasperation and turned on ᴛʜ
beams of her headlights, hoping to penetrate the sheets
of water. The knot in the back of her neck had hardened
to a new intensity, and she felt as though a marble was
being ground into the upper vertebrae of her spine. The
west of Ireland was certainly living up to its reputation
for lousy weather. The only consolation was that she
wouldn't feel guilty for staying inside for the whole
weekend rather than sampling the miles and miles of
hiking routes boasted by the health spa.

Just as she was beginning to wonder if she would
find the place before nightfall, she spotted a sign and
had to suddenly swing to the right. She turned into the
carpark and was greeted by the welcoming vision of a
long low building flanked by trees, huddled against the
side of a darkening hill. It reminded her bizarrely of a
fairy-tale dwelling, the squat wooden doorway looking
as if it led to another land.

There was a roaring fire burning in a huge fireplace
in the lobby and Alison could almost see the steam
rising off her clothes while she stood in front of it
waiting for her turn to check in. The scent of sandalwood
and lavender seemed to emanate from the curved
wooden walls. A woman who looked about ten years
younger than her was there before her, filling in forms
and asking loads of questions. She was wearing a classic
tailored trouser suit that accentuated her petite frame
but looked a bit formal to Alison. Her hair was bouncy
and shiny, but could have done with a highlight or
two. The woman waved her hands around, explaining

something, and Alison's eye was drawn to the huge sparkling diamond on her left hand. A white gold wedding ring nestled comfortably next to it. Alison rubbed her own bare finger with the tip of her thumb.

The woman turned away from the desk and picked up her bags, just as a porter was about to take them. "I'll be grand, thanks a million," she smiled at him and whisked off towards the staircase.

Alison went to the desk, and the receptionist greeted her.

"You found your way from the airport, no problem, then?" she asked, and Alison was impressed. She hadn't even opened her mouth yet. "You're our last arrival for today, so I'm assuming you're Mrs Harding from London?"

"Ms." Alison smiled at the woman, who was in her fifties with big glasses that dominated her face but highlighted soft blue eyes surrounded by the gentle wrinkles of experience.

"Sorry, Ms Harding. Now, have you got any questions, from the information we sent you?"

"Shall I book all my treatments now?" Alison had the list ready, so her personal timetable could be drawn up.

"Not at all, you can just potter around and do things at your leisure," said the receptionist, handing her a key on a fob. "Now, there's your key. You'll find your robe and slippers hanging on the back of the door, and if you want fresh towels at any time, just stick the used ones in the bath or on the floor, and the room attendant will replace them for you."

"Do you have guided tours?"

"Not really. It's not that big. If you get lost, just ask somebody. There's loads of us around the place. There's two wings." She gestured to her left. "That way for the treatment rooms, the pool and the dance studio. That way for the restaurant, and beyond it, the bedrooms. There's local maps for walks, over there on that stand, and we can organise pony trekking, surfing or fishing for you if you wish."

The porter picked up her bags, and Alison followed him, bemused by the lack of a timetable with tiny windows of time between classes, treatments and organised activities. In her room, a bowl of fresh fruit and a bottle of sparkling mineral water stood on a tiny table in front of the window. Outside there was complete darkness of an intensity she had only seen before in the middle of the desert on an overnight camel trip in Egypt. The porter nodded and disappeared without any hovering to show her the obvious features of the simple room. As soon as the door closed behind him, she stripped off her wet clothes, shivering suddenly. The robe was a pale lemon colour and smelled of fabric conditioner when she sank her face into the thick sleeve. The slippers were embroidered with an emblem that looked like a gorse flower on a thorny branch. She quickly towelled her hair, but it was almost dry already. The bathroom was sparkling clean, with only a tiny damp patch in the ceiling. It seemed small, until she realised that there was no bath, only a shower. It wouldn't be the same as a long hot bath, so she decided to find the sauna. She wanted to be warmed through to her bones, and then maybe have a Jacuzzi or a swim.

She grabbed an apple from the bowl and sank her teeth into it as she padded down the corridor, wondering if January was a busy time for the spa. Alison usually tried to avoid these places at this time of year, because they were full of well-intentioned people fulfilling their New Year's Resolutions, being all virtuous about eating the right things and getting loads of exercise, and making her feel guilty. She was lucky enough to be able to indulge herself on a health farm several times a year and as far as she was concerned it was a place to unwind and pamper herself, not a place of torture and self-denial. Her best friend Lisa had been here in the autumn and told Alison it was perfect, so here she was, savouring the prospect of relaxing completely even if it rained all weekend.

She passed through the reception area, a blast of cold air coming in with a guy carrying a pile of logs for the fire.

"Éamonn, would you ever close it behind you?" the receptionist scolded him.

He nodded. "Sorry, I didn't have a free hand."

"Lazy man's load," muttered the receptionist. She smiled and winked at Alison, and then turned to the fax machine, which had started beeping.

Alison followed the smell of chlorine, assuming that the sauna and Jacuzzi would be found in that general direction. There were a few people in the water, languidly stroking up and down the length of the pool. No fervent Olympic aspirants here, Alison thought with a sigh of relief. Another shiver assaulted her just as she noticed the wooden door of the sauna, and she stepped gratefully inside.

She loved the breath-catching moment that followed,

5

the heat searing her lungs, and the astringent pine scalding her nostrils. The coals had just been wet and were still sizzling. The other occupant was lying on the top level of shelving. Alison leant against the wooden wall, wrapped in her towel, and nodded towards her – only then realising the woman had her eyes closed.

Alison wondered would it be shocking if she went naked? She couldn't relax in the bulkiness of the towel, and liked to lie full length on the hot boards, eyes closed, transported by the smell and the heat to faraway desert places. She compromised, draping the towel across her midriff, and lay for a while, imagining the cells warming up inside her body, banishing the accumulating germ cells waiting to attack her after her soaking in the rain.

Then she was distracted. The love handles which had mysteriously appeared a few years ago, and would not be budged from her middle by the occasional binge diet or week of frantic exercise had somehow grown more pronounced since the last stocktake. She ran her hands down her sides, and across her tummy. Distinctly flabby was the only description that came to mind.

She sat up, the towel falling on the floor, and said out loud before she could stop herself, "This is not good enough."

"Sorry?" the other woman said dreamily, obviously coming back from her own faraway places.

"Oh, I'm terribly sorry," Alison said, stricken with guilt. She hated it when other people did that kind of thing. "I didn't mean to say it out loud. Sorry to disturb you. You looked very tranquil, lying there."

6

The other woman smiled. "I was just wondering what time it was, and if I could summon up the energy to find a phone to ring home and see how they're getting on."

"I think it's about 9.30," said Alison, wondering where home was for the woman, and who was in it, maybe missing her.

"Thanks. I think I'll have a dip and then I'll call it a day." She yawned, showing tiny white teeth, almost the size that Alison remembered putting under her pillow for the Tooth Fairy. The woman put her hand to her mouth, petite fingers stretched politely. The diamond glimmered.

"I'm Alison." She was determined to avoid a situation where they kept bumping into each other over the weekend, politely chatting but not knowing each other's name until it got too embarrassing to ask.

"Sophie Hanrahan. Hello, how are you," said the woman, reaching down from the higher shelf, and shaking her hand in a strangely formal way.

"Fine, thank you. This seems like a nice place."

"I haven't explored much, to be honest with you. I only got here a little while ago, and I came straight in for a sauna. I love them and I don't often get the chance these days."

"Me, too. I got soaked in the rain, so I came in here to warm up."

"That was a typical west of Ireland downpour, if you were never in one before," said Sophie, obviously noticing the English accent. "Mind you, it's forecast to rain for the next three days, so you'll soon be very familiar with it."

7

"Are you here for the weekend too?" Alison found herself warming to this tiny chatty woman.

Sophie was standing up, wrapping the towel around her. It seemed like it might even go around her twice.

"The two sisters packed me off, so they did. My first weekend away since the kids were born. Well, for years, to tell you the truth." She slipped her feet into a pair of flip-flops by the door, and pushed it open. "I might see you later?"

"Sure," Alison nodded, and lay back down. But she couldn't settle this time. The images she tried to conjure up of rolling golden sand-dunes were well and truly overridden by her own less than attractive undulations. She would have to do something about that before it got out of hand. Alison wasn't ready to settle into plump middle-age. It would be nice to throw on some more water and sizzle away the fat. She would walk out like a deliciously grilled sausage, leaving it all behind.

She stood up and decided to follow Sophie. She should really swim a few lengths first, to get a few endorphins flying around, and then enjoy the bubbles. But there was plenty of time for all that, she told herself, walking along the poolside towards the noisy cascade of water falling from a raised platform where the Jacuzzi was hidden in a simulated jungle of ferns.

Sophie grinned at her like a water nymph, the hair that had been pinned up in the sauna falling in damp curls around her heart-shaped face. "Couldn't take the heat?"

Alison smiled back. "No, and anyway one shouldn't stay longer than fifteen minutes in there. It's not good for you."

"And we have to be good to ourselves here – isn't that the whole point?" said Sophie, stretching up to put her hands behind her head in a parody of relaxation.

Alison admired the pearly nails as her toes floated to the surface. They weren't even polished.

"Were they all right, at home?" Alison eased herself into the bubbles, and positioned herself in between two pummelling streams of water.

"They're grand. They love Aunty Ger to bits. She spoils them rotten, so she does. Easily known she hasn't kids of her own."

"How old did you say they were?" Alison was wondering if there was a daddy on the scene, but didn't dare to ask.

"Five and four. Michelle, the older one, is due to start school in September."

"Both girls ?"

"No, one of each, thank God, so we didn't have to go again. They'd exhaust you. And it took us a while, so I wouldn't be fit for any more. I'm getting old."

Alison was astonished. She looked about thirty-two. And from what Alison had seen, she didn't have stretch marks or any other evidence of having had two children. Alison laughed, and Sophie looked at her.

"Seriously. I'm going to be forty this year."

"No way. *I'm* going to be forty this year and you look –"

"When?"

"The twelfth of December."

"I'm December too – the fifteenth," said Sophie. "Isn't it a sad state of affairs, when we're talking about

9

it nearly a year in advance? We're wishing our lives away, as my mother would say."

"That's true. We're only just thirty-nine." Alison was oddly cheered by this thought. A lot could happen in a year. Although babies did take nine months to make. And she didn't even have all the ingredients.

"Well, I don't think you look forty either, if it's any consolation. So, where are you from?" asked Sophie, thinking that Alison's hair looked a bit brassy, and she could probably do with wearing it a bit longer, to make her look more feminine. It was cut in quite a severe but well-sculpted bob. She had too many highlights for the lovely peachy tone of her skin. She should make more of those unusually large dark grey eyes, too.

"London," said Alison, wriggling and wondering if the power of the underwater jets could propel the love handles into retreat.

"That was a long way to come for a bit of pampering. Would you not have a health farm a bit nearer to you? I'm only down the road, in Galway. About an hour's drive away. Did you come through Galway?"

"No, I flew into Knock," Alison replied.

"What did you think of it? Weird, isn't it, an international airport out in the middle of nowhere. And all on account of a priest's determination to raise the investment funds."

"I thought it was great, although there was a distinct possibility at one point that we were going to be diverted to Shannon – is that far away?"

"Yes. You'd still be on the road now, if they had landed you there, but it happens a lot. Knock is

10

shrouded in fog half the time, because it's in a dip in the mountains. So you were lucky enough."

"The mountains are beautiful. I was glad it wasn't dark for that bit of the journey though, because I'm not used to driving without streetlights."

"I'd say the Maam mountains would be a bit of a change for you, all right," said Sophie. "I lived in London for a few years after I graduated. I loved every minute of it. But then I met Liam and we came back here, because he wanted to set up his own business, and it was a good time to be coming back, in the early nineties."

"Where did you live in London?" asked Alison, wondering if Sophie talked at this rate all the time. It could be quite exhausting.

"In Wimbledon," said Sophie. "I was working for a publishing company, doing translations mainly, and I could work from home a lot, so I didn't have to do much commuting. That bit of London life wasn't much fun, I will admit."

"I'm lucky because I live only about a mile from work. I can even walk along the river for part of the way." Alison was the envy of her friends, because she had invested in a house long before any of them were thinking of settling down, and now some of them were finding it difficult to move up the property ladder.

"I believe they've done a lot of development since we were over there. New bridges and everything. I heard the South Bank has really been perked up."

Sophie sounded a bit wistful, Alison thought. "It's great. There's a lot of investment going into riverside property. Particularly residential property. We have a lot of clients who are hoping to make a killing on it."

Alison sounded like she was a high flier in the city with a nanny and a housekeeper and a gardener, Sophie thought. She was worried she wouldn't know what to talk to her about. She felt the familiar twinge of inadequacy that struck her when Liam took her to Lions' Club dinners and one of the other wives tried to engage her in a debate about the war in Iraq or the US presidential campaign. "Mmmn," was her only reply.

Alison wondered why she had suddenly clammed up. Had she said something to offend her? "Is Galway a nice place to bring up children?" she said, in as friendly a tone as she could muster.

Sophie nodded. "It's great. Liam grew up here himself and he said if we ever came back it would be the only place he'd come to. I'm from Mayo, a little village not far from where Knock is."

"How did you two meet?"

"At the Irish club in Eaton Square, would you believe. I was going out with an English fella for a long time, but he didn't want to have a family so we parted company, and it was then I thought of going to the Irish club to see if I would meet anyone."

"Was it love at first sight?"

"It was definitely lust at first sight!" Sophie laughed, remembering the glance Liam had given her across the bar. He had black hair, sallow skin, big long eyelashes and dark eyebrows. She always thought of him as her own personal Pierce Brosnan, but a bit stockier. "I couldn't believe for ages that he wasn't already married off. He was twenty-eight but he looked older, and I was twenty-nine. God, that seems ages ago."

Alison nodded. "It *was* ages ago. I feel like a completely different person now, to the person I was at twenty-nine. I had so much energy then. I was doing a Master's, working really long hours and shagging my way through the night. I'm lucky if I get through the week without nodding off in a meeting, these days."

Sophie laughed. "Were you a bit of a wild one, then?"

"I was, in my twenties. I was such a goodie-goodie growing up, and all the way through University. I think I had my wild phase a bit late in life."

Sophie saw the tight lines of bravery in her smile. "And have you settled down now?"

"If you call being at home most nights, with the occasional foray out to galleries or for a civilised dinner with friends being settled down, then yes, most definitely." Alison tried not to sound resentful. "Work seems to have taken over somehow, without me realising."

"Me, too. 'Home-maker' they call us, now, don't they? I don't even get the occasional civilised dinner party," said Sophie ruefully. "Macaroni cheese with the kids at six o'clock, a glass of wine when they're in bed, and maybe I might see Liam before I crawl off to bed myself."

"Does he work very long hours?"

"Well, when you're running your own business, and especially in the building trade, when it's all about wining and dining the clients to get the next big job, your work and your social life kind of blur together." Sophie raised her eyebrows. "Put it this way. A lot of business gets done in the golf club, at the nineteenth hole."

Alison held up her wrinkled fingertip to Sophie. "Do you fancy a drink in the bar to replace some of the liquids we've lost?"

"Great idea."

Sophie stood up without the whale-like wave effect that Alison knew she would cause, so she waited until Sophie had climbed out before sliding herself along the underwater bench and easing herself upright on the steps.

They met in the bar half an hour later, and Alison was delighted she hadn't opted for the more ascetic health farm that had been the other one on her shortlist. A drink was most definitely in order. They sat in the curve of a bay window, and Alison was struck again by the blackness of the night, contrasted with the pale luminescence of moths flickering against the glass.

Sophie shivered. "Do you mind if I sit with my back to the window? I have a bit of a thing about moths."

"They are rather large," said Alison, feeling like she was on safari. She didn't mind the fat furry bodies hurling themselves softly towards the light, the beige and brown wings fanning out, folding, and finally flying away.

"I'll never forget one night as a child," Sophie went on, "when we had just got a new tent for the summer holidays, and we decided to try it out in the garden, to practise. I was about six and my sisters would have been ten and twelve, so they were going to mind me. We had torches and a midnight snack hidden under our pillows, and our new sleeping bags, and there was great excitement after Mammy came out to kiss us goodnight. We left the tent flap open, and the three of us were lying there, counting the stars. Denise put her torch on to see how far it would reach up into the darkness, and this huge moth, bigger than those fellas out there, came flying down out of the night like a torpedo, and he hit my face. I screamed, and I sat up and brushed him off, but then he was inside the tent, and the girls put on their lights to find him and of course that confused him so he kept blundering into us. I was hysterical by the time we got him out, and I ran up the path, crying. The back door was locked, and I felt trapped outside, convinced he was still flapping in my hair. I was banging my head and dancing up and down like Rumpelstiltskin when my mother finally came downstairs to let me in. She was mortified that she had locked the door automatically when she went inside, and it took her half an hour to calm me down. I refused to go camping that summer, and I ended up going to stay at my cousin's in Ballinrobe for the two weeks, while the others went off for a holiday with the French cousins."

"That is the kind of phobia I can totally understand." Alison raised her glass to Sophie. "So you won't be taking your kids on camping holidays then?"

"If Liam ever took two weeks off, I'd drag us to one of those *hot* all-inclusive places where your kids go into a crèche and you do water sports or have nice romantic lunches beside the pool," said Sophie laughing. "But chance would be a fine thing!"

"I've got a phobia about spiders," said Alison, "but it's a bit more prosaic than yours. I can't let the water out of the bath until I'm ready to leave the bathroom, in case a spider comes up the drainpipe."

"And instantly runs up the side of the bath, abseils over the edge onto the floor and makes a beeline for your feet!"

"Yes, and what he might do after that doesn't bear thinking about," said Alison.

The barman looked across and saw them wrapped in the cosiness of laughter, the dark sky stretching behind them not punctuated by a single star. He flicked the light switch, not wanting to disturb them, but eager to tidy up and get home to his wife, who was expecting a baby to drop any minute now.

Chapter Two

The morning brought some unexpected sunshine. Alison opened her curtains and stopped, staring. As far as she could see, there stretched a sea of gently waving grasses, a savanna of subtle golden shades. The sky was a high pale dome, coldly embracing the purple jagged hills in the distance. She opened the window to a chill silence, broken suddenly by a lark, a diminutive brown arrow shooting straight up, his tiny voice shrill on the air. She inhaled deeply, and felt the cold purity piercing through her. There was an unfamiliar tang of something she savoured like the bouquet of a Premier Cru, rolling it experimentally on her tongue. She shivered, still in her T-shirt, and closed the window. Perhaps she should have a walk straight after breakfast, if rain was forecast for later.

She found herself unusually hungry. One of her unhealthy habits was not to eat breakfast during the week, preferring to spend a bit longer on blow-drying her hair or touching up her nails. There never seemed to be time for food first thing in the day, and she liked to be in the office by 7.30. No stomach could cope with food much before nine, in her opinion. She would have a tall skinny latte and a Danish pastry at about eleven, and that would take her through to lunch. This morning, she found herself salivating on the way downstairs, as the smell of grilling bacon wafted up to greet her. What kind of a health farm was this, anyway, she wondered.

Sophie was already sitting at a table for two, and she gestured to Alison to join her.

"Sure you don't mind?" asked Alison.

"Not at all. It's nice to have the company. I ordered a bacon and mushroom sandwich. I know I shouldn't but . . ."

"Why ever not?" said Alison. "At least you don't have a stone in weight to lose. I'm the one who should be dieting. The smell of your bacon has set me off and I am happy to humbly follow in your footsteps. I'll start the diet when I get back home."

Sophie laughed. She didn't know why she had worried about what to talk about. Alison was great. "What are you planning for the day?" she asked. She had quickly checked the morning schedule and decided not to join the Legs, Bums and Tums toning session or the Aqua Splash exercise class. She was tempted to be a bit self-indulgent and have a pedicure, but her feet were very ticklish and she didn't want to make a show of herself.

"I think I'll have a walk," said Alison, "and then do

indoor things if it rains later. The air is incredible here. I took a big lungful of it through the window and it was like being on straight oxygen."

Sophie nodded. Visitors often said the Connemara air was different. "Did you sleep well, so?" Her French relations were always amazed at how well they slept when they came to visit.

"Like a log. You?"

"No. I couldn't believe it. I kept waking up thinking I could hear one of the kids crying 'Mammy, Mammy' and I'd shoot out of bed and then remember where I was, standing like an eejit in the middle of the room. I rang home first thing this morning, but they both slept through the night. Ger was delighted because I warned her she wouldn't get a wink of sleep with them. Typical!"

Sophie's extravagant hand-waving to accompany the story made Alison smile. She had mentioned French cousins and she looked a bit French herself, with her fine-boned gamine face, and her Gallic gestures. Alison wondered if the auburn glints in her hair were natural. The diamond was glittering brightly this morning, probably bleached by the chlorine in the pool.

"Would you be interested in a walk?"

"Grand, it would be good to get a bit of fresh air," said Sophie, biting into her juicy bacon sandwich with great relish. "I went for the wholemeal toast, at least," she said, delicately licking crumbs from the corner of her lip with the tip of her tongue. She reminded Alison of a kitten grooming itself after a feast of cream.

Alison didn't enjoy her sandwich quite as much. The

19

organic bacon tasted delicious, but somehow by the time she had finished, she could only think about the extra exercise she would have to do to burn off the calories. She savoured a cup of dark roasted coffee, making Sophie envious. She couldn't take coffee before mid-morning, preferring a strong cup of tea to kick-start her day.

Clouds were scudding across the sky as they left through wide French windows at the back of the building, which opened almost directly onto the bog as far as they could judge. Alison was highly amused as they floundered around on the soggy ground, trying to find any evidence of the alleged walking route mapped out in the lobby.

"It looks much nicer from a distance," she said to Sophie. "Maybe we should follow the lane down to the beach instead?"

"I must admit I'd prefer to be looking at the scenery from the firmness of the road, than to be walking along with my head down worrying about falling into a bog-hole," said Sophie gratefully. "We want to get value out of the walk, not be getting cross with the silly maps."

Alison agreed, and they set off down the lane, which in daylight boasted a very fine crown of thick grass and dandelions down the middle that she hadn't noticed the night before. The cold air bit their cheeks, but there was hardly any wind, and after a few minutes of walking, she could feel the warmth in her face.

"I've never seen a landscape quite like this," she said, "even in Scotland, which is the closest I can think of."

Sophie laughed, remembering a pen-pal from her teenage years. "I wrote to a Swiss boy called Eric for years, as a kid. He came over to visit once, and do you know what he spent the whole time doing?"

"What?"

"Staring at the sky, and taking photographs of sunsets and sunrises, and everything in between. He said he had never seen so much sky in his life. I was very taken with that idea, but it was only when I went to London that I realised what he meant."

"It's like that in Northumbria, near Newcastle, as well," said Alison. "You get the feeling they must have had when they thought the world was flat – the sky stretches so far into the distance you imagine there would be room for every place in the world to fit under it."

Another lark ascended, and even Sophie was silenced but only temporarily. "They can go up a thousand feet, did you know that?" she said, as they craned their necks to follow its trajectory.

"No, really?"

The song ritual finished, and the tiny bird plummeted back to the ground, disappearing in the waving sea of grass.

"They were my favourite bird when I was small," said Sophie "I loved the idea that such a tiny thing could have the power to shoot up in the air like a rocket, and then the control to come back down to land on the same spot."

"I've always liked albatrosses."

"Have you ever seen one?"

"Yes, and it confirmed everything I thought about them. Clumsy on the ground and so powerful and elegant in the air. As a child, I had a wooden albatross hanging in my room, with wings that flapped. At night, my Dad would pull the string to flap the wings and tell me stories about Albie carrying me far away across the ocean to meet his family. I even had a special harness to make sure I didn't fall into the Atlantic. Until one day I told Dad that I was big enough to hold on by myself. It was only years later I realised that was the last Albie story he told me."

"Your poor old dad!"

"What do you mean?" Alison had only recently explored her relationship with her father as part of her counselling, and she had found herself pouring out feelings of remoteness and rejection which had totally surprised her.

"You broke through the magic spell he had created around Albie. Maybe he felt silly telling you those stories after that."

"Now I'm supposed to feel guilty for growing up!" Alison retorted, tears springing up suddenly.

They stopped walking.

"Sorry, Alison, I didn't mean to intrude. I'm a bit of a nightmare for the amateur psychology I'm afraid." Sophie touched Alison's arm.

Alison was staring over the low bramble hedge, her eyes roaming unfocussed over the rough tussocks of grass. Red bullet-like blackberries were frozen in their unripeness. She turned back to Sophie. "I don't have a great relationship with my parents, to be honest, and

I'm trying to figure it all out. I'm always surprised at how close to the surface it is – I get upset whenever I talk about it."

Sophie saw her five-year-old daughter Michelle, wounded by an unfair scolding. She hugged Alison, their bulky coats a cushion from too much intimacy.

The fresh smell of Sophie's shampoo cut through the peaty wisps of smoke from a cottage at the end of the lane. Alison stood back after a moment. She wiped her nose on her glove, and then looked at it with revulsion as if it was attached to someone else. "Sorry."

"Not to worry. Let's go down to the rocks and see if we can see any seals before the weather closes in." Sophie just stopped herself from reaching out maternally to take Alison's hand as she led the way down the lane.

They covered two miles in easy silence, broken only by the occasional shriek of a seagull cruising on the thermals above the hills, carried away like an echo, almost as soon as it reached them. Shades of grey had crept into the paleness of the sky. A light breeze came up, carrying with it a hint of ozone, seaweed and endless miles of Atlantic emptiness beyond. Over the brow of the slight rise ahead of them, the surface of the lane deteriorated into a random stoniness. They picked their way across smooth sea-swept stones to a narrow strip of wet sand. Sophie pointed to a series of large rocks, the tops emerging from the water twenty metres away.

"Sometimes you can find seals over there. You have to really stare, they're so well camouflaged."

Alison's eyes ranged across the black slippery rocks. No dark movement betrayed any occupants besides a lone, gulping cormorant.

Their feet were sinking into the sand.

"Come on, you'll get salt stains on your lovely boots." Sophie took her hand and guided her to firmer ground. "We came here once when the kids were tiny, and a seal slid into the water and actually swam towards us. I'll never forget it. He had these big luminous brown eyes and beautiful silver whiskers. He just stared at us for ages, with the top of his head glistening in the sunlight. He was close enough for us to see the little droplets of water on the tips of his whiskers."

"Did the children like him?"

"They were entranced. That was part of the magic I think. They didn't move, or make a sound the whole time he was there. And then he ducked under the water and swam back to his friends on the rocks."

Alison shivered in the sharpening wind.

"Do you want to head back now, or get a bit more fresh air?" Sophie asked.

"Shall we go back? I can feel last night's chill coming back. I need to steam it out!"

"Good idea. I saw they were serving seared tuna and baby new potatoes for lunch."

"It's not fair! Obviously, you can eat as much as you want and still be slim!" said Alison, smiling so Sophie wouldn't take offence.

"You try running around and tidying up after two kids all day long, and you wouldn't need to be thinking about it either!" Sophie realised that might be a sore point as soon as the words were out. "No, seriously, the reason I'm eating so much here is that I'm not the one cooking. It tastes so much better. Come on, I'll race you to the top of the hill!"

Sophie suddenly broke into a run, and Alison followed before she thought about it. The last time she had run anywhere was to catch a plane when she had been waiting at the wrong gate. The disembodied and disapproving voice of the announcer had declared her name to the whole .world as the person delaying the departure of the flight. She had run from gate 14 to gate 41 in six minutes, her wheeled laptop case careening wildly behind her. It had taken the first half an hour of the flight to Barcelona for her heart rate to return to normal. She watched as Sophie sprinted up the slope, her hair flying out from under her woolly hat. Alison panted up to join her at the top, and they laughed, bending down to lean on their knees while they caught their breath.

"Thanks, Sophie," said Alison, unable to express anything more.

"Not at all," was the uncharacteristically brief reply.

They retraced their steps and Alison was curious about a tarpaulin-covered mound outside a picture-postcard thatched cottage at the end of the lane.

"What on earth is that?"

"Turf for the fire. Do you see over there?" Sophie pointed east, the direction from which Alison had arrived the previous night. There were raised brown scars stretching for several hundred metres, in between pools of dark water and islands of fibrous grasses.

"That's where they cut it, from the banks, and they stack it in little piles to dry, and then bring it home." She gestured to the miniature brown mountain leaning against the white wall of the house. "That will keep them going for the winter."

"Is that the lovely peaty, smoky smell I keep getting?" Alison sniffed the air like a hunting dog.

"I can't stand it, myself. When you're sitting in a room with a turf fire all evening, it gets into your hair and your clothes and everything. It seems to get into the pores of your skin." Sophie's grimace made her look even more elfin.

"What's wrong with it?" Alison quite liked the oddness of it.

"I used to get teased about it at school. Most of the town kids had central heating. They used to take a rise out of the ones who came in on the school bus, because they said we smelt of the bog."

"You poor things," said Alison, picturing three petite sisters in their school uniforms with their hair neatly tied up, teased by the townies.

"As if that wasn't bad enough, my father would sometimes cook our dinner for us, and he'd always use garlic of course, being French. None of the other kids knew what it was, except that it was used to chase away vampires, and it got all mixed up in their minds, so they used to call us the Frenchie vampires."

"Good grief!" said Alison. "You had a lot to contend with, didn't you?" Her memories of school days were full of giggling conversations, walking home slowly with her friends and doing homework in each other's houses. She had always been popular because she was bright, and willing to help when the others got stuck.

"We even used to bring back chocolate from our summer holidays, to make them like us, and we'd be very popular for a few days, and then it kind of wore off – the novelty I mean, and we'd be back to normal again."

"Are you bilingual then?"

"Yes, my dad always talks to us in French, and even Mammy sometimes. She went to Paris as an au pair, which was very unusual in those days and she met my dad. He came home with her on a visit and fell in love with Ireland. They decided to settle down here instead of in France."

"So you could have been a little French girl, if they had made a different decision," said Alison.

"Parisienne, too. I used to dream about that as a child. Especially when Ger and Denise moved up to secondary school and I was on my own on the school bus for a while. I had a little fantasy world where I was a beautiful French girl, abandoned by her parents in a strange land, trying to find her way home."

"Where are your parents now – still in Mayo?"

"No, they retired to France, a few years ago. It's great for holidays, but I miss having Mammy around for advice, and it would be nice for the kids to know them better. It's a bit artificial when you only see them for a couple of weeks a year."

"Do your kids speak French?"

"No. I'm disgusted with myself. I had every intention of talking to them in French as soon as they were born but I was so overwhelmed with lack of sleep and just surviving each day that I didn't get into the habit of it. Now, of course, because they realise how much it means to me, they refuse to play along."

"It's probably not too late."

"I know. But now it just feels like something else on the long list of things I should be doing, or would like to be doing, or am not doing right." Sophie sniffed and dashed away a tear.

Alison realised she had touched a sore point. "Well, in one short morning we've both managed to be in tears," she said, handing Sophie a clean tissue to replace the tattered one she had pulled from her coat pocket and was trying to blow her nose with.

"Must be part of the relaxation therapy," Sophie said.

They linked arms and went on, separating only to go through the front door, welcoming the warmth of the fire.

They were just in time for lunch, and Alison forced herself not to eat too much, although the potatoes literally melted in her mouth and she could have eaten the meal all over again.

"I'm going to have a manicure and pedicure this afternoon, to let the food settle down first, and then a swim and a steam," said Sophie, determined to have some physical evidence of her weekend of escape.

She would have a facial in the morning, and a whole body exfoliation. Liam hadn't been very interested in her lately, and she knew some of it was her own fault. Sex was very low on her list of priorities, with sleep way up there at the top. Liam had no idea how tiring her days were, but her biggest fear was of turning into a nagging, dissatisfied wife, so she didn't tell him. Liam hadn't changed at all. He was still the funny, gorgeous dynamic man she had met and married, not believing her luck. But running a business, employing people, borrowing loads of money to finance jobs and juggling the books seemed to have taken its toll. Sometimes she wondered if Michelle and Oisín were anything more than an irritant to him, keeping everyone awake at night, preventing Sophie from joining him at the golf club in the evenings, and causing a drop in the standard of shirt-ironing. He did see them at their worst, though, just before bed when Oisín was hyper, bouncing off every available surface, and Michelle was sleepy and cross. Most Saturdays and Sundays, he played a round of golf, insisting it was the only time he had to himself, to clear his head, and get some fresh air. Sophie could see his point, but he couldn't understand when she said that she didn't get time to herself.

"The kids are in playgroup three mornings a week," he would retort, as if something useful could be done in the one and a half hours she had between dropping them off and then turning around to go back and collect them. She was lucky if she got the weekly shopping done, and a couple of loads of laundry. Then there was the parish work. But Liam had no sympathy for complaints about that. It was her choice to spend her time organising the choir and getting involved in fund-raising for the new church roof. He was right, in a way. But it was her only tentative grip on the sanity of adult interaction. Without that reference point, she might forget how to hold a conversation using words of more than one syllable.

But here she was, in a place where she could spend two whole days just doing exactly as she wanted, reading, swimming, sitting staring into space, and she found herself spending every minute with Alison, a woman she was unlikely to meet ever again. Alison's loneliness surrounded her like an aura, seeping gently out through the polish of her conversation, yearning for a tuneful echo. Sophie was drawn to it, as she always was to neediness. She had forced herself to articulate her own choices for the afternoon first. If Alison chose to join her, Sophie would take it as a sign. She would listen, and empathise, and give her encouragement, if that was what Alison needed.

Because that was what Sophie did best. Ger and Denise were older than her, but they always came to her when things weren't going well. Ger had gone through a painful separation the year before, and had spent several months sleeping in Sophie and Liam's spare room while the sale of her house had gone through. Now she had enough money to buy a flat for herself, but she wouldn't take the step. At the age of forty-four, Ger thought she should be settled – married with two or three kids at school. No amount of counselling could convince her that she had to let go of that dream and find another one. Sophie bore the brunt of Ger's frustration because her life represented almost exactly what Ger felt was missing in her own. But she was fantastic with the kids, and Sophie had welcomed the extra pair of hands for a few months.

Denise had paid for this weekend to give Sophie a break and Ger had offered to have the children. They could see the signs. Sophie was at the end of her tether.

Just before Christmas, she had completely lost her temper with Liam, for the first time ever since they had got married. He had come home late, after promising to be back in time for her to get to the Carol Service. He had strolled in at 6.30, smelling of alcohol and radiating seasonal bonhomie. Sophie had her coat on, the kids bathed early and already in their pyjamas, his dinner warm in the oven. She went to peck him on the cheek as she passed him in the hall, determined not to show how angry she was. She didn't have time for a row, and anyway it was easier to let it pass. If she was very quick, she would arrive during the mince-pie interval and be there for the second half of the carol recital. Her solo wasn't until the end.

Liam looked at her in surprise. "Where are you off to, darling?" He looked at the kids, standing expectantly on the stairs, looking forward to stories with Daddy. He always told them really funny ones and he did faces and tickles to go with them. "I came home 'specially, to see the kids before . . ."

"The Carol Service was at six. It was in your diary to be home by quarter to. I don't ask much . . ."

Sophie was biting off the end of every word, and just stopped herself from going into full nag mode.

Liam's face fell temporarily, as he realised his mistake, but never a man to admit to one, he made the fatal error of bluffing it. "That's *next* week, darling – I do have it in my diary, for *next* Wednesday."

31

"Next Wednesday is Stephen's Day, Liam. Wednesday the 26th of December. It will be all over by then. And if you get in a few rounds of golf and a few nineteenth holes, you might even let the next week or so pass you by in a haze of drink and you won't have to think about it for another year."

She slammed the door, and stood outside on the step panting with rage and regret for not saying goodnight to the children. What if something happened in the night? Or she crashed the car and died and they never saw her again? She couldn't do it to them.

She put the key in the lock and turned it, to find Liam and the children frozen in a tableau in the hall. She briskly took the bottom three stairs, kissed the children, holding their little faces in her hands and said gently, "Night night, gorgeous," to Michelle, and "Night, Oisín, sleep well!"

She turned and flounced back out the front door, and Liam hadn't moved a muscle.

He had apparently finally got them to sleep by 9.30, and she had dealt with the grumpy fallout for the whole of the next day, negotiating every change of clothes, every meal, every wellie-wearing occasion. She had finally snapped just after tea, when Michelle had the most almighty tantrum about lumps in her yoghurt, and Sophie had frightened herself with the power of the anger that made her storm out and slam the dining-room door. The figures in the crib on the hall table had toppled onto the carpet, and she had cried as she put Baby Jesus back in his manger.

Denise had called shortly afterwards and, as Oisín

was engrossed in a video, Sophie was able to talk for
ten minutes uninterrupted. Denise and her husband Pat
had decided not to have kids, and lived the high life
with skiing holidays, city breaks and fancy meals out.
She couldn't understand why Sophie 'put up with' so
much. Whenever she told Sophie to stand up for herself
and stop being a skivvy, Sophie found herself
defending the idyllic life she had, not having to rush
out to work every morning, juggling child care and
cramming all the household jobs into the weekend.
Then her sister would sigh, and Sophie would sigh, and
they sometimes even laughed about it. "Go and bake a
chocolate cake and make yourself feel better," Denise
would urge, and Sophie would find herself engrossed
in lovingly grating dark crumbling mounds of 90%
cacao for the recipe that had seduced her husband in
the first place.

"Mind if I join you this afternoon?" Alison asked,
laying down her knife and fork. She noticed the tiniest
flicker of something in Sophie's face and kicked herself.
She was hogging Sophie's weekend. Did she somehow
think that some miraculous process of osmosis would
give her Sophie's figure and energy and optimism if
they spent the weekend together? They would say
goodbye on Monday morning and go their separate
ways, holding on to nice memories of good conversations
and some kind of shared wavelength. They would lose
touch after a few emails or phone calls, their real lives
taking over from this frozen moment of overlap. It
always happened that way, so why did she even
embark on the path in the first place? Her friend Lisa

said she had a fundamental need for constant reassurance that she was a nice person, and was far too worried about what other people thought. Her counsellor called it "being comfortable in your own skin", this indefinable nirvana she was supposed to be seeking. But then her counsellor was a size eight natural blonde with a PhD and a string of publications to her name, declaring her as someone to be impressed by.

"Well, maybe I'll see you later," she added hastily, standing up and pushing her chair back, narrowly missing knocking over the empty water carafe standing on a mahogany side table behind her.

"Join, me, do," said Sophie smiling. "I've never had a pedicure before and I'm afraid I'll make a show of myself with laughing. Will you come with me?"

The treatment rooms were arranged around a central atrium, furnished with chintz-cushioned bamboo sofas and tall jungle ferns. The tinkling fountain was barely audible above the strains of instrumental music Alison recognised from the bland classical compilation phase of her teenage music collection. Sophie was called first, so Alison sat for a few minutes, leaning back on the cushion and staring at the sky through the glass ceiling. She could feel eddies of cool air around her bare ankles as the heat from the radiator on the wall did battle with an insidious draught from under the door to the outside world. Specks of damp unconvincing rain flickered on the glass above her head. She closed her eyes and found herself drifting off into the grey white clouds.

Her mother was talking to her, interrogating her

about her latest boyfriend, each answer deeming him more or less suitable. His father had an acceptable position as a senior civil servant, but his mother worked too, and therefore was slightly suspect. He lived in the right part of town, but for some reason he went to the wrong school, and her mother couldn't understand how that had come about.

"But surely they could have sent him to St Bede's?" she had asked Alison, who had merely shrugged.

She knew that Craig's parents were a bit left-wing, and she vaguely remembered them making some reference to parents needing to make a statement, to support the local school. It was a matter of complete indifference to her, but she was resigned to sitting at the kitchen table, poking at the remains of her dinner until her mother had completed her investigations. At sixteen, she had learned that to endure this part of the process with good grace made everything easier later on. Her mother would call his mother, and they would agree that it was OK for the youngsters to go to the cinema and for him to walk her home. Alison's friends couldn't believe she told her mother every time she liked a boy. But she didn't like hiding things, or lying to her mother, and if she wanted to see him, that was the only alternative.

Her mother would like Craig, because he was polite, and clean, and well spoken. He was also very intelligent, which was Alison's main concern. She couldn't stand it when guys were barely articulate. Most of them expected to spend the evening snogging and groping, or watching a movie but unable to express any opinions afterwards about the acting or the direction, or even the plot. Craig was different. They talked about really important things, and he even wrote song lyrics. Alison would have called them poems, because there wasn't any music, but he was a guy, so he called them song lyrics, and that was fine with her. He wasn't the best-looking guy around, but he was funny and interesting, and that was much more important. She tuned back into her mother's voice.

"I suppose I should call his mother. What did you say her name was?"

Alison gave her all the details, scraped her plate and put it in the dishwasher. She kissed her mother on the cheek, and went upstairs to do her homework.

Still drifting in the clouds, Alison remembered sitting cross-legged on her bed, with Craig sitting on the beanbag on the floor, Dire Straits guitar riffs rippling around the room while they composed a song about truth and fallacy. She could only remember odd phrases: *"Ashes of truths that only cost philosophers an hour or two – I had striven, now I knew, the pulse of truth was beating near."* Not quite right. They always used to rhyme, as she recalled. Craig said it sounded much better. Her mother would have had no fears of illicit activities if she had been listening at the door, which she probably was. They were struggling with assonance rather than underwear. Of course they had snogged, but almost because one ought to. They were soul mates. Until Craig went off with tall, lanky Fiona from the Upper Sixth. He still wanted to be Alison's best friend, but she couldn't cope with that, and they had drifted apart. Craig had gone on to be an author, and whenever Alison saw one of his books, she read the biography wondering when she would find him *"living in Devon with his talented wife, two point four children and a Labrador"*. But by book three, he was still *"living in London, lecturing and writing on a wide range of subjects"*.

"Mrs Harding?"

"Ms. It's Ms," Alison said, opening her eyes to the disembodied voice hovering above her.

"Sorry, Ms Harding. Would you like to come through for your manicure now?" The slightly yellow tinge of the manicurist's make-up didn't suit her complexion, and Alison wondered if these professional beauty people ever gave each other advice. She followed the white-uniformed hour-glass figure into a salon with huge windows framing a stunning lake view, the dark water choppy in the rising wind.

Sophie waved from her semi-prone position, grinning while the pedicurist manipulated her toes gently. "This is the life!" she declared. "I am a convert to pedicures, that's for sure!" Several other women smiled at Sophie, nodding their agreement.

Alison sat at the manicurist's table, stretching her fingers out on the fluffy white hand-towel, and enjoying the gentle massage. The lake looked navy blue, reflecting the new darkness that had crept into the clouds. A group of five were pony-trekking in the distance, and she wondered if there would be a downpour before they got back. A rumble of thunder confirmed her suspicion that it was imminent.

"It's not looking too nice out there at the moment,"

ventured the beautician, not sure if this English lady was the conversational type. You got all sorts in here. Some people wouldn't shut up from one end of the day to the other, as if relaxing had uncorked some verbal outpouring that had to be spent. Others wanted complete silence, and wouldn't open their mouth to you, even to say hello. This woman seemed more like that – reserved, she would say.

"I think it looks amazing. I've never been anywhere quite so beautiful," said Alison, looking at the dark-haired twenty-three-year-old, and wondering if she were a local.

"I meant the weather, really."

"I know, but the weather is all part of the beauty, isn't it?"

That was a bit too profound for someone who had been soaked cycling to work this afternoon from the staff accommodation four miles away. "I suppose so," she said.

"Do you live nearby?" Alison was suddenly struck with curiosity as to where all the people working here could live, when there wasn't a town for twelve miles.

"Just over the brow of that hill there," she waved the emery board to the west. "There's a house with ten of us living in it."

"Wow, that must be fun!" said Alison, remembering her college days and thinking none of them looked older than their mid-twenties. They probably had parties every night.

"It is most of the time but it can get a bit lonely too, out here, if you haven't a car to get to town."

"I suppose so. Not too many nightclubs around!" Alison wondered if she sounded like a middle-aged lady trying to be amusing. They lapsed into silence, and she tuned in to Sophie's conversation with another mother.

"That's the problem, isn't it? You just get used to one stage, and you have your routine, and everything is going smoothly, when suddenly they grow into another phase and you're off again, trying to figure out what the best way is to deal with it."

The other woman was nodding fiercely. "How old is your boy? Because I believe the boys between four and six can have a testosterone surge, and it can sometimes have an impact on their behaviour. I was reading it in a book and I'm dreading it. My little fella is only two and we're having enough trouble as it is!"

Sophie laughed. "It's gas, isn't it? I bet our mothers never read a book in their lives about how to raise children, except of course Doctor Spock. He'd be down off the shelf, for every little blemish or bit of constipation."

"I know, and we turned out all right, didn't we?" The other woman opened her robe and gestured to her cellulite-ridden thighs. "Too much fat in the diet, though. Sure we lived off fish-fingers and chips and those Findus pancakes as kids. And bread and butter or stewed apple and custard to fill us up if we were still hungry after that. There was none of this 'five portions of fruit and veg a day' business then."

Alison looked out. Successive sheets of fine rain drifted on the breeze like muslin curtains being drawn across the lake. The pony-trekkers were nowhere to be seen. She shivered and the manicurist looked up.

"Are you all right? Is there a draught?" She was looking around to see if a window had been left open.

"No, I'm fine, thanks. I was just imagining being out in the rain. I got soaked last night and I keep getting the shivers." Alison smiled at her. This girl probably thought nothing of the rain, especially if she came from around here. It seemed like it was an occupational hazard.

"You should have a sauna or something to warm yourself up. Or a hot whiskey," the girl whispered mischievously.

Alison grinned at her. "Now you're talking," she said. She liked the colour of the nail-polish the manicurist had suggested. Somehow her usual 'vermilion rose' seemed crass in this place of mellow light and shade. Oyster-shell pink was much more fitting.

Manicure over, she thanked the girl and didn't disturb Sophie, who seemed to have drifted off, lying stretched out on her chair. The sauna beckoned, but Alison decided this time she would earn it, and swam a vigorous twenty lengths of the deserted pool. After only a few minutes in the sauna, she felt a rare calmness descending over her. The habitual knot at the back of her neck was just the memory of an ache. Lisa was right. She needed to create space for herself and be happy in it, instead of always trying to fill every minute of her life with other people. Even when Alison was alone in her house, she would have a radio on in one room, and the stereo in another.

She lay on the warm, scented boards, and focussed on the sizzling sound of the hot coals in the corner, and the occasional creaking of expanding wood. She practised the exercise her counsellor had taught her, imagining a maze of concentric circles. In the middle she was to place the problem that was worrying her, and imagine it as a round silver ball. Like a reversal of the children's game, the trick was to roll the ball further and further from the centre, until it fell out of the widest circle and disappeared. She imagined Dave, the twenty-eight-year-old new kid on the block at work, and gleefully rolled him up into a ball. He was so cocky that he was incapable of listening to advice. Alison had had to pick up the pieces with two long-term clients after his clumsy attempts to rush through a quick deal. The idea of slowly building a successful relationship didn't occur to him. The monthly commission number on his payslip was his furthest horizon. She kicked the ball so hard it ricocheted and bounced over the outer hedge of the maze and into the abyss. Lying there, Alison experienced a strange mixture of satisfaction and exhaustion, as if she really had booted him over the edge.

A blast of cooler air crossed her stomach and she grabbed the towel and sat up. Sophie slid onto the bench above her. "Are you cooked yet?" she asked, thinking Alison looked a bit flushed.

"I fell asleep, I think." Alison felt dehydrated and disoriented. "I'm going to have a shower and get changed. Fancy a drink in about an hour?"

Sophie nodded. "Perfect. I'll tell you the gossip I just

heard." Her eyes were closed but a tiny grin played around her mouth.

Alison enjoyed sitting at the bar, perched on a stool and watching everyone else go by as she waited for Sophie to join her. She guessed that most of the people here were about the same age as her, and they seemed to be in various states of fitness and flabbiness, which was reassuring. She had been to other health farms, frequented by the fabulously wealthy, and felt distinctly inadequate, but here she felt happy and relaxed.

Sophie came bounding down the stairs and joined her. "Feeling good?" she asked, reaching to pour herself a glass of iced water.

"Feeling great," said Alison. "I think I want to stay here forever and escape from reality! Did you enjoy the pedicure then? Let's have a look."

Sophie held up her left foot and wiggled it around to show off the polish. "That was the ultimate in decadence," she said. "It wasn't as ticklish as I thought." She sipped her water. "You know that girl who did your nails?"

Alison nodded.

Sophie lowered her voice to a conspiratorial whisper. "Apparently she's sleeping with the barman, whose wife is expecting a baby any minute. None of the other girls are talking to her."

"I'm not surprised," said Alison, wondering what it would be like to live in a place like this, your every movement known to everyone. "They probably all fancy him, though, don't you think? Maybe they're just jealous."

"Maybe," said Sophie. "He is quite fanciable."

"Excuse me, you're a married lady – don't you start," said Alison, winking at her. "Any eligible men floating around here are mine, so hands off!"

"It's not the kind of place you'll pick one up, unfortunately," said Sophie, looking around. "Ninety per cent women, and the men who are here are very much attached." She nodded towards the couple who seemed not to be able to keep their hands off each other. Alison and Sophie had had a laugh about them in the bar the night before, speculating about what time of the day they would appear out of the bedroom, if at all. The man was at least twenty-five years older than the woman, and spent the whole time groping her. She didn't seem to mind, and flashed her smile and flung her hair around in a very juvenile flirtation.

"I wonder if it's a boss taking his assistant away for a dirty weekend," Sophie had said. Alison had looked at her, wondering if she was serious.

"What?" Sophie had asked, her eyes wide in surprise at Alison's expression.

Alison had shaken her head. It was too difficult to unpack all the things she was thinking. It seemed that Sophie's world still had some clear delineations, and in Alison's all the lines were blurred in a muddle of political correctness and insecurity.

"Was that a really old-fashioned thing to say?" Sophie asked, without a hint of mockery. Alison smiled. "One of my best friends, Lisa, married a man the same age as her father. True love, if ever you saw it."

Sophie blushed. "Sorry, I didn't mean to . . ."

"Don't worry about me," said Alison, grinning. "I

was just thinking, though, that it's never too late to meet the right person, is it?"

"That's true. I wonder if the opposite is true too?"

"What do you mean?"

"That you could meet the right person too soon?"

"Do you think that's what happened to you with Liam?" Alison asked.

"Sometimes I do. Here I am, nearly forty –"

"Hey, what happened to our rule about living thirty-nine first?" Alison reminded her.

"OK, sorry. Here I am, thirty-nine, with two gorgeous kids, a lovely house, chair of the parish committee, wife of a successful businessman with enough money to go on holiday or buy a new car. Where else is there to go? Have I arrived already?"

"That's a nice problem to have."

"You're right. It's a lovely problem to have, and I feel so guilty when I have those thoughts. And do you know what else happens, if I allow myself to keep thinking like that?"

"You wonder about what disaster is about to strike you?"

"Exactly. In one of those pregnancy self-help books, a real all-American apple-pie one, the woman says that if you have an easy pregnancy, the gods look down and decide you deserve to have a nightmare kid for a few years to make up for it. So you don't get any sleep, or your child has colic or whatever. That's what happened to all of my friends, the ones who had babies at the same time as me – one or the other, an easy pregnancy, or an easy child."

"And which one did you get?"

"I got both. I wasn't sick once, I didn't put on loads of weight, Michelle and Oisín were both sleeping through the night by the time they were six weeks old. Not that they do it now, mind you, but that's different. My biggest fear is that something awful is waiting around the corner."

Alison nodded. "You are very lucky."

"And I count my blessings every day. I have nothing to ask for. I just thank God in my prayers every day for all that I have."

Alison envied her the simplicity of that. "If I still believed in God, which I don't think I do, I wouldn't be short of things to ask Him for."

"What would you ask Him for?" Sophie wondered if she was pushing too far, and added, "This is like a different version of 'What would you do if you won the Lotto?' isn't it?"

Alison took a sip of her drink and looked out at the lowering grey sky.

"A man to love, children, a better relationship with my parents."

Sophie was touched by the naked honesty of Alison's reply. "Not like the Lotto at all, then, really," she said, touching Alison's knee.

"It's really strange, Sophie," said Alison, her eyes coming back into focus. "I have never told anyone that before. Not even my best friend Lisa and I've known her forever, since school."

"She doesn't know that about you?"

"Of course she knows I'm desperate to find a man,

and have kids, but we joke about it. She invites me to dinner parties that she contrives just so she can introduce me to completely unsuitable single men. She has known me for over twenty years, and you should see the men she thinks I would like!" Alison was determined to strike a more jovial note. Poor Sophie would think she had acquired a socially inadequate stalker, at this rate.

"Is it time for a real drink yet? Is the sun gone over the yardarm?" asked Sophie, beckoning the barman.

"No sun, no yardarm, no rules!" said Alison. "Two gin and tonics, please, Éamonn," she said. "Could you charge them to Room 21? Thanks."

"What kind of man do you like then? Top three criteria," said Sophie, holding up three fingers. Then she shook her head. "Would you look at me, as if I was teaching you how to count! I need to get more adult company!"

Alison laughed. "Top three? Well, the first is definitely intelligence. I can't bear a conversation with someone who isn't on the same wavelength as me."

"Good. Next one?"

"I'm not that worried about looks any more. As long as he is taller than me, and a reasonably good dresser, I can cope with that."

"So is that on the list, or not?"

"Not, I suppose."

"Two more wishes from the matchmaker fairy," said Sophie.

"Wants to have a family," said Alison. "I hesitated about that one, because maybe I won't be able to have kids by the time I meet the right man. But just in case, I'll have that one in."

"Very wise," said Sophie. "I know loads of people who don't even ask the question until it's too late. Like your man Andrew, the guy I was telling you about. He was good-looking, earning loads of money and he even loved Ireland. But he never wanted to have kids. He was an only child and he hadn't a great relationship with his parents so he didn't see the point."

"Did you dump him because of that?" Alison asked.

"Yes, and I felt really bad about it, but the biological clock was ticking, and . . ."

"I know the feeling," said Alison. "Did I tell you I went out with an Irish guy once?"

"No, what was his name?"

"Ronan Murray." She rolled her 'r's and Sophie laughed. "An accountant. Sounds dull but he was such a sweetie. He would charm the birds off the trees, and he was so gorgeous I used to get palpitations every time I saw him."

"So what happened there?"

"Same as your guy. He wasn't ready to settle down. Your accent reminds me of him, actually. He was from Ballina. That's in Mayo, isn't it?"

"It is indeed. So what happened to him, then?"

"I had booked a holiday with some girlfriends, and I invited him to come but he couldn't afford it. He was a qualified accountant but he was just doing temp jobs in London, to earn enough to party and have a good time. I even offered to pay but Ronan said he didn't really fancy three weeks touring the Greek Islands with a bunch of women anyway, so I went without him. When I got back, he had left his room in Kensal Rise, and gone with no forwarding address. Even his flatmates didn't know where he was."

"Strange."

"Yes, I was devastated, even though deep down I suspected we wouldn't have stayed together long term. I probably talked too much about having a family, and scared him off. But even after all this time, it feels like unfinished business. I'd love to meet him again, just to close the chapter, really."

"How long did you go out with him?"

"Three years. I turned thirty while I was with him, and although I hated getting older, Ronan had this amazing ability to live for the day, and it rubbed off on me a bit. I was less stressed about work, and we could spend whole weekends just doing nothing. I couldn't do that now. No way. I have to be doing things all the time."

"I'm the same, usually. But look at us here – we've managed to do nothing for most of today."

"To doing nothing!" Alison raised her glass, and they chinked.

"Hang on a minute, there's still one wish left," said Sophie.

"There isn't one word for the next one," said Alison, stirring the lemon around in her gin and tonic. The ice cubes rattled. "I want someone who is gentle and caring, who wants to look after me. Does that sound pathetic?" She looked up at Sophie.

Sophie was surprised. Alison seemed so together, and independent. "Not at all. Like it or not, we are biological beings. We are programmed, by Darwinian theory or otherwise, to find a mate to provide for us, who is genetically strong enough for their offspring to survive. No matter how sophisticated we get, I think that's the bottom line."

"That's a nice way of putting it," said Alison. "Can you imagine a caveman coming home to the cave and stroking his woman's hair, and asking her if she had a good day with the kids?"

"I can't imagine Liam doing it, that's for sure," said Sophie, draining her drink.

"I thought he was the perfect man?" said Alison.

Sophie sighed. "He is, in lots of ways. He fulfils all the caveman criteria – strong, good provider, able to reproduce. I never see him though. I keep the cave warm and dry and I cook lots of caribou recipes and I make diligent use of the hoofs and other leftover bits, but he's never there. Hunting-gathering is his thing, and cave-keeping is mine."

"I read this hilarious article in the *Observer* a couple of weeks ago, where they reproduced sections of a nineteen-fifties cookery book, and it was incredible – the instructions included allowing fifteen minutes to change your dress and tidy your hair and make sure the children were clean and calm before your husband arrived, so that he would have a nice welcome home. One of the quotes was a classic: '*You may feel that you have lots to tell him, but don't forget that the events of his day at work are more important than yours, so allow him to tell you first.*'"

Sophie laughed. "That's ironic. I could have written

that chapter. A little while ago it occurred to me that maybe it was a bit too chaotic for him, to come home to the kids' leftover tea, and toys all over the floor, so I made some new rules, and now I make them tidy everything up by six o'clock and then we have bath time, so that when he comes in, they're sweet-smelling and calm. Still doesn't work. If I see him one night during the week, I'm lucky."

"Is he good with the kids?"

"Great. They love him. He never gives out to them, he just plays games and gives them piggy-backs and crawls around on the floor with them. They would do anything for him."

"That's a good start, then."

"Yes, but what about us? I don't want to slide into companionable middle-age. I'm not ready for that yet."

"I'm not a great one to give you advice on that," said Alison.

Over dinner, Sophie entertained Alison with stories about the kids.

"The other day when we were doing a jigsaw together, Michelle told me that dinosaurs disappeared a long time ago because God got bored with them and got bored with all the plants they liked to eat, so He got rid of them and started again."

Alison laughed and leaned across the table. "My friend's little boy told her that God was everywhere, even in her bottom."

Torrential rain poured down all night, and Alison woke

up and lay on the bed enjoying the angry sound of it drumming on the roof above her head. She imagined the rain sweeping out over the darkness of the Atlantic, its power dissipated as the waves absorbed it, swelling higher. She felt like a medieval explorer, visiting the outermost reaches of the known world to survey it and come back with an account of her findings. It was a beautiful place, untamed and elemental. She had found some peace here, and in Sophie she hoped she had found a new friend. But she was ready to go back to normal life. She wanted the hustle, the adrenalin rush of completing a deal. The storm was oddly comforting because too much peace and quiet unsettled her a bit.

Then she started thinking about what she had told Sophie about her parents. When she got back, she would go and visit them for a weekend. The estate in Hemel Hempstead was so dull, and their daily routines were so fixed now that it took a huge effort of will for her to go and spend any time with them. She could predict now, lying in the bed, how every minute of the weekend would go. If she called them in the morning, her mother would go to Safeway's on Tuesday for pensioners' discounts, and buy a string-tied pot roast for Saturday night, and a large chicken to roast for Sunday lunch. The vegetables would be cauliflower, carrots and peas. Half a fibrous grapefruit with a cherry in the middle for starters. Sherry trifle for dessert. Jersey cream biscuits with a cup of tea afterwards. They would talk about the dysfunctional teenagers living on one side, and the little old lady with the barking dogs on the other side. The council would have written an unsatisfactory letter back about her father's latest complaint – potholes, the library opening hours, the dog-poo in the park. The news headlines were always good for a half-an-hour discussion about how the world was topsy-turvy. A detailed analysis of the weather forecast would dictate the choice of a walk on Sunday afternoon, or a quiet doze with the papers on the sofa. Then Alison would have a quick cup of tea at four and leave, eager to salvage some small sliver of her weekend for herself. Guilt would assail her then, for her inability to rise above the petty frustrations and engage in more meaningful conversation with them. She could have told them some funny stories about clients viewing properties, or even about her friends, and their children. But as soon as she stepped in the front door, all her resolve that this visit would be different would leave her. The patterns of the carpet and the wallpaper in the hall, the smell of cauliflower, the neat row of shoes by the kitchen door oppressed her and she withdrew into the shell she had created for herself as a teenager. She had been allowed to paint her own room when she was fifteen, and had ripped down the flowery wallpaper that had been there since she was six. She had painted it magnolia, and put up framed prints from Athena, of dolphins leaping against a sunset sky, and deserted beaches. She would lie for hours on her bed pretending the frames were windows and that she could just open the door and walk barefoot out onto the sand. Or she would sit at her desk and study, determined to go to the furthest flung university that offered her a place. Now she never set foot in her old bedroom, but she suspected that it would look exactly the same. Her mother probably hoovered and dusted in there on Wednesdays, picking up the Disney snowstorm paperweight and the china dolphin off the mantelpiece to wipe underneath, pulling the dressing-table out to hoover the skirting-board behind. The beige curtains would still hang lifeless, framing the view of the neatly manicured back garden and the flaking back of the rundown house on Wilson Road.

Alison was their only child, and although her visits were a bit begrudging, they were a highlight in her mother's life.

As the storm raged outside, she had an inspiration. To break the pattern, next time she would take them out somewhere, and treat them to a special day. They could go to Waddesdon Manor and have lunch in the café, and then maybe go to see a film. She felt a warm pleasure in the thought, and fell back to sleep while the rain continued to fall.

Sophie lay under the duvet wondering if the children would be frightened by the thunder and lightning. Maybe it wouldn't even have reached as far as Galway. It might just be the ragged edge of an Atlantic storm, broken by the Twelve Pins and dissipated over the hills. She remembered nights cuddled up with her sisters in the huge bed shared by her parents, rolling thunder outside, and sheet lightning brightening the fields. Her mother would pull the curtains back and they would all lie there, watching it like a stage production until gradually their eyelids would droop and sleep would creep over them, the warm scent of their mother and father wafting up from the sheets, familiar and reassuring.

She was ready to go back to normality tomorrow, to have someone shouting through the bathroom door at her, needing a shoe-buckle undone or a plaster stuck on, if she tried to claim three minutes of privacy. She liked to be needed, and the self-indulgence of the weekend had an element of guilt tied up in it. The choir would sing without her in the morning, and she knew that they wouldn't have rehearsed on Friday evening without her there. The chit-chat would have overcome the need to practise the new hymn, so they would stumble through at ten o'clock without her there to smooth the cracks. No harm, she told herself. No one is indispensable, and it isn't the end of the world. She wondered if Ger had cooked for Liam last evening, or if they had had a Chinese takeaway, as Denise had suggested. He probably hadn't even bothered coming home after his golf game. He would seize the opportunity of a guilt-free Saturday night out at the club. Maybe next week she should ask the new girl next door to come and baby-sit, so they could go out for a meal. If she let things drift much further, without taking control, she and Liam would find themselves without a marriage. She would book a table at O'Grady's and surprise him. Usually when he suggested going out, she was too tired. She always suggested cooking a nice meal and having an evening in together, and he always acquiesced. They needed a bit more romance, and it was hard to create that at the kitchen table, no matter how exotic the recipe, or how fancy the wine. She opened the blind and watched the flickering sky until she felt sleep coming, and didn't wake until almost nine o'clock.

Chapter Three

"I love the smell of the air after a storm. It's so clean, isn't it?" said Alison when they took a stroll after breakfast. They just had time to walk around the perimeter of the lake before Sophie's departure.

"It's negative ions or something like that, I think," said Sophie. "Thanks for the chat yesterday evening. I'm going to make more of an effort with Liam, after this weekend. I can't just sit there blaming him for not being around. I have to change something."

"You made me think, too. I'm going to be a nicer daughter."

"I can't believe we didn't even know each other forty-eight hours ago," said Sophie. "Let's keep in touch – maybe you'd like to come to Galway for a weekend sometime?"

"I was going to invite you to London. Do you think you'd be able to wangle another weekend away from the kids, maybe in the spring?"

"That would really be lovely. I'll say yes now, and

work it out later. Denise would take the kids, if Ger has had enough of them this time! Don't I sound terrible, desperate to get away from them at every opportunity? It's not that really – it's the change of scene as much as anything – like the Town Mouse and the Country Mouse – they just needed a taste of the other life to remind them that they preferred their own."

Alison laughed. "This is certainly a change for me. I love it here, but I think it might be a bit *too* quiet for me, if I stayed for much longer."

They strolled around the lake, a gravelled path making it easier than wading through the sodden grass. A heron poised on the other side glided off across the grey choppy water when they got too close.

"There's something almost spiritual about this place," said Alison. "I have never been so relaxed. Not a text, not a message, not a beep from the real world, and I'm only having tiny, occasional withdrawal symptoms!"

Sophie laughed. "You'll have to come back in the autumn. It's really beautiful then, with the colour of the heather and the sky blue rather than grey and the sea calmer."

"Maybe I will," said Alison.

They hugged in the carpark, and Sophie drove off with a wave. Alison watched her little Nissan car rounding the bend and disappearing and she was glad they would meet again. She would show Sophie the best of London. They could firm up a date soon, and she would book a show, and dinner at the Oxo tower. Maybe she'd have a dinner party another night, and have some friends around to meet Sophie.

A cold breeze chased her inside. She joined a yoga class, and was soothed by the gentle movements, and the deep breathing. Only two other women were there, and she wondered if everyone else had gone back to their normal lives already. She sat at the bar for lunch and read the Sunday papers, feeling less self-conscious there than sitting alone at a table.

The drive to the airport was leisurely and this time she was able to appreciate the beauty of the scenery rather than being afraid of getting lost. The low winter afternoon sunlight laid golden tips on the grasses, and she listened to a classical music station on the car radio, enjoying the soft sibilance of the announcer's Cork accent.

Sophie arrived home to a calm orderliness she had not expected. Ger's idea of entertaining the children usually included getting out every toy and game in the house plus paintbrushes, easels and chalks. Sophie was ready to unbegrudgingly tidy it all up, still serene after her weekend of relaxation. But instead she was greeted by two heads down, the children diligently colouring in shapes with crayons. Ger was sitting with a cup of tea, watching over them. They looked up and smiled at her and, for a second, she could see that Michelle was torn. She wanted to finish what she was doing, but she jumped up and ran to Sophie, hugging her fiercely.

"Mammy, we're making a card for you to say welcome home!"

Sophie laughed. "That's lovely, pet. Do you want to

finish it then, while I give my big boy a hug, and talk to Ger?"

She bent over Oisín, and hugged him from behind, not wanting to disturb him when he was so uncharacteristically settled. He smiled at her, and in that moment looked the image of Liam.

She grabbed a mug, sat down and poured a cup of tea from the pot. "So, how did it go?" she asked Ger.

"We had a great time, didn't we, kids?"

"Yes, Auntie Ger," they chorused.

"Did you teach them to say that, or did you bribe them?" asked Sophie. "I presume my lovely husband is out on the golf course?"

"And where else would he be on a fine Sunday afternoon?" said Ger, managing with a huge effort of will not to say everything else she was thinking. She and Denise had had a chat on the phone the previous night, and they were agreed that Liam was treating Sophie like a complete doormat, and she just couldn't see it.

"The least he could do, with you looking after the kids, would be to come home on Saturday night," Denise had said when she called and discovered Ger was there on her own, having cooked herself an omelette for dinner. "Does he think the three of us are interchangeable, and that we were all put on the planet just to serve him?"

Ger recognised the signs. Her own marriage had failed because they hadn't paid any attention to it. She had been promoted several times in her job at the insurance company, and was now running the Galway office. Shane was on the road, only home a few nights a week anyway, and then he'd be out at darts one night, and playing five-a-side football another. They had tried for babies, and maybe kids would have kept them together, but without any glue at all the whole thing had just fallen apart. Sophie had her children, but her husband was never around. She could almost be a single mother.

"Are you going to say something to her, when she comes home?" Denise had asked.

Ger had thought about it. But now wasn't the right time. The whole point of them packing Sophie off to the health spa was for her to relax and to give her some time and space to think it out for herself. If she gave her a piece of her mind now, she would be defeating the purpose. Another time, she decided.

"I think the high life suits you," she said now, as she got up to rinse her mug in the sink. "We'll have to send you off again, somewhere nice."

"Well, now that you mention it," said Sophie, with that look on her face which Ger recognised from childhood. It was the grin she used to persuade her father to do something, like driving her into town on a Saturday afternoon when all he wanted to do was listen to the radio, or giving her extra pocket money when she had spent it all.

"What is it?" Ger asked, unable to resist. She had noticed Michelle using that look over the weekend too. It was kind of spooky how these things get passed on, subconsciously. Michelle had her dad wrapped around her little finger.

"I met a girl called Alison – I mentioned her on the phone to you . . ."

"The woman over from London?"

"Yes, we got on like a house on fire. She fell in love with the place, and I invited her to come to Galway for a weekend. I think she'd like it, but anyway she said why don't I come over to London for a weekend in the spring."

"Why not indeed?" Ger put her hands on her hips.

Sophie laughed. "Seriously, I'd love to see London. It's been ten years since I was there, I was thinking in the car on the way home. None of my friends from college are still there, so isn't it great that I would have a base, without having to stay in a hotel?"

"Very compelling arguments, my dear," Ger said with a French accent, imitating their father, who had always teased them as teenagers when the older girls tried to charm him. Then he would strike a deal for extra chores in exchange for the lift into town, or the extra pocket money.

Sophie thought she was winning.

"Why don't you get Liam to take you, and you could see your friend and have a romantic weekend with him as well." Ger paused, and then she couldn't resist adding, "You need to spend a bit more time together."

"I know. I decided last night I'm getting the girl next door to baby-sit next Saturday and I'm going to surprise him and we'll go out for dinner."

Ger bit her lip. "That's a very good start."

The front door opened then, and the kids went charging out to greet their father.

"I like the way I got a welcome like that," said Sophie, and she couldn't help wondering if getting taken for granted was her role in this family.

Liam came in and kissed her. "Enjoyed yourself? You look well on it, anyway," he said, grinning and swinging Oisín around by the arms at the same time. Oisín's foot knocked a glass off the table and it smashed. Then Liam lifted the children across the room so they wouldn't step on the broken glass in their stockinged feet, and Sophie got the dustpan and brush out, and then the hoover, just to be sure.

"Welcome home, Mammy," said Ger under her breath. "I'll head off, so."

Sophie stood up and hugged her. "Thanks a million, Ger. You're the bestest sister in the whole world."

"Don't let Denise hear you saying that, and she the one who paid for you!" said Ger, giving her sister a kiss on the cheek.

"Hang on a minute. Don't go, I have something for you," said Sophie, running upstairs to her room. In town the previous week, she had seen a beautiful presentation box with a calligraphy set in it and real Chinese inks and she knew that Ger would love it.

"Here, this is a little something to say thanks." She handed it over, and Ger unwrapped it.

"This is gorgeous, thanks!"

Ger waved to Liam through the sitting-room door and shouted goodbye to the kids, who were sitting on their father's knee, engrossed in a cartoon.

"Bye, Auntie Ger, see you soon," said Michelle, without taking her eyes off the screen. Oisín just grunted.

Liam smiled and thanked her, but in a distant way that made her feel like a paid baby-sitter rather than a member of the family.

She did know what Sophie saw in him, she thought as she drove home to her flat. He had many good qualities. He was a really hard worker, a good provider, and very ethical in the way he did business. He had taken years to build up the company, because he wouldn't compromise or take shortcuts. It had paid off, because he now had a reputation where people would come to him first. His building business had won best practice awards and ISO accreditation and he was chair of the Galway Chamber of Commerce. No fault with him there. He was very generous with his money too, and Sophie and the children lacked for nothing. The house was beautifully furnished, and they had nice clothes and holidays. The dream life. But Ger could see that Sophie wasn't happy. She loved being at home with the kids, but Liam took her completely for granted. Ger tried not to get angry. Sophie had to make her own choices, and their mother had told the older sisters not to interfere.

When Ger had pushed it, sitting at the Christmas dinner table, her mother had been uncharacteristically direct. "Listen, love, you didn't get it right yourself, so don't be judging Sophie for the way she's doing it."

Ger had sat for a minute like a sullen child, and her mother's heart went out to her. She should be having dinner with her husband and a few kids, over-excited by all the presents from Santa. Instead she had come to France for the holidays on her own, like a student home from university instead of a grown woman of forty-four.

"Did you and Papa go through patches like this when we were small?" Sophie had asked her mother on the phone only the previous evening, desperate for the reassurance that what she was experiencing was normal.

"Well, we had different tensions to deal with. Your father's work was in the house, of course, so we didn't have the problem of him not being around. I actually found it quite oppressive not to have any space to myself. When you were all at school, I used to go off to the library in Castlebar to read my book for a few hours, rather than sit in the house with him. He seemed to fill the place, not only with all his painting things, but with his personality too. I sometimes felt a bit overshadowed by him. But of course I still loved him."

"And I still love Liam," Sophie had said, and her mother wondered whether the emphatic tone was exaggerated by the telephone line or was Sophie's effort to convince herself.

"That's all right then, love. You'll get through it. Nobody ever said it was supposed to be easy all the time. Things that are worth having are worth fighting for."

Sophie had smiled. That had been her mother's adage all through their schooldays. Whenever one of the girls had failed an exam, or didn't get picked for the basketball team, she would allow them a little bit of time to be sad, and then she would ask them what they were going to do about it.

At times like this Sophie wished her mother was around the corner so she could go and have a cup of tea and a dose of the certainty her mother always had about things working out for the best. She had apologised to Liam for being cross about his being late when she had to be at the Carol Service, and they had made love on Christmas Eve for the first time in ages. She had woken on Christmas Day, optimistic that her mother was right. Liam made a real effort all day, and he loaded the dishwasher after the dinner, and even made her a cup of tea with the mince pies later on in the day. He kept it up for Stephen's Day and didn't even have his traditional round of golf. They had taken the kids down to the beach at Salthill, and sat huddled together on a coat spread on the rocks while Michelle and Oisín ran up and down with a new football. The weather had been lovely, and Sophie had been really happy, with Liam's arm around her, and her children laughing, like models in a children's catalogue of winter mittens and woolly hats.

On the way back to the airport, Alison hardly noticed it was getting dark but suddenly saw a light approaching in the middle of the road. She swerved to avoid it and felt the sickening grind as the underside of the car hit the edge of the ditch. The whole vehicle listed to one side and after the fear had passed she felt stupid, semi-suspended in the air, the driver's door at least three feet off the ground. What was she supposed to do now? The light had disappeared, and she registered the low diesel rumble of a tractor. It seemed to be quite close by, but she was afraid to twist her body around to look behind her in case she tipped the car over. She was a great fan of *The Italian Job* and even in the midst of the situation she could see herself at a dinner party, regaling her friends with the hilarious dilemma she faced. Should she open the sky-facing car door and dangle her legs down, trying to reach the road, and then slide out that way, or would she be able to open the passenger door, if it wasn't completely stuck in the bog, and crawl into the ditch? Her dilemma was answered when she suddenly found herself face to face with a man who had opened the sky door and was standing with his hand outstretched, offering to help her out. There was no elegant way of achieving this, so she allowed him to manhandle her onto the ground, and then she took a moment to push her skirt down and adjust her composure.

"Sorry, are you OK?" he asked solicitously, and despite his large build, he now looked like he was about sixteen, his face scarred with acne, and his hair plastered to his head with the rain. He had huge brown eyes, full of concern, and he stood there as if he didn't know what to do with himself.

"I'm really sorry. I didn't have my lights on," Alison said, immediately breaking the universal rule of not admitting fault in a road accident.

"There's never anyone on this road at this time of the evening. I was taking the tractor over to my uncle's for the morning and I . . ." He obviously hadn't registered that she was taking the blame. "Sorry, I . . . you won't tell on me, will you?" he stammered, looking around as if there was another soul within twenty miles of them. "It's the first time I was allowed out on my own with it. Dad would kill me."

"How old are you?" she asked. He seemed younger every minute.

"Fifteen."

She could see his vivid blush even in the gloomy light. "And you're allowed to drive a tractor?" What were his parents doing, letting him out on a public road with a huge vehicle like that? He could have killed himself, never mind anyone else who might get in his way.

"Not really, but Dad said he'd give me a go. To prove myself, like."

"Are you OK? Were you hurt?" She touched his shoulder.

"No, I just got a fright. Did I damage the car?" He was walking to the front of the car, and peering at the paintwork.

"Do you think you could help me to get this out?" she asked, waving at the helpless vehicle.

"I will, of course. I've a rope in the tractor. One second and I'll get it." The boy leapt on to the back of the tractor and reached to unhook a coil of rope from inside the cab.

He quickly tied it to the tow-bar of the tractor and on to the front bumper of the car. Then he realised he would need to get the tractor into a completely different position to enable it to pull out the car, so he had to untie it again, trying not to catch Alison's eye.

She didn't want to embarrass him further, and let him get on with it. Her mobile phone had absolutely no reception so she couldn't ring anyone for help. When he had reversed the tractor into a suitable position, she tied the rope back on and slung her leg up to climb back into the car. She edged herself carefully onto the tilted seat and signalled when she was ready behind the wheel. After much grinding of gears, he managed to move forward and haul the car out. It didn't look too badly damaged, from what she could see in the poor light, and she hoped the car rental company wouldn't charge her a fortune for the repairs. Surely it would be covered by the insurance?

"There you are. I'm very sorry again about that. I hope you get safely wherever you're going."

"Am I still on the right road for Knock airport?"

"You are indeed. It's about another nine and a half miles down this road, and you'll meet the dual carriageway. You can't go wrong after that."

"Thank you very much," Alison said, climbing back behind the wheel, shaking with the dispersal of redundant adrenalin. A loud honk of the horn and the disappearing taillights signalled the boy's departure, and she thought how relieved he would be to deliver the tractor safely to his uncle's house. She imagined him concocting some elaborate tale about why it had taken so long, so he would be allowed to drive alone again.

Her baby would have been fifteen this year. June the twenty-third. She wondered if it would have been a boy or a girl. Her counsellor had told her it was unwise to try to assign an identity to that lost baby. She would never come to terms with her decision to have an abortion if she kept imagining what the child would be doing now. It didn't exist as a person. It never had. She was deluding herself, exacerbating her guilt, not moving on. And that was what everyone was supposed to be able to do these days. Move on. But why? And to where? She blinked away tears and gripped the steering wheel. She had a plane to catch.

Chapter Four

Father O'Leary phoned just after ten on Monday morning, as Sophie was whisking the sheets off the guest bed having tidied the children's rooms. She loved the momentum of Monday mornings. She dropped Oisín and Michelle to the playgroup, changed the beds, tidied the playroom and had a quick cup of tea before going to collect them for swimming lessons at Leisureland. That passed another hour and a half, by the time they were dried and changed, and they always had their lunch in town as a treat. In the afternoon, one of her 'baby-friends' as Liam called them, would come for tea and the kids would entertain themselves for a couple of hours, with the novelty of a new face to distract them.

This morning she resented the interruption of the phone, and her abrupt greeting surprised the priest.

"Sophie, have you a minute?" he said tentatively.

She felt the familiar guilt when she behaved less than perfectly in his eyes. "Sorry, Father, I was just in the middle of –" she stopped herself. She was always gabbling on with details people didn't want to hear. "Can I help you, Father?" She cradled the phone to her ear and managed to put two fresh pillowcases on while she listened.

"The choir, yesterday. Well, to be honest, I've seen and heard better from them. I know it was through no fault of your own . . ."

"I can imagine, Father."

"Were you not well?"

"Did I forget to tell you, Father? I was away for the weekend." She managed not to divulge further unnecessary details, and was pleased with herself.

"Only I saw Liam and the children, and I wondered . . ."

"Yes, it was only myself away . . ."

"And isn't Liam a great man altogether, to be left with them for the whole weekend?"

Sophie smiled. "He is indeed, Father. Now, what can I do for you?"

"It was just the new hymn. I was wondering if there could be a bit more practice on it for next week? You'll remember of course we have the Bishop coming, to launch the new roof appeal for us. It would be nice to have everyone singing it out confidently and musically. Did you know it was the Bishop's brother-in-law wrote it?"

"I did, Father. Consider it done. We might get an extra rehearsal in this week, so." Sophie remembered perfectly well who had written it. Wasn't that the whole point of them learning it, for the Bishop's visit? She wondered if Father O'Leary was in the early stages of Alzheimer's or something. He often forgot about conversations they had

had. They exchanged a few more pleasantries, and she hung up, wondering which day would suit everyone and could she get them to come over to the house so she didn't have to organise a baby-sitter just for the hour. Would the singing keep the kids awake?

If she was quick she could get a few calls made before leaving for the playgroup. An hour later the upstairs of the house was in order, she had three definites for a rehearsal on Wednesday, and two messages left. She sent a quick email to Alison to say how much she had enjoyed the weekend, and that she was working on getting baby-sitting for the great London weekend.

The children gave her the welcome she had been hoping for the day before, and she had to waddle out of the playgroup with the two of them clinging to her legs in a rival attempt to demonstrate most affection, or demand most attention. She rolled her eyes to heaven at one of the other mothers, who had four-year-old twins, and said, "How do you do it?" The woman just smiled in acknowledgement of the universal rhetorical question.

The swimming lesson was a disaster, after Michelle swallowed a huge mouthful of water halfway through and then refused to let go of the side. Her brother, who usually kept her on her toes by being almost as good as her, went on strike too. Sophie sat squirming in the observation area, unable to reach them, or coax them into trying again, short of going and changing into her own swimsuit, or yelling like a fishwife. She could see Michelle's lips going blue with the cold and Oisín's teeth were chattering. She waved and gestured, trying to encourage them from a distance, but Michelle just screwed up her face and kept yelling, "What, Mammy?" until the teacher asked her to stop because she was distracting the other children.

Sophie bit her tongue as she dried them, determined not to be a pushy mother. She told herself it didn't matter if they took another six months to learn how to swim, even though everyone else in the class was making good progress. As long as they were enjoying it, that was all that mattered. The children took her silence as disapproval, and Oisín went into attention-seeking mode, climbing across the baby-changing units, banging locker doors and turning on all the hair-driers in a row. Sophie asked him to stop, conscious of the disapproving looks from other mothers. Easy to judge when your own child wasn't doing it, she thought to herself, knowing that if the roles were reversed she would be equally intolerant of other people's children.

She grabbed him on one of his forays past her, and held his wrist, looking into his eyes. "No treat for you after lunch, if you don't settle down," she said firmly.

"No, you settle down!" he defied her. The cheeky button was the one the children had learned through trial and error was the most fun to press, especially in public.

Sure enough, Sophie's eyes narrowed with the frustration of not wanting to make a show of herself in front of everybody else.

Oisín wriggled and said, "Ow, you're hurting me, Mammy!" He tugged hard, just as she let him go, and he fell on the floor, banging his head on the bottom of a locker door. Blood spurted from a cut on his temple. Her heart pounding, she picked him up and looked at it.

With the shock, he had gone limp and compliant, and Michelle's eyes widened when she saw the thick dark blood oozing from his head. "Is he going to die, Mammy?" she asked, her mouth open in a comic 'o' of surprise.

"Of course not, darling. Come here, Oisín. Look at me. Let me see your eyes."

Oisín turned and looked at her, and then he put his hand up to touch the cut. His fingers came away covered in blood, and he screamed in fear, "I'm bleeding Mammy. I'm bleeding!"

She shushed him. "Don't worry, pet. We might take you to the doctor just so he can have a little look at it. Sit there now, and I'll just get our bits and pieces." She frantically scrabbled in the locker, stuffed wet and dry things higgledy-piggledy into the rucksack. "Can you be a big strong girl for me now, Michelle, and carry that? I'm going to carry Oisín." She was moving in a robotic calm that even to herself seemed strange. Her ribcage felt as though a gremlin with a large mallet was inside, trying to escape. They made it to the car without incident and Oisín was ominously quiet, staring at his scarlet fingers until she strapped him into the car seat and wiped them clean. She wasn't sure if his eyes were in focus, and desperately tried to remember the symptoms of concussion. It was supposed to be better when they screamed, wasn't it? Better than this silence, like a surrender to some greater force. She plunged a children's tape of songs into the car stereo, as much to stop Michelle asking her questions as to distract Oisín. The drive to the doctor's surgery passed in a slow-motion haze of automatic gear changes, stopping at red traffic lights and changing lanes. She couldn't have recounted any of the details if someone had asked her. There were two other cars in the surgery carpark and she started rehearsing the lines she would use to skip the queue. She couldn't wait for half an hour to know he was all right. Maybe she should have gone straight to the hospital? She hadn't even called Liam yet. Should she call him now, or wait until she knew more? She got the children out of the car, locked it, got them through the door, somehow without speaking. Oisín's legs buckled as they got to the reception desk and she just caught him before he landed flat on the floor. She held him in her arms like the tiny baby he had been only three years ago.

The receptionist didn't need any prompting. She buzzed the doctor's call bell. "I think we have an emergency situation here," she muttered discreetly into the microphone when he answered.

The patient inside emerged within seconds, the doctor having cut short the amiable chit-chat for which he was the most popular GP in the area. He took Oisín from Sophie's arms and laid him on the couch.

"Michelle, will you play out here for a minute, until I come back?" Sophie said, injecting calmness and an expectation of obedience into her trembling voice.

"Yes, Mammy," Michelle said, like the adorable angel she was, and Sophie followed the doctor into his room.

"What happened to this little lad, then?" the doctor asked, gently palpating around the wound.

Oisín didn't react at all.

"He knocked his head against the corner of a locker door at the swimming-pool." Sophie could hardly breathe.

"About ten minutes ago. We came straight here." She paced up and down while the doctor looked into Oisín's eyes and checked his nostrils and ears.

"I think he'll be fine. He's suffering from shock but there's no sign of concussion. I'll put a couple of little butterfly stitches in it and a dressing on it." He washed his hands and prepared the items he needed on a small stainless-steel tray.

"Full of buck, was he, after his swim?" The doctor could smell the chlorine off Oisín's damp hair.

Sophie nodded. "I was trying to calm him down and I was holding him to talk to him and he pulled away as I let him go, so he really went flying."

"Well, he'll learn his lesson from it, anyway," said the doctor, winding up a musical mobile of vehicles that was hanging in a corner of the room to distract Oisín while he put in the stitches. He was very brave, with just a tiny whimper escaping.

Sophie felt leaden now, the adrenalin still in her system but drifting to her extremities. She sat down suddenly, and the doctor turned around.

"You're in shock yourself. I'll get Rachael to make you a cup of sweet tea before you go. Have you anyone you could call to drive you home?"

"I'll call Liam in a minute. I don't want to worry him." She sat with her head between her knees, and the doctor patted the back of her head.

"Don't blame yourself. These things happen all the time. Boys especially are all the time testing out their bodies, and they get themselves hurt while they're learning what they're capable of."

"I know, but I was holding on to him. If I hadn't done that, he wouldn't have fallen over."

"Not then, but he would have slipped off a bench two seconds later if you hadn't stopped him in his tracks by holding him." The doctor looked back at Oisín. "You gave yourself and your mammy a terrible fright. Will you promise me to behave yourself at the swimming-pool the next time?" His mock stern voice had the desired effect, and Oisín nodded. He tried to feel the stitches, but the doctor shook his head. "You need to leave them alone, Oisín." He turned to Sophie. "I'm going to put a little dressing on it, just for that reason – to stop him picking at them. The stitches will disappear themselves after about a week."

Sophie lifted up her head and nodded.

"Go out now and call your husband. I can't let you go home in this state," he said firmly, opening the door. "Rachael will give you tea," he said loud enough for his receptionist to hear, and when she looked up he nodded at her.

She took Sophie's arm and guided her to the bench seat beside Michelle, who was happily pottering in the plastic Wendy House. "Would you like a cup of tea, Mammy?" she asked solicitously, holding out a tiny pink cup through the window of the house.

"Thanks, love," Sophie said, taking it and wanting to cry. She dialled Liam's number and he answered immediately. She never called him at work. "Can you come to the doctor's surgery to collect us? Oisín had a bang on the head. He's fine but I'm not really able to drive."

"Ten minutes," he said.

Eight minutes later he came into the waiting room, breathless, and looked around. "Where's Oisín?" he asked, panicking when he couldn't see him.

"I'm in here, Daddy," came a gleeful little voice from inside the plastic playhouse in the corner.

"He's all right?" Liam asked Sophie, who had stood up when he came in but hadn't said a word.

"He's fine. Two stitches and he'll have a big bruise, probably." She smiled tentatively at him and he hugged her to his wide chest, belatedly sharing her fear, fighting off the thought of how much worse it could have been.

He drove them all home in his car and rang one of his lads to go and collect Sophie's and bring it to the house. Sophie made another cup of tea, and the children played uncharacteristically quietly together, piecing together a jigsaw puzzle.

"Jesus, it's terrible when you get a fright like that," said Liam, patting Sophie's hand where it lay on the table. He saw in her face the disapproval of his blasphemy. "Sorry."

"Thanks for coming to get us. I probably could have made it, but my legs were like jelly."

"No, you did the right thing. I'm glad you rang me instead of one of your friends."

Sophie suddenly remembered Maeve was due in twenty minutes with little Seán. She didn't think she could face being sociable so she sent her a text. "Thanks for reminding me," she said to Liam.

Her wan smile made Liam want to hug her and wrap her up in a blanket in front of an open fire. She was so strong and independent, sometimes he wondered if she thought he had any purpose in her life at all. Between the kids and the fund-raising for Father O'Leary, and the choir, she never seemed to have any energy left when he got home. He used to be able to tell her all his plans for the business, and they would sit with a glass of wine in the evening, talking about everything, dreaming about their future. Now she could barely summon a bit of conversation, and it was always about something Michelle said or Oisín did at the playgroup. They had a tacit agreement that Sophie didn't talk about the doings in the parish. He didn't go to Mass, and he wasn't interested. Liam had recently got into a bad habit of calling into the golf club for one drink on the way home from work, if he wasn't seeing Theresa. One drink always led to another, and he told himself that it was all part of building a business, keeping in touch with the right people. But the truth was, he had more than enough work lined up for the next two years. He could triple his turnover this year alone, without any bother at all. But Sophie didn't show the slightest interest in the business any more, and sometimes he was so hyped after a good day, and so full of news about things that were going on, he had to talk to someone. That was how it had all started with Theresa, if he was honest. She showed some interest in him. That was all he wanted, at the end of the day. Well, and the sex. That was pretty good too.

He stood behind Sophie's chair and massaged her shoulders, and she leaned her head briefly against his arm, loving the smell of him and the rough hairiness of his arm where he had pushed his sleeves up in agitation. He gently stroked her head, and thought how crude and uncouth his rough hand looked against the fineness of her hair and the delicate shell-curl of her ear.

"I love you," he bent to whisper, and she reached up and held her hand briefly against his cheek.

"Me, too," she said.

Liam told himself that if Sophie said she loved him a bit more often, he wouldn't feel the need for Theresa, but he knew he was only making excuses. "See you later, kids!" he shouted into the playroom, and they ignored him, engrossed in the final stages of the puzzle. The front door slammed and there was a brief silence before anarchy broke out, the two children fighting over who would put in the last piece to complete the picture.

"I had it first," wailed Oisín.

"But it's my turn," said Michelle, whacking him on the head with a teddy bear held by the foot.

"Michelle!" Sophie shouted, terrified that the stitches would break open.

Caught in the act, her daughter looked guiltily at the teddy she was still holding and handed over the last piece of the puzzle to Oisín.

"Tanks," he said, and then graciously allowed her to guide his hand to the right place. "See, we done it together," he said, generous in victory.

"Did it together," said Michelle and Sophie simultaneously in the exact same tone of voice.

Sophie couldn't help laughing.

"The health spa was unbelievable. You were right!"

Alison told Lisa on the phone when she got back on Sunday night.

"It's impossible not to relax there, isn't it?" said Lisa. Then she rushed on, "I've got news for you. We're having a baby!"

"Oh, my God, Lisa, that is fantastic! When are you due?"

"August the 9th, we think. It's very early days."

Alison had just worked out the maths. "What are you, about four weeks?"

"I know, I shouldn't have even told you. We promised each other we wouldn't say anything until at least nine or ten weeks, but how could I do that? I'm not telling anyone else. Michael is telling his mother, only because she's not well at all, and it will cheer her up. We finally made the decision over the weekend. She has to go into a Home. He's going to see her tomorrow evening to break the news."

"You've had a bit of a busy weekend then," said Alison, knowing that Lisa would be torn about the Home. Her mother-in-law lived only a five-minute walk away, and she felt obliged to go and see her every day, to check up on her and make her a cup of tea. They couldn't trust Edna to light the gas, so she had frozen microwave meals on wheels delivered three times a week. Her hands were crabbed with arthritis and they shook so much that she couldn't pour a kettle without scalding herself. Michael had known for months that they needed to find a better solution, but Lisa's pregnancy must have finally prompted him into action.

Lisa couldn't be expected to keep an eye on his eighty-nine-year-old mother. She had to concentrate on making this pregnancy successful. After two miscarriages, it might be their last chance. Alison could imagine the conversations they must have had over the weekend. Michael was such a sweetie, and he would be worrying that his mother would feel usurped by the unborn baby, relegated to a nursing home.

"Would you like to come over for supper at about 7.30 tomorrow? Michael said he would stay with his mum for the evening, to make sure she was all right."

Lisa sounded like she needed the company.

"I'll have to see how busy work is, after being out of the office on Thursday and Friday."

"OK."

Alison could hear the disappointment in her voice. "Tell you what, let's make it 8.30, and I'll bring a Chinese takeaway so you don't have to cook."

"Deal."

They sat at the kitchen table amongst the half-emptied tinfoil cartons and a two-litre bottle of fizzy water.

"You could have had wine, you know," said Lisa, wondering if the bloated indigestion she could feel coming on was from the pregnancy or the fizz or the poorly cooked food.

"I made a vow as I was leaving the spa. Instead of getting depressed about being nearly forty, I'm going to take myself in hand. I want to wake up on my fortieth birthday happy, fit and feeling good about myself. For me. Not for whoever may or may not be waking up in the bed beside me."

"So, no more alcohol?" Lisa asked incredulously. Alison was great for making resolutions, and even better at breaking them.

"Only at weekends. I should be able to stick to that, shouldn't I?"

"Well, I won't be drinking for a while either, so we can give each other moral support."

"That was dreadful food, wasn't it?"

Lisa nodded. "I didn't like to say anything. I can feel a monosodium glutamate revolution going on in my stomach already."

"Sorry, you'll probably get terrible heartburn. But maybe the baby will end up liking Chinese food?"

"Or not, as the case may be!"

"Changing the subject completely, I met this woman called Sophie at the spa. Half Irish, half French, thin as a whippet, two kids, and she's going to be forty three days after me. We had such a great chat. I really liked her."

"You always manage to find someone to make friends with, in these places," said Lisa enviously. She would never strike up a conversation with a complete stranger. Alison had been the one to talk to her while she was queuing up for a coffee on their first day at sixth-form college when she started her A levels.

"She talked non-stop, but she was very wise, I think," Alison went on. "We went for a few walks and had dinner together. I invited her to come over for a weekend when the weather gets a bit better."

"With her kids?" Alison's house was the most un-child-friendly place Lisa could imagine. Glass-topped tables, priceless vases and cream sofas and carpets.

"No, for a girlie shopping weekend. She lived in Wimbledon for a while but she hasn't been back for ages. She was laughing, saying we were like the Town Mouse and the Country Mouse. I've done the country, which was lovely, and now she can come and do the town.".

"So you liked the country better than the Town Mouse did?"

"Oh, I was ready to come back! The peace and quiet would drive me mad after a while. Great for somewhere to escape to, but I need my urban hustle!"

"I'm the same. I wonder if I'll still love London when I have a child. Someone said to me that you get very protective, and anxious about traffic fumes and things like that."

"Well, you've got two lovely parks near you, and loads of coffee shops full of mothers with their pushchairs having coffee at ten o'clock in the morning!"

Lisa grinned. "I shouldn't get too far ahead of myself. But this one feels different. More settled, or something. Mind you, it's hard to tell with that Chinese food wreaking havoc." She burped loudly, putting her hand on her stomach. "Sorry, how rude!"

Alison checked the time. "Listen, do you mind if I don't wait until Michael gets back? I have an early start tomorrow, so I should get home. If I have a late night I'll cancel out all the benefits of the weekend in one fell swoop."

They hugged and Alison patted Lisa's stomach. "This one will be fine," she said.

Later, Alison sat on the edge of her bed, trying to figure out why she felt a bit unsettled. She should be feeling great. She had called her parents to say she would come at the weekend. She was so delighted for Lisa about the baby and felt optimistic that this time all would be well. She had even received an email from Sophie about coming for a weekend around Easter time. So what was the problem? The day at work had been a bit dull, if she was honest. The deals she was doing these days were so big that they took months to pull off, and months to execute. There wasn't the rush and pressure of monthly targets, and the buzz of hitting them. Since she had been promoted last year, to work with the 'strategic' clients, developing project briefs, and pulling together ever more complex financing arrangements, she had gradually moved away from the work she really enjoyed. Her salary had increased, and she had lots more share options, but it wasn't so much fun any more.

Should she bring it up in the meeting with her boss the next day? She couldn't go back into her old job in the team. That would look like a demotion. But she didn't really have any alternatives to suggest, so her boss would think she was just being negative. Eloise had just come back from maternity leave and had wangled herself a three-day week. It had been announced that Dave was off to Dubrovnik in March to manage an amazing new coastal resort development with a marina and apartments. The project would take at least six months so he would have the summer there, shagging lots of Croatian girls no doubt, while Alison slogged her way through the compliance implications of the new money-laundering regulations. It was brain-stretching stuff, but to what end? She flopped backwards onto the bed and lay down. She stared at a bunched-up spider in the corner of the ceiling, trying to recapture the serenity and certainty she had felt only twenty-four hours before.

Chapter Five

The choir made a fair attempt at the hymn written by the Bishop's brother-in-law, and Father O'Leary thanked Sophie after Mass, as he stood shaking hands with his parishioners on the way out. He held her hand in both of his, thinking how petite and soft it was, compared to the big chapped hands of some of the women.

"Is everything all right with you?" he asked *sotto voce*. He had noticed a strain around her eyes, and a sense of discontentment that hadn't been there before. Sophie's positive energy was one of the things that defined her, and she hadn't been quite so bubbly recently.

"Grand, thanks, Father, and yourself?" she said automatically, hardly meeting his eye.

It wasn't the time or the place, so he made a mental note to give her a ring during the week, or to pop in for a cup of tea one morning, when the children were at their playgroup. Sometimes it was the strong ones who fell the hardest and he didn't like to take anything for granted.

"Come on, kids. Daddy will be waiting for us," Sophie said, taking their hands and walking across the carpark.

Father O'Leary watched them go, and felt sad that Liam never came to Mass with his family. The golf seemed to be his release from the day-to-day stresses. The priest wondered if there was any tension between himself and herself, with Sophie taking all the responsibility for the children's spiritual development. Soon they would be asking questions about why Daddy didn't go to Mass. The previous generation of parents didn't have to worry about it. Everyone went to Mass, and that was that. He would fully admit to himself, but not aloud, that the power of the twitching net curtain had prevailed in those days as much as the power of God. These days nobody really cared what the neighbours thought, so they only went to Mass if they wanted to. He watched the last of his congregation starting up their cars, and waved as they passed. His stomach was rumbling. He loved this moment of anticipation after twelve o'clock Mass on a Sunday. He had said three Masses this morning, and now Mrs Raftery would have a well-deserved roast dinner ready for him. In the afternoon, he would make a few home visits to give Holy Communion to the sick and elderly, and then come back for scones and jam, and a snooze in the armchair. Benediction at seven o'clock would be attended by no more than four or five stalwarts, and he would go back home at eight to his cosy sitting-room, fulfilled after a good day's work. He hung the vestments carefully in the sacristy, and walked slowly down the path to the presbytery, greeted by a waft of roast-beef-scented air as he passed the kitchen window.

Sophie got home to a message on the answering machine from Liam. He was going for a quick drink after his round of golf. She turned the oven down low. At three o'clock, when she couldn't bear the grizzling of the hungry children, she carved the chicken and they ate their lunch in silence. The children sensed her disappointment. Nothing felt right. Sunday lunch was the only meal where the family sat down together. Today it felt like every other weekday meal, sitting with their mother at the kitchen table instead of in the dining-room. They had yoghurt for dessert and then Sophie allowed them to get down from the table and play while she tidied up. A lone dinner plate sat on the hob, waiting for Liam to come home and eat his dinner. In the fridge, a Waterford-glass dish of dark chocolate mousse acquired a slight skin but it would still be delicious underneath.

They watched videos for an hour, although Sophie knew that she would pay the price with high jinks later. Sundays were supposed to be different, but she didn't have the energy to think up games to play and things to make. If she took the children out to the woods or the beach, Liam would come home and find the house empty. When she came back they would have an argument and the rest of day would be ruined for sure.

She was close to tears, but watching Bob the Builder fixing everything in sight was sufficiently anodyne to keep her emotions in check.

"That's like Daddy, building the house," said Oisín, pointing excitedly when Bob finished the roof on Farmer Pickle's extension.

"Yes, sweetheart, it is," said Sophie, savouring the warmth of their bodies snuggled up against her on the sofa. She closed her eyes, and said a little prayer that Liam was all right, and that he would come home soon. In a couple of hours it would be time for tea, followed by the battle of bath-time and pyjamas. She knew it would be worse because the children had had no fresh air or exercise and would suddenly come to life at seven o'clock when she wanted them to be settling down to sleep.

"Where is he?" she muttered, not meaning to say it aloud.

"He's there, Mammy, look, on the roof!" Michelle said, pointing at Spud, the naughty scarecrow who was always getting into trouble.

"Oh, yes, so he is," she said, stroking Michelle's head.

"Get off, Mammy!" She wriggled away to the other side of the sofa, and Oisín clambered across his mother's lap to follow her.

Sophie sighed. There was no point in shouting at them. "Who wants to go for an adventure in the woods?" she asked, glancing out to make sure the sky wasn't too grey.

"Me!" said Oisín.

"Not me!" said Michelle. "I want to play Mammies and Daddies."

"You always want to do that, 'shelle. It's so boooring!" Oisín had recently mastered a particularly provoking tone of voice, calculated to wind his sister up to the point of distraction.

"Maameee, he said I was boooring!" Michelle wailed.

Sophie was in the hall, getting their shoes and coats out of the cupboard. "Come on. Let's go before it gets too dark," she said, hoping that if there was some momentum, Michelle might forget her protest.

"But I don't want to go!" Michelle stamped her foot.

Sophie bit her lip very hard and counted to ten under her breath. "I know! Let's put Tiny Tears in her pushchair and take her for a walk!" She managed to sound like she had had the bright idea of the day.

Michelle decided she would be the Mammy, Oisín could be the Daddy, and Sophie could be the big sister. After only seven and a half minutes, they had their coats and shoes on, and Tiny Tears was safely strapped into her pushchair with her hat on and a blanket in case she got chilly. Sophie opened the front door and Liam was standing there, his hand up with the key, about to insert it.

"I have to take them out for some exercise. They're climbing the walls. Dinner is on top of the cooker. Give it about three minutes in the microwave. Dessert is in the fridge." Sophie didn't kiss him.

The children hardly seemed to notice he was there, absorbed in their game.

"I'm going to push it first, and then you can lift it over the puddle at the gate, like a real Daddy, and then it will be my turn again," said Michelle.

Oisín nodded, happy to be henpecked as long as he was included.

They walked to the gate, and Sophie didn't look back. Oisín and Michelle managed to get the pushchair over the cattle grid, and Michelle allowed him to put his hand on the handle, to help her to steer.

Liam stood on the front step and watched them go. He would have time for a shower now, which was a relief. If Sophie had come close enough to kiss him she might have smelt more than smoke off him. He had smoked a couple of cigarettes on the way home to cancel out Theresa's perfume. Sophie would think he had been at the golf club with a few of the guys, and disapproved of the smoking so much that she never seemed to notice anything else.

He went up to the bathroom and stripped off. He stood in front of the full-length mirror and reassured himself that he was still in good shape. Sophie might not think he was attractive, but there were plenty of women who did. She was always asleep when he got into bed, and he was a man with needs. Before the kids came along, they would make love three or four times a week. Now he was lucky if it was once a month. Theresa smiled when he came into the office, and she asked him how he was, with that little grin playing around her lips. She gave all the signals that she fancied him, and if he was honest, he needed that. Theresa had a certain look that she gave him while she held his dick in her long fingers, looking into his eyes while she teased him into hardness. He would fully admit that the danger element added to the sexual appeal. Theresa had come on to him so strong, he was in no doubt about what she wanted. The first time, they had sex on the meeting-room table, and another time, in the back of the car, like teenagers. Sophie was a missionary-position girl, which was fine in itself, but it got a bit boring after a while. She never slid her hand down his thigh in bed, or stroked his stomach with the tip of her nail like Theresa did, making him wait and wait until she was ready. He climbed into the shower stall, and soaped himself all over. Sometimes he was surprised at how easily he had slipped into this double life, seeing Theresa and then coming home to his family. Sometimes in the middle of the night, he woke up sweating, feeling guilty and tossing and turning until the morning. Then when he went into the office and saw Theresa, and she smiled at him, it all seemed almost normal, and he would go on for another while, thinking maybe it was possible to have the best of both worlds, as long as he could keep them completely separate . . .

He pushed away the mental image of Sophie's face if she ever found out. She would never understand that sexual drive could be separate from love. He still loved her, of course he did, and he wouldn't want to hurt her. He just couldn't stop himself when temptation was put in his way. He nearly spent more time in Theresa's company than he did in Sophie's. She worked long hours in the office, and it was on one of those late evenings when they had just finalised the accounts for the month, that Theresa pulled out a bottle of wine from the bag of shopping she had got at lunch-time, and asked if he wanted a drink. One thing had led to another. But she had definitely started it, and he wasn't sure if he would have the willpower to stop it.

Today had been the first time Theresa had come into the golf club, but it had been a nice surprise all right to see her sitting there in the bay window, waiting for him. He had come in with John for a quick pint after their Sunday morning eighteen holes. He only had half an hour, he had said to John, because Sophie liked them all to sit down for the Sunday dinner at one o'clock. John had nodded his agreement, and gone up to the bar to buy the round.

"Unusual to see you in here," Liam had said to Theresa, standing close to her table and wondering who she was with. She said she had come especially to see him. Liam wondered if that could be dangerous. At the office there would always be a reason for them to be talking, sorting out the diary, arranging meetings, her typing a letter for him. Here, her red plunging top and the painted nails seemed out of place. All the other women here on a Sunday were waiting for the afternoon women-only session, kitted out in their sports wear, talking about handicaps and the Captain's Prize.

Theresa had patted the banquette beside her. "Come and join me," she had said as John came back with the pints.

"Oh, sorry, can I get you something?" John had asked politely. He didn't know who she was.

"Hi, I'm Theresa, Liam's assistant." She stretched

out her fingers for him to hold rather than shake. "I'd love another gin and tonic, if you don't mind?"

"One second, so," said John, turning back to the bar.

Liam whispered, "Theresa, you know we need to be careful, don't you?" She looked different today. Predatory was the word that came to mind and it made him feel uncomfortable. Theresa had to understand that she had a particular place in his life. And she couldn't be going around turning up at the club, or in other places where she would stand out like a sore thumb.

"Of course, darling," she whispered back, just as John came back to the table. "So, how do you two know each other?" she asked, raising her glass and nodding to thank John.

"John is one of my oldest friends," said Liam.

"We went to St Enda's together," said John. "I was Liam's best man." He sensed that this woman needed to be given the message that Liam wasn't available.

"We've only known each other three or four months, since I started working for Liam," she said, looking across at him.

Liam seemed a bit embarrassed. She kept on giving him meaningful looks and little smiles out of the side of her mouth. John didn't want to be rude if Theresa was an employee of Liam's but he didn't like her. He got up to leave after the one pint, mildly curious when Liam didn't follow suit, especially because Liam had emptied his glass first.

"See you next Sunday, so," said Liam.

"Is it not Saturday night that you're coming over to us for dinner?" asked John, unsure of the date.

"Could be. Sophie is the keeper of the social diary," said Liam, laughing. "Next week, anyway, one way or the other."

He had waved as John passed the window on the way to the car. Liam was cruising for trouble by the looks of things. John wasn't sure if he should tell Ann, or if he should wait and see how things panned out. She might feel obliged tell Sophie, and then all hell would break loose.

Liam had waited until John's car disappeared out the gate. The bar was empty now, in the post-lunch lull.

Then he had hissed at Theresa, "Never do that to me again!"

"What?" She looked all innocent, with her eyebrows curved in a question mark.

He couldn't talk to her properly here. The barman would notice if they hung around much longer. He had to get her straight on some facts, before they got into this any deeper. There had to be some rules.

"Come with me," he had said abruptly, and she followed him meekly to the car. He had driven to the office, so they wouldn't be seen together. It was bad enough that they had been seen at the club already. The heating was off for the weekend, and the office was freezing. Theresa shivered, standing there in her coat, and something snapped in him. He kissed her hard on the red lips, and pushed her back down against his desk, pulling off her coat and her blouse, grabbing her breasts. He couldn't get enough of her perfume and the taste of her skin.

Afterwards she went to the ladies' and he sat on his

chair, looking out the window. What could he say to her now?

She came back, her make-up repaired, her shiny blonde hair brushed smooth and she kissed him sweetly on the lips. "That was lovely. It always seems more *exciting* when we make love at the office." Everyone said that married men didn't leave their wives, but in this day and age anything could happen. Liam didn't seem to be happy with Sophie, so maybe they weren't right for each other. Theresa knew she could make him happy. Liam loved her and, given the chance, Theresa could make a lovely home for them. One that he wouldn't want to stray from. She looked deep into his eyes, wondering what he was really thinking. She wanted more than just the sex. That was only the beginning. She had so much more to give him, if he would just let her in.

Liam nodded distractedly. Of the rules he had rehearsed in the car on the way here, he could only summon one. "We can't do that again. Not on a Sunday."

She agreed demurely.

He wondered if she was mocking him. Sunday was the only day that Sophie asked was kept for the family. She didn't mind him playing golf in the morning while they were at Mass, but the rest of the day was for the four of them to spend together. How could he explain that to Theresa without sounding hypocritical? He was happy to shag her any other day of the week, but Sunday was reserved for his wife and kids?

"Afraid that God wouldn't approve?" said Theresa. "I thought doing it on a Sunday would add another bit of excitement."

She traced the tip of her nail along his lip, and then kissed him again, the blended smell of sex and perfume rising from her cleavage.

He moved away. "God has nothing to do with it," he said. "My rules. We don't do it on Sundays. And don't come to the golf club again."

"I'm going to be put in a little box in your life, am I? To be taken out at your pleasure, but not when I might interfere with anything else. Is that it?" A tear slid down her cheek, belying the sarcasm she was using to hide the hurt.

He had kissed her tear away, stroked her hair. "I just have some things to work out, that's all. It will be much easier if we do things my way. Trust me."

He had held her face in his hands, and looked into her eyes. He wasn't sure what he saw there, but he knew he was getting in deep.

He finished showering, his heart pounding. Keeping Theresa in his life was going to lead to trouble – that was for sure. And how could he get out of it? If he fired her, or broke off the relationship, she might tell Sophie, out of spite. If he kept going, Sophie was bound to find out. Theresa was starting to look for more than he was prepared to give. He ate his reheated dinner, feeling like a schoolboy who was being punished, and then caught the end of the afternoon's sports on TV. He heard the front door opening. He heard Sophie telling them to take their wellies off in the hall, and then shouting at Oisín, who obviously hadn't. Then she ushered the kids straight upstairs. Oisín's stomping footsteps moved up the stairs and then to the bathroom, and the hysterical wailing of Sunday night hair-washing started. He dozed on the sofa, looking forward to their sweet-smelling arrival on his lap for a story before bedtime.

Chapter Six

Alison put on some fresh lipstick and eyeliner, leaning forward to check the progress of the tiny crow's feet around her eyes. Not much worse, she thought, wondering if the carrageen eye cream was actually doing the trick. Her boss was taking her out to lunch at Quaglino's as a thank-you for her work on the Fisher Quay deal. The development would be amazing. She might even sell her house on Tremaine Street, and move to one of the riverside apartments.

They chatted in the taxi about their weekend and although Steve had never struck her as a man who would be interested, he asked her lots of questions about the Irish spa she had been to a couple of weeks before.

"The most striking thing about it is the complete and utter peace. I suppose it might be the time of year. January isn't exactly peak season in the west of Ireland. Maybe the roads are busy with tourists in the summer, but I didn't pass one other car on the way from the airport, once I came off the dual carriageway," she said. "Within an hour of landing, you could literally be on another planet. Even the vegetation seems foreign."

He laughed. "So you're a big fan, then?"

"Most definitely. I might just have to go back again and again, and forget about all the other health farms on my list to try!"

He held the taxi door for her while she climbed out, and opened the restaurant door too. He was being uncharacteristically solicitous, and a frisson of anxiety went through her. Was there more to this lunch than a simple thank-you? When she had started in the job nearly five years ago, Steve had made it very clear that he was attracted to her. She had told him in no uncertain terms that married men were off limits for her, irrespective of how attractive they might be. He was tall and very muscular, a regular squash player and footballer. His round face was slightly plumper five years on, and he had lost some hair, but he was still handsome, and he was certainly bright. Recently his wife had left him, taking their two kids to Scotland, and Alison had felt really sorry for him. Maybe Steve had misunderstood her offer of a shoulder to cry on. It hadn't occurred to her before this moment that he might still be interested in her. Now as she stepped past him into the lobby of the restaurant, slipping off her coat to hand it to the receptionist, she was suddenly conscious of every movement. Was he watching her from behind? She tucked her hair behind her ears, and quickly moistened her lips with the tip of her tongue. She stood up straighter, glad she was wearing the new aubergine suit from Jigsaw. It made her eyes look bigger and even darker, and she had just had her hair highlighted. He was fumbling his wallet out of his coat pocket, not even looking at her. As she walked to their table ahead of him, sashaying her hips just slightly as she weaved between the intense conversations of businessmen and lovers, she wondered what was going to happen.

The waiter presented the menus with a flourish and Alison made a mental check of her diary for the afternoon. She had one appointment at four . . .

"So, Alison," he started, after they had ordered their food. He sipped his sparkling mineral water. She did too. Steve noticed the hazel flecks in the grey eyes contemplating him and thought how unusual they were. It was a shame they had never got it together. He really enjoyed Alison's company, and she was quite sexy, in an understated sort of way. But now she was looking expectantly at him, so he had better get on with it.

"How do you think your job is going at the moment?" he asked, and she looked surprised. "Sorry, of course, I should start by saying thank you, of course. The Fisher Quay development is the biggest project you've brought in yet, and we, that is the partners and I, are very pleased with it. And with you, of course," he added as an afterthought.

"Of course," she smiled. Did he have any idea how often he said that? Once they had run a book on it in the team, and she had won a tenner. Thirty-four times in one meeting was the record.

"Your bonus this year will obviously reflect that success, of course."

She nodded. "Thank you, Steve." He seemed to be struggling a bit. Curiosity had replaced the burst bubble of her brief sexual fantasy.

"I had a meeting with the partners last week. A strategy meeting, in actual fact."

"Oh yes?"

"Yes, as you know, we are about to embark on that new project in Croatia. We see that market has real potential. It's the up-and-coming Riviera of Eastern Europe."

"Yes, no doubt Dave will make a huge success of it," she said dryly. She would have liked to learn to sail in Dubrovnik. That would have been another tick against her wish list before hitting the big four zero. It was still a man's world. It was all about sinking pints in the Forest and Firkin after work. She wouldn't play that game. Life was too short. Alison didn't need to earn more money, and she didn't care about her job title. But she did hate being bored. Their starters arrived and as Steve moved his hands from the table, She noticed that he had started biting his nails. She hated bitten nails on a man.

"The thing is, Alison . . ." he said, and she had a momentary flutter.

He sounded so tentative. Maybe this lunch was a come-on after all. She looked up.

"There is another strategic market I want to get into."

Bitten nails were not the end of the world, she thought ironically. "Yes?"

"And you came up in discussions as the best person to do it."

"Yes?"

"Because you bring so much to the team. It's not only me who thinks that."

"Oh, yes?"

"It was James who said it first."

"Said what?"

"That you would be perfect for it."

Alison blushed and stared at the olive-oil-coated leaf of lollo rosso on her plate. Maybe they were going to send her to Croatia instead of Dave? Or to Bulgaria, maybe? Not as exciting, but it had potential.

"Expansion in Ireland. It's having such a boom, and we are missing out. Galway, on the west coast, is the fastest growing city in Europe."

Alison choked on the pine-nut she had been nibbling. She coughed it up onto her plate and grabbed her glass of water, glad she could buy some time to suppress her incredulity.

"Sorry," Steve said weakly. She had seemed so enthusiastic about Ireland in the taxi, he had thrown away the carefully planned script to sell this job to Alison in a really positive way. Good for her development as a manager, good for her career with the firm. More of the kind of work she enjoyed doing. The opportunity to make her mark on a blank sheet of paper. All the prepared phrases had been abandoned, and now she was sitting in front of him, completely aghast. She looked as if she might even walk out of the restaurant.

"You want me to go to Ireland?" she spluttered, in between gulps of water.

"It will be a great opportunity to make your mark, to –"

"Have you *been* to Ireland?" she asked.

"Well, no, but everyone says –"

"It's lovely. The people are so great. They're warm and friendly. The Celtic Tiger is going mad. They have money to burn."

"Yes, yes." Maybe she wasn't so upset after all.

"But Steve, it's so *dull.* There is one theatre in Galway. Cinemas, OK. Restaurants, OK. No galleries, no museums, no Wembley arena, no comedy club. Crap public transport. It's not a city, it's a town."

"I believe it's very picturesque," he said.

"I believe Dubrovnik is very picturesque, too."

"Alison, it's been decided. We're going to give Maurice a go at the strategic kind of work you've done so well for the last year. It's a building block and we need to expose everyone on the team to that kind of stuff."

"What if I say no?"

"You could go back into the team, take on Maurice's clients?" He didn't even have the conviction to erase the question mark.

Alison wiped her lips with the linen napkin. "I just need to visit the ladies'," she said. She managed to extricate herself and get her handbag from underneath the table, and walked through the restaurant with her head held high, not caring this time who was watching her.

"*Alison?* Hello, how *are* you?" a confident and half-familiar voice greeted her as she passed the last table in her bid to escape to the coolness of white tiles and mirrors.

She turned, and there was the crooked smile, the dark eyebrows and the long-fingered hands of Ronan

Murray. He was half-rising from his chair, reaching out his hand to her. How do you greet your absent lover after ten years apart?

They kissed on the cheek, and he introduced her to his companion, a grey-haired man in his fifties in a very smart blazer.

"I'm only over here for a couple of days. Business, you know," Ronan said, and he still had that easy familiarity she remembered. He was wearing a single-breasted navy linen suit with a white T-shirt underneath. One day's stubble darkened his cheeks.

"You're looking well. What are you doing these days?" he asked, unashamedly running his eyes up and down her body.

She sucked in her tummy slightly. Ronan had exactly the same effect on her, all these years later. "Legs to mush," was the phrase she and Lisa had invented for that liquid, uncontrollable sexual attraction.

She smiled. "Same old, same old."

"Rich?"

They had shared a joke that she would be rich before him, with her uncanny knack for spotting a good opportunity and closing a profitable deal.

"Fairly."

"Big house?"

She laughed. When they were together she had fantasised about a huge house in the country, with loads of kids and dogs and a pony. Alison always suspected that she had scared him off. "Yes." She fought the urge to fill the gaps. Let him think she had found the dream with someone else. "And you?"

His gaze flickered. "Dogs, kids, a pony."

So he remembered? "Nice."

"Well, he's more of a donkey, actually." Ronan grinned. His companion laughed.

"Lovely to see you," she said. There would be no pretence of staying in touch. "Nice to meet you," she said to the man whose name she had already forgotten. Ronan had that effect. He eclipsed the people around him. Although he was tall, he wasn't particularly handsome – slightly wavy almost black hair, a high forehead and bluey-green eyes – but he had charisma. When he laughed, the whole room was filled with it.

She managed to walk to the door of the Ladies' without looking around. She fought the sensation of a magnet drawing her back.

She sat on a pink wing-backed chair in the powder room, and picked at its gold brocade. Her reflection didn't help so she turned away from the harried-looking red-cheeked woman with the suddenly flat hair and slumped shoulders. So, the Ronan chapter was well and truly closed – happily married with numerous kids. Ironic. Ten years wasn't such a long time, after all. He must have found someone else very quickly. She was still looking for Mr Right.

And as for work, what options did she have? She could just walk back out to Steve and resign. She could be in another job within a week. Or even take a break for a few months, and go travelling, and do something different when she came back. That was quite exciting. Then there was the demotion option, which had nothing going for it. She could go and talk to James and the other partners and tell them she would sue them for sex discrimination, unless they acknowledged that they were treating her less favourably than the young studs coming up through the ranks. Not much going for that option except the immense satisfaction of making a fuck-off speech to get it all off her chest. And then there was the option of toeing the line, doing the Ireland thing. It was a lovely place, but she just couldn't imagine slowing down her pace of life that much – and what about Lisa and the baby, and her own new-found resolution to see more of her parents? That would all go out the window. But if she did it for a year, max, then she could come back to London and claim her rightful place on the senior management team.

In the meantime, Steve was sitting out there with his lunch getting cold in front of him if he had any manners at all. She couldn't believe she had thought even for a moment that he was coming on to her. Cringe. She stood up and brushed herself down, repaired her make-up and combed her hair until her scalp was tingling. She was a woman in charge of her own destiny, and nobody was going to tell her what to do. She marched out of the Ladies' and nearly crashed into Ronan, who was standing up to go. She just nodded and kept going, as if it was the most normal thing in the world.

She rejoined Steve at the table.

"Sorry about that. Bumped into an old friend," she said, and noticed that he had actually started eating his meal. Her place was empty and a waiter immediately hovered, asking if she was ready for her main course now? She shook her head. "No, I don't think I'm hungry any more, thank you. I'll just have a double espresso, please."

Steve looked humble. "I'll wait," he said.

"For what?"

"For your food to come."

"No, you go ahead. That looks delicious. I'm not hungry, honestly. I'll have a coffee to keep you company." Having decided not to storm out and resign there was no point in antagonising him.

The coffee arrived.

"Steve, can I have the weekend to think about it? It's obviously a very big decision, and I need to give it some time." She gave him the deal-closing smile that always worked with clients.

"Of course," he said.

Sophie spent an hour on the phone to Ger, who for once had the wit to just listen rather than give advice. But after she had off-loaded all her frustrations with Liam, with the way Father O'Leary seemed to rely on her for everything and with her life in general, Ger couldn't resist any longer.

"Get onto the internet and book yourself that weekend in London. I'll give you five hundred euro as an early fortieth present to go on a shopping spree. Ring up your English friend and get yourself organised. I'll take the kids for the weekend. You'll feel much better when you have something to look forward to."

Sophie sighed. That was only one part of it. Ger of all people should know the pain of feeling unloved.

Spending money and keeping busy were only distractions. They were like taking an aspirin to kill the pain of a brain tumour. She had thrown herself into the parish work as a way of keeping her sanity when the kids were tiny, and now that they were getting more independent, Father O'Leary seemed to think she had more time to sell raffle tickets for the church roof and organise the annual Community Mass. Half the people on the road never showed their faces in the church, but he seemed to think she would just go and knock on their doors and not only get them to come to the Mass, but to help with the flowers, or the readings or the prayers of the faithful. The saddest thing of all was that at least three families had moved into the road over the last year and she hadn't a clue who they were. Some neighbour she was. As a child, she had always been struck by her mother's generous nature. When anyone new came to the neighbourhood, or someone was coming home from hospital after having a baby, she would bring over a casserole dish to them, and bake an extra cake for them when she would be baking for the family. Sophie hadn't even rung the doorbell to say welcome to these new people and now they would think she was some kind of evangelist, trying to lure them into the church.

She spent the rest of the day, in between making and clearing up after meals, two loads of laundry and Michelle's reading practice, mulling over what she would say to them.

Liam had promised, for what it was worth, to be home by seven, so she could go and knock on a couple of doors before it got too late. They were all working people, so they weren't around during the day. She kept an ear open for the sound of Liam's car door slamming, so she could hush him at the door. The kids were already asleep. Typical, she had thought at 6.30 when Michelle started rubbing her eyes and asking to go upstairs. They'll be tucked up in bed when he gets in, and he'll wonder what on earth is so difficult about my idyllic life. Sure enough, the door slammed at 7.05 and she swallowed her irritation at his noisy entry, just glad that he had kept his promise about the time.

"They're asleep. Keep an ear out for Michelle – she might be coming down with a bug. She was very crotchety and tired today. I'm just going to the new bungalow next door to Caseys' and the one across from Walshes'," she said, kissing him briefly on the cheek.

She welcomed the blast of sea air after half an hour in the steamy bathroom fighting damp little legs into pyjamas. She felt an urge to keep walking past the lit windows of her target houses, right down to the beach. Ten minutes later she stood, listening to the rhythm of the small waves sucking and pulling at the sand. A grey peace settled over her. She breathed through her mouth, not wanting the stale seaweed smell from the washed-up heaps behind her to spoil the purity of the moment. Her feet slowly sank further into the wet sand and she wondered how deep her weight would settle if she didn't move again. Was it possible to drown vertically? She pulled her soaking feet out of their sink-holes, thinking that Oisín would love the monster-like suction sound they made. She jumped over the line of dry seaweed waiting to be revived by the returning tide.

"You're in your element," her mother had said, when Sophie had complained about being taken for granted. "You were always great at organising things. When you were a little girl, you had all the other kids at your beck and call. The shows, the stall for lemonade in the back garden – everything was organised by you."

"Maybe I'm fed up with organising my husband's shirts and my children's social life," Sophie had moaned.

Michelle had been to other children's houses for lunch twice this week, so Sophie had picked up Oisín, gone home for an hour or two, and then gone out again in the car to collect Michelle. Surely you weren't supposed to turn into a taxi driver until your children were teenagers? Sophie had just bought a family calendar, so she could keep track of the swimming lessons, the party invitations and whom she needed to invite back for tea.

"It's just a phase, love. Wait until they're both at school and you'll have loads of time on your hands. Aren't you lucky you're at home with them instead of out working?"

She sighed. Her mother was right. The grass was always greener, she supposed. She knocked at the first house and was pleasantly surprised when a woman about her own age opened the door. She had assumed it would be a young professional couple and she'd have nothing in common with them.

The woman smiled. "Hello, you're from down the road, aren't you? Come in. Come in." she held the door wide and Sophie stepped onto an immaculate beige carpet that made her want to take her shoes off. She had visions of squelching damp sand through the hall. She looked down.

"Kick them off there, if you want to," said the woman, "but don't feel you have to."

Sophie smiled. "With kids you get so used to taking shoes off, sometimes you forget how adult visitors should behave."

The woman led her to a huge kitchen at the back of the house with French windows overlooking a beautifully landscaped garden with night-lights glowing along a gravelled path.

"That's gorgeous," said Sophie. She had unsuccessfully craned her neck so often, passing the house, trying to see what they had done with the back garden.

"Thanks. Well, it would want to be, since it's what we do for a living," the woman said, putting on the kettle. She turned around. "Sorry, I'm awful rude. My name is Rachael Comerford. My husband Ciarán is out at the moment. He'll be sorry he missed you." She held out her hand.

Sophie shook it. "Lovely to meet you. I'm Sophie Hanrahan. I'm sorry I didn't come down to welcome you sooner."

"Not at all, it's nice to see you. A cup of tea?"

Sophie wondered how she could broach the subject of the Mass. "That would be nice, thanks. I just got the kids off to bed, and came straight out."

"A glass of wine, so?" said her neighbour, and Sophie couldn't help grinning. "My kids are older, but I remember that stage so well. Coming down the stairs at half eight gasping for a glass of wine." She opened the fridge and poured a glass of Sauvignon Blanc into a large goblet.

"Sláinte," said Sophie, and they clinked glasses. "How old are your children?" She had never noticed any kids on the road or in the garden.

"A girl, seventeen, and a boy, fifteen," said Rachael.

Sophie couldn't imagine her kids being that old. "You must have started young, so," she said, and Rachael nodded.

"It was hard work at the time, when you're young and you don't know anything, but now it's really lovely. I'm nearly friends with them sometimes. They come and ask for advice, and I hope that if they got into problems they'd confide in me." She held up her crossed fingers.

"I haven't even seen them around," said Sophie.

"They're gone early in the morning with their dad. He gives them a lift into town so they don't have to hang around at the end of the road for the school bus. In the spring Orla might cycle, but the weather has been so miserable, you wouldn't want them out in it."

Sophie sipped the wine and the inclination to tell Rachael about the Mass slipped even further away. If they were going to be friendly, she could bring it up another time, she decided. It would be almost rude to mention it now, when she was halfway down the glass. At quarter to nine, after another drop of wine, she finally stood up to go. They had traded anecdotes and worked out that teenagers were just toddlers in bigger bodies, full of unreasonable demands, insecurities and downright disobedience. Rachael said they should collaborate on a book revealing the secrets of positive parenting. Sophie decided she could hardly turn up at the other neighbours' house breathing alcohol fumes to compound her intrusion, so she stumbled in the dark up the road to home.

Liam was in his usual position in front of the television, and she felt a profound sense of sadness that her first inclination was to go straight to bed rather than snuggle up beside him and talk about the day. She suppressed the urge to sneak upstairs and popped her head around the door.

"Cup of tea?" she asked, and he nodded, not taking his eyes off the screen.

She joined him on the sofa just as the football coverage finished.

Liam took his mug of tea. "Thanks, love," he said, and stroked her cheek with his fingertip. "Good day?"

Sophie looked at him over the rim of the mug. "Yes. You?" She was hoping he wouldn't ask what she had managed to rope the neighbours into doing. The Mass was only six weeks away and she had been moaning the night before about all the planning she had to do. That was why he had volunteered to come home early.

"Did you get the prayers of the faithful doled out?" he said.

Oh, dear. She shook her head. "I sat in one house for the whole evening drinking wine. Rachael and Ciarán are the couple in the big bungalow. Two kids, a boy and a girl, teenagers, and they run a landscaping business together. She was lovely."

"Sure you can ask her again, another time, can't you?" he said, knowing she would be feeling bad after not achieving her mission. Sophie was a woman not easily deflected, and that was one of the things he loved about her. He did really love her, he told himself, as the guilt rose in his gullet.

"I can, of course. I invited them down for dinner on Saturday night."

"Saturday? We're supposed to be seeing John and Ann that night at their house, aren't we?"

"No, that's the following week."

"Grand, so." He sipped his tea contentedly. It would be nice if Sophie made a friend on the road. Sometimes she got a bit lonely, and then she got unsettled. Then she looked around for things to keep her busy and her life got even more hectic.

"You could always say to Father O'Leary that you don't think the community Mass is a good idea. What was wrong with the old-fashioned Stations going around to everyone's house?"

"Liam, you know perfectly well what was wrong with it! People spent six months painting the house and doing up the garden and going into hock buying new furniture in case the neighbours might look down their noses at them!"

Liam laughed at her. "I know, but sure it went on for generations. You could say to Father O'Leary that what was good enough for our parents and grandparents should be good enough for us. At least when it was one family hosting it, everyone else didn't have to get stressed out."

Sophie hated the mocking tone he used to say Father O'Leary's name.

"I'm only teasing you," he said, when he saw Sophie's face. She used to laugh at his jokes and share his sense of irony about these things. She seemed to take everything very seriously these days.

"I know," she said, and kissed his dark, stubbled cheek. She was sometimes hard on him.

Chapter Seven

Alison suppressed her anxiety about work, determined to make a success of the weekend with her parents. She bought a bunch of flowers for her mother from the florist's on the corner near the train station, deliberately choosing something not too flamboyant. Her mother passed the stall every day on her way to the shops. She would know the price of the out-of-season gerberas and think it a shocking waste of money. Tulips were closer to the mark. Alison wheeled her weekend case carefully behind her and felt like a flight attendant in her long dark navy coat. Would her parents have liked her to do a job like that, rather than trying to compete in the male-dominated world of property development? Had they looked at her in her school uniform, sucking her pencil while she did her sums, wondering how she would turn out? She suspected that their apparent indifference was a careful avoidance of putting pressure on her. Alison had always been allowed to make her own choices – about continuing piano lessons, about leaving the school swimming squad, about which 'A' levels to take. But the corollary of that freedom was the loneliness of making all those decisions alone. Their hands-off style of parenting had just made her feel remote and at times, unloved. She sighed. The net curtains in the front room shivered, and she knew her mother had been watching for her arrival. Alison would ring the bell and her mother would answer the door, feigning surprise.

Inside, she hugged her mother briefly and noticed how frail she seemed. They went through to the kitchen just as the kettle whistled to the boil. Her mother would have used the thirty seconds between leaving the front window and answering the door to put it on the hob.

The tray of tea things was laid out already with digestive biscuits arranged in precise concentric overlapping circles. The good china cups were sitting primly on their gilt-rimmed saucers. The silver teaspoons shone. In recent years Alison had acquired the guest status reserved for visiting aunts and certain friends. At first she had been upset. She would have much preferred her tea in her favourite Marks & Spencer's flowery mug. But her mother enjoyed the ritual of taking the carefully stacked china cups and saucers from the walnut cabinet and rinsing and drying them before laying them on the lacy tray cloth with their matching plates. There were not too many occasions warranting such ceremony, and Alison wouldn't deny her that little pleasure by asking for a mug. Now her mother precisely placed the teapot on the tray and carried it to the breakfast room. Most of the other people on the road had knocked the kitchen through years ago, absorbing this old-fashioned red-tiled room and installing modern kitchen fittings. Her parents' kitchen still had green-painted wooden cupboard doors with chrome inlaid black handles and chequerboard yellow and pale green lino floor tiles. It only just missed the chic of being retro.

Alison loved the breakfast room, the familiar pictures and tapestries reminding her of her childhood tea parties. The embroidered heart with 'Sarah and Dennis, 1959' in pink swirly writing had been a wedding present to her parents from great aunt Libby, and Alison had thought it very romantic when she was little. Wooden French doors opened onto the patio, which was a riot of colour with polyanthus, winter pansies and narcissi crammed into pots of every size and shape.

"This is nice," she said. "Where's Dad?"

"He's having a little lie-down, darling," her mother said, her lips narrow with concentration as she tipped the heavy teapot and poured. There was a slight shake in her hand.

"Is he not well?"

"No, he's not, really. We have something to tell you, and he wanted me to break the news first."

Alison felt as though the bite of digestive biscuit in her mouth might choke her.

"It's his bowels," her mother said in the same tone she had used with Alison as a child to make sure she was 'keeping regular'. She didn't meet Alison's eye.

"Is it cancer?"

Her mother nodded.

"Do they know . . . ?"

"How long he has? A few months to a year, they said."

"Can't they operate?"

"It's quite advanced. He's had some problems for a while now, but he didn't like to talk about it, even to the doctor, and now it seems it's too late for intervention."

Alison sat staring at the daffodils waving in the breeze. "When were you going to tell me, if I hadn't come to see you?"

"Well, it's not something for the telephone, is it?" Her mother sipped her tea.

Would they have patiently waited for months and months while the poisonous cells invaded his body, wondering when she would decide to call?

"It takes some getting used to," her mother said, after a few minutes of silence.

Alison couldn't speak so she nodded furiously, biting the trembling in her lip. If she let go even a tiny bit, she would surrender to a grief much greater than that of her father's loss. The sadness she felt was for the years and years of her mute intolerance of him while she was still living at home as a teenager. For all the times she had competed in swimming events or won certificates, and she hadn't shared her success with him. He had seemed not to care. She had decided when she was thirteen that it was better if he wasn't there. Other dads jumped up and down on the sidelines at Sports Day, clapped at swimming galas, hugged their triumphant daughters when they completed a complicated gymnastic routine.

He sat there, straight-faced. When she was eight, his indifference had made her try harder. Maybe he thought it was easy to swim four hundred metres, so she would swim six hundred metres next time. By the time she was ten she wondered if she should be on grade eight piano instead of just grade six. She would practise her pieces for hours, and she desperately wanted him to ask her to play. He never seemed to have the time to sit and listen to her. At the age of twelve, she had been elected as prefect of her class, and had proudly worn the shield-shaped badge, waiting for him to notice at teatime. He hadn't said a word. That was when she had given up trying to impress him. Twenty-seven years later, Alison wondered how he had felt, to be excluded from all her triumphs. Then she remembered her university graduation day, and felt the familiar resentment that had coloured her view of him for so long. Her parents had taken the event very seriously, dressing smartly and taking her out for a nice lunch when she would have preferred to go to the pub with the friends whose parents hadn't bothered to come to the ceremony. She had stood in her mortarboard and gown, holding her degree scroll at the requisite angle for the photographer, smiling into the lens. Her father had been quiet all day, and out of the side of her eye, she watched him as he stood in the quadrangle, waiting for her to be finished. He was overawed by the ancient ivy-covered bricks that echoed centuries of privilege and learning. She was cross with him for looking like someone who had never set foot in a university before. How dare he humiliate her on her special day? Her mother had taken her arm as they strolled through the gated arch to return her rented cap and gown before lunch. Her simple exclamations of pleasure in the grandeur of the surroundings soothed Alison. She shouldn't be so condescending. Her parents had never had the opportunity of going to university. They had supported her as best they could over the last three years, although she had to take on a part-time job as well, because there just wasn't enough money to cover everything. She didn't resent any of that. It was her father's apparent inability to rise to the occasion yet again that revived all her teenage insecurities. By the time they got to the restaurant she had reconciled herself to the fact that seeing her parents' imperfections was part of growing up and she needed to let go of her own hang-ups. After lunch her father had said how proud he was. That was enough to keep her going for quite a while.

Her mother spoke again. "Do you want to go up and see him?"

Alison looked at her. It was the last thing she wanted to do, but he would have heard the doorbell, calculated the time for a cup of tea, and the news to be broken. Now he would be up there wondering when she was coming to talk to him.

Alison didn't want to see him lying on the candlewick bedspread. She wanted him to be out weeding the vegetable patch and talking about what seeds he was hardening off in the greenhouse.

She stood up. "I won't wake him if he's asleep."

"Oh, he won't be asleep," her mother said, collecting the crumbs from the table into her hand. "The birds will enjoy these," she said, as she always did, opening the lock on the French window to throw them out.

Alison wondered if she was imagining the smell of old age as she climbed the stairs. Was she just projecting her new perception of her parents as ageing mortal beings onto the familiar smells of lavender, furniture polish and toilet freshener that had always permeated these walls? She trailed her hand along the dado rail out of habit and was surprised to find her fingertips dusty, like some Mary Poppins test of good housekeeping. She bought some time by going to the loo and washing her hands. He would hear the flush and the kick-start of the extractor fan, ticking away the seconds until he had to face her. She went to their bedroom door and tapped gently on the varnished wood.

"Come in," he said in a tiny strangled voice that irritated her despite her best intentions. She had always suspected him of being a hypochondriac, making the most of every tiny illness to have her mother running up and down stairs after him.

"Hello, Dad," she said with a smile in her voice as she pushed the door open.

She was glad she had uttered the words before going in. He looked much worse than she had imagined. He had lost lots of weight since Christmas – only six weeks ago. His skin was slightly yellowed, and he looked about ten years older. The worry would do that, she supposed. Then she realised that this was a physical deterioration of his whole body, not just the pinched expression of anxiety on his face.

"Hello, Alison," he said, and he looked away, not

wanting to see her shock reflecting his own worry about the speed of his decline. Day to day he could convince himself that he wasn't looking too bad. Alison's expression now denied his tenuous hold on that hope.

She sat on the edge of the bed, and took his hand. "I don't know what to say," she said, and he smiled bravely.

"I didn't know either, that's why I got your mum to tell you," he said. "I bottled out."

"I would have, too," she said. How could she ask him how he was feeling without sounding flippant? What an insult to the enormity of what faced him. 'How do you feel about looking into the jaws of death?' 'How does it feel to have to lie down for a snooze at eleven o' clock in the morning, when you've always been an early riser, ready for anything?' She squeezed his hand.

"I know, love. I know," he said.

She could see the chasm of grief in the grey depths of his eyes and she realised with a shock that she had inherited the stormy-sea colouring of hers and those long lashes from him. "I'm sorry," she said.

"Don't be sorry. We have to be brave about it. Make the most of the time left. I might get a whole year. We might even get another Christmas."

That brought the tears. She would be forty next Christmas, probably without a father. They kept coming, huge droplets rolling down her cheeks and neck, while she tried to control the jerky sobbing. He squeezed her hand now, and passed her a fistful of tissues from the bedside table. She kicked off her shoes and lay on the bed beside him, alternately blowing her nose, and staring at the beige-tinted ceiling.

"It needs freshening up," he said, as if he was about to go and get the stepladder and his pot of paint, and start doing it now. "I've never noticed it in the night-light, but it looks downright grubby when you're lying here in daylight."

The daytime rest must be part of his routine now, she supposed. Her father would find that really frustrating, especially at this time of year, when he would want to be digging the soil and planting for the spring.

"How are you feeling?" Somehow the question didn't seem so loaded now.

"It's pretty uncomfortable. I have painkillers, but it's the worry about the end, you know, the indignity, that bothers me the most."

"Mmmn." He was a very private man, and reserved. He wouldn't even want his wife of forty-seven years to have to care for him in that very personal way.

"I often wondered which way I would prefer to die – you know, your body or your mind going first. I suspected that it would be worse to have your mind go – in case you started doing really ridiculous things, or calling people nasty names because you had lost control of your mental faculties. Now that it's happened the other way, I wonder if it would be a blessed relief not to be aware of what's ahead."

"I know what you mean," said Alison. She was seeing for the very first time what had made him seem indifferent to her every cry for attention. Embarrassment would have stopped him jumping up and down in the spectators' gallery of the swimming-pool, even if she had won a gold medal. His battle with self-consciousness was what she had seen on her graduation day – on unfamiliar territory he had withdrawn into sullen silence. They lay together for an hour, semi-dozing and then he suggested that she go downstairs.

"Will you be all right?" she asked, and he gestured urgently towards the bathroom, so she left smartly, leaving him that dignity intact at least.

"How did you find him?" her mother asked, stopping in the middle of setting the table for lunch. The smell of pot roast filled the kitchen. Steam from the vigorously boiling carrots dulled the windowpanes.

"He's lost an awful lot of weight since I saw him last," said Alison, looking at the food curiously. Saturday lunch was usually soup and sandwiches.

"We eat the main meal in the middle of the day now. He finds it easier on the digestion," her mother said, noticing her look.

Alison braced herself to eat a full lunch. Her stomach felt as though it had shrunk with the shock of the morning's news. She could hear her father shuffling downstairs. He looked old when he came into the kitchen, the rubber-soled tartan slippers slapping off his heels as he walked. He touched her arm, and she felt closer to him than she had for years. Just when she was about to lose him. They sat down to lunch, drinking the tinned reconstituted orange juice her parents preferred to any other adult beverage she had ever tried to introduce. They didn't like bubbles, herbs, slight flavours of peach or citrus, or anything dressed up in a fancy bottle. Her mother opened a fresh tin, added four tins of water to the jug, and filled their glasses – free from the petrol station, she announced. This time Alison joined them without the customary twinge of irritation about how set they were in their ways. Who was she to criticise them after half a century together?

Sophie's message on the answering machine cheered Alison immediately, when she got home on Sunday afternoon.

"I know it's a bit cheeky, but could we put a date in the diary for our girlie weekend?"

Alison picked up the phone to call Sophie immediately, partly because she needed to postpone thinking about work for a bit longer. She was delighted that Sophie had got in touch.

"Hi, I got your message," she said when Sophie answered.

"Great. My sister said she'll take the kids whenever it suits," Sophie enthused.

They settled on the weekend before Easter, agreeing that London was at its best on cold bright spring days.

"How's life, anyway?" asked Sophie, hoping that if she got in first, Alison wouldn't ask her. She didn't know if she had the energy to pretend that life was rosy for her.

"I got some bad news about my dad over the weekend. He's been diagnosed with bowel cancer, and he wasn't looking too good," said Alison, rehearsing the phrase she would repeat again and again over the coming months.

"Oh, I'm very sorry to hear that," said Sophie, feeling as if her own problems had shrunk to insignificance.

"I haven't really got my head around it yet," said Alison. "You think your parents will go on forever, don't you, even when you're our age?"

"I suppose we're lucky really, that they've been in our lives for this long, to see us settled, and . . . doing well at work, and things."

"So, do you like musicals?" Alison went into social organising mode.

"I prefer a good play, to be honest," Sophie replied. She found it irritating when everyone burst into song and the story went on hold while the entire cast waxed musically lyrical.

"OK – I'll book something for the Saturday night. We can have a bite to eat beforehand in the West End, and make a night of it."

"Sounds great," said Sophie, and then she heard squeals of frustration from Michelle and shouting from Oisín. "I think I'll have to go. Anarchy is breaking out here. Listen, thanks a million, and I'll email you when I have the flight booked. Sorry about your dad."

Alison could postpone the moment no longer. She had to make the decision about work the same way as she always made big decisions. She rooted around in her bedside cabinet for a pen to make a list of pros and cons. She asked herself why she hadn't mentioned the prospect of the move to Galway to Sophie. Because she didn't want to be told that it was the right move? Because she didn't want to disappoint Sophie if she decided not to go? She wasn't sure.

The pros.

If Steve kept his word, and it was only for a year, she could move up the ladder at work more quickly than if she stayed in London. Meeting new people. Interesting to work in a new market. The location was nice, if pedestrian. She arrowed the word 'pedestrian' into the 'cons' column.

The cons.

Being far away from her parents. On Friday she would have put that down as a pro, because she wouldn't feel guilty for not visiting them every weekend if she was living in Galway. Now they needed her so she would feel guilty. Missing friends, like Lisa. Missing the buzz of London. Her house being empty (she couldn't bear to let it to strangers). Being out of the loop with the London office politics. That could be lethal for her career.

The cons were mounting up.

Learning to sail! She could really do that in a year.

What if her father died while she was away?

She could get cheap flights home every month or so.

Escaping a fortieth birthday party in London. Lisa was bound to organise something, despite Alison's pleadings to ignore her birthday this year. She could hardly do a surprise party if Alison wasn't around. Going to the spa in Connemara would be nice, but she wouldn't be doing it every week.

The lists were even. She was no further ahead. Her parents would tell her to do what was right for her. Lisa would tell her to stay, Sophie would want her to come. What did she want herself? Alison wanted to call someone to talk about it, but she couldn't think of anyone objective. If there was a man in her life, would it be any easier? She suspected not – he would just be another interested party with his own agenda.

Alison tossed and turned all night. Crazy images of herself paragliding in a wetsuit overlapped with Dave bonking Croatian beauties and Steve's smiling face looming out of the darkness to say, "Well done, Alison. You can stay in Galway for another year."

She shot awake when the alarm rang and was surprised she had ever got to sleep. There was a feeling in her stomach of facing the inevitable – those pre-exam nerves that scream, 'I don't want to do it, but I have to!'

She went to work dressed in her sharpest suit and high-heeled black boots. She had a meeting with Steve at ten, and she spent two hours reviewing her project notes, wondering what timescale Steve had in mind, and how Maurice could possibly cope with her clients. She nibbled a wholewheat cracker and drank a carton of fresh orange juice. No more Danish pastries mid-morning. She had felt slightly too plump when Ronan was eyeing her up and down, so she was going to do something about it instead of overcompensating with expensive suits and manicures.

She walked into Steve's office at exactly ten o'clock, with fresh lipstick and a squirt of Issi Miyake to boost her.

"Hi, how was your weekend?" he asked, pointing to the chair in front of his desk. No cosy chat at the low coffee table then, cross-legged like the guys did, with their Starbucks coffee mugs and their football banter.

"Not great, to be honest," Alison said, knowing that the answer was irrelevant to Steve. This was just a task that he was doing for the partners and he could be very single-minded.

He shuffled the papers in front of him, and absent-mindedly glanced at his BlackBerry screen when it pinged to tell him he had a new email.

"Tough decision?" he asked, finally looking at her.

She nodded. She wouldn't share her dilemmas with him. A man wouldn't. "I'll go, but I have some terms."

"Oh, yes?" he said in the tone a parent would use to a child offering to be good if they can have a treat.

"I don't want to go for longer than a year, because I'm not renting out my house and I don't want to leave it empty."

"Mmmmn." He even managed to convey this non-syllable with some condescension.

"I want a centrally located apartment, expenses paid, and flights back to London once a month."

He just stopped himself from laughing. Alison didn't seem to realise that the whole Galway thing was just a way of sidelining her. Maurice's father was a huge investor in the firm, and had let the partners know what career path he expected for his son. Alison didn't have any such leverage with the partners. She wasn't in a position to negotiate terms.

"I've just found out that my father is dying of cancer. You need to make leaving the country an attractive proposition for me"

Silence.

"I want to go on a reconnaissance trip, to find

somewhere to live and I'll need a few days off. I've used up my holiday entitlement for this fiscal year."

"Yes, that would be the three-week trip to Egypt, wouldn't it?"

Why did he have to be so cruel about this? Was there some need to prove his supremacy?

"Is it a deal?" she asked, wanting to sound in control but feeling like the kid holding out her hand for an ice cream.

He stood up and shook her hand. "Deal. First of April OK?"

Alison agreed, and he called Maurice to join them as they went through her client files.

She broke the news to her mother when she called her during the week, and got a characteristically low-key reaction.

"That sounds like a nice change, love," her mother said, with not a hint of resentment.

"I've negotiated flights back every month so I can come and see you." Alison felt the need to show she had taken them into account.

"That will be lovely," her mother said. "You liked it in Ireland, didn't you?"

"Yes, it was lovely. I'm a bit nervous about working there, though. It's very different to London."

"That's no harm. You could do with getting more fresh air and exercise. It will probably be a much healthier lifestyle."

"You're right, Mum. Maybe you and Dad could

come and visit, when I've found somewhere to live."

"Maybe indeed," said her mother.

"The sea air would be nice for him."

"So when are you off?"

"They want me to start on the first of April."

"You haven't much time to get organised."

She knew her mother was wondering if she would manage another visit before she left.

"No, but once you make a decision like this, it's better to get on with it."

"We've always encouraged you to be independent. You have to do what's right for you."

Alison had noticed they often slipped into parallel conversations, with only passing reference to the other's input.

"Thanks, Mum. I'll come and see you in a couple of weeks."

"That would be nice."

The conversation with Lisa was much more difficult. "What about Charlie? He'll be born while you're away!" She sat back on the sofa, stroking her stomach.

"I'm coming back once a month," said Alison. "A year will fly."

"But I want you to be godmother!" Lisa blurted out, knowing she was being selfish.

"Lisa, don't make it worse." Alison wanted to cry. She had gone through the pretence of weighing up the pros and cons, just to give herself the illusion of making a decision. She didn't really have a choice. To move firms now, when she was on the brink of making it onto the senior team would be stupid. She would be back at square one in another firm, proving herself for years before they accepted her into the upper ranks. "I'll come back when he's born, and I'll come back for the christening."

"It might just be a naming ceremony."

"Whatever." Alison was getting frustrated now. The child wasn't even born, and they were haggling about such trivia. "It's only just over an hour on a plane. If you moved to Wales like you keep threatening, you'd be four hours away from London. It's not a big deal, Lisa."

"Alison, you know perfectly well it's a big deal. I'm trying to get you to think. You don't want to go, so why are you pretending?"

Lisa was able to say all the things her mother couldn't.

"I have to do it, Lisa. The glass ceiling is bloody tough enough to get through. If I don't take this job, my card will be marked, and that's the end of my career."

Lisa had the wit not to say, 'So what?' There was a line in the sand, even in their friendship.

"It might be fun," she said instead. "You might meet a nice Irishman!"

"I forgot to tell you, with all the stuff about Dad and work. I bumped into Ronan last week!"

Lisa screeched. "How could you forget such a thing? How did he look? Was he as gorgeous as ever?"

"He looked older, definitely, and he had a bit more style about him. He's aged well. Married, kids, dog, donkey."

"Donkey?"

"Long story."

"And did he take the time to tell you his long story?" Lisa teased.

"He was with a colleague. I was with Steve. There wasn't time. Anyway, what would be the point?"

"Yeah, right," said Lisa. "Admit it, you'd love to know what he's up to, and what kind of a wife he went for, and why he left in the first place. But you're being very sensible. No point in getting hurt by opening old wounds. Your friend Sophie will be disappointed if you go to Galway."

"If I *go*? Why?"

"You were supposed to be showing her a good time in London, weren't you?"

"Lisa, will you get it into your thick skull? This is not an Arctic expedition. Galway is an hour and twenty minutes from Luton Airport. That's quicker than getting the train to Newcastle. I'm not giving up the house. My life is not going to end. I can still invite Sophie to London for the weekend."

She handed Lisa the list of pros and cons she had written.

"Good positives," said Lisa. It was an old trick they had invented years ago, to dispel their doubts about new men, new jobs, new situations. Focus on the positives. It could be very effective.

"When the baby is born, you could even come over and chill out with me for a while. The beaches are great."

"Alison, newborn babies don't do beaches. They guzzle milk and sleep all day."

"I was talking about you. You could sunbathe and breastfeed and read all those books you've been saving up."

"Sounds idyllic." Didn't it rain all the time in Ireland? Lisa was trying really hard. She didn't want Alison to go, but it wasn't fair to be bitchy about it.

They arranged to meet again for coffee and shopping the following Saturday. Alison wanted to buy some new work-clothes. She wanted to impress, and clothes always helped. Anything to suppress the nervous feeling in her stomach. What if she failed?

Sophie was over the moon when she heard that Alison was moving to Galway. "When you come over for your reconnaissance weekend, will you stay with us? We'd love to have you," she enthused. "I can get some details of apartments in town, and make appointments for you, if you like?"

Alison was overwhelmed. "Are you sure it won't be too much trouble?"

"Not at all, I'd be delighted. Give me the dates and I'll get it organised for you. Have you a budget?" Sophie got a pen and pad, and took down all the details. Alison felt a bit embarrassed, as if she was treating Sophie as a secretary.

"I'd love to do it," said Sophie mischievously. "I'm such a nosey-parker, I'll have a great time finding out about all the new apartments."

Chapter Eight

Three weeks later, armed with her digital camera and a weekend bag, Alison sat in the tiny propeller plane as it circled Galway airport, suppressing an urge to be sick. In a small plane there was no escaping the counter-intuitive physics of metal tubes being able to fly. There was some turbulence, but finally they landed on the single runway strip, and taxied to the airport building.

Inside, she just stopped herself from laughing when she saw the luggage carousel. It bore no resemblance to a carousel but was a single strip of conveyor belt, emerging from a hole in the wall, through which she could see the luggage handlers pushing the bags they had just unloaded from the plane. It was the fastest luggage turnaround she had ever seen, and five minutes after landing she went through the Arrivals door.

Alison had insisted that she would get a taxi. "Second on the left after the turn to Silver Strand? Is

that really it?" she had asked when Sophie had told her
how to direct the taxi-driver.

"You'll see when you get here. It's pretty obvious,"
Sophie had said. "You don't have to do 'the knowledge'
to be a taxi-driver in Galway." She had always been
amazed at the rigour of the training that black-cab drivers
in London had, and their ability to find the tiniest back
street with no directions.

Alison spotted two children sitting on the front
doorstep as the taxi pulled up, but they disappeared like
rabbits down a burrow as soon as they saw her, with only
the soles of their shoes showing as they raced inside.

Sophie emerged from the house looking like the
quintessential housewife, drying her hands on a tea
towel, as Alison turned away from paying the fare.

"Look at me!" Sophie said, throwing the tea towel
aside. She hugged Alison. "You made fantastic time. I
thought you'd be another half an hour yet." She waved
at the taxi-driver, who had reversed through the gate,
and beeped as he sped off.

Alison took a deep breath of the salty air. "You're
really close to the sea, here, aren't you?" Between the
passing cars, she thought she could hear the breaking of
waves.

"Two minutes down the lane. Come in and have a
cup of tea, or do you want something more substantial?"

"No, I'm fine, honestly. My tummy is always a bit
funny when I fly. That's such a short trip, isn't it?"

"It's great, but you're only up and you're coming
down again, so it can upset your tummy." She yelled,
"Kids! Come and meet Alison!" They peered around the

living-room door like cartoon characters, one head above the other, their fingers gripping the door frame. Both were smiling.

"Hi guys, do you want to see what I have in my bag?" Alison asked, knowing they were at an age where curiosity would overcome shyness in a very short time. She passed by, following Sophie to the kitchen, and she sensed them following, full of suppressed giggles. Ten minutes later, Oisín was pushing her trolley bag down the length of the hall, ostensibly taking it to her room, but enjoying the diversion of pretending it was a forklift truck. He and Michelle had munched through Alison's chocolate offerings in very fast order and now she was firmly established in the kitchen, sipping her tea.

"Does your mother give you the good china cups when you visit now?" Alison asked.

Sophie laughed. "Do you know what? She did for a couple of years after I married Liam, and I teased her that I felt like a visitor. Then the kids came along and I think she was terrified the china would get broken, so she stopped."

Alison couldn't imagine teasing her mother about anything. It was unlikely that she would have kids as an excuse either, so she was probably destined to drink from fine china cups forever.

"How's your dad doing?" Sophie asked, sensing Alison's reflective mood.

"Not great. I went to see them a couple of days ago, and he was resting again. I think it's hit him harder than they're letting on."

"They spend their whole lives protecting us, don't they? It doesn't stop because you're forty . . . or in our case, thirty-nine!"

Alison smiled at Sophie's brave attempt to cheer her up. "I promise I won't be a Miserable Minnie while I'm here. I'm really looking forward to the weekend!"

"The bad news is that we have to take the kids to the two apartment-viewing appointments this afternoon, because my friend Maeve who was going to look after them has one of her kids at home with chicken-pox."

"No problem. They seem as good as gold," said Alison, watching Michelle colouring in a Disney princess picture, her tongue protruding with the effort of staying inside the lines.

Sophie smiled at her daughter's endeavours. "We're big princess fans, aren't we, Michelle?" she asked, and the little girl nodded, not wanting to be diverted from her purpose.

Oisín's forklift sound-effects wafted down the hall, as he wheeled the bag to park it at the bottom of the stairs.

"Will he be all right?" Alison asked anxiously. "The stairs?"

"He'll be grand," said Sophie. "He won't go up with it."

Michelle finished colouring in the picture, and presented it to Alison with a flourish and a blush. It was Ariel, the mermaid, surrounded by her underwater friends, the dolphin, the lobster and the little fish. The creatures were coloured in every iridescent shade, and Ariel had scarlet hair and a bright green tail.

"Wow, that's fantastic, thank you!" said Alison. "Is she your favourite princess?"

Michelle shook her head shyly.

"Tell Alison who's your favourite, sweet-pea," said Sophie, rubbing her daughter's back as if to infuse her with confidence.

Michelle didn't raise her eyes above the floor, but she whispered, "Snow White, because she makes friends with the little animals and the dwarfs."

Alison was impressed. "Do you like little animals, then?"

"Yes, I like dogs and cats the best."

This was hotting up into a real conversation. "Are you going to help me choose a nice place to live while I'm staying in Galway?"

Michelle nodded.

"Do you know what I'm going to do, as soon as I choose the right place?"

Michelle shook her head.

"I'm going to get some Blu Tack and stick this picture up in my bedroom, or maybe on my fridge door."

Michelle's face lit up and she hugged Alison. "I can do lots more for you, if you want," she said, imagining a new gallery for her art-work. The kitchen walls were already full, and Sophie couldn't bring herself to cull the pictures. Each one was special. She could remember the ones they had made at home, and the ones from the playgroup. When Michelle started school in September, she would do a big clear-out, she supposed, and put them all in scrapbooks. If she ever had the time.

"Let's get ready to go then," she said. "The first

appointment is at two – you have time to freshen up and then we can head off. Michelle, will you show Alison which room she's sleeping in?"

Michelle took Alison's hand and led her to the stairs.

Sophie quickly cleared the dishes and wiped down the table. She hated coming back to a mess. Tea was already prepared, and in the oven with the timer set to come on at four. The kids would be hungry when they got back and she wouldn't expose Alison to the half an hour of hell that would ensue if food didn't immediately appear on the table.

Alison was pleasantly surprised as they drove the length of a wide, well-kept promenade. "It's like Brighton, or Bournemouth," she said, "but without all the Victorian houses."

Sophie grimaced. "When I was young it was even nicer. It was all green on the other side of the road, but they're putting up apartment blocks and hotels all along it now. Galway is very popular."

When they reached the other end of the promenade, Alison could see similarities with less attractive south-coast towns. Arcades and shabby hotels predominated, interspersed with fast-food joints.

"This is where the students used to come clubbing when I was at college," said Sophie, "but the activity is much more focussed on the middle of town now, so this place has never really smartened itself up. It's lovely in the summer, because somehow you don't notice the tat so much, but it's a bit sad in the winter."

Five minutes later Sophie was manoeuvring the car into a multi-storey carpark in the centre of town. "We can walk to the two places from here. It's easier than trying to find somewhere else to park."

As the children climbed out, competing to hold Alison's hand, Sophie bent down to look them in the eye. "Remember the deal?" They nodded solemnly, but Michelle had a twinkle in her eye that didn't guarantee good behaviour.

"What's the deal?" Alison asked.

"If they're very very good while we're looking around, they can have a comic each." Sophie tried to sound stern.

Michelle and Oisín walked very sweetly on either side of Alison, until they got to the lift, when they started bickering about who was going to press the button. Alison got them to agree that Michelle would press the down button and Oisín the up button on the way back. But Sophie could see through Michelle's strategy. She was counting on Oisín forgetting the arrangement, so she would get to do it twice. Fine, as long as they weren't making a show of her. Alison seemed to be quite impressed so far.

The first apartment was in a converted warehouse on Abbeygate Street, and Alison loved the stone walls and the curved windows. She had dreaded the thought of being in an anonymous concrete block like some of those she had seen on the way through town. The street was narrow, almost medieval in feel, with pavements that could only take one person at a time. They walked single file to the entrance, and Alison spotted the Estate

Agent immediately, as she waited outside. They shook hands, and the woman was very friendly, making a point of saying hello to the kids as well.

Sophie tried to catch Michelle's eye for a last-minute reminder, but they were through the door, and running up the stairs before she got a chance. Delighted squeals drifted down from the first landing.

"Don't worry, they can't do anything too dangerous," reassured the Estate Agent. "My own two are the same age. You can't keep them contained."

Sophie climbed the stairs and ushered the children up to the third floor, where they arrived just as Alison and the other woman came out of the lift. There was only one other apartment on this level.

"It's a single guy of about forty-five in there. He's been here about a year. Works in Boston Scientific, above on the Tuam Road," said the Estate Agent, unlocking the apartment door.

Alison wondered if she was trying to match-make, or if giving a potted life history of other tenants was normal in Ireland. She made a mental note not to tell too much about herself. The apartment was delightful, with lots of natural light, solid wood floors and modern minimalist furniture. It was decorated just exactly how Alison would have chosen and she didn't need to see any more.

"How much is the rent on this one?" she asked, not even caring whether she sounded too keen. This wasn't work, this was life, and the place felt right.

"One thousand five hundred a month," said the woman, not even blinking. For a second Alison forgot she was talking about euros and just managed to not let her jaw drop.

"And the deposits and things?"

"Two months in advance, and we like to have a standing order set up for the monthly payments. It saves chasing and processing cheques."

"Fine," said Alison. "I'll take it."

"You don't want to see the other one?" Sophie and the woman asked, almost simultaneously.

Alison kicked herself. She wasn't used to being organised by someone else. She had always made her own decisions, without having to consult. But Sophie had gone to a lot of trouble to arrange everything, and it would be ungrateful to treat the decision about where to live so lightly, as if the apartment was a commodity, and she had money to throw around. The firm had given her a budget of seven hundred and fifty pounds a month, and she didn't mind topping it up for the right place, but perhaps she should look at the other apartment, just to be sure.

"Yes, of course, I should. I'm sorry. I just meant that I really like it, and if the other one isn't better, I'd be happy in this one."

It sounded feeble but Sophie's face relaxed and she went to retrieve the children from the bathroom where Oisín had unerringly found the bidet control and had sprayed the tiled wall with a jet of water.

"Look, Mammy, a bottom cleaner!" said Michelle. "It's like the one in Grandmama's house in France."

"Why can't we have one of those?" Oisín asked, only slightly chastened by Sophie's fiercely whispered scolding.

There was a hand towel on the rail and she used it to dry the walls. "Get into the hall right now and stand still," she hissed, pushing them in front of her. "Do not move until I tell you!"

Alison and the woman were waiting.

"Off to the next one?" Sophie said brightly, and her children recognised that best-behaviour tone of voice that even mammies use sometimes. They behaved well for a full ten minutes, until Michelle said her legs were tired. They were walking around the edge of the old Galway docks, to a development that faced the sea, just where the river Corrib flowed into it. Oisín was fascinated by the ships on the moorings. A coastguard vessel was entering the dock as they reached the end of the footpath, and he stood, transfixed. Sophie stayed with him, thinking it was better on balance to keep them amused outside than to get them to traipse around another apartment. But she had really wanted to see Alison's initial reaction to this one.

Alison walked with the woman to the corner of the modern white stone-clad building, fascinated at the use of the brown-field site. It had probably been a shabby storage area or coal depot like the one she could see just around the corner, and its value must have increased tenfold now, with a hotel, apartments, and what looked like a marina club house.

When she stepped into the fifth-floor apartment, she was stunned. A picture window in the living-room faced the sea, and to her right the river flowed quite vigorously, host to hundreds of swans bobbing serenely on its dark waters. To her left she could just see the grey stone walls of old converted warehouses and the entrance to the docks. Across the sea loomed purple grey mountains, which she couldn't identify until the Estate Agent explained it was County Clare, the southern side of Galway Bay. Alison could imagine herself sitting at that window for hours, not reading, or doing anything but watching the changing light of sky and sea.

"This one obviously has a premium on it because of the view," the woman started her sales spiel.

Alison nodded, her commercial instincts finally kicking in and stopping her from jumping up and down.

"It's two thousand a month, but of course you have the extra room as well," the woman said. Alison hadn't even registered that it was a three-bedroom place. "So, if you wanted to, you could get a flatmate . . ."

Alison couldn't imagine having a flatmate after all this time on her own, but she nodded, wanting to keep agreeing with this woman, justifying to herself the outrageous expense of living here. Two thousand, that was about fifteen hundred in real money, she found herself thinking, which meant she would have to pay seven fifty a month herself. She could afford it. What else did she have to spend her money on?

"Is it available from the first of April?" she asked.

The agent nodded. "As you can see, it's a vacant let, so it could be all ready for you as soon as you like."

"I'll take it."

"Sure?"

The woman probably had her down as a serial mind-changer, and wouldn't believe she had done the deal until she had a deposit cheque in her hand.

"Final answer!" said Alison, smiling.

Obviously the agent didn't watch *Who wants to be a Millionaire?* so she didn't get it and just smiled back uncertainly.

Alison's doubts about spending a year of penal servitude in Galway were fast diminishing. She imagined Lisa and the new baby in the spare room, or her parents, with lots of space, and loads of places for gentle walks for her dad. Or he could just sit and watch the boats. Her mum would love the shopping on the little streets they had passed on the way here.

The agent had a briefcase. She perched on the edge of one of the dining chairs to take out the paperwork with her long elegant fingers, while Alison stood at the full-length window and imagined twinkling lights across the bay and a gin and tonic in her hand. She signed up for a year's lease, and wrote out a cheque for the deposit. The woman's face gradually relaxed, and Alison knew she was counting her commission. Easy money, but it would be with such a property. Who wouldn't fall in love with it? In just one afternoon, Alison was starting to get a feel for the opportunities that Galway offered. She would make a go of this job, and she would go back covered in glory. And in the meantime she would learn how to sail on that serene and beautiful bay.

The agent was staying behind to call her office and finalise the clearance of the payment. They shook hands, and she said, "Well, I wish you every happiness here, and I hope you love it."

"I do, thanks," Alison grinned at her, feeling like she was twenty-two and moving into her very first flat.

She bounded down the stairs instead of waiting for the lift.

"I got it!" she yelled across to Sophie, who was trying to restrain Oisín from getting too close to the edge of the dock. Only a one-foot metal barrier stood between him and the deep oil-stained water.

"You'd never have kids in a place like this; you'd be a nervous wreck!" said Sophie, standing up, but holding onto the back of Oisín's fleece. "You got it! Now, aren't you glad you didn't just take the first one?"

Alison nodded. "Thanks, Sophie, I really appreciate all you've done to organise this. Do we need to cancel other appointments?"

"No," Sophie looked sheepish. "These were by far the best two, and I had a feeling you'd fall for one of them, so I only had the other estate agent on standby. I pretended there might be a problem with you getting a flight."

"You could make a career out of this!" said Alison. "I'd give you a job tomorrow."

A gust of wind whirled around the side of the building. "That's the down side of it," said Sophie. "I noticed it was windy the last time I came as well. But you're not trying to keep a garden or anything, and there's parking underground, so you don't have to be out in it if you don't want to."

"Very true," said Alison. "Are the kids up to walking the long way around so we can see the swans?"

"Swans, I love swans!" said Michelle, racing off around the side of the building. They all followed, with even Oisín distracted from the boats by the prospect of the swans.

"This is fabulous," said Alison, as they turned the corner. Opposite, across the river and a canal, there nestled an old-fashioned grey stone church, and on the bank, almost in front of it, was a line of rowing boats, drying on the grass. "We're in the middle of a town, and it feels like a village."

"This was the original fishing village, called the Claddagh," said Sophie, pointing to a terrace of narrow houses painted in a rainbow of colours. "That's where Claddagh rings come from. There's some amazing sepia photographs of the women in the old days in their black shawls and their red dresses, waiting for the men to come home from the fishing."

Now it was obvious that the cottages had become trendy townhouses, with Audis and Golf GTi's parked outside, but as they walked the length of the pier, Alison could imagine the half-doors standing open, and the shawled women watching the horizon for the silhouettes of the returning boats. Sophie was constantly running to keep Oisín away from the edge, and encouraging Michelle to walk on the inside footpath. Alison watched two kayaking students negotiate the current under the arched stone bridge ahead of her and the swans, floating aloof from the indignities of human endeavour. A small whitewashed building declared itself the Galway museum, and she promised herself a look inside as one of her first ports of call. The history of this place was probably quite interesting. There were the obvious remains of a high grey granite town wall to her right, so the town must have had some substance as a trading or military post as well as from its fishing activities. She felt a sense of contentment settling on top of the excitement she had experienced in the apartment. She caught up with the others, and they meandered through some more tiny streets, the smell of cooking emerging from bars and restaurants which were coming alive for the evening trade.

"Come on kids. Let's get the comics here, and then you can read them in the car," Sophie encouraged them, as their legs flagged after a lot of running, jumping and climbing on steps.

"They must have covered at least twice the distance we did!" said Alison, amazed that they were still going.

"The main thing now is to keep them awake in the car, until we get them home and fed. Then they can be as tired as they want," Sophie muttered as she paid for the comics. "Come on, lads. Let's go!" She was like a football coach, constantly on their case and perking them up. They got back to the car, and both children were silent for ten minutes as they flicked through the comics, deciding what stories they were going to have at bedtime.

Alison thanked Sophie again. "I'm really glad you made me wait to see that one. I think I'm going to be really happy here."

"Good," said Sophie. "You haven't even seen the half of it yet. Liam says we can go out on the town tomorrow night, just us girls, and he'll baby-sit."

"Great." Alison had to resist putting her head back and dozing off for a few minutes herself, but she suspected that wouldn't be popular, so she started a sing-song with the children. It had the desired effect, and they made it home without anyone falling asleep. The smell of macaroni cheese greeted them at the front door, and Alison realised she had worked up quite an appetite. She was making complimentary noises about the tea, when Sophie told her she was having scallops and potatoes dauphinoise, but they wouldn't eat until the kids were in bed, so she could have a little spoonful of macaroni to 'keep her going'. Alison sat at the table with the children and relished the familiar but long forgotten taste. She wondered why adults never made macaroni cheese for themselves. It would be much healthier than some frozen ready meal, and much more filling. Alison always ended up eating two of those at a time, defeating the calorie-controlled element as well as the enjoyment element. She would sit there, feeling guilty while the second one spun around in the microwave, knowing it wouldn't taste as good as the first one, but still hungry enough to do it.

Sophie said she would break her own rule of no wine before seven o'clock if Alison would join her.

"To pastures new?" said Sophie.

They clinked glasses. "To pastures new," they said simultaneously, and the children insisted on bashing their plastic cups and joining in.

Liam was impressed by the glossy brochure for the apartment. "Much as I hate to say it, they've really done a good job on that development," he muttered about the rival building firm.

"Sure you're in a completely different market, aren't

you?" said Sophie. "You're much more geared up for the family homes. Those ones out on the Headford Road are selling really well, aren't they?"

"Eighty per cent of them were sold off the plans." He smiled and lifted his glass to Alison. "Enjoy Galway. It has a lot going for it."

He wasn't exactly sure what job she was going to be doing, but Sophie had probably told him. He wasn't going to ask any questions, in case he looked stupid. Sometimes Sophie was so glad for adult company when he came home that she downloaded her whole day in about ten minutes of gabbling as soon as he was in the door. Liam would freely admit that half of it went in one ear and out the other. She looked good tonight, he thought, not as tired as usual, and she had some of her old spark about her. Alison seemed to bring out the best in her.

"How were the kids today?" he asked. He hadn't made it home before bedtime. He had stayed chatting to Theresa for an hour after everyone else was gone. They hadn't done anything, just had a cup of tea. It was nice to unwind like that at the end of a busy day. The kids' bath-time and the hysterics just before bed were the last thing he wanted, so he tried to avoid it as much as possible without making it too obvious to Sophie that he was shirking. He usually got away with three or four nights a week, coming home at about eight when they were fast asleep. They looked gorgeous then, and he loved standing at the door of the bedroom inhaling the fresh smell of them, and watching them breathing gently, eyelashes resting on their smooth cheeks.

"They were fine," Sophie said.

Alison chipped in, "I thought they were great. I had a lovely welcome, and we had a nice game before bed. I even got to read a bedtime story to Michelle."

"Oh, you have a great fan there," said Sophie, jealously. Michelle had asked Alison all about her job, and what kind of clothes she wore for work. She had admired the line of cosmetic creams and potions that Alison had laid neatly out on the dressing-table in the guest room, fascinated by them. Sophie was lucky if she had time to slap on a bit of moisturiser in the morning before rushing out with the kids, and she certainly didn't have exfoliation cream and under-eye cream and cuticle cream. Alison had sat on the edge of her bed with Michelle and patiently explained what everything did. Alison had painted Michelle's toenails with a garish red polish that Sophie didn't particularly like, so she drew the line at fingernails. "You're not allowed to have it on at the playgroup, darling," Sophie had said. "On your toes is fine because no one will see it."

Oisín had been feeling neglected because all the girls were doing boring girl stuff, so he had taken down one of his puzzles and completed it on the floor of his bedroom without any help. Alison had been suitably impressed, so he had condescended to show her his mini-beast collection. It was the easiest hour before bedtime that Sophie had had for years, and she wondered, if Liam came home earlier a bit more often, how much more pleasant life could be.

They sat over their meal, chatting. "This is lovely, thanks," said Liam, grateful not to be eating the leftover macaroni cheese he had seen in the fridge when he went to get a beer.

Alison looked at the married couple, their faces softened by candlelight, smiling and laughing about various escapades the kids had got up to, and telling her stories about their time in London together. She had sensed from Sophie that everything was not completely rosy, but looking at them now, they seemed content, and she wondered how long you have to know someone, to have that easiness and familiarity. All her relationships had been fairly stormy, with the balance of power shifting from one person to the other, the uncertainty of how long it would last always looming in the wings. She had never felt totally relaxed with a man – there was always something to be proven – her independence, her intelligence, even her soft side. In her counselling sessions, Alison had come to realise that her relationship with her father was a big part of this insecurity in her. Sophie didn't seem to have that need – she was the quintessential organiser, a fantastic mother, a loving wife and now was showing that she was a good friend too. But there was no guile about her – she was a nice person with it, and Alison envied her naturalness.

At 11.30 she suppressed a yawn, "Sorry guys, I'm going to have to go to bed. Travelling always tires me out, and I've had a lot of excitement today."

Sophie nodded from her position on the sofa, her head resting in the crook of Liam's arm. "See you in the morning. A bit of shopping while the kids are out?" She was relieved that Alison wasn't going to be one of those visitors who kept you up half the night, forgetting that kids don't need alarm-clocks to be up at half past six in the morning.

Alison was happy to go along with Sophie's plans. Now that she had somewhere to live, she could relax a bit. Work loomed on Thursday, with a very busy agenda for the day. Tomorrow she would just take things as they came, as long as Sophie delivered her to the airport on time for her flight.

Alison's first conscious thought was that she was being attacked. A heavy weight rested on her chest and there was a high-pitched sound piercing her left ear. She opened her eyes in shock, her heart pounding. On her chest, Michelle was spread-eagled, her head almost on the pillow, and she was screaming at Oisín, who had just launched himself off the floor to try and wrestle his sister.

"Get off! Get off!" Michelle was screeching, while she kicked wildly at Oisín. He wailed as her heel made contact with his chin. Luckily he decided that telling Mammy was the best option, and raced out of the room, crying loudly. Michelle had to be there to defend herself if he was going to tell tales, so she levered herself off the bed, her elbow briefly compressing Alison's windpipe on the way. Alison lay there gasping for a moment, and then laughed out loud. The occasional shocking assault was a useful reminder that kids were a mixed blessing. She had gone to sleep with an ache of loneliness that wasn't just prompted by the cosy scene of Liam and Sophie snuggled together on the couch. She had popped her head briefly into the kids' bedrooms as she passed, and inhaled the peace and innocence of their night-lighted world. She had felt like a spectator who would never know the joy of really participating, and it had hurt. Now she could hear Sophie scolding, and the children wailing. There was probably an eighty-twenty rule for enjoying children, and she suspected that the eighty per cent hard work was very hard work.

Sophie knocked at the door. "Tea?" she asked, holding a steaming mug. Alison smiled. "They didn't wake you, did they?" Sophie put it down on the bedside cabinet, using a cork coaster to protect the walnut veneer.

"Not at all, I was ready to get up," Alison lied. She sipped the tea. "How long have I got?"

Sophie checked her watch. "I'll have them at the front door ready to go in about half an hour."

"Great. I don't do breakfast, so I'll be ready then too."

The sound of the shower in the en suite bathroom drowned out the noises of running bare feet, screams, shouted instructions and *Fireman Sam* music that were the staples of Sophie's mornings. Alison emerged and took twenty minutes to carefully administer all her potions and put on her make-up.

Michelle peeped around the door while she sat at the dressing-table in her underwear and silk kimono. "You look like a princess getting ready for the ball," said the little girl, admiring Alison's mascara brush from afar. She had been told not to set foot in Alison's room, so she made sure that not even her big toe crossed the threshold. "Mammy never does all that. She puts on a bit of lipstick and mascara, and sometimes she puts on nail polish if she's going out with Daddy."

Alison wondered what Michelle would make of the cellulite on her thighs, and the dry flaky skin on her shins that she had to keep regularly moisturised. Her mother didn't have those either. She smiled at Michelle in the mirror, as she plucked a stray hair from her eyebrow line. "Your mummy is beautiful already, isn't she?" Alison waved the mascara wand over the dressing-table and wondered if they did all suddenly disappear, would she look so different? They had become the habit of a lifetime. She had suffered terribly with acne as a teenager, and her experimentation with the elixirs of life had started then. Most of them were useless, but the carrageen moss exfoliant she had bought at the spa was working a treat, and she thought the kelp extract moisturiser was also having an effect.

"I think you're beautiful," said Michelle, and Alison guessed she had just had a 'twenty per cent' moment.

"Thanks. Tell your mummy I'll be there in two minutes, will you?" She had to find a pretext for Michelle to disappear while she slipped off her kimono and pulled on some clothes. Michelle was back almost instantly, curious about what Alison was going to wear. Her favourite cashmere jumper and Kaliko trousers seemed to go down quite well, but the pointy strappy shoes were a firm favourite. Michelle asked breathlessly if she could try them on when she came home from playschool if she was a very good girl and Alison reassured her that she could. They walked hand in hand down the hall, and Michelle insisted on leading Alison step by step down the stairs.

"Control freak, like her mother," whispered Sophie as Alison arrived at the bottom and her hand was grabbed once again so Michelle could steer her to the door. "Ready then? Sure you don't want to take a piece of toast?" Sophie was slipping Oisín's coat on over his arms while he was distracted by a spider running along the top of the front door.

"No, I'm fine, thanks." Sophie's hair was rough-dried, and she had only a tiny bit of make-up on, but she still looked ten years younger than the reflection Alison had just left in her mirror. Surely kids were supposed to age you, not make you look younger?

Alison followed her escort to the car, and sat in the front seat, as instructed.

"You're the visitor and you're an adult so you sit in the front," Michelle told her, while she climbed onto her own booster seat in the back and strapped herself in.

"I saw this great card in the newsagent's the other day, and I think I'll send it to you," said Alison as Sophie slid into the driver's seat, and handed Alison two tiny rucksacks, her handbag and a bottle of water. "A little girl is sitting on her mother's knee looking very thoughtful. It says 'Mummy, I bet you can't wait until you're young enough to know everything.'"

Sophie laughed and then spent five minutes trying to explain to Michelle why it was funny. She raised her eyes to Alison. "Sometimes, God forgive me, I don't talk at all, because whatever I say, I have to go to such great lengths to explain it, I'm exhausted."

"It's bound to be a sign of intelligence, don't you think? An insatiable curiosity?"

"Well, I don't do intelligent conversations until I've had some tea, and that, my dear, is exactly what we're doing after we drop these two reprobates off."

"Mammy, what's a retrobrate?" came Michelle's voice from the back seat.

They sat in a little cobbled courtyard on Kirwan's Lane, Alison relishing her tall latte and Sophie delicately sipping her first cup of tea of the morning. The almond croissants had been irresistible.

Alison didn't even feel her usual 'day of departure' anxiety. Her flight wasn't until 6.40, but normally she would have a knot in her stomach from the moment she woke up until she was sitting safely on the plane. Here, in the bright March sunshine, there was no need to worry about anything at all.

"I thought in the middle of my shower this morning of how I can get the flat paid for by the firm," she said.

"Really? I thought they'd given you a fairly tight budget?"

"They have, but they're also assuming that I'll rent an office space. I can use the third bedroom, get it set up with fax and internet access, and work from there."

"What about when you have clients visiting? It would be very intrusive, if you're living there as well, wouldn't it?"

"Most client meetings happen on site, or I can meet them in hotels or restaurants. A lot of it is wining and dining anyway. The communication is mostly done by email, and as long as I have a fast enough broadband connection, I can send and receive drawings and pictures as well. It will save the firm a fortune."

"Sounds like a good idea, then. As long as you wouldn't end up eating, sleeping and breathing the job."

Alison had worried about that too. She wasn't going to try and make lots of new friends if she was only staying a year, and she couldn't just assume that Sophie would be around when she wanted to go out. Sophie had a busy life too. So she planned to sign up for sailing lessons, and maybe do some jogging on that lovely promenade. It went all the way around the edge of the bay, so she could run for about five miles with a view of the sea. What could be better? She would go back to London a different woman. This could be a whole year of detox, away from the temptations of dinner invitations, drinks after work and lazy Sundays reading the papers. She would exercise, eat more healthily and get lots of fresh air, just like her mother had said.

She grinned at her friend. "There's no danger of that. I've got great plans for turning myself into a new woman."

They avoided the shopping centres, because Sophie somehow knew that Alison would be a boutique kind of girl, so they browsed through some smaller shops, and Alison managed to spend a few hundred pounds on shoes and a handbag. Sophie envied the careless way she handed over her credit card. Alison was spending her own money and didn't have to have the slightest pang of guilt about spending it on herself. Alison was surprised when Sophie didn't buy the lovely little pink pumps she tried on in Karl Scarpa. "They look gorgeous on you. They'd be great for the summer. Just slip them on with any old skirt and you'd look really smart," Alison encouraged her.

Sophie shrugged. "There's no point. Honestly." Alison didn't really get the fact that she didn't have any reason to look 'smart' in her day-to-day life. Sophie had loads of nice shoes and sandals for going out, for the rare times she did, but her Birkenstock slip-ons were the most glamorous thing she would wear on her feet during the day. Faced with milk and food blobs, saltwater stains from the beach, a dusting of flour, and some mud from Oisín's digging patch when she went out to rescue her cutlery from burial, the pink pumps wouldn't stand a chance.

She put the pumps back on the shelf. She spent the ninety-five euros further down Shop Street, on a gorgeous summer dress for Michelle with a matching hair-band, and a pretty embroidered lamb's wool cardigan.

Alison raised her eyebrow. "Do you ever buy anything for yourself?" She admired Sophie's selflessness. Would she be the same if she had children? She bit her lip. She had to stop projecting herself into a different life.

"I love buying things for the kids."

Even though Liam was always telling her that his money was their money, Sophie felt uncomfortable whenever she bought clothes she didn't really need for herself. Buying for the children wasn't the same, though, so she went to town on dressing them in lovely little outfits, and they always had French shoes. There was some cathartic pleasure in that, without any of the guilt of self-indulgence.

"Michelle will be in a school uniform from September, so I'm going to make the most of dressing her for now. She'll soon be getting all stroppy about what she'll wear and won't wear. *Carpe diem* and all that."

"I need to do a bit more of that, I think," Alison said. Seizing the day. Another self-improvement target to add to her list for the year.

They had lunch in a restaurant overlooking the bay, and Alison sighed with satisfaction after a delicious crab salad and Irish brown bread. "Sophie, I have eaten more food since this morning than I would normally eat in the whole day. You are a bad influence!"

"It's all healthy stuff though. I bet you feel good on it. I was like you when I was working. Black coffee on an empty stomach as soon as I got to the office, and then nothing for hours. How I didn't get an ulcer I will never know."

"I thought you worked from home?"

"My first job when I went over to London was doing European telesales for a conference hotel near Wembley. I got in at eight, worked until about seven in the evening and then I took an hour to get home. I was a wreck. I was so determined to have a job that used my languages that I didn't see the wood for the trees. The money was crap, my life was crap, and one day I woke up and decided I didn't want to do it any more. I took the translation work for the publishing company and got even less money but I felt much better in myself, and I didn't have to commute."

"I think you had the life-changing moment a bit earlier than me, then," said Alison. "About ten years earlier."

"But ten years on, you've got your own flat, a fantastic life, independence, money to go wherever you want on holiday, a real profession. You're a person in your own right. On my bad days I feel like I'm just an appendage to Liam and my children."

"But you have the family, and you could go back to work if you wanted to. I don't even have a man, so I could end up a rich and lonely old spinster." Alison laughed to dispel the gloominess that was descending.

"Choices, choices." Sophie sipped her mineral water. It was good to be reminded that she did have some. Being at home with the children was her choice, and she enjoyed it most of the time.

"It's much simpler for men, isn't it?" Alison said reflectively. "I don't want to go off on some feminist kick, but they never have to compromise, do they? Their careers are very rarely affected by whether or not they have a family."

Three of the guys in Alison's office had kids, two of them in the last year. There was no change in their working pattern. They had bags under their eyes for a couple of months but the only thing that changed in the office was the screensaver on the computer. Cherub-cheeked babies had replaced the tigers or dynamic dots. All their wives had gone back to work. She imagined them, packing bags for the childminder or nursery in the morning, with nappies, changes of clothes, emergency juice supplies, while he shaved at the usual time. She would shove mushed-up Weetabix down the baby, trying not to get vomit on her jacket while he took his carefully pressed suit from the wardrobe, kissed her goodbye, and slammed the front door. She would drop off the child, precision timing essential to her getting to her first meeting on time, feeling bad that she was only reading the papers for the first time on the Tube journey, trying to sound credible and engaged when her afternoon meeting went on and on and she had to excuse herself at five o'clock to go and collect the kid again.

In Alison's office the only working mother was Eloise, and she was increasingly given the low-key, back-office jobs, because it wouldn't do if she had to rush out of a client meeting at five, and she only worked three days a week anyway. She had definitely lost some of her edge. She often seemed to drift off somewhere else during a conversation, and Alison couldn't get through. She knew it was probably lack of sleep, and changed priorities, but Alison couldn't help it. Her respect for Eloise had diminished a little bit. Her opinions seemed less grounded, her arguments were less well thought out. She was sliding into career oblivion. And once she got there, there was no climbing back. The next generation of hungry young things was already biting at their heels, waiting for their chance to take the big clients, and make the big commissions. Sophie looked at the expressions flitting across Alison's face as she stared at the sea, and wondered what thoughts were driving them.

Chapter Nine

The office looked just as it had when she left on Monday, and Alison was strangely unsettled by that. She already felt different, disengaged in some way. It didn't help that Maurice was handing out invitations for a riverboat party in May, for his girlfriend's twenty-first birthday.

Twenty-first! Alison felt ancient as she stood at the coffee machine waiting for the frother to put the top on her cappuccino.

"Sorry, Ali, I didn't do one for you – you'll be gone, won't you?"

Alison was just about to say she would be back regularly at weekends, and she was sure she could fit it in, but instead, she took her coffee out and said cheerfully, "Only three more weeks and I'm off to pastures new." She looked over her shoulder. "Give Karen my best for her birthday."

"When can we start the handover?" Maurice asked

as she walked away, and she mentally gave herself a point. He was really desperate to get his hands on the big strategic projects. Wait until he realised how dull it could be! "I was thinking we could spend a couple of days next week – Wednesday and Thursday suit you? We could just block out the days, and really focus."

"Will it take that long?" He looked completely dismayed. Probably by the thought of being closeted away with her in a meeting-room for two whole days.

"I should think so, and perhaps a day or two the following week?" What did he think she did all day? Things that could be handed over with a five-minute chat? "The devil is in the detail with these things," she said, knowing she was irritating him.

He nodded, but the flush around his bobbing Adam's apple gave him away. Alison went to her desk and opened up the project management software programme to run a critical path analysis on her three biggest projects. She was determined that the handover files would be very impressive. She would copy Steve in. If Maurice failed, it wouldn't be her fault. The morning flew by and at two o' clock she stopped for a quick bite of sushi. It was the nearest thing to a crab salad that she could find in the Marks & Spencer's in the basement of the building. She could hardly believe that less than twenty-four hours before she had been sitting looking at the Atlantic Ocean, feeling completely relaxed. Her stomach was in its usual knot, and the sushi slid down without touching the sides. She might as well have eaten tapioca. She went for a stroll and walked against the traffic of people flooding over

London Bridge back to their offices after their lunch breaks. Dull suits, flat shoes, mobile phones permanently glued to their ears. She didn't see one smile and she must have passed over a hundred people in the ten minutes it took to get to Hay's Galleria. She loved the high atrium and the palm trees, the crafty shops and the Italian ice-cream stall. On the black sail of the galleon sculpture with its mechanically moving oars, a red balloon was caught by its string. Standing at the base of the fountain, a small boy was looking longingly up, not wailing or making a fuss, but very obviously trying to work out how he could retrieve his balloon. A young nanny was sitting at a table outside Café Rouge, in animated Spanish conversation. She hadn't noticed what had happened, and the boy wasn't trying to get her attention. Maybe he already knew at the age of four that interrupting a conversation like that was fruitless. Alison was struck by his patience. She went into a stationery shop to buy a thank-you card for Sophie, and when she came out, he was gone. She wondered if he had managed to get his balloon. She glanced at the table where the young girl had been sitting, and she was still there, talking. There was no sign of the boy. Alison glanced around the courtyard area, but couldn't see him anywhere. Then she looked up. There he was, edging along one of the metal oars, holding on by his fingertips to a spar above his head that he could barely reach. Alison shouted to the woman, pointed, and ran to the fountain. The nanny screamed, and threw down her phone. That was her sole contribution in the next five minutes, while Alison talked gently to the boy, got him to stop and then reached up to hold him as he edged back down. She hugged him as soon as he was close enough, and in his dilated pupils and pale skin she could see the residual fear.

"It's OK sweetheart; we'll get you another one," she said, over and over, in answer to his wails of, "My balloon, my balloon!" There was the sound of clapping and when Alison looked up, all the customers sitting near the windows of Café Rouge were standing and applauding her. She blushed. The nanny scolded the boy in Spanish, and he finally released the pent-up tears. Alison felt powerless to intervene, but she just wanted to hug the boy again, to reassure him that he was brave, that everything was all right now. The nanny was probably terrified that someone would report her and she would lose her job. She only looked about eighteen – still a girl herself. Alison sat her down on the edge of the fountain, and got her a coffee. The boy was delighted with a strawberry ice cream and one of the waitresses from the restaurant came out with a new balloon.

Alison left them and walked back to the office, where the quiet hum of the photocopier and the air-conditioned coolness belied the existence of any other kind of life going on outside.

Sophie was frantically beating the choux pastry to make profiteroles when the phone rang. It was Rachael confirming they would be around at 8.30 for dinner. The pastry mix looked too runny, and even as she was spooning it onto the baking tray, Sophie was racking her brain for emergency alternatives. She had some trifle sponges, and the cream, and a tin of fruit salad. That would do at a push, and she could sprinkle it with hundreds and thousands and say she was doing a 'seventies' dessert. Ridiculous that it wasn't cool to serve trifle, unless you called it retro. Everyone loved it but they couldn't admit it. These celebrity chefs had a lot to answer for. They had made food into a fashion. The food should be nice, of course, but wasn't the company more important? Nobody was expecting to eat gourmet food when they went to someone's house. But at the same time, she would want to make them feel welcome, as if she had made a bit of an effort for them. She wondered if Liam and the husband would get on. Liam was making a bit of an effort this weekend, and had taken the kids to Leisureland for a swim while she got everything ready. The most stressful bit of a dinner party, although she could hardly call having the neighbours round a dinner party, was the preparation, with kids running around your ankles. This time, even the absence of the children hadn't helped, and she knew when she turned the oven light on and peered in, that the profiteroles would be disappointing flat pancakes of dough. She took out the trifle sponges and soaked them in sherry. The kids could put jam on the profiteroles and have them at tea-time. They wouldn't know the difference. She turned on the radio and hit on three songs from the eighties in a row. She laughed out loud as Rod Stewart's "Hot Legs" blared out, and she was twirling around the kitchen conducting him with a dripping wooden spoon when the children came tumbling through the back door.

"Mammy, what *are* you doing?" Michelle asked in the shrill tone Sophie used herself when they were up to mischief.

"Just having fun, is that OK?" Sophie grabbed her daughter and tried to tickle her.

"No, it's not OK. Mammy, can have a biscuit please?" Michelle wriggled away. She hated tickles.

"After tea," Sophie said, echoed by Liam as he followed with an armful of coats and bags.

He smiled at her. "Do you want me to hang these up on the line?" he asked, shaking the wet swimsuits and towels out of the bag onto the table along with a shower of sand from a previous beach outing.

Sophie grimaced. She had just polished the glass top on the table and had planned to put a plastic cloth on for the children's tea which she could then just whip off, before setting it for dinner. "Yes, please," she said. She wondered how much of women's time was spent not doing or saying things, to keep the peace. Or was it just her? Maybe Ger was right and she was really a doormat. But Liam had just gone outside to hang up the swimming things. Was that significant, or just the ordinary actions of an ordinary husband? Her father had cooked and cleaned and even done some sewing when she was a child, but she knew that wasn't typical. Liam's father had certainly been very traditional. He had never picked up a dishcloth in his life, and his tea was always on the table when he got in from work. Liam's mother expected her three daughters to help with the housework and but the two sons lolled around being waited on hand and foot. Well, that wasn't strictly true. They had to get in coal, cut the grass and put out the bin. Men's work. And to be fair to Liam, he was very good at all the physical stuff around the house. He wasn't like lots of other builders too, who let their own houses fall into rack and ruin because they were too tired after working on other people's houses all day. He took pride in every brick and fitting, and was always quick to fix things when they got broken.

Oisín stood outside with him now, handing him up the towels to put on the line, happy to be helping with man's work. She and Liam would have to be careful not to fall into the same trap of stereotyping their expectations of the kids. She already had Oisín doing 'baking' which he loved, but in his mind she suspected it wasn't much different to playing with Plasticine. He certainly hadn't developed the light, cool touch of the pastry chef yet. His lumpy baked offerings were grey and hard, but anything tastes good covered in sweet icing. She extracted the tray of flat profiteroles and got Michelle to spread jam on them. As a special treat she was allowed to put on some silver balls too. The boys started playing football in the back garden, and Sophie watched them for a minute. Oisín's body movements were so strikingly an echo of his father's that she never ceased to be fascinated. Temperamentally, the children shared equally their parents' genes, with Michelle tending towards Sophie's curiosity and determination, but with Liam's short temper, and Oisín being softer, more even-tempered, with Liam's interest in things rather than people.

"Mammy, can I stick two together to make a sort of sandwich?" Michelle asked, interrupting her thoughts, and Sophie was brought back to the reality of finishing the trifle, making the starter, and taking the meat out of the marinade before the kids' teatime.

Liam looked at Sophie in the candlelight, slightly flushed from the heat of the oven and her third glass of wine. She was talking to Ciarán, waving her tiny expressive hands, laughing the way she used to laugh with him. He was only half listening to Rachael's description of the new apartments down at the pier. She assumed that was all he wanted to talk about, just because that's what he did for a living. Did she want to talk about gardens all the time? He was trying to listen to Sophie. She was telling Ciarán a story and she had the look of someone trying not to laugh before they get to the punch line. She put her hand on Ciarán's forearm, where it rested on the table. It was a tiny gesture, but he was surprised at the surge of jealousy that rose in him. Ciarán was a nice guy, seemed fairly interesting, and in a woman's book, probably not bad-looking. His hair was grey, but some women liked that, and he had the steely blue eyes of a Robert Newman and the tan of someone who works outside all day. But then so did he, so what did she see in this guy? He remembered feeling like this when the girl he had taken to the end-of-school dinner dance started chatting up Neil O'Hare, who was sitting across from her at the table. He poured some more wine and filled Rachael's glass too.

"Feel like we're at someone else's party?" she muttered to him.

He had almost convinced himself that he was imagining that chemistry. It was broken when Sophie stood up to finish off the sauce for the main course, and discreetly nodded to Liam to clear the plates. Feeling like a waiter under instruction, he stacked them in the dishwasher, and went back to the table, quickly starting a golfing story. After that, they had a four-way conversation for the rest of the evening, and as the guests left, he agreed with Sophie that it had been a success, and they were very nice neighbours to have. They had even been offered the baby-sitting services of Orla, the seventeen-year-old, who had suddenly developed a voracious need for lots of pocket money, and was eager to earn as much as possible at the weekends.

Liam had decided not to say anything to Sophie about her flirting with Ciarán. He didn't want to spoil the nice evening, and maybe he was imagining it, anyway. He helped to pile the dishes, soak the pots and he even rinsed the wineglasses. They left the rest until the morning. He made a vow to get up early and finish the clearing up so that Sophie wouldn't have to face it before Mass.

They went to bed, and although Liam had been tempted earlier in the evening to make love to his wife, somehow the urge had gone off him, and he turned his back to go to sleep.

Sophie lay awake thinking how nice it had been to talk to Ciarán, a man who knew very little about her, but who seemed to be interested in who she was as a person, not what she did as a mother, or a wife, or a model parishioner. She remembered with irritation that she had forgotten to mention the Community Mass again.

Sunday was sunny and bright, and Sophie felt hugely optimistic when she looked out at the clear sky. A slight hangover would be banished by two Paracetamol and, best of all, she could hear Liam clearing up downstairs. He had taken the kids and plonked them in front of the TV, which wasn't great, but at least they hadn't woken her up. It was 8.30 and she could have a leisurely bath and still have time for breakfast before Mass. She filled the bath and put in bubbles, feeling very self-indulgent, but half listening out for little footsteps climbing the stairs. The children had some inbuilt radar that told them she was awake, but in a different room and not giving them attention. Oisín could be happily playing in the garden while she was at the kitchen sink, looking out, but as soon as she stepped out of sight, he would run through the house in his muddy wellies, with some compelling question to ask, prefixed by "Mammy, Mammy, Mammy?"

She slid into the bubbles, already feeling the positive effect of the tablets, and to her shame, thinking about how muscular Ciarán's arm was, when she touched it.

Chapter Ten

Alison looked around at her friends, and felt an odd mixture of regret and excitement. She wondered how many of them, apart from Lisa, would really miss her while she was away. Everyone's lives were so hectic, and planned so far in advance, she had been pleasantly surprised how many had turned up to her leaving-do, organised at fairly short notice. Lisa had insisted that she have a party, but she hated being the centre of attention. The pub was great, with the patio heaters on the terrace luring people out to watch the passing river traffic. Lisa had promised faithfully that she wouldn't make a speech or start shouting for Alison to do one, so she was quite relaxed. It wasn't often she had lots of her friends together in one place, and they all seemed to be getting on great. She moved around from one little group to another, and everyone was congratulating her on the new adventure. She had splashed out on a couple of cases of champagne, to get everyone started.

"Lisa, thanks. You were right. This is great," she said, hugging her friend, whose bump seemed to have grown exponentially in less than a month.

"Sometimes I think you need to be reminded how nice you are, and how many lovely friends you have," said Lisa, eyeing Alison's glass. "Do you think the baby could tell the difference between water fizz and champagne fizz?"

"Go on, I'm sure a little bit of indulgence won't do any harm." Alison held out her glass. Lisa rolled the champagne on her tongue. "Elixir of life! I don't care if I'm breast-feeding, I told Michael I want a bottle of champagne on ice for when I come home from hospital. I'm having severe withdrawal symptoms!"

"Well, if I know you two, the child will be spoiled rotten from day one, so he might as well know what champagne tastes like from an early age!"

"Do you think it's a boy then?" Lisa stroked her bump. They had told the radiologist at the twenty-week scan that they wanted a surprise, so Lisa spent endless hours dithering about choosing the colour scheme for the nursery and deciding what kind of pushchair to buy. But secretly she was sure it was a boy, and had nicknamed him Charlie.

"You're still not really showing from behind, are you?" said Alison, turning her friend around.

Lisa twirled and then turned back to a shocked expression on Alison's face. "What?" she asked.

Alison whispered urgently in her ear. "I think you have some blood on your dress."

They hurried into the ladies', followed by Michael,

who had seen Lisa's reaction from across the room. He stood helpless at the door after Alison chased him out. She opened the door again and whispered, "I'll look after her. Call an ambulance."

The blood was dripping down Lisa's leg when she lifted her dress. She sat down suddenly, all the colour draining from her face. "But there's no pain, so it can't be bad, can it? It's not like the other times."

Alison nodded. "It's probably nothing. Maybe you've just been overdoing it and you need some rest. Michael's going to get help."

She lay her friend down on the patterned carpet, making a pillow from her lilac cashmere wrap. Eloise from the office came in with a glass of water, and relayed a message from Michael that the ambulance was on the way.

"He called an ambulance? I don't need one, I'm sure. I just need to rest. I'll be fine, really," gabbled Lisa. Her hands were shaking when she took the glass.

Alison held it for her as she sipped, wondering if she should cancel her flight to Ireland for the following day. Whatever happened, Lisa would need to rest for a few days, and she might want some company. She stroked Lisa's cheek, and reassured her that everything would be all right. The ambulance was there in eight minutes, and finally, Michael was allowed in to help Lisa down to the front door.

"I don't need a stretcher!" she had shouted when the paramedics appeared, and they had decided that it was better not to distress her by insisting. Michael practically carried her down single-handed. She was tucked into the back of the ambulance and he rode with her, holding her hand. Alison ran back upstairs, to tell everyone what was happening. There was a subdued silence punctuated by the odd mumbled comment.

Then someone said, "Alison, don't feel you have to stay here. Go with Lisa, if you want to."

She had been torn between following the ambulance in a taxi, and returning to her social obligations. There wasn't going to be much of a party now, anyway, she supposed. "I'm really sorry it's ended this way, everyone, and thank you so much for coming. It's been fantastic to catch up with you all, and I promise to keep in touch. Do stay and enjoy the rest of the evening, but I'll go, I think, if you don't mind."

People weren't sure whether or not to clap, so they all smiled at her, and some came to kiss her goodbye.

Eloise had retrieved her wrap from the floor of the Ladies', and handed it to Alison. "I'll settle the bill, and let you know by email on Monday, shall I?" she whispered.

"Thanks, Eloise. I'll send you a cheque. See you in May, for our dinner date?" Eloise nodded. "Will you take my flowers? I can't take them to the hospital." Alison waved briefly and went outside to get a taxi.

Noisy groups of twenty-somethings were standing around in the bar downstairs, drinking steadily and rivalling each other in gales of laughter and punching arms. Some couples were sitting at the tables, heads close together, fingers entwined, their little worlds sufficiently engaging to block out the interference from everyone else. Alison felt a huge sense of loneliness as she stood on the kerb waiting to see the yellow glow of a cab light. Lisa didn't really need her. Michael was there. She would probably have to sit outside the hospital room, not next of kin, not partner or lover, just best friend, waiting for news. She wasn't the most important person in anyone's life. It wasn't an ego thing – that wasn't what bothered her. Alison just felt like she had so much to give, and nobody to give it to. She finally saw a cab through the blur of tears, and waved it down.

"Guy's Hospital please," she said, glad she had had the presence of mind to ask the ambulance crew where they were going. The cab driver was mercifully reticent, and she closed her eyes, resting her head against the cold leather seat cover. What a turn life could take in seconds! She looked at her watch. Less than half an hour ago, she and Lisa had been talking about champagne bubbles. She desperately sent up a prayer to a God she hadn't acknowledged for years, suddenly feeling the huge importance of talking to Him. She had had a childhood superstition about asking for things for herself, but it was always OK to ask for other people. Lisa deserved to keep this baby; she had done everything by the book this time, resting, giving up work even though she couldn't really afford to, sleeping every afternoon, not drinking. *Please, please God, let the baby be OK*, she begged, squeezing her hands together tightly.

"Which entrance, love?" the taxi driver interrupted as he swung the taxi round.

"A&E, I think," she said, and paid him a three-pound tip so she wouldn't have to wait while he fumbled for change.

"Cheers, love," he shouted as she ran in the door.

It took five minutes to find out where Lisa had been taken, and then Alison had to go out of the building and enter by a different door. The warren of corridors was badly mapped, and she frantically ran up and down several hallways before finding the lifts to the right level. There was an orderly in the lift with an empty gurney. Had he delivered someone to an operating theatre, or was he going to take a body to the morgue? She couldn't escape the circle of morbid thoughts while they took forever to go up four floors. She muttered thanks to the man as she left, as if he had done something for her. She saw Michael pacing up and down and ran to him.

"Where is she? Is she all right?"

He held Alison for a minute. "She's in there. I don't know. They took her in there." His usual eloquence as a barrister had left him.

They couldn't sit still. The wails of a woman in labour sounded eerily from further down the corridor. The cheerful pastel shades of the walls seemed incongruous. Half an hour later, Michael leapt to his feet as soon as he saw the door of the theatre opening an inch. A doctor appeared. He looked from Michael to Alison.

"It's all right. Tell me." Michael reached for Alison's hand, and squeezed it so hard she gasped.

"The baby was distressed. We've had to do an emergency C-section," the doctor said. Alison's ears were buzzing. "Mother and baby are stable."

Michael slid down the wall, exhaling. He let go of Alison's hand and she looked down at her crushed, whitened fingers. He was completely limp, and laughing uncontrollably. Alison watched the doctor standing there, waiting for Michael to register that there was more news. He cleared his throat, wondering whether to sit on the chair next to Michael and talk to him at floor level, or wait a bit longer for him to stand up again.

"Michael," Alison said gently, touching his shoulder. His cheeks were wet. She put her hand under his elbow and he stood up awkwardly.

"Sorry." He coughed, and took out a pristinely folded white handkerchief to blow his nose. "Can I see her? Them?"

The doctor nodded. "You understand, of course, that the baby is very premature. At twenty-six weeks, she still has a lot of development and growing to do."

"It's a girl?" Lisa and Michael hadn't managed to agree on a girl's name yet.

"Yes, you have a little girl."

Michael was pushing the door. "Can I go in? Can I see?"

"The baby has been taken to the special care unit. She is very vulnerable. You won't be able to touch her or hold her for some time. The risk would be too great."

"Lisa?" Michael was through the door, not listening.

The doctor gave Alison a sympathetic glance before following Michael, still trying to explain to him the fine thread on which his daughter's life was hanging.

Alison sat on a plastic chair, staring at an abstract print of desert browns and yellows, the wavy vertical lines alternately forming a mother and child or a sweeping sandstorm. In focus, out of focus. Dream or reality?

Minutes or hours later, Alison looked up when Michael came out again. "She's fine. They've given her a sedative. I've asked if you can come with me to the special care unit and they've given permission."

Alison walked by his side, following a nurse with a Scottish accent and a very big bum, accentuated by the tightness of her white dress, and the blue elasticised belt at her waist.

They passed several delivery rooms, and the quiet efficient bustle of the nursing station. UV light glowed through the glass viewing window and Alison felt as if she was travelling through time. The nurse gave them gowns and masks, and they had to slip on fabric covers over their shoes. She pointed to a dispenser and they washed their hands with an antiseptic gel, the evaporating alcohol cooling Alison's sweaty palms.

They shuffled inside the room, the incubators looking like tiny glass cases for museum exhibits. Michael and Alison stopped when the nurse pointed to one of the incubators. "Here she is, the little poppet."

Inside, the tiniest baby lay on her back, naked but for a nappy, tubes inserted to feed her and help her to breathe. Alison touched the glass with her fingertip, desperately wanting to connect with her, to reassure her that the world was not as harsh as it must seem. She would have love and laughter and sunshine and cuddles.

Michael put the palm of his hand flat against the glass. "Hello, princess," he said softly. She opened her eyes and seemed to look at him.

Alison suppressed the slight shudder that passed through her. Was it unnatural to wonder if science should be allowed to override nature? There was the precious tiny person that Lisa and Michael had conceived, alone in a sterile box that was supposed to replace the warmth and comfort of the womb. Was man presumptuous to suppose that the miracle of life could be so easily replicated by machinery? Lisa's body had failed to do what nature intended, so medical science had taken over. She had been given medication to make her sleep, to take away the pain, while her baby was being nursed by a thermometer and an oxygen tube. Alison struggled to smile.

"Thanks, Alison. I needed you," Michael said, putting his arm around her shoulder. He was already asserting the Alpha maleness which had temporarily deserted him. Mate and offspring were warm and secure. Another female member of the herd needed some reassurance. He was there.

"I'll leave you with her for a minute, so you can bond," Alison said, slipping away.

As she took off all the paraphernalia, the Scottish nurse said, "It's a bit overwhelming the first time you see such a wee one. Think of it as another kind of miracle."

Alison was touched by her perceptiveness. She wondered if they would let her see Lisa, and found her way back to the nursing station.

"She's resting now, love," said a big Nigerian nurse. "Stable, so you don't need to worry about her. She'll be full of beans in the morning. A lovely little baby. They will be just fine. Just fine."

Michael appeared then. They shared a taxi, and Alison was dropped off first. The pub they passed on the way was in complete darkness. Even the windows of the landlord's flat above showed no sign of life. The day was over. It was tomorrow. She had completely forgotten about cancelling the flight. She should be checking in at Luton Airport in about seven hours' time.

There were several messages on her answering machine. People saying thank you, and good luck, and asking for Lisa. She sat and watched an Open University programme about relativity, as bemused by the theory as she had been at school. She was about to switch off the television and try to get some sleep, when the next documentary started. They were following two professors who were trying to track down the location of Einstein's brain, which had been preserved after his death for scientific research. Unbelievably, the pathologist who had carried out the post-mortem on Einstein had kept his brain for study, so that scientists could slice it up to see if it had any physical characteristics that could explain his genius. They suspected that he could have been autistic, because of his poor social skills and inability to relate to people, and they had found an enlarged part of his brain in the area which dealt with spatial relations. They speculated about whether it had been bigger when he was born, or whether like any muscle it had grown so big with exercise. Alison watched them holding up thin slices of Einstein's brain, and was saddened that his legacy could be reduced to the physical nature of his brain cells.

By the time Lisa's baby had grown up, the 'miracle' of her birth would probably be commonplace. Alison was profoundly depressed by the thought. Did being born fourteen weeks early count as healthy? Less time in the womb to grow, less time for your mother and father to think of a name for you. More time on this strange planet called Earth.

Alison was surprised when the alarm woke her at seven. She still had her clothes on. The now-crumpled dress she had bought for her leaving party would never seem the same again. She stepped into the shower, thoughts flitting from calling Steve to say she couldn't fly to Ireland to start the new job for at least another week, to calling Michael to ask about Lisa, to not waking him, to calling the airline, to calling the hospital. After a shot of espresso from the pristine coffee machine she rarely used, the thoughts were marshalled into sequential order. She delayed the flight by 24 hours, left a message on Steve's voicemail at work to let him know, and called the hospital. Lisa had had a good night, and had just woken up. She could have visitors after nine o'clock.

Alison finished the last-minute packing, laid out a fresh suit and emptied the last bits of perishable food out of the fridge. Now she could spend the day with Lisa, and be ready for action in the morning

Chapter Eleven

Sophie was looking forward to seeing Alison. Liam had offered to put the kids to bed, so she was putting on her make-up at seven o'clock instead of being up to her elbows in bubble-bath. The usual screeches about shampoo in eyes and the sound of soggy footsteps running across the upstairs corridor did not bother her at all. The sound that startled her was her own contented humming. It had been a while. She went upstairs. Liam summoned a smile despite his generally frazzled expression, and she kissed the kids goodnight. There was a surprising air of calm, and Sophie had a moment of doubt at the front door. Nobody seemed to be too bothered that she was going out. She wasn't sure if she liked it.

There were lots of parking spaces near Alison's apartment, to Sophie's relief. The hotel that was in the same block wasn't too busy during the week. Rain was pouring down, and the time she had spent blow-drying her hair was cancelled out in five steps through the downpour. She was surprised to see no light shining from Alison's apartment when she glanced up, but maybe she was in the hotel lounge already. They were going to treat themselves to a glass of champagne there first, and Sophie had brought another bottle and some nibbles so they could later sit and watch the sea from Alison's picture window. They hadn't taken darkness and torrential rain into account, but what the hell, she thought, shaking out her coat in the hotel lobby.

A pianist was creating a mellow mood with a Nina Simone number, and there were a few people sitting at the bar. No sign of Alison. Her mobile had been switched off all day, but Sophie had just assumed it was because she was travelling, and had forgotten to turn it back on. She didn't know the number for the apartment. After a couple of minutes, she went up to the bar and got a soda-water and lime. Even sipping it really slowly, she only managed to make it last for ten minutes, and then decided to go and ring Alison's doorbell, just in case she had fallen asleep in the bath or something. There was no answer. The mobile was still switched off. Sophie decided to leave a note but then found she had no notebook or paper in her bag.

She was just picking her way through the puddles back to the hotel, when she heard a familiar voice.

Ciarán, her neighbour, was just coming out of the bar.

"I thought it was your car I had seen," he said. "Where's Liam?"

"He's at home with the children. I was supposed to be meeting a friend who's just moved into one of those apartments upstairs. We had planned to have a drink in the hotel lounge. She's not in, so I was going to get a bit of paper from reception and leave a note under her door."

"You look a bit disappointed," Ciarán said, following her into the hotel.

"I'm a bit worried, to be honest. Alison was due to fly over from London today, and she starts her new job tomorrow. I haven't heard from her, so I was assuming the plan hadn't changed. But here I am and here she's not!"

"It seems a shame to waste your night out. Why don't we have a drink together and wait a little while longer in case she turns up?" Ciarán was steering her towards the lounge, assuming her assent.

"Where's Rachael?" it was Sophie's turn to ask.

"Bridge. She's in a weekend tournament and she wasn't expecting to get to the final, so we were going to have dinner. But she's still stuck there, so I thought I'd have a drink while I'm in town."

"We can keep each other company, so," said Sophie, not dreaming that they were doing anything but that.

Two hours later, Sophie realised with a shock that she had had three gin and tonics without even thinking. Liam always drove when they were out in the evening because her night vision wasn't great. Here she was, well over the limit, and she would have to abandon the car in town until the morning and get a taxi home. Ciarán had slid into an unattractive monologue about how his life was a bit dull, and she suspected that he had had one or two drinks earlier on before he met her.

He was great for a chat, and she had been flattered by his attention at the dinner party, but he was fundamentally quite boring. She gestured to the barman and asked him to order her a taxi.

"What are you going to do, Ciarán?" she asked him, hoping he wouldn't want to share the cab.

"I'll come with you," he slurred. "Rachael must have forgotten about me like your friend forgot about you."

Sophie had a guilty start. What if something terrible had happened to Alison, and she had been sitting here drinking gin and tonics? She quickly dialled Alison's number and, finally, it rang. Alison's bleary voice sounded like she had just been woken up.

"Are you all right?" Sophie asked.

"Oh my God, Sophie, I am so sorry!" her friend exclaimed. "I'm still in London. It's a very long story. Lisa had to have an emergency C-section and I've been at the hospital all day but I completely forgot about our arrangement. You're not still waiting for me, are you?"

"No. I am at the hotel, but don't worry, I'm fine."

Ciarán took it into his head to grab the phone. "She's fine. I've been looking after her."

Sophie snatched it back, mortified.

"Who's that?" asked Alison, thinking it didn't sound like Liam.

"Long story. I'll call you tomorrow, and I'm just glad you're all right. Is Lisa OK? And the baby?"

"Both fine. Thanks, and sorry, and I'll talk to you tomorrow. Bye."

The taxi came, and Ciarán just followed her out and climbed into the back seat beside her as if she had agreed to his suggestion. Sophie wasn't annoyed enough to make a fuss. She could drop him off outside his house. It wasn't a big deal. She wondered what Liam would think if he knew she had spent the evening with Ciarán. Probably best not to tell him. But then she'd have to lie about seeing Alison, or else say that she had sat for two and a half hours waiting by herself. She had nothing to hide but she had noticed the look on Liam's face when Ciarán was flirting with her the other evening. He would not be happy. She was looking out the streaming taxi window at the big waves crashing over the wall of the prom, assuming that Ciarán had nodded off to sleep. Then she felt him lurching towards her across the seat.

"Are you all right?" she asked, pushing him back by the shoulder, pretending the movement of the taxi had unbalanced him.

His hand reached out and quickly stroked her leg, just a glancing caress. "I'm fine. You?"

"I think you've had a bit too much to drink," she said, edging herself closer to the door, and turning slightly away from him. She stared at a rivulet of water running down in front of her face, and prayed: *Please, please God, don't let him do anything else!*

His leather jacked creaked. Her body tensed. The tips of his fingers caressed the end of her hair, and glanced the back of her neck. He hadn't moved, but his arm had stretched across the gap between them. Ambassador. Advance reconnaissance. Invasion. She shuddered.

He took his hand away. "Sorry," he mumbled.

She didn't turn around. She was holding the door

handle so hard that she thought it might open and hurl her onto the speeding black tarmac. The taxi-driver was oblivious, tapping on his steering wheel in time to the dreadful country and western song warbling from his radio. The remote crackle of the controller's voice occasionally interrupted. Sophie counted to a hundred twenty-three times before they turned into the road. She directed the driver to stop at Ciarán's house. Inside the lit window of the living-room, Rachael was curled up on the sofa, flicking through a magazine. She glanced up when the car stopped, and waved casually when Ciarán emerged. She went back to her reading and Sophie wondered if she had noticed another head in the back seat, or if she assumed the taxi was just going to the end of the road to turn around. She finally let go of the door handle, and her curled fingers were white and stiff. Her forearms felt like lead bars.

Liam came to the front door, alarmed that she wasn't in her own car. "Are you all right? He hugged her, and she sank into his big bulk, just wanting him to carry her upstairs and tuck her in.

"What happened? Did you have an accident? Why didn't you call me?"

"No, I just drank too much and I couldn't drive."

He half-carried her in and she wouldn't lift her head to look at him when he sat her on the sofa.

"That's OK. We've all done that," he said, stroking her cheek and her hair. "As long as you're all right."

"It was very irresponsible. I won't be able to get the car until the morning, and the kids will miss playschool, and –"

"Lighten up, Sophie. Did you have a good time?"

"I did."

"And you're safe and you didn't do anything silly like driving home drunk, so everything is fine. Come on. I'll make you some hot chocolate." He pulled her hand and she followed him into the kitchen.

"Do you think Alison will be happy in the apartment?" He stirred the milk in the pan, preferring not to use the microwave. The ritual was as soothing as the end result.

"Why wouldn't she be? It's lovely. The hotel is a great place for a drink, too. Nice and quiet."

"We should go in there one evening. Just the two of us. Now that we have Orla down the road, let's make the most of the baby-sitting, and get our social life back." He handed her the steaming mug.

"Thanks, Liam. How were the kids?"

"Grand. Two stories each and they were out for the count."

"They're always very good for you. I have to tell them about four or five before they settle down."

"You're far too soft. That's your problem." He kissed her on the top of the head and went to lock the back door.

Sophie burned her lip trying to gulp down the drink. She just wanted to go to bed so she wouldn't have to tell any more lies, even if they were by omission. Liam switched off all the lights and they went upstairs together. It was only when they were in bed and she looked at the radio alarm-clock that she realised it was only 10.30. Liam's finger traced the line of her silky nightie and she couldn't help the cynical thoughts that crept into her head while he rolled her over towards him. Men were only after one thing, and they would do whatever they had to, to get it.

Alison rang Sophie from the airport, full of apologies. "I was completely distracted, Sophie. Please forgive me."

"Honest to God, it's not a problem. Lisa needed you."

"I could have called though. I was so focussed on work and packing and the hospital I forgot about you."

"Forget it. Listen, I won't be able to do our champagne date tonight though. Liam will be late back from work, and our newly acquired baby-sitter only does weekends."

"Not a worry. I'm exhausted anyway. I stayed up most of the night on Saturday, so I'll just crash when I get to the apartment. Maybe we can catch up at the weekend? From what you said in your last call, it sounds like you've got something to tell me?"

Sophie couldn't match the lightness of her tone. "Nightmare. I'll tell you all about it when I see you."

Her friend Maeve had kindly collected the kids this morning, and Sophie waited at the end of the road for the town bus, feeling stupid. She was wasting a whole morning retrieving her car, for the sake of a couple of drinks. And look what trouble it had got her into. She hadn't been able to sleep all night, wondering if Ciarán had told Rachael, or Rachael had noticed her in the taxi, or if anyone had seen them together in the hotel bar. The taxi-driver could have seen everything in his rear-view mirror. And what if Liam was chatting to Alison sometime and it came out in conversation? How did people have real affairs, without being discovered? She had nothing to hide and she was behaving like a criminal, mentally retracing her steps and counting up the possible witnesses. She was too embarrassed to tell Liam now, because by hiding it last night she had given the whole thing more substance. Ciarán had been drunk and he had made a stupid mistake, but there was nothing more to it. She didn't want any awkwardness with Rachael and Ciarán, and it was best to just forget the whole thing. He probably wouldn't even remember it this morning.

There was a big dollop of seagull poo on her windscreen, which she hoped would be the full extent of her divine punishment. She used up three tissues from her handbag, and the glass was still dull and smeared. The windscreen-wiper fluid bottle was empty so she went to a carwash on the way home. The blue fuzzy brushes swept over her head and at the side windows, giving her the momentary claustrophobic panic she had always experienced as a child. Her sisters had loved it when they were kids, and it was a special treat to have a dry too, with the hot air blowing the water bubbles across the windows until they disappeared. She used to discreetly put her head down, scared that the brushes would break through the glass like aliens from *Doctor Who* and sweep the family away to infinity. As an adult she just closed her eyes, and waited for the beeping noise to tell her it was time to drive off. Oisín would notice that she had been to the carwash without him, and would kick up a fuss. She popped into the newsagent's in the village, knowing that she shouldn't resort to bribery, but not in the mood for an argument. Her mother's advice about not drinking gin when you're feeling a bit low came back to her now, and she wished that she could have replayed the evening and just got into her car and driven home instead of staying with Ciarán.

When she got back into the car, her mobile phone was beeping. A text message from Ciarán. How had he got her number? *"Great time last night we must do it again xx C."* She threw the phone back onto the passenger seat and it bounced onto the floor.

"*Stupid* man! What is it with men?" she shouted at the empty road, craning her neck to make sure there was no traffic before pulling out.

Father O'Leary's battered Nissan Micra was bearing down on her and she desperately hoped he wasn't coming to see her. He tooted and waved, pointing towards her house. She groaned, and followed him down the road. He turned into her driveway, oblivious to the fact that he was now blocking her from getting into the parking space in front of the house. She sighed in exasperation and parked on the grass verge outside.

He hailed her with a wave. "Great, Sophie, I'm glad I caught you. I was actually on my way out to Inverin but you are so busy these days I have to grab you when I can!"

She offered him a cup of coffee, and they went inside.

They chatted while she made coffee for him and a cup of tea for herself.

Then he went straight in for the kill.

"So, may I ask how much success you're having with the Community Mass?" he asked, as if she had sole responsibility for the event. "Only a few weeks to go now."

"I have the O'Tooles lined up for the Prayers of the Faithful, and the Walsh kids said they'd bring up the offerings."

"Great. That's fantastic. Anyone to host it yet?"

"Host it? Aren't we having it in the church?" Sophie gulped down her tea, scalding her sore lip again.

"No, sure isn't that the whole point, that it is in the community, and of the community? I thought you knew."

She could see his eyes roving around her own kitchen imagining the tea and sandwiches laid out here, and calculating how many people she could squeeze into her living-room. "Anyone come to mind?" he asked.

"But, Father, nobody will want to host it, especially at short notice." She refused to be drawn. She might be a sucker for volunteering but there was a line in the sand, even for her. Line in the sand . . . that was it! "Why don't we have it down on the beach, Father? It would be like a Mass in the Penal Days. We could use a big rock for an altar! The children would love it."

"It would be a bit chilly, wouldn't it?" He had visions of being soaked by a wave, and the altar cloth blowing away.

"Well, do we have to have it in April? We've just had the Bishop's Mass. We should spread our pleasures. Why don't we do it in August when the weather would be a bit better?" The further away the better, as far as Sophie was concerned.

"I'll certainly think about it," said the priest doubtfully. He couldn't force it on them, and Sophie was the only one willing to do any organising, so he had to have her on his side.

"I'll have to go and collect the children in a minute." Sophie stood up with her cup and took his mug. She rinsed both of them under the tap. He would happily pour himself another drop from the cafetière if she left the mug in front of him. He had told her once that her house was the only one where he got real coffee.

He was still sitting there, not taking the hint, when her phone beeped again. She picked it up.

"Missing you already. When can I see you? xxx C"

"It's the playschool, Father. I need to go and get Oisín. He's upset about something."

The priest eased himself out of the chair. That was a shame – he had been looking forward to a gossip. The old lady he had to go out and see in Inverin was an ex-parishioner, who had moved to be closer to her daughter but still liked to have her Holy Communion brought to her. He didn't enjoy the mid-weekly outing. Her personal hygiene left a lot to be desired, and although the daughter did her best, the old woman should really be in a hospice at this stage. She would talk the hind legs off a donkey and he would be out there for the best part of two hours trying not to breathe through his nose, without a drop of tea or coffee, before he could come back and have a late lunch.

"I'll think about the beach idea," he said, already determined that it wouldn't work. But you have to make people think you are considering their suggestions, or you'll get nothing out of them. That was the nature of the Lord's work. Building His kingdom was a slow and tedious business, sometimes. He shuffled back out to his car. His sciatica was really playing up today and he could do without driving. But he wasn't a man to complain.

"Thanks for the coffee," he said, waving through the open car window. He reversed out and narrowly missed skimming the side panel of Sophie's car as he swept off up the road. She stood on the doorstep, wondering what she was going to do about Ciarán. Her hope that it was a drunken aberration was obviously a futile one. She wouldn't text anything back. That was a dangerous game. She had read in a magazine that more affairs were discovered through mobile phone records and text messages than by any other means. Wives didn't have to go digging through suit pockets for dodgy receipts any more, or sniff collars for a hint of foreign perfume. A quick look at the message inbox, or the phone bill, and Bob's your uncle. She deleted the two messages from her in-box, feeling like a criminal again. Why the hell hadn't she just told Liam? Then she wouldn't be standing here feeling like a teenager caught by the nuns behind the bicycle shed with her knickers down.

Alison sat staring at the dark choppy sea for an hour, nursing a glass of wine, wondering if this would be a moment to look back on with fondness or regret. One didn't often get a chance to press the 'pause' button in life, and take stock. She was disconcerted by the mixture of anxiety and excitement she felt. The next year was going to be a test of more than just her business ability. As of tomorrow, she was 'The Irish Office' of Porter, May and Stock. The computer had been delivered, and she had managed to connect the printer and the internet without too much hassle. She would have business cards and headed paper back from Jaycee printers by the end of the week. There were a couple of lunch dates with prospective clients in the diary. A conference call with the London team was booked for Friday. That was the easy bit.

But tonight she had been too scared to go out running, even though she had changed into her trainers and Nike running shorts. It was impossible to get lost on the straight run along the prom. There were so many people out jogging and walking their dogs that she was in no danger of being mugged. Nobody knew her so it didn't matter that her bum looked a bit big in the shorts.

Alison couldn't explain the fear that had overtaken her at the front door and made her turn back. She had kicked off her trainers, grabbed her favourite soft fleecy blanket, and curled up on the big recliner chair with a drink. She watched the lights outside flickering on as dusk settled, and the slight heave of the deep water as the tide turned.

Sophie had phoned earlier and Alison had been really upbeat about the view from the window of her new 'office' and the fantastic bread and olives she'd bought from the street market for lunch.

"You have no idea how great this is," she had enthused. "I've unpacked nearly everything, and this apartment feels like home already."

Sophie had been impressed. "You're well organised. I thought you said you were really bad at things like this."

"I am, usually. But I only brought my clothes, work things and a few bits and pieces from the house. There's no point in dragging loads of stuff over here."

"True."

Sophie wondered idly which parts of her home she could leave behind for a year. That would be a good challenge. If you didn't use something for that long, you probably didn't need it. She envied the simplicity of Alison's choices. She could pick up a few suitcases and start a new life in a different country, just like that. Sophie had always had a secret yearning to bring the children up in France, not only to be closer to her parents, but to give the kids an alternative perspective, and the chance to be bilingual. Liam didn't speak French though, and he was too embarrassed by his accent to even try when they went on holiday. The children picked up on that, and refused to co-operate when Sophie tried to teach them French words. Sophie could see the disappointment in her father's eyes. He had worked so hard to show his own girls what it was to be partly French. Now they didn't even come to France to visit as often as he would like. With no other grandchildren on the horizon, Michelle and Oisín were his great hope for the next generation, and Sophie had failed to inculcate even a hint of their Gallic heritage in them. But what could she do? Liam had to earn a living, and the best place for him to do it was in Ireland. When the children were older, they could go over to France for the summer holidays and hopefully it would rub off on them. Sometimes Sophie felt that she was on an uphill and single-handed struggle. Liam had a very masculine approach to childrearing that didn't involve too much thinking about their spiritual and cultural development.

"So, we're on for Friday night, then?" Alison had interrupted her thoughts.

"Yes, I'll come into town and pick you up and we can go for a bite to eat."

"Liam won't mind?"

"I haven't even asked him. I've booked the girl from down the road to baby-sit. She'll be here for seven o'clock, so he can do whatever he wants."

Alison admired Sophie's pragmatism. So many couples with kids seemed to tie themselves in knots trying to juggle time out together, so that they couldn't make time for their own individual friends any more. Lots of her friends were in cosy couples, either suffering from baby-induced lack of sleep, and not entertaining at all, or trying to get to know the parents of their children's friends by having them around instead. Lisa wouldn't be like that, of course, and Alison still had a few girlfriends who were single and enjoyed a good night out at the theatre or a film. But she had this horrible vision of still being the odd one out in ten years' time, introduced as Lisa's *oldest friend* in a tone that was supposed to explain her singleness and her lack of children. Being a godmother would be lovely, but a bit like a consolation prize if she didn't have her own kids. These were the morbid thoughts that welled up as she sat in the growing darkness, disinclined to move from the warm hollow she had created in the chair. The clean sheets and the new duvet cover from Selfridges were not enough of a draw to the strange bed, and she wanted to postpone that moment of surrender for a little while longer. When she woke up in the morning, she would be starting the new life that was supposed to be the answer to all her troubles, and she was scared.

"You've got to confront him," was Alison's advice when Sophie told her that Ciarán was sending five or six texts a day.

"I was hoping he would just give up after a while."

"He's certainly persistent. You haven't sent him any messages at all?"

"Not one. The thing is, today Rachael invited Liam and me back there for dinner, and I'm terrified what will happen. I waffled away that I couldn't lay my hands on my diary, and I'd ring her back. I'll have to talk to her tomorrow to set a date."

"Could you send him just one text, telling him you're not interested?"

"I could, but I still have to sit at their dinner table, acting normal. There's no easy way around this. Should I just be honest with Liam, at this stage? I have nothing to hide, but I feel the longer it goes on, the more I have to explain."

"If you decide not to tell him, I'll back you up and pretend we were together that night."

"Then the lie is even bigger. I think I have to tell him. It's ridiculous that it's even got this far."

"How do you think he'll react? Would he go round and punch Ciarán's lights out?" Alison was laughing but Sophie suddenly looked serious.

"This is going to sound really stupid, but I actually don't know what he would do. Years ago, like ten years ago, there was a guy from Tullamore who fancied me when I was going out with Liam first. He was a regular at the Irish club, too, and sometimes we'd have a chat and a drink at one of the socials. He was lovely, but not my type. We were just friends, really, although he would have liked it to be more. Dermot was his name. One time when I was waiting for Liam to come and meet me at the club, I saw Dermot and I went over for a chat. He seemed really nervous and he kept looking over my shoulder at the door. I asked him what the matter was and he said, 'I'm just looking out for your bodyguard'. I laughed but he said really seriously that he wouldn't want to cross Liam, and a minute later he sidled off. When I turned around, Liam was there. I told Liam what he had said as a joke, but Liam just nodded at me and took a drink out of his pint. 'That's good,' he said, and I suppose I was kind of pleased that he was so possessive of me. It was early in the relationship, so you make allowances, don't you?"

"Has he ever done anything else?"

"No, but there hasn't been any reason for him to worry. I wouldn't look sideways at another fella." She put her hand on the top of her head. "Even on the days when I'm up to here with him, I wouldn't be tempted.

Marriage is for life in my book, and that's not maybe. I love him to bits, for all his faults."

"Sounds like you need to tell him, before he has any reason to suspect the worst."

"Thanks, Alison. I couldn't talk to anyone else like Maeve about it because it's too close to home, and you wouldn't know where people might be gossiping. Imagine if Liam heard it somewhere else first."

"Your secret is safe with me," said Alison.

Liam was enjoying a guilt-free evening with Theresa. Orla was baby-sitting, and he wouldn't have to face the look on Sophie's face that was part martyr and part Friday-night exhaustion. As long as he was home by 10.30, he could be on the couch with a cup of tea when Sophie got in after her evening out with Alison, and he could offer to make her some hot chocolate. She would be full of news about Alison and mellow after a few drinks. It would make a nice change. Theresa was deftly undoing his shirt buttons while she was talking dirty to him. He loved the sensation of her long nails gliding across his skin, a promise of the intensity to come. She slid one finger into the waistband of his boxers, and he grabbed her and kissed her hard. Her pushiness was such a turn-on. Theresa never waited, compliant like Sophie, for him to initiate sex. She demanded it, and he liked giving it to her.

Sophie peered through the front window, her hands on her hips in an unconscious gesture of disbelief.

Stretched out on the sofa, with a blanket borrowed from the airing cupboard, was poor old Orla, fast asleep like a Babe in the Wood. Sophie looked at her watch again to double-check the time. 12.15. She had been fully expecting to be locked out, because she had forgotten her house keys, and Liam would probably be in bed. But instead, Orla was still here, on her first baby-sitting night, out for the count. She must have been frozen, the poor thing, to be hunting around the house for a blanket. The central heating timer went off at eleven and Sophie hadn't told her how to switch it back on. Why would she? Liam was never this late on a Friday.

Liam woke with a start and untangled himself from Theresa's sleep-heavy limbs. That was one aspect of her intensity that he struggled with. Sometimes he felt trapped when she pulled him deeper inside, her legs and arms clamping him to her. Now she stirred and moaned as he leaned across to squint at the tiny travel clock on her bedside table.

"Shit!" He jumped out, feeling around him on the floor for his shorts and socks.

"Whassamatter?" she mumbled.

"It's nearly one o'clock in the morning. I can't believe I slept that long."

"Well, we were very busy," she said, with the cat-like grin he loved.

Liam missed it, as he stretched under her bed to retrieve his shirt. How had it got there? He pulled a muscle in his shoulder as he twisted out again.

"I hate it when you leave me!" she whined.

"That's the downside of shagging a married man," he said harshly, because his watch seemed to have completely disappeared. Theresa made him take it off because it scratched her. Her carefully crafted rolling tear drop was wasted on him too. He was pulling out the bedside table. A Japanese paper lamp fell on his head as he stooped to retrieve the watch which was jammed against the skirting-board.

"Fuck!" he shouted, throwing the lamp across the room. The bulb smashed on the heel of Theresa's shoe, abandoned on the carpet. The black electric cord stretched to its limit and the lamp lay pierced through by the blood-red stiletto.

"Sorry." He didn't even bend down to kiss her, just grabbed his jacket from the chair and ran downstairs, feeling in his pockets for the car keys.

Theresa had been here before, and she recognised the signs. She was competing with someone who offered much more than sex, and it was just a matter of time before the novelty wore off for Liam. The tears that soaked her pillow were real as she admitted to herself that the only way to save her dignity would be to finish with him first.

Sophie was full of apologies as a tousle-haired Orla opened the front door, blushing with embarrassment at being found asleep.

"Orla, don't worry about it. If we were at home, we would be asleep as well. You're not expected to be sitting up listening for every sound at this time of night."

"Sorry, though. It doesn't look very good on my first time, does it?"

"I'm only mortified that I'm home this late. I thought Liam would be in before me. Tell your mammy it wouldn't usually be after midnight, will you?"

"She won't mind. I stay up this late at the weekends anyway." Sophie could hear in the tone of defiance that Orla was even more embarrassed by the reference to her mother. She pressed thirty euros into Orla's hand. "Thanks a million. Will I walk you down the road?"

"I'll be grand. There's no one out at this time."

Sophie stood at the gate and watched until the teenager turned into her own house, and in the silence of the night, she could hear the rattle of Orla's keys as she took them out of her bag. Where the hell was Liam? She was really cross with him. The one and only night she was out, he had to go one better, and stay out longer. She pottered around the kitchen, tidying up the crayons and Lego the children must have used with Orla. She was very much a teenager still, with no sense of responsibility for tidying up. Sophie found the activity calming, as she went through all the options. The golf club was the only place he could still be at this hour of the night, unless he had gone home with John for a nightcap. But they lived on the other side of town, and Liam would be unlikely to do that, with the Gardai out in force this week with their breathalysers. They were due to see John and Ann the following night anyway.

Sophie finally climbed the stairs and checked on the children. She kissed Oisín on the cheek, but didn't dare to step into Michelle's room. She was such a light sleeper that even the rustle of clothes could wake her. Sophie peered around the door, and saw the pile of soft toys Michelle insisted on taking to bed every night, and in the middle of all the brown and white and pink fur, there was her little round face, her mouth open and her hands at either side of her head, in the abandoned pose of a tiny baby. Orla had said they had behaved very well for her, so Sophie would give them each a star on the chart tomorrow. Michelle was aiming for a My Little Pony, with twenty stars, and Oisín wanted a Star Wars light sabre.

She undressed and lay down, unable to sleep. There were no messages flashing on the answering machine, and nothing on her mobile. She wondered, as she always did when Liam was late, at what point she should let in the worry that was niggling in the periphery of her thoughts. After how many hours do you start ringing around the hospitals, or call the Guards to find out if there have been any accidents? Do you wait until the morning, and then face the fact that he hasn't come home all night, or do you act like a paranoid wife, causing mayhem, when actually he is conked out on the sofa in John's sitting-room, too drunk to phone home?

Then she heard the car. Had he driven home drunk, or was it a taxi?

It stopped, and she heard his characteristic door-slam.

"Thank God, he's safe," she muttered under her breath. That was all that mattered. It was better if she pretended to be asleep, and then she could decide how cross to be with him in the morning. Two o'clock was too late to be arguing. She turned to face away from the bedroom door, and by the time he slid between the sheets she was so close to sleep that she didn't have to pretend. She murmured hello, and drifted off.

Liam lay on his pillow facing Sophie, looking at the lines of her lovely face. Her hand was curled up beside her cheek, and he slid his thumb into the curved space of her palm and felt her responding, squeezing gently. That was how they used to fall asleep when they were lovers, before marriage, before children, before life got complicated. He sighed with relief, and Sophie vaguely thought she smelt lemongrass and coriander on his breath

Chapter Twelve

Alison had had two meetings with prospective clients, and she wasn't sure how well they had gone. In London, that kind of meeting, whether it was lunch, or more formal, would have had an outcome. Usually, both parties would agree to pursue their interest, or investigate financing, or talk to colleagues. Emails would be sent afterwards, clarifying things, and confirming actions. In Ireland, it seemed to be different. At her Wednesday lunch with a local investor, which had been very pleasant, there had been absolutely no reference at all to the hotel and leisure centre development in Salthill that they were supposed to be discussing. Politics had featured, and she had learned a lot about the Irish tribunal system for investigating allegations of fraud. They had talked about their plans for summer holidays, and Alison had found out that Irish kids get much longer holidays, with a full three months off school. Then there was the chat about the Galway Chamber of Commerce, which she had been encouraged to join, as a good networking opportunity. Other topics had included the closure of the main post office for renovations, the police or, she should say, the Guards' recent clamp-down on drink-driving, and the latest spending scandal in the County Council. All very interesting and illuminating, but where did she stand? The guy had been involved in several residential developments, financed by syndicates of local business people with some spare cash to invest. Now he wanted to go solo and make big money on a project of his own, so that he could retire in comfort. That had been the basis of his interest in having lunch. He knew James, one of the partners in May, Stock and Porter, from a joint venture years before, and he was the only lead the firm had given her to launch the Irish business. Steve would want feedback for the team debrief on Friday and she wasn't sure what to say.

Thursday's meeting had been even more disconcerting because she spent most of the time wondering if the guy was flirting with her. They had met in the bar of Jury's Hotel, which was just across the courtyard from her apartment. She had been mildly surprised when he ordered an Irish coffee at eleven o'clock in the morning. Maybe that should have set alarm bells going, but he seemed very pleasant. Not bad-looking, either, although he had a bit of a beer belly. Hardly surprising if he was drinking whiskey and cream in his coffee that early in the day. He had recently acquired some land on the sea-facing side of the coast road out past Spiddal, and he was interested in creating a holiday village. Alison thought it was sad that everyone's idea of development was to copy the worst aspects of Mediterranean coastal eyesores. There was no easy answer, and she had to admit that such a development would be very exciting. If the architect could come up with something a bit different, she might even trump Dave's Dubrovnic project. The client was a self-made and self-declared millionaire, who had made his fortune building houses in the nineties, and proudly told her he had covered more than three square miles out on the east side of Galway, with town houses and apartments that were selling like hotcakes.

"I want to do something a bit different now, and that's why I wanted to talk to you. For a different perspective, like."

She wasn't sure if he was eyeing up her cleavage, so she nodded, took notes and promised to go out and do an initial survey the following week.

"Take the second turn after the VG shop. Down to the left. You can't miss it. If you see tennis courts, you're gone past it and you need to turn around and come back at it."

Alison wondered what a VG shop was, but didn't dare to ask. They agreed to meet the following Wednesday, and she made a mental note to avoid meeting him in a bar. Seán Kelly was his name, and she felt she had made some progress with him, although he was vague on the details of his plan. The project seemed to be almost a hobby to him, and she wondered if it would peter out to nothing. He held her hand a second too long for comfort when they parted.

Still, the first week had gone quite well, and when Sophie and she had dinner, there was a lot to talk about.

Sophie was unduly anxious about the horny neighbour, in her opinion. These guys just needed to be told firmly, and they went away. Not that she could claim a great track record on that front. She sat in her office room on Saturday morning, munching a croissant and browsing on the internet to find a cheap flight to London to go and see her parents.

Her mum wasn't saying much on the phone but she sensed that her dad was not doing well. If there was any way he could travel, Alison was convinced he would love the sea air and the change of scene. The second bedroom was big enough for them to stay, and she was sure they would respect her working space and let her get on with things. Maybe she could make up for her lack of attention to them for so long.

She picked up the phone, and her mother was delighted to hear her voice.

"Well, how has your first week been, love?" she asked.

"Interesting, I would say. It's very different. Work is going OK, and the flat is lovely, or 'apartment' I should say. It's a funny mixture of American and European influences here. Not what I expected at all."

"What? Were you thinking it would be like England in the nineteen-fifties?" her mother asked, laughing.

"Not quite that bad, but you know, not full of internet cafés and trendy boutiques and satellite channels. I suppose I thought they were a few years behind us, at least."

"Well, it sounds like it will be an interesting experience, anyway," said her mother, in a voice that sounded quite wistful.

"I was wondering if you and Dad would like to come over, to stay for a little while?" Alison asked. She couldn't understand why her voice was cracking as if she was asking a guy out for a date, or something equally bizarre.

"I don't think your father would be able to cope, darling," came the answer – the words Alison didn't want to hear.

She so desperately wanted to share this new experience, and for them to understand why she had left them, just when they needed her.

"He likes his routine and, you know, not being too far away from places that are familiar."

Why had she thought that. Why had she thought that he would suddenly want to fly to Ireland for an adventure now? She would never understand him, despite her momentary flash of understanding when she had been lying on the bed beside him, staring at the beige, cracked ceiling.

"I suppose you're right," she said, feeling sad for her mother too. Whenever her parents ventured abroad, her mother always came back full of vivid descriptions of their discoveries. "I was just looking at flights, and I thought I'd come and see you for the first bank holiday weekend in May – it gives me an extra day."

"That's not far away, is it?" her mother sounded like her old self, her optimism overcoming every hurdle she encountered in life.

Alison was determined to make this weekend different,

and not to slip into the habit of watching too much TV, eating too much, and making the jobs around the house last longer than they needed to, just to pass the time. Her weeknights in London had always been busy with the friends who were happy to grab a quick meal and a drink after work, but there was often an emptiness in her weekends that she couldn't fill, even with visits to galleries and museums. She had tried, but they were boring without someone else to talk to. Halfway around an exhibition, she would suddenly notice that Turner paints the sun halfway up the canvas and structures the foreground and the sky in a balance that draws the eye to the centre, conveying vast distances and depth by using delicate shades of yellowing grey. "So what?" her brain would ask the other side of itself, to be met with an internal shrug. "Just thought it was interesting, that's all."

This year in Galway was going to be Alison's metamorphosis, and she was determined to emerge more independent, more interesting and, of course, thinner. She put on her running things, grabbed a bottle of water from the fridge, and slammed the front door, not pausing to analyse the tremor of remembered anxiety from Tuesday night. The swans felt like friends now, their routines becoming as familiar as her own. There was a man who fed them from the pier every evening at six o'clock and they would gently cruise towards his spot as the time approached, pretending casual lack of interest, but eagerly stretching out their necks as soon as his hand plunged into the rustling plastic bags. Alison wondered if he bought the bread specially, or got it from a shop that was throwing it out, because he seemed to have six or seven loaves every day. She loved to see the swans curving their necks to tuck their beaks in and sleep as darkness fell, bobbing gently on the waves where the salty sea met the tumbling brown water of the Corrib. Now as she jogged along the edge of the pier, trying to set a rhythm she could maintain, there were some children throwing stale crusts and she wondered if the birds' appetites would be spoiled, and the man would wonder later at their indifference to him. There was a gravelled path running along the very edge of the sea front, and Alison thudded along, wishing she had remembered her ipod and her pedometer. Still, there was plenty of time to measure the distance along the prom. She planned to run every evening, as the days got longer. She had been struck by how much later the sun went down here, and realised she was eight hundred kilometres or more further west than London. She couldn't remember the maths, but that was probably enough to make a time difference, although of course she was still on Greenwich Mean Time. The prom was crowded. To her horror she realised after a few hundred metres that one of the popular local entertainments was people-watching from the comfort of a heated car. She counted loads of them, mostly older women, sitting chatting in the front seats, pointing, laughing and gossiping about all the people going past. They were probably judging the poor woman up ahead, battling with a screaming toddler who was refusing to get into the pushchair. They probably disapproved of the teenagers who were managing to walk, arms entwined, their tongues down each other's throats while still making forward progress. What would they say about her sagging bum as she thudded past? Still, she didn't know them, and who cared what they thought? Despite these internal reassurances, she swerved to run on the side of the footpath nearest to the sea. She consoled herself with the thought that by the end of the year, they would be eyeing her up jealously, wishing they had bothered to get fit when they were only forty – thirty-nine, she told herself, smiling – rather than descending into middle-age slobbishness. When Alison got back, she was on an endorphin high, and had to stop herself eating everything in the fridge as a reward for her efforts. She made a healthy wholemeal sandwich and allowed herself some crisps, but she drank tea rather than Coke, and felt very virtuous.

She spent the afternoon browsing through the shops on Quay Street, trying to find something that would appeal to her father as a gift when she went home. Finally she settled on a carved black cat made from hundred-year-old wood excavated from the bog. It was surprisingly animated, and would remind him of the cat they had had when she was a little girl. She wondered idly why they hadn't got another one when it died. Sooty had been a real character, so they probably thought he was irreplaceable. His funniest trick had been to leap at the French doors in the breakfast room, forgetting they were made of glass, trying to catch the birds as they ate the morning crusts on the patio. Once, she had been convinced that a magpie was doing a victory dance right in front of the windows, taunting Sooty for his bruised nose and dignity. Maybe she should buy them a real live kitten? Her dad might enjoy that, since he was pretty much housebound now. She made a mental note to contact Battersea Dogs' and Cats' Home, to see if they were expecting any kittens.

Chapter Thirteen

Liam was surprised at how lightly he had got away with his Friday night out. He had rehearsed a story about Captain's Night at the golf club, knowing that Sophie paid little attention to the affairs of the club, and wouldn't have a clue. But she didn't even ask. By lunch-time on Saturday, Liam was wondering if he should have volunteered something, to make it seem more natural, but then he talked himself out of it, deciding to let sleeping dogs lie. Sophie wasn't even giving him the frosty disapproval that he sometimes endured. She was pottering around the house and he had even heard her humming. They were going over to see John and Ann later, and he was looking forward to that. Ann was a great cook, and they would have something exotic out of a cookery book that she was trying for the first time, but was guaranteed to be delicious. Their kids were much older, so Ann seemed to have a bit more free time than Sophie, and she loved experimenting. She was

221

thinking of giving lessons at the college, and John was encouraging her. That would be much more rewarding than being at the beck and call of the old priest who relied far too heavily on Sophie's goodwill. But Sophie wouldn't listen to Liam. She was disappointed he wouldn't come to Mass on Sundays but he thought it was hypocritical, and there were enough hypocrites in the world already. Sophie said it was for the sake of the children, but in his opinion Michelle and Oisín would be better off thinking for themselves instead of swallowing the whole Catholic package of sin and guilt that would only screw them up in later life. Sophie said they could leave the Church when they were older, if that's what they decided, but if they had never known it, they were unlikely to find it by accident. Life was too materialistic and busy to make time for God, she said, but if He was in their lives already, there was some chance they might keep Him there. Liam just didn't get it, but he respected her faith, and who was he to lay down the law on something that meant so much to her? Also, from a selfish point of view, he got Sunday mornings to himself without feeling guilty. For the last couple of weeks, he had been spending them with Theresa instead of playing golf, and he hoped that John wouldn't land him in it tonight by making some comment about not seeing him much at the club these days. As far as Sophie was concerned, he practically lived in the place. It was the perfect cover. Maybe he should have a quiet word with John and ask him to be discreet. But then John would only give him a hard time about being unfaithful to Sophie, and he didn't need to hear it. Suddenly, Michelle landed on his stomach, winding him, and he shouted with shock. She burst into tears, wailing loudly, and Sophie came running in, wondering what had happened.

"I didn't even hear her coming into the room. She must have launched herself from the door and landed on me!" Liam could feel a bruise on his sternum.

"Michelle, you're getting to be a big girl now and you're heavy, love – you shouldn't be jumping on people like that."

"Daddy was asleep and I wanted to give him a surprise," she mumbled, knowing it was no defence.

"You big heffalump!" shouted Oisín in glee, glad not to be the one in trouble for a change.

"Am not!" she shouted back.

"Oh, yes, you *are*!" He ran upstairs with Michelle flying after him, screaming blue murder.

"Will you take them out for a little while, to get rid of some of their buck?" Sophie asked, and he smiled and said of course he would.

Sophie was planning to ring Rachael and she wanted Liam out of the way in case Ciarán answered the phone. She had rehearsed what she would say, and she was almost hoping that he would answer, so she could get it off her chest. Silence settled on the house and she put on the kettle for a quiet cup of tea. She dialled his number on her mobile. Ciarán did answer, but words failed her as soon as she heard his voice.

"Sophie, how are you?" he said in the false voice of someone with something to hide. Rachael must be close by. Sophie wouldn't risk saying anything to him now.

"Fine thanks, I was just ringing about our dinner date." She could sense from his silence that he thought she was talking about just them, and he was wondering how to respond, in his wife's hearing. Sophie let him squirm for a few seconds. "Is Rachael there? She gave me a few dates, and I had to check with Liam first."

He handed the phone over, saying, "Talk to you soon then?"

Sophie chatted to Rachael and even screwed up the courage to ask her to do a reading at the Community Mass. "It won't be until August now, so you don't need to worry about it yet, but it's good to have names down against the jobs. Then there's less to worry about nearer the time."

Rachael agreed, and Sophie was delighted with herself. At least she had achieved one thing with the phone call. She should just text Ciarán telling him to stop, and then behave as normal. She sent him a text message that minute, sipping her tea and concentrating hard, wondering how teenagers found this a satisfactory way of communicating. *"pls stop snding mssges. S"*. She was proud of her 'text speak,' and she thought that the message was sufficiently anonymous to prevent Rachael from identifying her, if she should happen to read it. Two seconds after she pressed the 'send' button, the mobile beeped. She groaned.

It was a text message. *"Who are you?"* it demanded peremptorily.

Sophie's heart was pounding. She should never have sent a message! Rachael had obviously picked up his mobile and was on the trail. Hopefully, as she hadn't used Ciarán's name, Rachael might conclude it was someone using a wrong number. She put the mobile in her handbag, to hide it from view. Even the chocolate-covered Kimberley biscuit with her tea didn't make her feel any better. This was worse than being a teenager. She had half an hour of peace and she was just dozing off on the sofa in the warmth of the sun in the conservatory when she heard the front door slam followed by wellied footsteps running down the hall. Michelle managed to stop herself just in time, her heels squealing on the laminate floor as she braked, remembering not to leap full length on her mother's prone body. "Hallo, Mammy. We found a great shell, look!" she said, breathlessly.

"Oh, that's lovely," Sophie said, admiring the perfect whorls of the yellow periwinkle. "He's a big fella, isn't he?" said Michelle, adding him to her glass jar of shells. They were going to decorate a plant pot with putty and shells when they had enough special ones. They would take it to Grandpapa in France in the summer. It was to remind him of Irish beaches. Sophie was going to show Michelle how to varnish it when the putty was set, to hold the shells in place. She had a vivid memory of a summer spent collecting shells and decorating pots, when she and her sisters had thought they would raise money for the local orphanage. They had gone with their classes from school at Christmas time, to sing carols and donate their 'clean, nicely kept soft toys' to the poor children. Denise had been struck by the loneliness the orphans must feel, even though the nuns who minded them were lovely, friendly, cuddly ones. It was her idea to raise money to send the orphans on holiday, and the three sisters had cleaned windows, cut grass and sold the pots on a stall in the village. They had raised a hundred and fifty-seven pounds, which seemed a fortune, and had earned them an article and their photo in *The Mayo News*, but no one had ever told them that it wouldn't even cover the hire of a bus to take the orphans out on a day trip.

"I'm starving, Mammy. I don't think I'll make it until dinner-time. Can I have a biscuit to keep me going?"

Michelle had recently developed a wheedling tone that irritated Sophie, and she had to suppress the urge to scold her. Michelle had spotted the wrapper from her own biscuit so she could hardly refuse her. She stood up and took two biscuits out of the tin.

"*Two?*" said Michelle with wide eyes, and Sophie gave her a withering look.

"One for Oisín," said Michelle, without further prompting.

When Liam came in, smelling of fresh air, his cheeks reddened from the wind on the beach, Sophie knew she just *had* to tell him about Ciarán. She put a video on for the children and they were amazed at being allowed to eat their biscuits in the sitting-room in front of the telly on a Saturday afternoon. Life didn't get much better than that.

"Listen, Liam, about the other night . . ." she started.

Liam felt oddly relieved that he could get his story out while it was fresh in his mind. "Sorry, I know I was very late. It was —"

Sophie shook her head. "No, I'm talking about a few

weeks ago, when I was out with Alison. Or not out with Alison, as the case may be . . ."

"What do you mean?" he asked, completely thrown.

"Alison's first night?"

He nodded.

"She didn't turn up that night at all. She was delayed in London, and I was just coming back into the hotel after checking for her at the apartment, when I bumped into Ciarán from down the road."

Liam sat up straight. That was the night she had come home drunk, in the taxi. What the hell had she been doing? That Ciarán was dangerous. He fancied Sophie – that was obvious. What had he done?

"He offered to wait with me for a while, and I said I'd wait another half an hour or so. I don't know where the time went, but I kept on drinking, kind of forgetting I had the car with me, because you always drive when we're out . . ."

"And did you think you were out with me?" He couldn't help the sarcastic tone.

"Not at all, of course not. Anyway, he kind of joined me in the taxi before I knew where we were, and . . ."

"What did he do?"

"Nothing, he didn't do anything, honestly, but he'd had a few to drink, and he got a bit carried away with himself."

"Carried away with himself *how*?"

"He kind of made a move on me." This wasn't coming out at all how Sophie had thought. She should have rehearsed it a bit more, knowing how Liam was likely to react.

"What kind of a move?"

"He just put his hand on my leg and I told him he had had too much to drink, and I thought that would be the end of it, but he seems to think that he likes me, and now he keeps on sending me text messages and I don't know how to stop him without causing major ructions."

"I'll give him major ructions!" shouted Liam, standing up and heading for the back door.

"No, Liam, don't be stupid! Nothing happened. I'm only telling you because I'd hate if you thought something was going on, and it isn't. I wouldn't be in the least bit tempted by him. Don't do anything. Sit down, please?"

Liam stopped but he couldn't sit down. The thought of that man putting even a finger on Sophie. The cheek of him. Didn't they say you shouldn't piss in your own backyard? And yer man, only three houses down the road, thinking he could have a bit on the side maybe, during the day when Liam would be out at work . . .

He looked at Sophie, sitting at the table with her head in her tiny hands, and she looked so like a little girl. She was this worried about telling him something she said hadn't even happened, and he was betraying her every day, fantasising about Theresa and shagging her at every available opportunity.

He stood behind her, and stroked her hair. "Don't worry, sweetheart. I won't do anything stupid. The thought of it, though . . ."

"I know. I couldn't decide whether to tell you or not, and then you just assumed I had seen Alison so I didn't put you right on it, and the longer it went on, the bigger it got, until I felt like I had done something and I was feeling guilty. And that's not right, is it?" She put her hand on top of his, and stroked it.

He shook his head, but he couldn't speak.

"I don't know if we can just go for dinner there, and act normal?" She was asking him, he knew, not worried about herself, but only whether he would make a show of her by throwing a punch at Ciarán, or something equally 'inappropriate'.

Liam shrugged. "I suppose I could pretend to know nothing, and you could send him a message saying you're not interested?"

She took out her mobile. "I tried that. I think Rachael sent this one back." She showed him Rachael's text.

"Oh, shit! I didn't think of that."

Sophie felt comforted. They were in it together, and even if they ended up not speaking to the neighbours after all this, they would still be together.

"Send one back saying 'If you don't know who I am, then I won't be expecting any more messages?'" Liam could see the funny side now, but Sophie was still anxious.

"What do we do about Rachael?"

"Nothing. She's already noticed that Ciarán fancies you like mad. She won't want to hear it from the horse's mouth."

Sophie was amazed. "Where on earth did you get that idea from?"

"When they were here. Ciarán was all over you, and Rachael and I had a little exchange on the subject." Liam grinned sheepishly.

"I'm obviously out of practice at picking up the

vibes," she said, secretly delighted that Liam had noticed the spark. She felt completely taken for granted most of the time, and although she didn't want him to go and confront Ciarán, it was no harm if Liam felt threatened. He might appreciate her a bit more.

She stood up and he hugged her close, towering over her. It was completely different to holding Theresa, who was up to his shoulders and he barely had to bend his neck to kiss her. Sophie just reached up to his chest, and he loved the feeling of holding her, protecting her. Unwittingly, she had released in him a flood of the guilt that usually only visited at night. Standing there, consoling her, Liam wondered how he had got himself into a situation where he had betrayed that complete and utter trust she had in him.

Seán Kelly was bringing his 'Finance Man' to this meeting, and Alison was relieved that there would be a chaperon. She didn't relish the prospect of fighting off Seán's advances while trying to move the negotiations on to the next stage. She had been to survey the land, and it was on a very attractive strip of the coast, facing the Clare mountains, with an uninterrupted view out to the Atlantic and the Aran islands. She was amazed that planning permission had been granted. She had been doing her research, and the County Council was supposed to be preserving the coast side of the road from development. At least they had the foresight to set the rules. Maybe they just didn't have the willpower to stick to them.

They were meeting in a hotel that she guessed

would be a prime competitor, if the development went ahead, as she noticed a cluster of white cottages in the grounds behind the main building. They were stark and new, the white paint glaring without the softening of mature foliage and grass. Neat gravel driveways with room for two cars led to bright red doorways, and the windows were placed at strange angles so that each room could catch a view of the sea. They were ugly, in Alison's opinion, and she was intrigued to see Seán's ideas for his own holiday village.

She had arrived early at the hotel after allowing extra time for getting lost. She was used to having an A-Z map to get around London, without relying on other people's directions. Even for party invitations, people in London sent photocopied maps with a circle around their house and the nearest Tube station. You couldn't go wrong. Here, directions seemed to depend on people's knowledge of local pubs, shops and five-barred gates. Some of the lanes were so tiny she wasn't sure if they were driveways or real roads. Still, she was here now, and she was salivating at the thought of real seafood chowder and some Irish brown bread. The hotel was perched on a hill, with a fantastic view of the bay.

Seán was a few minutes late, and she was wondering whether to order a pot of tea, when she saw a huge black Mercedes sweeping into the carpark beneath the window. That would be him. She quickly whipped out a mirror to check her lipstick and hair, and she was sitting casually contemplating some papers when she heard Seán's booming voice as he talked to the head waiter. She looked up with a welcoming smile, and nearly died.

Ronan Murray was standing there with Seán, grinning with delight at her discomfort.

"Do you two know each other?" Even the self-centred Seán could sense the electricity between them.

"From years ago," said Ronan, leaning down to kiss Alison. His eyes said so much more than the polite peck on each cheek to greet an old acquaintance.

They sat down.

She was determined not to lose it in front of Seán, so she said casually, "It certainly was a long time ago. London, in '91?" She sipped her Ballygowan.

"It was '92," Ronan said, winking, his dark-roast-coffee voice conjuring memories Alison had long ago abandoned.

"So, you're the finance guy, are you?" she said, trying not to sound mocking. Ronan had been such a timewaster in London, hardly holding down jobs for more than a few months at a time. She had nagged him about wasting his ability and talents, and he had said there was plenty of time for all that. London was a place to have fun, not to be earning a living. Which was easy for him to say when he pretty much lived in her flat, and ate all her food. The room he rented smelt damp and musty and she had hated going there.

"I am indeed." He handed his fine dark wool coat to the waiter, revealing what looked like the same suit she had seen in the restaurant in London.

"This is a bizarre coincidence," Alison said. "Bumping into you twice in such a short time."

"It certainly is," he said, as the waiter hovered to take their drinks orders. "Almost as if it was meant to be. Champagne?"

Alison felt slightly bemused.

"To celebrate our new association," he said, looking at Seán for confirmation.

"I hereby appoint you as Project Manager for the most amazing holiday village in the West of Ireland," said Seán, laughing.

Alison couldn't decide whether to be relieved that she had a brand-new client, or terrified at the prospect of working closely with Ronan. The hairs on her forearms were standing to attention.

The champagne was poured and they toasted the new venture. By the end of the lunch Alison was still trying to figure out what exactly Ronan's role was, but one thing was certain. She was going to see a lot of him.

"I don't believe you!" screeched Lisa down the phone when Alison rang her, knowing she would never be forgiven for not passing on this juicy titbit immediately.

"Large as life. I nearly dropped my glass on the floor. But first, tell me about you, and how's . . .?"

"We decided on a name last night. April Rose."

"Lovely, so how is she doing?" said Alison moving swiftly on. She hoped they were only going to use the first name. People might think she was a celebrity child with a name like that. What planet was Lisa on?

"She's putting on an ounce a day, which is great, apparently. It's really strange, spending the whole day sitting there staring at her. I haven't held her or even touched her yet. She still seems like someone else's baby, somehow. Isn't that a horrible thing to say?"

"Not at all, Lisa. You'll bond just as soon as she's sturdy enough to come out of the incubator. She won't know any different. Does she wave her little hands and feet around?"

"Yes. She's gorgeous. I love babies' little hands, but hers are even tinier and she even has nails, the most beautiful little curved nails. She seems more miraculous in a way, seeing her in there, growing and getting stronger."

"I can imagine. Have you recovered? Are you getting enough rest?"

"Yes, thank you, Mummy! I've got Michael looking after me. He is such a sweetie. He was really scared about this whole baby thing, and he's just turned to mush. He talks to her through the glass, and makes funny faces and things she can't even see."

"And do they have any idea when April can come out of the incubator?" The name didn't sound so bad now that she'd said it out loud. April Carmichael. Media type? Actress? Politician? Finance director? It was a big enough name to cope with all those eventualities, Alison decided. It made her wonder all over again how Michael's parents could have called him Michael Carmichael. He had become a barrister despite a name that should have graced a cartoon car mechanic.

"They said at least four weeks, and then they'll assess her progress. Four weeks feels like forever, but I suppose we've already done ten days."

Ten days. April had come into the world ten days ago, and Alison had changed her life so much it was almost unrecognisable. She hadn't even spoken to Lisa in that time, only sending her text messages she could read when she came out of the hospital late every night. Alison read the replies in the morning, sitting at her breakfast bar munching healthy cereal.

"I'll be home before then. I've booked some tickets already. Dad doesn't sound too good."

"Oh, you poor thing. Well, give us a ring when you know how much time you've got and we'll put a date in the diary. Now, back to the important topic of 'Alison and Ronan meet again'. Did you suss him out on the whole wife and kids thing?"

Alison snorted. "Lisa, it was a business meeting. I was hardly going to interrogate him in front of Seán, who seems to have the hots for me, which is a tad awkward."

"It might be your scintillating personality, your radiant good looks, your fantastic body."

"Yes, or he thinks that any single woman he comes across is fair game."

"What happened to your resolution to think more positively about yourself? I reckon there's more to this than meets the eye. How did Ronan suddenly appear out of the woodwork and land up working with you? I smell a rat."

"Lisa, even in my very short time here, I've realised that Ireland is just unbelievably small. Never mind the theory that everyone is only six people removed from someone you know. In Ireland you're probably bonking their second cousin. It's all about scratching each other's backs, and a bit of nudge, nudge wink, wink, and how's your father?"

Lisa laughed. "The Irish accent is coming along nicely."

"We're having dinner tomorrow night."

"Another business meeting?" Lisa said scornfully.

"No, he suggested we should have dinner to catch up on old times. He is *soooo* gorgeous!" She ended on a teenage shriek, and Lisa laughed again. "I'll have to really restrain myself to stick to my vow of not flirting with married men!"

"Make sure you do, young lady," Lisa mocked her.

Chapter Fourteen

Sophie was lying soaking in the bath, surveying the faint stretch-marks on her stomach, and doing a mental inventory of the body parts that had changed since having children. There was still a bit of flab on her tummy but it was easily hidden with the right clothes. Her bras had never come back down to her pre-baby size, but someone said your diaphragm actually got bigger when you were pregnant, so you had a wider back. Sounded a bit far-fetched, but she was definitely a different shape. Her boobs weren't too saggy, considering she had breast-fed two kids. She did a quick routine feel around. She was never quite sure of the point of this, but she did it every month, like you were supposed to. It was a bit like doing a glass test for meningitis on the children's rashes. She wasn't really sure what to look for. The doctor at the clinic had told her to put her first three fingers together, then roll them gently across her breast, palpating for any abnormalities. He had said she should get into the routine of doing it at the same point in her cycle, but she didn't always remember. She closed her eyes to concentrate better. Under the tip of her index finger, there was something not quite right. She probed. Sometimes in the last few years, there were temporary swellings in her glands, and she always felt them obsessively for two or three days and they seemed to go down. This felt different. Harder and more defined. It was a lump.

She sat up, the warm, lavender-scented water sloughing off her shoulders. She felt again, and at this angle it was less defined. She slid back under. It was still there. How long had it been since she checked? At the health spa? Before Christmas? It could have been growing for months. She stood up, unable to lie still. It was ten o'clock at night so she could hardly call the doctor's surgery. There was that book, the one about looking after yourself postnatally. There was a paragraph in there about breasts, she was sure. She wrapped a towel around herself and ran downstairs.

Liam put his key in the front door, surprised that all the lights were on this late. He found Sophie sitting on the carpet in the living-room, surrounded by a pile of books she had pulled off the shelves. She looked like some kind of refugee, her hair hanging damply around her face, her green eyes enlarged with fear, and the huge navy-blue towel dwarfing her. She didn't speak when he came in.

"What are you doing, love?" he asked, not wanting

to get too close in case she smelled Theresa's perfume. He always had a shower before going to bed, and usually Sophie was fast asleep when he got in any time after eleven. She looked up at him, and let the towel fall from her. Was this some kind of sexual come-on? Liam was completely confused. He wanted to hold her but he stood frozen on the spot, torn.

"Feel this," she said, holding out her hand to him.

He couldn't move. He wouldn't make love to her with the smell of Theresa still on him. He just couldn't do it. "I'll be back in a minute, love," he said, sprinting upstairs, his heart pounding.

For a second Sophie thought the sound of the shower motor was just the buzzing noise in her ears that she sometimes got when she was overtired. Then it went on and on and Liam still wasn't coming back, and she sank back onto her heels, without even the inclination to pull the towel back up around her shoulders to stop her trembling. He came bounding back down, bringing steamy lime-scented air with him, his hair wet. He knelt beside her, and started caressing her, and she shook her head, like a bewildered child. She took his hand, and directed it.

"No, here," she said insistently, and he was surprised by her assertiveness. Her pupils were huge. Had she taken drugs? There was no smell of alcohol on her breath but she was behaving so strangely. He didn't think he could make love to her. He placed his hand on her breast, where she told him and then he could feel it. A smartie-sized lump. It was hard, and resistant to the pressure of his fingertip.

"Jesus Christ!" he said, taking his hand away as if an electric current had run through his whole body.

A fat tear rolled down her cheek. He must think it was bad, too. His face was full of the shock she felt herself. Liam couldn't believe the baseness in himself. He had never sunk so low. Sex had been the only thing on his mind, when Sophie was trying to tell him that she had cancer. He would have made love to her, thinking she was trying to win him back by being more assertive, more sexually demanding, to turn him on. Her hand had been reaching up, asking him for help, and he had fleetingly wished her nails were longer. In the shower he had asked himself why tonight of all nights? He had already come twice with Theresa. She had been very attentive this evening. Now he was kneeling on the floor, shivering with cold and fear, wanting to abase himself in front of Sophie, to put his hands and forehead on the floor, and beg her forgiveness. She sat motionless, her legs folded under her, like a white marble Rodin sculpture, her simple passivity berating him. He stood up and gently lifted her, his hands under her armpits and her knees, and he carried her upstairs like a sleeping child unfolded from the car seat after a long journey. He gently dressed her in her silky nightie, and tucked her in. Then he lay beside her, and she curled into the warmth of his deep chest, her breath barely caressing his skin. They hadn't spoken a word.

The first sound that penetrated Sophie's deep, dark sleep was a moan from Michelle. She shot awake and ran into her little girl's room, arriving before her brain had really woken up.

"I had a bad dream," Michelle wailed. Sophie sat on the bed and stroked her hair, making soothing noises. She never asked the children what they dreamt about, because in the description they scared themselves all over again. She kissed Michelle's damp cheek, the sweet smell of childish night sweat rising from her hair. After a few minutes, when Michelle was beginning to doze off again, she said "Night, night, love. See you in the morning."

She was standing at the door, looking back when Michelle muttered, "That was my bad dream. You weren't there in the morning."

"I'll be there, love. I'll be there." Sophie managed to keep her voice neutral and calm. She pulled Michelle's door until it stood slightly ajar. She was gulping air convulsively. Was it a sign? She leaned against the wall and had to use every ounce of will not to sink down onto the floor, sobbing. Liam was sound asleep when she slid between the sheets. He had never woken for the children when they were babies, and nowadays he seemed even more tired than ever. She couldn't get back to sleep, wondering how quickly she could get an appointment, and a referral for tests. The children were due at playschool only for one more day before the Easter holidays, so she would have to organise childcare. Her friend Maeve was going away to Euro Disney with her kids. Ger was off to Majorca for a spring break. Denise was on a business trip. Liam would have to take some time off. But she wanted him with her. This was scary.

Much scarier than baby scans. What if she had to have a breast removed? What if it didn't work and the cancer came back? It happened a lot, she had heard. Liam wouldn't make love to her if she was deformed. Did women take their false breasts off at night? She stared at the digital clock as it silently changed the shapes of its green lines. Four, five, six, seven, eight, nine, zero. The faint row of pale green eights lay hidden behind, waiting to march out as the next hour and the next minute passed.

The radio jolted her from a light doze, and she automatically nudged Liam, who was not a morning person, and liked to lie for a few minutes before getting out of bed. He groaned and rolled over, turning his back to her. Then she could see his shoulders tensing, as his memory returned.

He lay for another second, marshalling his thoughts, and then he turned and said, "We'll get it checked out straight away. It will be fine, honestly." He touched her cheek gently and she nodded. She had felt the lump again this morning, unable to resist, like a tongue worrying a loose tooth. It was still there, solid and resisting. How could something like that be growing in your body without you knowing? Where did the cells come from, and how did they get there? She didn't talk to Liam, but got dressed and went downstairs. This was too big for words. If she had it tested and it was fine, then they could get back to normal. If it wasn't fine, there was no room in her head for daily pleasantries. The children noticed her pre-occupation and for a blessed change, they ate their breakfast like angels, without bickering and she even managed to brush their teeth and get their shoes on without a single word of protest. Michelle was shadow-eyed with tiredness. She said, as she sat on the bottom step of the stairs while Sophie did up her buckle, "You were right, Mammy. You are here in the morning. In the night-time you imagine things, don't you?"

"Yes, darling, you do." Sophie kissed the top of her head.

"Well, how are you?" Dr Magee asked, surprised when Liam followed Sophie into the surgery. Maybe they wanted to talk about birth control, now that they had two kids. He smiled at them, anticipating their embarrassment. It might be against the rules of the Church but in this day and age people had to be practical. He tried to make it easier for people by creating a relaxed tone, but he wasn't going to lead them into the discussion. It had to come from themselves. He sat forward, expectantly.

"I have a lump on my breast, doctor," Sophie said.

Liam was holding her hand but he was staring fixedly at the red plastic pot of pens on the mahogany desk. It often took the men that way, in Dr Magee's experience. They couldn't get their minds around the idea of cancer invading their partner's body. They sometimes went into a bit of a distant state, to remove themselves from the situation, and not have to face the harsh reality.

"Could you go behind the screen for me, and slip off your top and your bra?" he said gently, and Sophie stood up.

Liam held on to her fingertips for a long second, and then he let her go.

The doctor tried to give Liam a reassuring smile, but he couldn't make eye contact. He rubbed his hands together briskly. "Just warming up my hands a bit," he said, stepping behind the screen. Sophie was perched on the couch, her legs hanging over the edge like a child.

"Which side is it?"

She pointed to her left breast. He placed one gloved hand flat on her back and used the other to gently palpate her breast. It took only a second. She saw the discovery registering in his eyes. They narrowed as he concentrated on feeling the rest of her breast. Then he swapped sides and checked the right breast. "There seems to be only the one, that I can feel," he said. "Slip on your things again, and come out when you're ready."

Liam was fiddling with a pen he had taken from the pot, clicking it up and down, up and down in a regular rhythm.

"She won't be a minute," the doctor said, pulling his swivel-chair out from behind the desk so he could talk to them both.

Sophie rejoined her husband and they sat there mutely, looking at him.

"I'd like to refer you for a biopsy," said Doctor Magee, and he could see Liam's fingers tensing as he squeezed Sophie's hand. "Very often these lumps are benign. The biopsy will tell us. Can I just take some notes?"

Sophie nodded.

"When did you first notice the lump?"

"Last night."

"And how often do you check your breasts?"

"Not very often, to be honest. I can't remember when I last did it. I found it when I was in the bath. It was more prominent when I was lying down."

The doctor nodded, writing incomprehensible scribbles on a pad. "Have you noticed any other changes in your breasts, recently? In the texture of the skin, in your nipples, or even in the general shape of your breasts?"

She shook her head. The questions went on, and he filled two pages of case history. She wasn't aware of any family predisposition to breast cancer, she didn't smoke, she had been thirteen when she got her first period . . . on and on.

Liam blew out a huge breath when they left the surgery. "He's very thorough, anyway," he said. "It will be fine. You'll have the biopsy within the week, and then we'll celebrate next weekend. Let's go away somewhere. We'll get Ger to take the kids."

"It's Easter." Sophie couldn't summon the energy to give him the litany of reasons why they couldn't go away.

"The weekend after, then."

Maeve and her husband were coming for dinner that weekend. Liam's only concession to planning ahead was to run a diary at work. He never bothered to read the family calendar she kept so carefully updated. He relied on her to remind him of everything important, including his mother's birthday and their own wedding anniversary. She bought the cards, he signed them.

Sophie just shook her head.

"I have to go into the office, just for a little while today. The architect is coming down from Dublin 'specially."

"Well, you can't let the architect from Dublin down, can you?" Sophie said, and he was too preoccupied to notice the sarcasm.

There was no meeting with the architect. He would have to break it off with Theresa. He couldn't continue for another day without finishing with her. It was eleven o'clock. He would go into the office and say he wanted to take her out for an early lunch. He would break the news, ask her to pack up her desk and he'd pay her a couple of months' notice. It wouldn't be good for her to hang around. He would get a temp in from tomorrow to answer the phones and then he'd worry about finding someone else. He wondered if Theresa would go back to Cork. She had often said that but for him she would be very homesick, and he was the only reason she stayed in Galway. Maybe he should pay her a bit extra and suggest that she go back home. Less risk of anything nasty developing. He had a horrible feeling it wouldn't be as straightforward as he hoped, but money solved most problems. Everyone had their price. He kissed Sophie at the front door, and got back into the car, promising to be back by three o'clock.

"You're late," Theresa simpered at him when he got in. "Late night?"

How had he ever found her garish red lips

attractive? She should wear something softer like Sophie, a sort of pearly pink. He made sure the foreman wasn't in the canteen next door before saying, "I thought we could nip down to the Salthill hotel for lunch?"

But, just as he spoke, the door opened and one of the leading hands came in to pick up some plans from the table, with an apologetic nod in their direction.

As the guy left, he heard Theresa saying, "That's a good idea. I have something I want to discuss with you." She didn't sound in the least like she was talking about work.

They all suspected something was going on between the boss and Theresa. Some of the lads were disgusted with Liam. They had known Sophie for years and they couldn't believe that Liam would be looking elsewhere for his oats. A few of the others said that Theresa was a real goer, and they would do the same, if they got half the chance. The leading hand laid out the plans, double-checking the location of a water tank, and he couldn't resist telling the foreman that the boss was taking Theresa out for lunch. The foreman winked. He was one of Theresa's fans.

Ten minutes later, Liam and Theresa came out, putting their coats on.

"We won't be long," shouted Liam across to the foreman, who just nodded.

"I bet you won't," he muttered under his breath. Some guys had it all – that was for sure.

The hotel bar was quiet, before the buzz of the lunch-time trade. Liam didn't want them to be seen, so he picked a booth in the corner furthest from the door.

"You're getting very secretive, all of a sudden," said Theresa, placing her hand on top of his, to stop the drumming of his fingers.

"I need to talk to you," he said, finding it difficult to get started. He cleared his throat. The barman came over to the table with his pint of Guinness and a 7Up and lime for Theresa. She would usually have gone for a vodka and tonic, but he supposed it was a bit early in the day. He waited until the barman was well out of earshot.

"Can I go first?" She was fidgeting on the seat.

What was the matter with her? He had asked her out for lunch, told her he had something to say, and here she was, just like a woman, hijacking the conversation. It was hard enough to summon up the courage, without her interrupting him. Sophie was the same, sometimes. It drove him crazy. He held his breath. He didn't want to be horrible to Theresa, or hurt her any more than was necessary. He nodded. She was probably going to come up with some wild idea of a dirty weekend away together. She was always dropping hints. Sometimes she seemed to conveniently forget that he was married.

"We're going to have a baby!" she said.

As he stared in horror, she clapped her hands and all but jumped up and down on the seat.

"What did you say?" He looked around wildly to make sure no one else had come in.

"I did a test last night, after you went. I just knew it, and I was right!" She rummaged in her handbag.

He couldn't believe it. She was holding up a white plastic pregnancy stick with a blue line on it.

"Put that away!" He slapped it out of her hand, and it fell on the floor. He leaned over and picked it up. It had fluff on it from the carpet. The last time he had held one of these was when he and Sophie were expecting Michelle, their miracle first baby, after years of trying. They hadn't bothered testing when Oisín was coming. They just knew by then. He shoved it violently back into the bottom of her handbag.

"I can't deal with this now," he said.

"We'll work something out, darling. Don't worry," she reassured him.

"Look, Theresa, I brought you out for lunch to tell you that I can't see you any more."

The shock registered on her face. "No, Liam. You can't say that. Not now."

Liam gulped. "I was going to give you your notice today. Pay you a couple of months' wages, maybe to the end of June, to tide you over until you find something else. I'll have to rethink all that now, but we still can't go on seeing each other. Will you give me a forwarding address?"

"Forwarding address? What? You know my address. Liam. You know where I live. We make love in my bed, darling."

"Theresa, you can't keep on working in the office. It's too difficult, especially now. I need time to think. I'll be in touch." He stood up and for a moment his legs were trapped under the table, so he leaned forward as he eased out.

His face was close to hers and she saw the determination in his eyes. She knew that her tears and remonstrations would have no effect. Something had changed, and it wasn't just the news about the baby that was making him behave like this.

"We made a baby together," she whispered fiercely. "It is *our* baby, whether you like it or not."

Liam was close to cracking and he didn't want to show her any weakness, until he figured out what the hell to do. He would give her the benefit of the doubt that she hadn't done it on purpose. "Theresa, love, it's been really great being with you, and we've had some lovely times together, but it has to finish now. And you can't continue to work for me. Give me a few days and I'll ring you."

He walked out and he didn't look behind. If he had, he would have seen Theresa sitting bolt upright, sipping her drink through a straw. The barman thought she looked like a woman not to be crossed.

Sophie was playing with the kids when Liam got back. They were surrounded by Lego, and Oisín was making a fair attempt at a fire station. Liam sat down on Michelle's pink beanbag, and caused snorts of laughter when he fell backwards.

"Your bottom is too big, Daddy!" teased Michelle, and Oisín pretended to be a crane, helping to lift him up off the floor.

Sophie looked tired, and Liam wondered was he imagining it, or did her face look a bit gaunt? Was he already imagining her wasting away, her cells blasted by radiotherapy, before they even had confirmation that the bloody lump was malignant? A strange calm lay over the family as they clicked together the pieces of coloured plastic to build a whole village. Liam was commissioned to construct a baker's shop for doughnuts, and a fruit and vegetable shop. Michelle took on the ambitious task of building the church, which had a very interesting steeple made of alternating blue and white stripes. Sophie made a flat blue duck-pond and some park benches. Oisín completed the fire station. When it was finished, Liam wondered how they had subconsciously created a kind of cartoon English village. Liam had yet to see an Irish village with a pond and a baker's shop. Then Michelle got her 'Playmobil' people and they acted out a story together, each one putting on silly squeaky voices. They laughed when Oisín insisted that there must be a fire in the story so he could open the hinged doors of the fire station. They all had tea together, and Liam took the children upstairs for their bath while Sophie tidied up. Soon, sleep reigned in the dimly lit children's bedrooms.

Sophie and Liam sat together on the sofa. "Should we tell anyone yet?" she asked, in an ironic echo of the question she had asked when they discovered she was pregnant with Michelle.

"It's early days," he said, echoing his old reply.

"We'll wait for the biopsy results."

"I wonder how long they'll take?"

"Probably weeks."

After a few minutes of desultory speculations, they

resorted to the television. The question of the future was too big to contemplate. Too big to find the words to talk about it.

Liam was paying no attention to the home-decorating programme. It was sufficiently anodyne for him to be able to comment occasionally without engaging his brain. He was trying to work out what Theresa might do. He suspected she had a nasty streak. What if she rang up Sophie and told her everything, to get her revenge? She had hinted in the golf club, that time when John was there, that she was capable of something like that. He could see now that part of her attraction for him had been the element of danger she presented. But he had never considered his 'exit strategy' as they said in business, because Theresa seemed to be relatively content to be his mistress. She had often said she didn't believe in marriage, and Liam had been reassured that she wasn't trying to lure him away from Sophie. She liked her independence. That was why she worked and earned her own money. Theresa could never be a married woman just sitting at home, she had once told him with a slight sneer, referring to Sophie. But now it sounded as if she was trying to blackmail him into some kind of commitment. "We made a baby together," she had said. "It is *our* baby, whether you like it or not." He remembered how she had clapped her hands and waved that plastic stick about. As if she was overjoyed about the pregnancy. What was she playing at? He felt bewildered.

He must be firm – make it clear there was no hope of continuing the relationship. Then maybe she would go back to Cork and he could put the whole episode behind him. He would pay for her trip to England to have the abortion, of course, if that's what she decided. He should at least take responsibility for that.

He had tempted fate by being unfaithful to Sophie. Now was the time to put it right. He would make it up to her. He was so lucky to have her. And the kids. Just the two. He could feel his blood pressure rising. There was no way that Theresa was going to take this lying down. If she wanted to, she could make things very nasty indeed.

Sophie was curled up under his arm, her head resting on his chest. He could feel it getting heavier and heavier as she relaxed into sleep. He sat for two hours, not moving a muscle, even to reach the remote control. She would need all the sleep she could get. *Who Wants to be a Millionaire?* was followed by some inane sitcom. It all washed over him.

Chapter Fifteen

Alison was surprised that Sophie hadn't returned her calls for a couple of days. She hoped it wasn't because she disapproved of her going out for dinner with Ronan. She had warned Alison to be careful.

"Don't worry, Sophie. As I said to Lisa, I am not in the business of dating married men. It is purely for the sake of old times."

"That must be the oldest line in the book!" Sophie teased. She had been racking her brain trying to think where she knew the name Ronan Murphy from. Alison had said he was from Ballina, so maybe it was a childhood memory that was niggling at her. But she had a feeling it was more recent than that.

"I'll ring you after I see him, just to reassure you that I haven't done anything naughty," Alison said. "Do you fancy a drink next week to plan our weekend in London? There's a UK bank holiday the last week in May – we could aim for that."

Sophie had agreed, but now she didn't seem to be around. Alison hoped there was nothing wrong with the kids. Sophie did tend to get a bit wrapped up in them sometimes, and forget to have a life of her own. The jury was out for Alison on whether she liked Liam or not. The guys she was used to working with in London were all younger, so it was difficult to compare him with them. Maybe Liam was just an old-fashioned bloke, who expected to be the sole breadwinner, with all the attached privileges of hot meals, laundry and metaphorical warming of the slippers. There was nothing wrong with that, if it worked for both parties, but Alison sensed a huge frustration in Sophie. Alison wanted to tell her not to let her life revolve too much around the kids. As lovable as they were, they would ultimately do their own thing, and Sophie could be left with no sense of purpose at all if she didn't develop her own interests now. Alison thought of her own mother, and had a guilty pang about her selfish decision to come to Ireland instead of being close by.

"Sophie, give me a ring when you get a minute. I hope the kids are fine? Talk to you soon, bye."

That was her third message. She felt like a chat, so she decided to try Lisa, in case she was home from the hospital.

"Hi, please leave a message and we'll call you back."

"Lisa, it's me, I . . ."

Lisa snatched up the phone. "Hello! I've just got in the door. Sooo . . . how was it?"

"Kind of scary."

"Why on earth was it scary? You still fancy Ronan

255

like mad, and you think you might succumb to his irresistible charms?"

"Yes. And the really scary bit is that he's not married any more."

"*What?*"

The evening had been quite surreal. Ronan had suggested a restaurant in town, and Alison had met him there, grateful that there was quite a buzz in the place. She hated stilted conversation in a very quiet restaurant. Even though she hadn't been facing the door, Alison knew when Ronan walked in. His electricity filled any space he occupied. Even if the back of her neck hadn't tingled, the drooling expression on the waitress's face told all.

Ronan kissed her, a perfunctory, brother-like peck on the cheek.

"So, how are you?" He flicked his white linen napkin out, put it across his knee, and picked up the wine list with the other hand. He had developed real poise to complement his natural grace. The ten years sat well on him, with just a hint of grey at the temples, and a firming of his features. He lifted his left eyebrow in the cute way that had always made her want to giggle. He reminded her of a spaniel, begging for friendship with soulful eyes and a wrinkled forehead.

"Fine, thanks. How are the family?" The line she had settled on to establish the rules of engagement seemed gauche and defensive. He might not even fancy her, for heaven's sake.

"They're in great form. I had them over to me for the weekend. We took *Gráinne Uaile* out for a spring sail." He was talking as if she was intimate with every detail of his life. Why was he saying, 'had them for the weekend'? Who, or what, was 'Groinewail'?

He wasn't looking at her, but studying the wine list with great concentration, so she glanced at his hand. No wedding ring, but he probably wouldn't wear one anyway. She squinted, looking for the pale tell-tale shadow of a recently abandoned ring. Not a hint.

"Red or white?" He suddenly looked up, and followed her glance.

"I need to decide what I'm eating first." Alison was relieved that the menu was a huge one, so she could hide behind it to conceal the pink flush on her neck.

"No wedding ring?" he asked, lifting that quirky eyebrow again.

"Yes," she admitted to checking him over for one.

"Where is it then?" he asked.

"Oh, you mean me? No, *I'm* not married," she said. She could hardly hide completely behind the menu, but she had a desperate urge to fan herself with it.

"Neither am I. Well, not strictly speaking, anyway."

Here we go, thought Alison. The predictable spiel about the wife not understanding him, the fact that they had drifted apart, were living different lives, sharing a roof but not a bed, for the sake of the children . . .

"We're separated. Only six more months to go and I can apply for a divorce. The rules over here are a bit stricter than they are in England."

"That's sad," said Alison. Did that make him available?

"It's very hard on the kids. I have them some weekends, and half of the school holidays. That's the difficult bit, to be honest. The logistics are a nightmare."

"Where do they live the rest of the time?"

"In Athlone. That's where we settled. We bought the big house, just outside town. Two acres around it. It's a huge old Georgian thing, from the days of the Plantations, no doubt."

She didn't haul him up on his casual blending of architectural and political history. "Lots of space for the dogs and the pony, then."

"Yes, indeed. But I was very busy, working hard to make the money. You know what it's like. It becomes a kind of fever, and it's very hard to switch off. I never took enough holidays. The kids were starting school before I even noticed them."

"How old are they now?"

"Nine, seven and six. They're great now, very easy to spend time with. Like we went out on the boat yesterday, just the four of us, and they were a big help. The youngest one, Nancy, can be a bit of a hazard. You have to keep an eye on her. But the boys are great. Real little sailors."

He sipped the wine he had ordered, rolling it on his tongue, sloshing it forward to the taste-buds at the front of his mouth. Alison had always found this ritual pretentious when her other friends did it. Somehow it suited the newly sophisticated Ronan. He seemed like a man of substance, not afraid to reject the wine if it didn't suit his palate. He nodded, and the waiter poured for her. The wine was delicious, light and crisp.

"What are the boys' names?" Alison was desperately trying to stop herself doing the maths.

"Brian and Dara".

"Lovely names," said Alison, trying to distract herself.

Ronan was staring at the tablecloth, and tugging his ear, a nervous habit he hadn't lost. His casual sophistication had vanished temporarily. "Before you ask, and it won't take you long to work it out, that was why I left you so abruptly. Sinéad was pregnant with Brian."

Alison didn't say anything. Ronan must have been two-timing her, but she was oddly relieved that he hadn't just got bored with her. Her confidence in later relationships had been knocked by constantly wondering if she was interesting, or sexy, or challenging enough. She had forgotten how to just be herself.

"I came back to Ireland with Sinéad. She said she would prefer to face the shame of having a baby here, than to have one growing up over there."

Alison looked down at the plate of nibbles that had mysteriously appeared on the table. "That's putting it bluntly," she muttered.

"No offence," said Ronan. He had always been a straight talker, for all his charm.

"You obviously got married, so where's the shame in that?" she asked.

"Well, Sinéad came back home with a six-month bump. The wedding photos are not exactly the ones you imagine when you're a little girl deciding whether you want to be a nun, or marry a handsome prince in a big flouncy wedding dress."

"Did you wear a big flouncy wedding dress?"

He laughed. "That's what I love about you, Alison . . ."

"So what went wrong?" She wasn't quite ready to succumb to his smile yet.

"Sinéad was a recruitment consultant in London, earning really good money. Ironically, that's how we met. You were nagging me to go and get a job, and when I went in for an interview at the agency, there she was. We went out a couple of times . . ."

"And you couldn't resist her charms?" Alison didn't really want a blow-by-blow account. She wanted to go straight to the unhappy ending bit.

"You went off to Greece and the next night when I met her for a drink, Sinéad told me she was nearly four months pregnant. I felt like I had to stick by her." He stopped abruptly and leaned across the table, dropping all pretence of being casually dismissive of his marriage. "You know, all I could think of was how upset you were when you told me about the . . . abortion."

Alison gulped and put her hands under the table to hide the shaking.

"You were in bits about it," he went on, "and you felt so guilty, and . . ."

She nodded.

Ronan went on. "You told me that the father didn't want to have anything to do with the baby, or you, when you told him you were pregnant, and I'll never forget the look on your face when you were telling me. And you said you didn't have the courage to have the baby on your own, and you would always regret it."

Alison couldn't bear to see the tears in Ronan's eyes reflecting her own.

"I couldn't do that to Sinéad, so I had to make a choice. It was the hardest decision I ever made in my life."

He reached across, wanting to touch her, but Alison couldn't move. She stared at his long fingers, and remembered their caress, and the turmoil inside her was worse, not better, for knowing why he had left her.

He took her silence as an invitation to continue. "When we came back here, we had no money in the beginning so we had to live with Sinéad's parents in Mullingar. It was a nightmare. Her mother kept giving me these dirty looks, for getting her daughter into trouble, and the father kept taking me down to the pub for man-to-man talks about how he expected me to make an honest woman of his daughter at the earliest opportunity. The two of us got on like a house on fire, so we'd have a few pints and we'd come home to a very frosty reception from the two women. I should have seen the writing on the wall. They say you should always look at the mother to see how the daughter will turn out. The signs were all there for me to read, but I ignored them."

"So she turned into a nasty nag, and you left her?" Alison couldn't quite equate the 'happy families' image he had conjured up about his children, with the story he was telling. "There must have been some good bits in between."

"There's loads in between. To keep a long story short, I got a job locally in an accountant's office doing fairly menial things like the tax returns for the smaller clients – the farmers and the local businesses. I discovered I had a flair for it and before long the clients were asking for me because I seemed to be able to identify ways for them to reduce their tax bills."

"Tax evasion?"

"No, just tax avoidance. It's a completely different thing. You just have to know the rules really well. There are lots of legal ways of paying less tax. Eventually I was able to set up my own firm, and after a few years –"

"And a few babies," interjected Alison.

"Yes. After a few years we had enough money to buy the dream house and live a bit more comfortably."

"I bet the father-in-law was pleased."

"He was, and we still get on, even now. He took me to one side a few months ago and he said to me he understands why I left."

Alison couldn't quite get that one, so she let it go. The father-in-law approving of his daughter's abandonment? Could she believe him? He seemed to be telling the truth, but how could she ever know? Had Sinéad kicked him out, or had he gone of his own accord?

"So what went wrong?"

"Sinéad got bored at home, I think. On the one hand she had it very easy, looking after the kids and running the house, but I will admit I wasn't around much so she had a lot on her plate, especially when they were small. She started drinking."

Alison wondered how much of this was embroidered by Ronan to make himself look good.

"It never turned into a really bad problem, so I won't

try and blame it on the drink, because that wouldn't be fair on her."

How very noble of him. Alison's right and left brain were having a punch-up. Her hormones were zinging. The cavewoman in her wanted to be dragged off by the hair, right now. The rest of her was standing, legs akimbo, waving red warning lanterns: *Do not pass this point. You will only get hurt.*

"Are you OK?" Ronan was looking into her eyes.

She wondered what he could see. "Yes, of course. Sorry. Go on." She tried to sound interested but dispassionate. It was a struggle.

"One day, I just woke up and realised that there was more to life. It's not OK to just let circumstances dictate how you live your life. Sinéad wasn't happy, and neither was I. We both felt trapped by the situation. I'm a much better father now than I ever was when I lived with them. We get much more –"

"Quality time." Alison just stopped herself putting on a corny American accent.

"Exactly. I never thought about what they were interested in when I was with Sinéad. That was her job. She decided where we went on holiday, she went to the kids' sports days and organised their social life. I only feel like I'm getting to know them in the last year or so."

"But why did you have to leave them, to find out?"

"I tried. I really did. But to keep the peace, everyone deferred to Sinéad, including the kids. She could be very moody if she didn't get her own way. If I ever suggested something, like going out on the boat together, there would always be a reason why we couldn't. Nancy had a cold, or Brian should be doing his homework. Now, if I have them for the weekend, I get to make the decisions. I love it. They tell me stuff that they never would have told me before."

"And of course you don't have to worry about nappies and routines and formula milk."

He missed the irony. "That's exactly it. We're well past that stage. They're half-reared." He paused. "Have you decided what you're going to eat? Have I told you that you look fantastic?" He twinkled at her across the top of his menu.

Alison had the overwhelming feeling that he had offloaded everything, and now he thought the way was clear to start the charm offensive. He had always been single-minded. Even when he had been in London, and Alison thought he was just being flaky, he had actually been single-mindedly having a good time. Then he'd had his successful career, then become 'Dad of the Year', and now, what?

"Thanks," she said. "I'm having the scallops, followed by the shank of lamb."

"Sounds good."

A waiter was hovering to take their order. Ronan took control and ordered for her, even remembering that she loved sugar snap peas and asparagus tips.

She couldn't eat much, but the food was a good distraction. They managed to chat about her work, and a show they had both seen in London, and laugh about the latest antics in the Whitehouse. He was as entertaining as ever, regaling her with stories about various clients without disclosing anything confidential, but giving her a sense that he had put his inherent talent with numbers to very effective use.

"So, did he come back to yours, or did he lure you for a nightcap in his sumptuous penthouse apartment somewhere?" Lisa demanded.

"No, we had a very virtuous little kiss at the end of the evening, and he put me into a taxi. He lives in the opposite direction."

"Going to see him again?"

"I'm not sure. He asked me all about what I had been doing for ten years, and when I didn't really have much to say, I wasn't sure if he'd lost interest. He probably thought I was really boring. And if he did ever get my clothes off, he would find a less than attractive sight underneath."

"Well, I consider it a good sign that you're fantasising about getting naked with him, girl," said Lisa. "Keep up the diet and the jogging."

"I wasn't sure if I *liked* him any more, Lisa. I really fancy him – God, do I fancy him, but he's got a hard edge to him, and he's a bit self-absorbed. A bit more arrogant than I remember, as well."

"You're only there for a year, Alison. If he's good for a bonk, and you're up for it, don't worry about it too much. He sounds like he's very confident in his own ability, but he clearly has a soft side to him too – he's good with his kids, and he fully admitted that he was sorry for hurting you."

"Lisa, I just know I could fall head over heels in love

with him again. I don't want to get hurt, if it's not going anywhere."

"You're getting risk-averse in your old age. Live for the moment, instead of worrying about the consequences."

Alison remembered making a similar speech to Lisa when she was trying to get pregnant again, but scared of going through another miscarriage. "Sex is more than just about making babies, you know," she had lectured. "You are so lucky to have a man like Michael to make love to. Enjoy it. Cherish him. If you're meant to have babies, you will. If not, you still have him. Live for the moment."

Alison yawned. "I'm going now. I have an early meeting on site tomorrow. Thanks for the chat."

"You're welcome. Any time."

As Alison hung up, she was struck with guilt that she hadn't asked how April was. She dialled again. "How's April?"

She could hear the smile in Lisa's voice. "She's gorgeous. Her face is filling out now, and she looks more like a little girl. Thanks for asking. Night, night. Sweet dreams!"

Chapter Sixteen

Sophie had a blissful moment of forgetfulness, just as she emerged from sleep. She woke up at 6.30 from habit, to the sound of birds singing, and for just one second, she was happy. Spring was in the air. Her tongue ran across her furry teeth. Why hadn't she brushed them last night? Then the anvil settled on her chest, pinning her to the bed. She had taken to imagining all kinds of twinges and pains, most of them on the left side of her body. This morning, she had to sit up to breathe. She felt as though the winter-weight duvet was smothering her. She swung her legs out to the side of the bed, taking gulps of air. She was so scared. Michelle came wandering into the bedroom, her hair tousled, and stumbled across to the bed for a hug. Sophie sat there, holding her daughter, inhaling her sleepy cotton-sheets smell. This was the beginning of the fight, she decided. Nothing or nobody was going to take her away from these precious children. She asked God to give her the strength to fight, and to show them no fear. *Let me hide from them the depth of my fear. Make me strong. Let me not even entertain a negative thought. Give me positive energy, and the will to fight.*

She straightened up and patted Michelle on the head. "Will we go down and make breakfast for the boys as a surprise?" she whispered.

Michelle nodded, loving any kind of conspiracy. They went downstairs hand in hand, whispering as they passed Oisín's door. Michelle helped her to lay the table, and although the thought of a boiled egg made Sophie retch, she went along with Michelle's menu suggestion, and put on a pot of water to boil.

"This is like Christmas," said Michelle delightedly. She rarely got her mother to herself, and in such a good mood.

"Why is it like Christmas, love?" Sophie asked, bending down and looking into her eyes.

Mammy never did that, thought Michelle. She was always busy doing other things, or bossing her to tidy up. "Because it feels like we're waiting for something to happen," she said.

Sophie stood up and it took every ounce of her willpower to say, "That's right. We're going to surprise the boys, aren't we?"

Liam ate his egg in silence, and the children sensed that something wasn't quite right. Daddy was usually gone to work long before they got up. He was going to take them to playschool, and spend the day with Mammy. "That will be nice for you, Mammy. You won't be lonely today," said Oisín. "Can we stay at home too?"

"No, Oisín, they want to do *adult* things, like talking and pottering around," bossed Michelle. Liam and Sophie's eyes met across the table and they struggled not to laugh – Michelle was such a little mimic. Focussing on the children would get them through this if nothing else did.

When Liam came back in the car, Sophie had a cup of tea ready for him. "Liam, this could go on for a long time. You have to go to work. We can't put the world on hold while we're waiting for the results."

"I don't want you to be on your own," he said, putting his hand on top of hers.

"I'll ring Alison and see if she's free for lunch. I think I can talk to her without telling her anything. Maeve would get it out of me in one second flat."

"If she's free, I'll go into work for a few hours, so," said Liam, gulping back the tea. The lady who ran the playgroup was going to keep the kids until four o'clock. He had told her there was a family emergency and she had been all ears. She would interrogate the children, no doubt, to get to the bottom of it. She liked nothing better than a crisis.

Alison was delighted to hear from Sophie. "I can do one o'clock," she said. "Do you fancy a quick sandwich and then a walk along the prom?"

"Wow, are you on a health kick, or something?" Sophie asked.

"Yes, as a matter of fact. I'll tell you all, when I see you."

Liam kissed Sophie softly on the lips, in a way that he hadn't done for a long time, and she wanted to shout at him, "Don't give up on me yet – I'm not dying!" It had felt like some kind of blessing he was bestowing on her, or a tender farewell.

There was a stiff breeze coming in off the sea, and Sophie took a scarf out of the glove compartment to wrap around her head. She hated getting earache. Alison was striding towards her, waving. They sat in the lee of the huge sand-retaining rocks and ate the sandwiches Alison had brought. "Goat's cheese and parma ham is probably not the most calorie-friendly lunch in the world," she said, "but there have to be some pleasures in life."

"I love apricots too. I can't believe you got them at this time of the year." Sophie sank her teeth into her second one, throwing the stone from the first one high into the air, to land in the choppy water.

"There are no seasons any more, in this wonderful global economy," said Alison. Sophie was very subdued today, she thought. She wasn't sure whether to tell her about Ronan. "Are you OK?"

Sophie nodded, but she wasn't looking at Alison. "Fine, thanks. A bit tired, from not sleeping well last night, but otherwise, fine."

"You don't seem yourself."

"I feel a bit like I'm somebody else, to be honest. Like I'm living in Limbo." Sophie abandoned her resolve to keep the news to herself. "I have a lump on my breast. We're waiting for the biopsy results."

Alison dropped the last bit of her sandwich, which

suddenly tasted sour. The crusts, flaked with goat's cheese, fell apart and tumbled down the rocks, landing in a crevice.

"Oh, my God, Sophie. When did you find it?"

"A couple of days ago. The doctor gave me a referral for a biopsy straight away. It feels like an eternity though, waiting for the results."

Alison put her arm around Sophie's shoulder and they sat there until the chill of the rocks penetrated through the raincoat they had spread out to sit on.

"Do you want to walk?" Alison asked, shivering. She was glad she didn't have a meeting this afternoon. She could take out as much time as Sophie needed. They stood up and shook off the crumbs, and Alison pulled on the windcheater.

"Let's have a really brisk walk, and then have a cup of tea at the other end," she said. She was sure that Sophie wouldn't want to be treated like an invalid. Anyway, the tests might say it was benign. It was the waiting that must be difficult. Her parents had done all that waiting alone, without involving her, just in case the news was good, and she would never need to know. Her mother had told her they had three weeks of hell, and it was almost a relief to get the news about her father's cancer, so they knew what they were dealing with.

Sophie didn't seem inclined to talk. Alison strode out, setting a fast pace, but aware that Sophie was much shorter than her, so she cut her strides to match.

Sophie was glad of the wind, which didn't make conversation easy. She wanted time to think, but not to be alone. Liam's long face just made her think the worst. In her cynical moments she could see him wondering how he would cope with the kids if she wasn't there. He couldn't even manage to look after them for a weekend, never mind the rest of their lives. Maybe the weekend in London was a bad idea. She should spend every moment possible with the children, just in case, in case . . .

"Do you know what, Alison?" she said, out of the blue.

"What?"

"Do you remember us in January, both so hung up on turning forty this year? We spend our time looking around to see what everyone else is doing, and thinking the grass is greener. We haven't actually stopped, either of us, to look at what we have, and savour it. Being dead is a lot worse than being forty."

Alison didn't know what to say.

"It's true, though, isn't it? If this thing turns out to be just a scare, I hope I remember this feeling, afterwards."

They were striding along Grattan Road, and they could just see the windows of Alison's apartment block in the distance.

"Look at us. I have a lovely husband, and two fantastic kids and a house. You have a great career, a cool apartment, a man running after you by the sound of things, and neither of us think that is good enough. We spend our time looking at what everyone else has and thinking we're missing out. I hope I don't die, but if I do, this is the life I have lived so far, and there's no changing it."

"You won't die. But sometimes it's good to take stock. A shock like the lump on your breast or Lisa's scare with Baby April does make you stop and think."

"I called into the church on the way over here. It's not often I go in there on my own, when there's no crowd for Mass and no Father O'Leary nagging me about things."

"I can imagine."

"It was so peaceful. That church has been there for hundreds of years. I think it's a Norman one. I don't know my architecture, but anyway, it doesn't matter. Those stones have seen it all: grief, persecution, death, marriage, birth, despair and hope. Those walls must have heard the confessions of a million people by now. Father O'Leary, me, the kids, anyone else who goes in there to pray – we're all just so many human beings passing through. The stones just sit there, unchanging, maybe weathering a bit on the outside. And we come and go."

"Did you pray?"

"I did. I keep asking God for strength – not for myself, but to make it easier for everybody else. I think I was expecting some kind of sign from Him. Some reassurance that He won't let me die yet because I have something important to do for Him."

"And did you see the sign?"

"Nothing. It was as silent as the grave." She slowed down, holding a stitch in her side. Her left side again. "Unfortunate metaphor, sorry."

"Don't say sorry to me. I wish I could do something. When will you hear?"

273

"Could be days, could be weeks. Sometimes I think the longer it takes, the less urgently they're treating it, so it must be good news. Then I remember that it's just a test tube labelled with my name, among hundreds of other test tubes. They'll get around to it when they get around to it. I'm not entitled to any kind of special treatment."

"It will be fine. I'm sure there must be loads of people who get lumps and they turn out to be benign."

"I wasn't very good at checking though. I've always just taken my health for granted. Horrible things happen to other people, but not to me. Maybe if I had found the lump sooner . . ."

"Sophie, you have to stop this. You're torturing yourself for no reason. It might be fine."

"But whatever happens, good or bad, I have something to learn from this. That's what I'm saying."

Alison just hugged her. They had a cup of tea, and Alison tried to lighten the mood by telling Sophie about Ronan, but everything she said seemed to carry such heavy import. Ronan had discovered the ability to relate to his kids. Sinéad wasn't needed so much, by him, or by her children. Even as one of life's eternal optimists, Sophie would hardly miss the comparisons. Characteristically, she focussed on the positive.

"It sounds like he's grown up a lot since you were with him before," she said.

That thought had crossed Alison's mind. "I know, but I'm having trouble reconciling the Ronan who left me to stick by his pregnant girlfriend, and the one who has just walked away from all his responsibilities."

"Not all of them, Alison. He has the kids every

second weekend, and in the holidays. That's unusual. He must be something special."

"He's definitely something special. I'm scared though, Sophie. What if I fall in love with him, and then I have to go back to London?"

"Take it one step at a time. Maybe you won't want to go back to England."

"There's a job waiting for me, though. Someone else would get it, if I didn't go back."

"So what? Is the job the most important thing in your life?"

"Well, yes, it is."

"Only because you haven't had anything else to replace it. Alison, if you had met the right guy, at the right time, are you telling me that you wouldn't have had a family by now? You are so good with kids, you'd be a natural."

"What if his kids hate me? They might think I'm some kind of Wicked Stepmother."

"Alison! You're jumping ahead ever so slightly here. You've had one date with the guy. You fancy him but you're not even sure if you still like him. Or if he likes you. You don't have to go out and reinvent yourself as a stepmother yet. Try having a nice time as a girlfriend, first."

"I've always done this with men. I think it's what puts them off. I'm so busy imagining the next step in the relationship that I don't stop to enjoy what's happening. After the first date, I start to worry about what his parents will think of me, or which of his friends will be the best man!"

Sophie laughed. "What kind of wedding dress are you going to have?"

Alison smiled. "Long, ivory, and with a short curvy train."

They walked back to Sophie's car. "I wasn't going to tell anyone, until I got the results. Don't mention it to anyone, will you?" she asked.

Alison wondered who on earth Sophie thought she would tell.

"I feel a bit superstitious about it, as if talking about it will make it come true."

"I understand. Call me as soon as you have a result."

"Of course, I will."

They hadn't talked about the weekend in London. Everything might be fine.

Chapter Seventeen

There was a bouquet of lilies and roses waiting for Alison when she got back from her evening run. That was her sixth in a row, which was a record. She stood on her doorstep, panting. She picked up the hand-tied cellophane bundle and unlocked her door. The card just said, *"Thank you for a lovely evening last week . . . can we go for a repeat performance?"*

It was their old joke. Thirteen years old, to be precise, but Alison knew exactly what he meant. The morning after they had made love for the first time, Ronan had gone out to buy the Sunday papers, and come back with croissants and a bunch of daffodils she knew he had nicked from the local park. He had scribbled those words on a torn piece of brown paper, and wrapped it around the daffodils. He delivered the flowers and breakfast in bed. Alison had scolded him, saying "It's all right for you; you don't live here. I'm the one who'll have to suffer the dirty looks from the little old ladies who saw you picking them."

"I might just have to move in, to protect you then," he had said, pushing the tray aside, and slipping back into bed. The repeat performance had been fantastic, and he had sort of never left, until he left for good.

She arranged the flowers in a tall vase. Sophie was right. She should just take it one step at a time. Enjoy being with him, and see what happened next. The phone rang and she wondered if it was Ronan. She was smiling when she answered.

"Alison, can you come home, darling?" Her mother hadn't meant to sound so desperate. She had rehearsed a little speech – 'nothing to be alarmed about, but it would be good to have you here, your dad would appreciate it . . . '

"What's happened, Mum?"

"Your dad's taken a turn for the worse. They've taken him to hospital. I'm going there now, but I'll call you tonight to let you know . . ."

"Mum, I'll get on to the airline now, and book a flight. I'll leave a message on your home phone to let you know when I can be there."

"Thanks, love. See you soon." Her mother's voice was choked with tears.

Alison booked a flight and within an hour, she was packed and in a taxi on the way to the airport. It would be tight, but if traffic wasn't too bad, she would make it. Her phone beeped.

"Surprise! See you tonight? R."

*"Can't. Dad in hosp. Flying home. Thanx for lovely flwrs.
CU soon."*

She should call him, she knew, but there was no
room in her head for conversation. What if she didn't
make it on time? Her mother was going through this all
on her own. Why the hell had she been so selfish? She
should have just knuckled under, stayed in London, let
Dave go to Dubrovnic, let Maurice do her job. What did
any of it matter? The last call for boarding was echoing
around the terminal when she ran inside. The check-in
desk still had four people in the queue. It was as if
Galway airport was so huge that people needed fifteen
minutes to walk to their departure gate. There was only
one gate – a door from the departure lounge straight
onto the tarmac. Passengers had to walk a few yards to
board the plane. She got to the top of the queue and
checked in. "Go straight to the departure gate," she was
told, and she nodded, too distracted to make a joke
about it. She crossed the tiny terminal building and put
her bag through the security check. Twenty people were
waiting in the departure lounge.

"They have delusions of grandeur in this place," one
woman said to her when she caught her eye. "They
made the final call about ten minutes ago, as if the plane
was ready to take off. It hasn't even landed yet!"

Alison smiled. They watched the turbo-prop plane
circle once above the airport and then come in to land.

"I love this airport," she said to the woman, trying to
distract herself from thinking about her father by
making conversation. But the woman had turned away

and was busy ranting to someone else about the lack of a duty-free shop.

The 'hospital feeling' settled on Alison as soon as she stepped inside the main entrance. *Déjà vu* of her experience with Lisa, as she walked the corridors trying to find the right ward. She found her mother sitting by her father's bed. Two ancient-looking men were in the other beds, wizened and waiting. Why had her parents never paid for BUPA or something? This was humiliating for her father. He had been brought so low by his illness, and now he had to share a smelly, noisy space with two complete strangers. It wasn't even a room with a door, but an alcove leading off a corridor. Her anger overwhelmed her fear, just for a moment. She briefly hugged her mother, and they sat watching his sleeping face. A drip was feeding into his emaciated, bluish arm.

"He's lost weight again," she whispered to her mother, who nodded.

A clanging trolley went past, a care assistant whistling as if to ward off the gloom of imminent death.

Her father's eyes opened and he smiled a thin-lipped greeting. "Sorry not to be more chipper," he whispered, his usual apologetic manner not irritating her today.

"It's OK, Dad. How are you doing?" She had to be brave for him. That was the idea of visiting in hospital, wasn't it? Self-indulgent thoughts about how guilty she would feel when he died were not the order of the day.

"Not bad, love, considering," he grimaced.

"Let's tell her straight, Dennis," her mother urged, holding his hand. He nodded.

"You tell her," he said.

"We haven't got long, have we, love?" she said, looking between him and their daughter.

He shook his head. "A week, maybe," he said.

How could they talk about it like this? Their resignation to their fate was the thing that had frustrated her most when she was growing up. They would write their letters of complaint to monolithic customer service departments as a matter of principle, but that was as far as it ever went. As if the act of protest was an end in itself, and they lost sight of the real goal. Why wasn't he fighting? Who had told him he had a week to live? How dare they? She fought the anger, squeezing her mother's free hand. Then she gently took her father's other hand, the one that lay flat on the bed, fingers curled, the wrist weighed down with a drip. The three of them sat, connected, for a long time without speaking. Theirs had always been a relationship of few words. There was a tacit understanding that they loved one another, a tacit agreement never to argue. Her teenage resistance had been endured, but never discussed. Alison had sometimes wondered if they even noticed what she was doing, and she wanted to scream at them, to shatter their comfortable delusions. She had thought about dyeing her hair green, or even becoming a full punk and piercing her tongue, just to make them blink, and acknowledge her right to be different. But she didn't want to be too different. She must have inherited their compliance genes after all.

At ten o'clock, a nurse came to say that family visiting hours were over. The arrival of her father's meal had briefly distracted them, and they had analysed the contents in detail. "I think that's broccoli," her mother had said, pointing at a soggy green mess that could equally have been cabbage.

It didn't matter. He wasn't eating it anyway. Alison covered it up after a while as the contents of the plate kept drawing her eye, and she wanted to heave. Her mother said they should go to the cafeteria for something to eat, but she shook her head. She went to the coffee machine and got drinks and a bar of chocolate for them to share. Her mother nibbled around the edges of the squares like a child trying to make a treat last for longer. Her eyes were sunk in her head, and circled by black shadows. She looked old too. Her parents had moved to a new place in her perception, and Alison didn't want them to be there. She insisted on paying for a cab home, despite her mother's protestations.

"We've got to keep our energy up for Dad," Alison said, and finally prevailed. They got back to the house, which smelt of stale milk. The breakfast table was still laid, two bowls of high-fibre cereal, the covered milk jug, two glasses of precisely matching quantities of orange juice. A toast rack with two slices of toast, cut into triangles with the crusts taken off. The crusts lay on the breadboard.

"We had to dash out so quickly I didn't have time to tidy up."

"It's OK, Mum," said Alison. She started to put things away.

"The birds missed their breakfast," her mother said, opening the French windows. "They can have a late snack."

Rats were more likely, thought Alison, but she didn't say anything. They had a hug on the landing before going to bed.

The phone rang in the middle of the night.

"I knew I shouldn't have left him," her mother wailed as she ran downstairs, her slippers flapping on each step.

"Be careful, Mum. Don't fall," Alison called, following her.

She just stood there, holding the receiver, shaking her head. In the hall light, Alison could see the narrow outline of her mother's body through her full-length cotton nightie. She heard the dialling tone, and took the phone gently from her mother and hung it up.

"He's gone," her mother sobbed, leaning against her. Alison held her by the shoulders and led her gently into the living-room. They sat on the sofa together, Alison muttering soothing wordless sounds and stroking her mother's soft, light hair. Dawn broke and they were still sitting there, Alison stiff with holding her shoulder at a comfortable angle to support her mother's head. She had eventually slipped off into a doze, and Alison wondered how many sleepless nights she'd had in recent months, listening out for her father, or just lying there worrying about him.

"Oh, sorry," her mother said, sitting up suddenly. "I didn't mean to sleep."

"You needed it, Mum."

Her mother wiped saliva from her mouth. She was embarrassed to see she had dribbled on her daughter's sleeve, but she didn't say anything.

"Let's put the kettle on."

They watched the light seeping into the sky over the back hedge, clutching their mugs of tea. No china cups and saucers for a day like this, thought Alison. This was the first day of her life without a father.

"It wasn't nice for him, at the end," her mother said, breaking their long silence. "He was a private man, and that kind of an illness is not nice, if you . . ."

"I know, Mum. I'm really sorry I wasn't here to help."

"He wouldn't have wanted you to see him like that. He hated the idea of you even seeing him in hospital."

"But why, Mum?" He was always keeping her at arm's length.

"He said to me when you were still tiny, that he wanted to be your hero."

Alison was stunned.

"He wanted you to look up to him."

"I did," said Alison, remembering the excitement she would feel, coming home from school, waiting to show him what she had been doing. He didn't seem to be interested so gradually she had stopped.

"You looked up to him when you were little. He was so proud of you, too. Then as you got older, you didn't need him so much, and that hurt him."

"But he was . . ." It wasn't fair. Alison had never found the words to articulate this confusion when he was alive, so how could she explain it to her mother now? Her mother had just lost the man she had loved for forty-seven years. Where had the cycle of misunderstanding begun? Had she shunned her father once, when he expressed an interest? Or had he been uninterested one day when Alison particularly wanted him to pay attention? Who knew? It was lost in the family memory. Now she wouldn't get a chance to put things straight.

"I loved him," she said.

"I know." It was her mother's turn to be strong. "We have a busy day ahead. Would you like to use the bathroom first?" For once, the offer didn't sound like the politeness owed to a visitor. Alison went upstairs and showered, wondering how long ago her father had tiled the walls, and how many times he had re-grouted the seal around the bath. He had provided a warm, comfortable and safe home. He had been a solid and reliable husband and a steady earner even when times were tough and he had to go and do delivery jobs to pay the bills. His ego had never got in the way of doing the right thing by his family. Alison watched the soapy water swirling around her recently pedicured feet before disappearing down the plughole. She had also had a bikini wax before her dinner date with Ronan. She had told herself they were just to boost her confidence, and not because she was planning to sleep with him. Now, after the flowers, and his message, it was just a matter of when. Sophie said she should take it a day at a time, and maybe that was right. But maybe the legacy her father had really left her was the quest for someone like him – someone to love Alison as her father had loved her mother. Was she likely to find that person in Ronan, who had already walked away from his family?

The day passed in a whirl of activity. They went to the hospital one last time, to see her father laid out in the Chapel of Rest.

"He looks better already," her mother said, and then, bizarrely, they laughed. As if he needed to look his best for the journey through the underworld. Like the Egyptian Pharaohs, welcomed by Isis with her hawk and her cobra. Alison left her mother there for a few minutes to say goodbye in private, and collected the death certificate to give to the undertaker. She was glad he wanted to be cremated. It fitted better with her image of her father being transported to a better place, subsumed by flames rather than rotting underground.

They walked arm in arm down the high street, neither of them able to remember exactly where the funeral parlour was.

"It's the kind of place you walk past unnoticed unless you need it, like a pawnbroker's shop," her mother said.

"Did you ever have to use one?" Alison asked, surprised at the reference.

"Only the once. That's why it has stuck in my mind, I suppose. Remember that time when the silver tea service disappeared for a while, and I told you it was having a special clean?"

Alison remembered it really well. It was around the time her father had worked nights. She had been angry that her father couldn't come to the end-of-year show at school, because his shift started at eight. She had told her friends that he was ill, because she was too embarrassed by his manual job, fitting air-conditioning units in offices.

"We managed to redeem it after three months, which wasn't too bad. That was a difficult time, really."

Alison knew that part of her mother's memory of that time would be her own outrageous behaviour. She had started smoking, and occasionally playing truant. That was as far as Alison had ever taken her rebellion, and she hadn't even enjoyed it. She had just felt a really strong need to show them she was different. They were so boring and conservative and dull, she had screamed at them that evening, as her father left the house for work.

"Sorry I made things difficult for you then," she said, wishing she had told her father that she loved him before he died.

"It was just part of growing up," her mother said.

Chapter Eighteen

Liam wasn't going to pick up the children from a party for another hour and Sophie planned to have a cup of tea and then a little nap. She wasn't sleeping at all, worrying herself through the hours of every night about what would happen if the results were positive. The weariness she felt now reminded her of the afternoons when she was pregnant with Michelle. She would lie on the bed, just staring at the leaves on the trees outside, or reading the week-by-week pregnancy book with its fruit imagery, imagining how big a strawberry or a peach would be inside her. Sometimes she would doze off, and would wake up an hour later, full of energy and ready for anything. She had made curtains, varnished the living-room floor, and made three little cot covers, with embroidered ducks and rabbits. She had been lucky to have a huge translation project from the university, which kept her busy in the mornings. The months had flown by. That was over five years ago, she realised. She didn't have the luxury of afternoon naps when she was pregnant with Oisín. As a toddler, Michelle never seemed to sleep during the day. She was like a little motor, running all the time until she collapsed in a heap at 6.30, when Sophie had felt like doing the same.

Liam was standing in the kitchen, and Sophie wondered if he was waiting for a cup of tea, or something. He had that expectant look on his face. He could just put the kettle on himself. He might have to learn self-sufficiency soon enough.

"Sophie," he said, too gently. He put his hands on her arms. "Do you want to sit down?"

"Why would I want to sit down?" she demanded, even though suddenly her knees felt wobbly.

"Doctor Magee called."

"Is there news?" she asked, thinking what a relief it would be, just to know.

"He wants us to go in and see him this afternoon. He'll tell us the results."

"We can't. There isn't time before we have to pick up the kids –"

"Maeve is going to collect them. She'll give them their tea."

"What did you tell her?" Sophie felt completely out of control. Liam didn't organise things. She did. That was her job. What would Maeve be thinking, with Liam ringing her in the middle of the day?

"I told her nothing. I just said I'd really appreciate it if she collected them, and she said no problem. Her two are at the party as well."

It must be the worst news possible. The doctor wouldn't have asked them to come in, otherwise.

Sophie and Liam were sitting, waiting to go into the doctor's surgery. There was nobody else in the room, and the ticking of the huge clock over the mantelpiece was the only sound. Sophie was staring at a poster about pre-school booster injections, trying to remember if that was what Michelle had had in January, or was that just a meningitis one? She had it all written down in the little book from the Western Health Board – she would check when she got home. A red car pulled into the carpark, and she noticed a woman getting out. Sophie hoped they would get in to see the doctor soon. She couldn't face making small talk with someone now. The woman pushed open the outside door and stepped up to the reception desk. Sophie thought she recognised the voice as she spoke to the receptionist. Yes, it was Theresa from the office. She wondered who would be answering the phone if both Liam and she were out. She turned to Liam to nudge him, thinking Theresa might be embarrassed to be caught out of work. Not that there was anywhere for Liam to hide himself.

Theresa turned around and smiled but she looked a bit awkward. Sophie had always found her very sociable. But she wouldn't be inclined to tell Theresa any of her business. She was known to be a bit of a gossip. What would Theresa be thinking now, seeing herself and Liam sitting here?

"Hello, Theresa," Liam said in the very measured

tone he used when he was controlling his temper. He must be raging that she had left the office unattended.

"Hello, Liam," she said, a bit frostily, which Sophie thought was strange.

"I'm just coming in for a check-up," Theresa said, stroking her stomach in the universal gesture of motherhood.

"Are you having a baby?" said Sophie. She turned to Liam. "You never told me that!" Then to Theresa again, "Congratulations! When are you due?"

Theresa smiled. "Thanks. I'm just over two months gone. Due in late December, early January. I'll know for sure after the scan."

Liam was sitting there quietly, but he must have known because he didn't look surprised. He must be feeling awkward, thought Sophie. Maybe Theresa had wanted it kept secret until after the scan. Usually you would wait until the three-month mark to be telling people. That was only normal, and she admired Liam for keeping the confidence. She had never heard him mentioning a boyfriend, and Theresa wasn't wearing a ring. But she seemed happy enough, and that was the main thing. People didn't have to be embarrassed in this day and age.

The doctor came out then, ushering a patient who was clutching a prescription.

"Sophie, Liam, come in," he said solicitously, shaking his head at the receptionist so she would know they were not to be disturbed for any reason.

Half an hour later, they came out, and Theresa was still

sitting there. She was flicking through a magazine, her red nails immaculate. Sophie's brain was full of new words. Adjuvant therapy, cytoxic drugs, tamoxifen. They would go for chemotherapy first. Mastectomy would be a last resort. There was no room for anything else in her mind, so she nodded briefly at Theresa and the receptionist, and Liam led her by the arm out to the car. He dialled Ger's number on Sophie's mobile. She heard him making arrangements, and she wanted to stop him, to tell him that normality would be the best distraction, but her arm felt too heavy to lift, and her tongue felt swollen. The effort of speech was too great. He reached across her and clicked on her safety belt. It crossed the right side of her chest, and she shrank back against the seat, not wanting to imagine the shape of her body with no left breast. She flinched when he touched her cheek.

"We'll get through this, together, Sophie."

She nodded. *'Til death do us part.* Those words had seemed to Sophie to convey a notion of gently slipping into companionable old age together. '*In sickness and in health*' was so bland. Wrenching, tearing, searing loss didn't feature in the vows of marriage. What if she didn't die, but Liam stopped loving her? Things between them hadn't been fantastic recently, but she had thought it was just a minor blip – a phase in their relationship and in their lives. Their whole lives, that they planned to spend together. What if they didn't get a chance to fix things? If he stopped fancying her, if all her hair fell out, or her skin went a funny colour, or if she did end up losing a breast. Or two breasts?

Liam was driving along the familiar road to home,

but it seemed to Sophie as if they were travelling through a 3-D movie set, wearing glasses with red and green lenses. Trees loomed at the side of the road, their twigs tipped with the iridescent green of newly opening buds. The sea was purple, swollen. Clouds hung low and darkly. Liam's voice was coming at her in waves, but she couldn't process the sounds into words. She shook her head.

There were messages bleeping on the phone when they got in, and Liam checked them while Sophie rushed to the loo. Ger confirming she would collect the kids from Maeve's house and keep them overnight. She had spare clothes for the children, not to worry. She would call later to see if Sophie or Liam needed anything else. She was praying for them.

Alison saying her father had died and she was staying in England until after the funeral.

Maeve ringing to say she didn't think it was anything to worry about, but Oisín seemed to have a rash on his lower back that might need to be checked out.

Liam sat down, exhaling through pursed lips.

The phone rang again, and after a moment's hesitation he let the answering machine take it.

"Just to let you know, the date is confirmed. December the twenty-fourth is the big day." Theresa hung up. What was she playing at, leaving a message on the home phone? He deleted the message with clumsy fingers.

"What were the messages?" Sophie asked. The house was too quiet without the kids. She wished Liam had let them come home, instead of asking Ger to take them. Then she would have had to summon the energy and courage to act normally. This way, there was nothing else to talk about. They would endlessly analyse the permutations, and debate who to tell, and how much to tell them. She needed more time to let the idea of the cancer invade her mind, as well as her body.

He held up three fingers. "Ger, not to worry about the kids," He folded down one finger. "Alison . . ." He stopped. Poor Sophie couldn't take much more bad news.

"What about Alison?" He was looking a bit funny.

He took a deep breath. "I'm sorry, darling. Her father died. She's in England and she won't be back for a week or ten days."

"Oh, my God! She'll be so upset. She was hoping to have more time, to get on a better footing with him. They didn't have a great relationship when she was growing up."

"We all have those doubts, about whether we've been good enough, and done the right thing," said Liam.

Unusually philosophical for him, Sophie thought. "Did she leave a number?" Sophie didn't know where Alison's parents lived, exactly.

"Sophie, don't worry about her. She'll be fine. It's you we have to worry about," said Liam, raising his voice. She was always thinking about other people first.

"Liam, the world has not ended because I've got breast cancer! We have to keep going. Doing all the things we do, and living our lives. We'll deal with it. Alison might need me." Sophie was getting really agitated.

"Alison's got lots of other friends in England. I'm sure they'll call her, and go and see her. You are not responsible for everyone and everything!"

They were shouting at each other, standing at opposite ends of the sofa. Sophie burst into tears. Liam strode across the gap and held her, and they stood there, rocking gently to their own rhythm. The first time they had danced together at the Irish club, they had swayed to the slow set, not even moving their feet, just joined together in one long gyrating embrace.

Liam made tea and they watched *Educating Rita,* and ate a whole packet of chocolate biscuits. The usual pattern of Sophie's day dissolved. 6.30 bath-time passed, 7.30 story-time went unnoticed. Later, the phone rang and Ger told them the children were sound asleep, tummies full of pasta, tired out by the adventures of the day. "I didn't give them a bath, but I thought missing one wouldn't hurt them."

"Not at all, thanks a million for coming to the rescue." There was a pause. "We don't want to talk about it," said Sophie, slurring through the haze of her second glass of wine on a nearly empty stomach. "Tomorrow is another day."

Ger said she loved her and hung up before she let herself cry. Liam had broken the news earlier, and Ger had managed to be brave all afternoon in front of the kids. Hearing Sophie's voice had opened the floodgates.

All night, Sophie tossed and turned, worrying about Alison and feeling bad that she hadn't tried to track her down and speak to her. Still, she would have asked if Sophie had any news, and then Sophie would have had to tell her. She would have to call France in the morning and tell her parents. Ger would tell Denise but she had told her not to say anything to anyone else. This was Sophie's news, and she didn't want it generally known. If the drugs worked, she might not need to have an operation. That was how she would break the news to her mother. One step at a time. She felt the lump and wondered how she could have missed it for so long. She was so familiar with its shape now, having explored it from every angle over the last few weeks, that it truly felt like part of her body, not some invasive army of cells attacking her. She remembered the term 'hostage syndrome' from one of the drama serials on TV. After some time in captivity, the hostage starts to identify with the captor, and wants to do things to please them. It was a psychological mechanism to cope with the lack of control over their destiny. Maybe her horror at the thought of a surgeon cutting out part of her breast was a version of that syndrome. Those cells were part of her now.

Liam was looking at her when she woke up in the morning. That was the second time she had caught him contemplating her in a loving but detached way that she found quite disconcerting. She smiled at him.

"Another day," he said, stroking her hair.

Sophie felt claustrophobic. Being nurtured was nice, but Liam was being so intense. She told him to have a little lie-in and she would shower first. Had he made arrangements with Ger for this morning? She really wanted to see the kids, but there were a few calls to make first, and it would be better if they weren't around. Ger was so good to take time off work at short notice, and Sophie didn't want to take advantage.

"Will I just take them straight to the playgroup and tell them that you'll come at 12.30 as usual?" Ger asked, deliberately focussing on the logistics rather than asking Sophie how she was doing. That way, it was easier for both of them to be brave.

"Grand, thanks. I'm going to call Mammy and Papa now, and poor old Alison has lost her dad, so I want to try and speak to her, and then . . ."

"Just tell me you're OK with all this," Ger interrupted.

"As fine as can be expected. I'll call you this evening and tell you all the gory details about the treatment and everything."

"Love you."

"Me too."

She made breakfast and a list of things to do at the same time. At 8.30 when Liam came down freshly smelling of shaving soap, there was a bacon sandwich and a cup of tea waiting for him, and Sophie was sitting eating toast and marmalade, looking pretty normal.

"You go in to work today. I have loads to do, and not much time before I get the kids." She was sucking the tip of a pen, and adding to the list.

Card for Alison.
Michelle booster?
Collect side of lamb from butcher

Liam was totally intimidated by her ability to cope. He couldn't imagine getting any work done, but he couldn't let things slide for another day. The lads were hardworking but there was a limit.

"I'll get back by six," he said, kissing her cheek on the way out. She wiped the slightly greasy trace of his lips from her skin and waved out the front window as he drove away.

As usual Liam had been too lazy to delete the messages on the phone. He would let them mount up until the tape was full. The first two messages she deleted after hearing them. Then Maeve's message set her pulse racing. Oisín had a rash, and he hadn't had a bath last night, so Ger wouldn't have noticed anything. But if he was feverish, surely she would have said something? But he was naturally quite pale-skinned, so a slight flush wouldn't have seemed abnormal, especially with all the excitement of going to Auntie Ger's house. Should she ring Maeve first, or Ger? Find out what the rash looked like yesterday, or get Ger to go straight to the doctor's with him now? She felt trapped without the car. Liam's had a flat battery, so he had taken hers, and was sending a mechanic to recharge the battery before she had to go and collect the children. She rang Ger's mobile. She had to stop her before she dropped off the kids. If it was something contagious, the playschool wouldn't thank her. It went straight to voicemail.

She called Liam. "You forgot the message about Oisín's rash," she accused him. "Can you go and intercept Ger when she arrives at the playschool and take Oisín straight to the doctor."

"That's a bit melodramatic, isn't it?" Liam was just pulling into the car parking space outside the office. He was distracted. Theresa's car was parked in her old space. She wasn't sitting in it, so she must be waiting for him inside.

"It could be meningitis," Sophie said.

"Ger didn't say anything."

"Ger wouldn't have noticed it. I tried to phone her but I can't get hold of her. It's on his lower back. Liam, can you just do it, please?"

He swung the car around and drove out again, the tyres screeching as he accelerated away in the wrong gear. Sophie was overreacting, but it was understandable. He wondered if there was any counselling she could get to help her to come to terms with this cancer. She was so used to being in control of everything, and this was one thing that she couldn't control. She might lose it completely, if she didn't get help. He saw Ger's car up ahead as he approached the nursery school. He was just in time. Oisín ran across to him and gave him a big bear hug around his knees.

"This is a nice surprise, Daddy," said Michelle in a very grown-up voice, reaching up for her hug. She liked to be lifted up so she could put her arms around his neck and cuddle him properly.

Ger was confused. "Did I get the wrong end of the stick?" she asked, handing over a plastic bag with their clothes from the day before.

"Not at all, thanks Ger. I just need to have a quick look at Oisín." Liam knelt down on the tarmac, a stray pebble grinding into his knee, as he lifted up Oisín's

SK8 sweatshirt. Oisín wriggled. "Ouch, Daddy your hands are cold! What are you doing?"

There was a pronounced rash, spreading across his pelvis and up the centre of his back. Ger put her hands up to her face. "Oh my God, I didn't notice that at all!"

Liam made a face behind Oisín's back, and shook his head. "It's grand, wee man, but I think we'll just go and see the doctor. You have a little rash on your back."

Michelle craned her neck to see. "Uggh, Oisín, you're all spotty," she said, and he started to wail.

"Ger, could you do me a favour and take Michelle in? I'll go to the doctor and call the teachers later."

He kissed the top of Michelle's head. "You be Daddy's best girl and go in, now, and Oisín will be back later, probably."

Oisín followed him to the car, calmed by the whispered prospect of jelly tots in the glove compartment.

Doctor Magee pretended it was the most normal thing in the world to see Liam for the third time in a month. Theresa Nolan had also told him when she was in for a six-week pregnancy check-up that Liam was the father of her baby, but he took it with a pinch of salt. She struck him as an opportunist, and she might be trying it on.

"So, what have we here?" he asked Oisín, whose mouth was full of a congealed mess of jelly tots.

Oisín gurgled and a multi-coloured dribble emerged as he grinned.

"He has a rash on his back. The kids stayed with

their auntie last night, and we didn't get a good look at it until this morning . . ." Liam lifted up the sweatshirt.

The doctor pressed the area, and Oisín didn't flinch. "Is it itchy?" he asked, and Oisín nodded, still mutely chewing. He absent-mindedly rubbed himself with the cuff of his sleeve. The rash reddened deeper for a moment.

"I think it's an allergic reaction to something," the doctor said. "Has he been sleepy or lethargic at all, or whimpering, or narrowing his eyes to bright light?"

Liam shook his head. "I don't think so, but as I say, he was staying somewhere else last night."

"Oisín, look into the light, will you?" The doctor held a light and looked carefully into his eyes, ears and throat. "Could he have been in contact with something unusual, during the course of yesterday?"

Liam shrugged. He had no idea if Ger had anything in her flat that could have caused it. It was frightening that he couldn't really account in detail for Oisín's last twenty-four hours.

Ger might not have noticed if Oisín was behaving strangely, but surely Maeve, who had two kids of her own, would have? Liam decided to call and ask. Maeve had only noticed the rash, she said, but nothing else. They had been playing out in the garden, so maybe he had picked up something there? "He was really chirpy, and running around the place, full of buck," she said.

Now for Ger. She was at work, and full of apologies that she hadn't noticed the rash. "Was there anything else? Was he extra tired, or complaining of a headache or anything?" Liam was terse.

"Not at all, he was in great form. He ate a big bowl

of pasta and pesto, and we had a game of Ludo. He was grand."

Liam was trying to decipher her tone. Was there an element of defensiveness? Was she afraid to say she had noticed something, and done nothing about it? "Thanks, Ger, we'll talk to you later," he said, sighing as he put his phone away. The doctor was making a call to the hospital. Liam gulped, and then grinned at Oisín, who had noticed a change in the atmosphere. He was bored with the toys in Doctor Magee's box of tricks under the desk, and he was fiddling with the paper clips he had found in a glass dish.

"I want you to take him to the children's unit for observation," said the doctor. "There's nothing to worry about, I'm sure, but the rash is not completely disappearing when I press it. That's known as a purpuric rash, and it can be caused by a number of things, including an allergy. But to be on the safe side, he should be monitored for a few hours, to make sure his temperature is stable, and no other symptoms present themselves. They're expecting you."

Liam took Oisín by the hand. "Come on, little fella. We have to go and play with some more toys in another place," he said, glad that Oisín wasn't old enough to recognise the falseness of his smile and the brittleness of his tone.

"Sorry, Liam, but it's better to play it safe." The doctor shook his hand. That man had a lot on his plate.

Liam drove quickly to the hospital and was pathetically grateful to see someone driving out of the carpark, leaving a space. It was usually really difficult to find one and he had had visions of driving around for half an hour, trying to keep Oisín entertained while suppressing his anxiety and frustration. They walked into the children's unit, and a friendly-faced young nurse came to meet them and took Oisín's hand. Liam hadn't expected this, and was slightly taken aback.

"Oisín, isn't it?" she said, and his son happily walked through a swinging door with the woman, Liam walking two steps behind, wondering if he was supposed to follow. There were at least four other people waiting with their children. Would they think he was skipping the queue? The nurse lifted Oisín up onto a gurney, and gave him a coloured windmill to blow. He was delighted, and held it up for Liam to see, while the nurse examined his back, and took his temperature. Liam answered all the same questions that Doctor Magee had asked, and the answers were noted on a fresh patient record sheet. The nurse was very thorough, and explained to Liam that they would need to monitor Oisín for at least four hours.

"You can sit in the special room in here," she said to Oisín, and Liam wondered if it was some kind of isolation ward. They could hardly have a kid with potential meningitis playing around with the other kids. Bean-bags littered the floor, and there was a shelf full of worn-out books. A plastic Wendy house had seen better days, and the cooker inside was full of bits of plastic food.

Liam sat down and Oisín made him a surprisingly realistic egg sandwich and a cup of tea in a red cup with a yellow saucer. There was a television, and they watched endless episodes of *Noddy* and *Rugrats*. Oisín was delighted with himself. His temperature was checked every twenty minutes by the nurse. Liam paced up and down, unable to use his mobile phone, trapped in this brightly coloured space that denied the existence of illness and death. Sophie would be beside herself. He should have asked to use a phone. He wanted to wait until Oisín got the all-clear, rather than worrying her even more. Finally at one o'clock, a doctor came in, her white coat seeming extra clinical in this rainbow-coloured room.

"Hello, how are you? I'm Doctor McCormack. I'm pleased to let you know that Oisín is fine. I suspect he has had a reaction to something he has touched or eaten in the last twenty-four hours. If the rash doesn't clear in forty-eight hours, go and see your GP again, but we don't believe it is anything sinister."

Liam whooped with joy and picked up Oisín to give him a bear hug.

"Daddy, get off. I want to see the end of this," Oisín whined, wriggling to see the television screen.

The doctor smiled, and Liam shook her hand. "You have no idea how happy I am," he said.

She left, and Liam sat down on one of the blue bean-bags with Oisín snuggled in between his legs until the tinkling music declared that Noddy and his red and yellow car had finished their latest adventure.

Chapter Nineteen

Alison was standing in the front pew with her mother, desperately trying not to sob out loud. Behind them, twenty or thirty people stood respectfully waiting for the coffin to be carried up the aisle. Her father's ex-colleagues from work, some neighbours, a few cousins and even three of the guys from Alison's office had turned up. Evelyn had said she couldn't make it because the baby had chicken-pox. Lisa was expected but hadn't turned up yet. She was always late. Alison had a strange sense of detachment from all these people, even her mother. She felt the presence of her father very strongly, which was disconcerting. They hadn't been regular churchgoers when she was growing up, and her belief system, if she could call it that, wasn't really a spiritual one. She thought there was a force of some kind, encompassing the earth. One book had called it Gaia, which she liked. A kind of balancing power within nature and the elements. But after death, that was it. No reincarnation, no eternal life, no higher planes of existence. So why was her father's voice silently calling in the corners of her mind? He was gone, and after the cremation, there would be nothing left but his fairly meagre possessions, and the memory of him in other people's minds.

The vicar's eulogy was brief. He hadn't known her father well, but he managed to convey the faithfulness and integrity of the man in a way that impressed Alison. Her mother had been to see the vicar the evening before, wanting to go alone. Her father didn't have a long list of achievements. He wasn't accomplished in any particular way. He hadn't left a rich endowment to education or the arts. Alison had wondered what the vicar could possibly say about him.

"Dennis was a man dedicated to supporting and loving his wife Sarah and his daughter Alison, who are here to grieve for his passing and to acknowledge the beginning of another life for him. A life with God, free from the pain he has experienced during his last months. We often underestimate the simple power of living a good life. Just like a drop of rain in an endless lake, the ripples can pass outwards, touching people and events well beyond our expectations. We may not ever know the effect we have on someone else's life. Dennis was a humble man, who would never claim to have dramatically changed the world. He was proud of his daughter, Alison, standing here today, and in her, he has left a part of himself to continue in this world, and who knows where the ripples of his life are yet to touch? Let us pray . . ."

Alison sat down, the words of the next hymn washing over her. She daren't look at her mother. Her hands were gripping tightly, her knuckles as white as the laminated funeral service sheet. A tear was snaking its way down the wrinkle that cleaved her mother's cheek. She looked so old. She mustn't be eating properly. The weight was falling off her. Alison wondered if she could persuade her to come to Galway for a break. To get away from the house, with all the memories. To get some fresh air. That way, Alison could make sure she was looking after herself.

Finally, the service ended, and she and her mother followed the coffin down the aisle, their arms linked. Alison realised they had touched each other more in the last few days than they had for years. She glanced at the people in the pews, mentally calculating whether they had provided enough catering at the local pub. Lisa was standing right at the back, embarrassed that she had only just turned up. Alison's eye was drawn to her, and then she did a double-take. The tall, dark-coated man two rows from the back of the church was Ronan. His hands were reverentially held in front of him, and he nodded respectfully as they passed. Lisa waved apologetically and Alison smiled wanly at her. She felt as though the notes of the organ music from the gallery above her were landing like the blows of a mallet on the top of her head, thumping her into the ground, until she would disappear under the Minton tiles, like a scene from *Alice in Wonderland*. Her mother's arm was still firmly linked to hers, and they shook hands with the line of people who filed out silently, offering their condolences.

Maurice from the office gave Alison a half-hug, awkward. "Listen, we need to get back to work, but we just wanted to . . ."

"Thanks, Maurice, I really appreciate it." She included Steve and James in her smile. "Talk to you at the end of the week, probably," she said.

There wasn't much to report. Things seemed to move very slowly in Ireland. You could have a meeting, and everything seemed to be very positive, and then three or four weeks would go by, with nothing happening. Liam had reassured her one evening when she had gone over for dinner to their house that it was normal, and it would all come together eventually. The London office would be looking for something a bit more tangible, and soon.

But for now, she had other things to worry about. One of them was coming now.

"Ronan, this is a surprise," she said. How had he even known where the funeral was? She had called him to tell him that her father had passed away so she wouldn't be back for a while, but she was absolutely sure she hadn't told him about the details of the funeral.

"I had to come. To pay my respects." He solemnly shook her mother's hand. "Mrs Harding, I'm sorry for your trouble."

What a strange phrase, thought Alison.

Lisa was hovering behind Ronan. "Sorry for your loss. It was probably a relief in the end, wasn't it?" she asked solicitously.

She hadn't seen Alison's mother for years, not since

Alison had left home. She thought she had really aged. Mrs Harding nodded, sniffing genteelly and touching her nose with an embroidered hankie. Lisa hadn't realised people still used them. Alison was blushing like mad in the presence of Ronan, and Lisa couldn't blame her. Alison was right, the extra few years suited him. He looked very well off. The coat was immaculately tailored and his fingernails were manicured, if she wasn't mistaken. A very different proposition to the slightly harum-scarum Ronan of yesteryear.

"Mum, this is Ronan." Alison couldn't avoid it any longer. She just hoped her mother wouldn't come out with some inappropriate comment, like, 'You mean, *the* Ronan?'

Her mother just nodded. "Nice to meet you, Ronan. Thank you for coming. There will be some drinks and food at the pub afterwards if you would care to join us."

There was something to be said for impeccable manners in the place of spontaneity, Alison thought gratefully.

Ronan didn't try to hijack her at the pub, respecting her need to circulate among the mourners. He stood at the bar with a pint of Guinness, chatting to various people as they came up to order drinks.

Lisa couldn't resist. She hardly knew anybody else there, so she went up and gave him a peck on the cheek. "Ronan, long time no see," she said, mischievously.

He smiled. "Lisa, you're looking well," he said graciously, holding up his pint in a salute. "Can I get you a drink?"

"Red wine please." She could have asked the barman herself but she appreciated that Ronan was playing the gentleman.

"How is the little one? It was a girl you had, wasn't it?" he asked, handing her the drink.

Lisa was impressed. Alison must have filled him in. "April. She's doing well, thanks. She should be able to come home from hospital in the middle of June, all going well. I can't wait to hold her properly."

"That must be very hard, all right," he said. "But she arrived safely, which is the main thing, considering how premature she was."

This man was nothing like the devil-may-care Ronan that Lisa remembered. He had been too busy having a good time to worry about other people. Lisa had thought at the time that Alison was better off without him even though her friend was devastated. But now he seemed to have grown up. If Alison had asked him to come to the funeral, things must have moved on further than she was letting on to Lisa.

"So, are you here on business?" Lisa asked. Nothing ventured, nothing gained. If he had come of his own accord, that was even more impressive.

"I must admit, I had to be over in London yesterday anyway. I rang all the local funeral parlours around here until I found the right one, and I thought I'd come and pay my respects." He drained his glass with great relish, holding eye contact with her.

He was a very sexy man. Still, he deserved credit for the effort, thought Lisa. He was going to great lengths if he was just after a shag with Alison.

He checked his watch. A Rolex. "I have to go and catch a plane, so I'll just say my goodbyes," he said.

Lisa nodded. "Nice to see you again."

"And you. Good luck with the baby, and everything."

He went to Alison, and touched her elbow to get her attention. An elderly aunt was holding forth about the vicar's lovely words.

"Excuse me a minute," Alison said, turning to Ronan.

"Thanks for coming," she said.

"I wanted to be here for you, but I don't want to intrude." He kissed her cheek, and whispered in her ear. "Dinner, when you get back?"

She nodded. "I'm not sure when."

"Ring me." He nodded across the room and waved to Alison's mother, who waved back. He left, the pub door swinging shut behind him, and Alison wondered if she was imagining a slight drop in the temperature. She shivered.

"A handsome young man," warbled the aunt, and Alison nodded, moving absent-mindedly across to the bar to talk to Lisa, not caring that her aunt might think her rude.

"'Cloud nine' would sum it up," said Lisa.

Alison shook her head. "I can't believe I'm floating around lusting after Ronan at my father's funeral."

"You could hardly avoid it. You're right. He's changed. But I think it's for the better, personally."

"How do you think my mother looks?" Alison asked anxiously, watching her talking to the aged aunt.

"Old," said Lisa.

"I'm hoping to persuade her to come to Ireland for a

break. I don't know if she'll leave the house, but I think it would do her the world of good."

"That might scotch your plans for wicked doings with the lovely Ronan," said Lisa.

"My mum is more important, just now. She needs a change of scene."

"It's a great idea. You've got the space."

"I need to get back to work. Steve has been sending me emails wanting progress updates. Everything takes forever in Ireland. They want to put something in the annual report about our expansion into Europe. I need a quick win."

"Isn't Ronan the key man on one of your projects? Why don't you get him to speed things up for you?"

"I don't like mixing business and pleasure," Alison said. "I wish we didn't have to work together. It complicates things."

"I know what you mean. But if you have to work with him, you might as well get the most out of it."

Lisa was always very pragmatic about these things.

The rest of the day passed quickly, and Alison and her mother sat on the sofa drinking a cup of Horlicks at 10.30, winding down. She decided to broach the subject of her return to Ireland.

"Mum, do you think you'd fancy a little visit to see me? I've got a spare room. I could show you the sights, and you'd have time to potter around during the day while I'm working . . ."

"Maybe soon, love. I think for now I need to be here.

I have to get used to the idea of your dad not being around. When people are ill for a long time and they go into a hospice or something, there's time to get used to the idea of them not being around the house. Dennis went so fast, I still expect to go upstairs and find him dozing on the bed."

Alison nodded. "But maybe if you were in a different place, it would be easier?"

"No, I'll stay put thanks, love. You have to get back to your life, and I need to get on with mine."

"Sure?"

"Yes, I'm sure." She paused. "Was that *the* Ronan? I didn't like to ask."

"Yes. He's separated from his wife. He left me because she was pregnant, and they got married. It didn't work out."

"Seems to be quite common, these days," her mother mused. "Just be careful you don't get hurt, that's all."

"I will. Thanks. He seems to have changed a bit. Even Lisa thought so."

"Are you sure it's for the better?" her mother asked, and Alison had to admit to herself that she wasn't sure.

Chapter Twenty

Liam put the children to bed, glad for the opportunity to escape into fairy tales. Sophie had been distraught when he finally called from the hospital carpark to say that Oisín had the all-clear. She had understood why he waited so long to call, but she couldn't help crying. Liam thought how difficult it must be for her not to feel in control. He had forgotten completely to ring the mechanic and get him to charge the battery on the car. Maeve had collected Michelle and delivered her home after Sophie called her in a panic. Liam fully admitted he was crap at juggling all the logistics of kids' whereabouts. He was filled with even more admiration for what Sophie coped with every day. Going in to work was ten times easier for him. That reminded him suddenly of Theresa's car parked outside the office. He hadn't made it in to work. By the time he drove Oisín back home, it wasn't worth going in. The foreman, Robbie, had assured him that everything was under control. But that could mean anything. That fella was as crooked as a ten-bob note. He was probably making hay while the sun was shining, or playing while the cat was away, or whatever. Liam wondered if Theresa had seen his car arriving, and then suddenly turning away. She might think she had him tied down, with her message about the Christmas Eve due date. He felt completely trapped by things he couldn't control. Sophie's cancer and Theresa's baby were growing every day, and he was supposed to act like normal. He would have to figure out what to do for Theresa. He would have to meet her and sort it out, otherwise she'd ring the house again, and Sophie might answer the phone. He couldn't believe he had been so stupid, and all over a bit of sex. Theresa obviously had bigger plans in mind all along, and he hadn't even suspected a thing. He had believed her when she said there were no strings attached.

He felt a tugging on his arm. "Daddy, Daddy, turn the page," Michelle was urging him. He had stopped reading, the wolf poised outside the brick house to blow it down. "Sorry, love." He turned over. "*I'll huff, and I'll puff, and I'll blow your house down!*" he said.

"Do the wolfy voice," she pleaded.

He growled the words again, and Michelle giggled, savouring the anticipation of the wolf burning his bottom in the big pot of boiling water.

Sophie was dozing on the sofa when he came downstairs. She didn't usually sleep during the day, at least not since when she was pregnant, and Liam thought how drawn she looked, even in sleep. The laughter lines that animated her waking face now looked like nothing more glamorous than crows' feet. The shadows under her eyes had deepened. Today must have been exhausting for her, trapped in the house and powerless to do anything for her children. He must do more with the kids. There were some things he could influence, and making Sophie's life a bit easier was one of them. He found that the more time he spent with Michelle and Oisín, the more fun they were, because he could tune in to their wavelength, and he knew what they were on about, instead of being irritated by their seemingly irrelevant questions and their little in-jokes. He made tea, and placed Sophie's mug on the tiny table by the side of the sofa. He had always hated its spindly legs, expecting every time he passed it to knock it down, incurring Sophie's wrath for a red wine or coffee stain. That stupid little table made him feel clumsy and inadequate. One of the things he had loved about Sophie when they met was the way she made him feel so manly. When they danced together, her petite frame was enclosed in his muscular arms, and he felt as if he would take on the whole world to protect her. She was full of bounce, and he was the steady one. Together they could do anything. He never gave her credit for it, but his business wouldn't have taken off without her. She wasn't afraid to make phone calls to people she hadn't seen for years, when they came back to settle in Galway. She made fliers and went around putting them in people's doors. She had got him into the Chamber of Commerce, and said he should join the golf club. She had been right. The business took off, and it hadn't looked back. Liam employed fourteen permanent lads now, with casual labourers as well, on the big jobs. The turnover had doubled this year, and he was known as a serious player. But as soon as the kids had come along, Sophie stopped asking so many questions about his day, and didn't seem to take such an interest in the business any more. In the early days of motherhood, she could regale him for hours with the minutiae of food and sleep, as if he was interested in how many spoonfuls of baby rice Michelle had eaten the first time, or Oisín's two-hour nap. Now, he had to admit, the kids were much more interesting, and you could have a chat with them about lots of things. They were more like little people.

After kissing Michelle good night, he had checked on Oisín, asleep with a contented smile on his face after an idyllic day – telly, toys and his dad's undivided attention. What could be better for a four-year-old? Liam envied the children's simplistic ability to live in each day, ignorant of the sinister undertones of colourful hospital wards, and solicitous questions from nice doctors.

Sophie woke up and stretched. Liam was looking at her again, this time standing in the doorway of the living-room. She wondered how long he had been there. She was irritated, feeling like some kind of museum exhibit, constantly under his scrutiny. Was he looking for signs of her imminent demise? Was he trying to create an image in his head of what she looked like now, so that when she only had one breast, he could remember the old Sophie? She summoned a smile.

"There's a cup of camomile tea there for you," he said, pointing at the table beside her.

"Oh, thanks, love," she said, reaching for it. She would need it to help her to get to sleep again for the night, having taken the edge off her tiredness. "I think I just got myself a bit worked up today, and tired myself out with worrying."

Liam sat gingerly beside her on the sofa, as if the pressure of his bum on the cushions would disturb her in some way.

"I'm not a china doll, Liam. I'm not going to break if you touch me."

He was silent.

"Thank God, Oisín is all right," Sophie breathed for the twentieth time since they had got home.

Why couldn't she think about herself and worry about what was happening to her for a change? Liam thought. She was in denial. It wasn't for him to remind her. She would start her treatment on Tuesday, and they were both to go to a counselling session on Monday to prepare them for the next few months. Liam was quite impressed when the specialist told them it was a standard part of the process, to support people dealing with cancer. But it meant that he wouldn't really get any work done until Wednesday next week, and there was a lot on. He wondered if Robbie could be persuaded to take on some more responsibility for the next little while. Liam could pay him cash in hand, and he was saving to get married, so it might suit him to have the extra money. But could he be trusted? Liam still wasn't sure but he didn't have much choice. He was determined to get home by 6.30 every evening to help with the kids, so Sophie wouldn't get too tired. He had to help her to fight this thing. If they lost the battle, what was the point of anything else? He stroked her hair back from her narrow forehead, and the eyes that looked out at him were scared. She snuggled against his chest, and he felt again like her big, strong man. He stared at the ceiling, her hair tickling his chin, and wished that he could protect Sophie from the things on the inside as well as the outside.

Sophie answered the door to Father O'Leary, and kicked herself for not checking first who was ringing the doorbell. She had been known to hide in Michelle's bedroom at the back of the house when she saw his car coming, pretending to be out. You had to be in the mood for him, and she definitely wasn't ready for him today.

"Sophie, hello, how are you?" he asked in his breathy way, and she knew he was going to ask her for something.

It was so hard to do, but she held the front door, not opening it to invite him in.

"Not too good today, Father. I'm a bit under the weather, so I'm taking it easy."

"Sorry to hear that," he said, with one foot lifted, ready to come over the step for his cup of real coffee.

"What can I do for you?" Sophie asked.

"Well, it's about the Community Mass," he said, and she nodded.

"I was hoping that we could make a contingency plan, if the weather was inclement . . ."

Sophie couldn't imagine how she would be feeling two weeks ahead, never mind in August, so there was no way she was volunteering to host it. "Maybe in the church?" she said. It wasn't original, but it was certainly practical. It wouldn't be fair to expect anybody to be on standby for a bad weather invasion of at least thirty people, even if the food and everything was already organised.

"I hadn't thought of that," he said, his upper body moving forward again, hinting at his desperation for the coffee.

Sophie held firm.

"Did you hear from anybody else on the road?" he asked.

"I think most of them will come, Father, but it's so far away. It's not top of their minds at the moment." Would he understand what she was trying to say?

"You're right. They will all be thinking about their summer holidays and the children being off school and everything. You will be able to talk to them maybe in a few weeks' time, and have a better idea."

"Yes. I will. Are you off to Inverin?" Sophie found herself narrowing the gap in the door. Why didn't he just go away?

"I am. Duty calls. I must dash." He finally stood back off the doorstep, his wispy white hair caught in the sea breeze, an egg-stain down the front of his dark grey cardigan. Sophie relented.

"Have you time for a coffee, Father? The kettle is on."

Chapter Twenty-one

Alison was nervous. Despite all the jogging up and down the prom every evening, and her diet, Ronan was bound to think that, ten years on, she wasn't quite as firm and luscious as her thirty-year-old self. They were having a nightcap after a romantic dinner in town, the lights of the boats riding on the waves beyond the window of her apartment creating a soothing rhythm. The brandy fumes rose warmly to her nostrils, and she tried to relax. The one advantage of not having children was that she had no stretch marks. His ex-wife probably had loads, after giving birth to three kids in quick succession. Alison's boobs were still reasonably pert, although she always seemed to carry some of her extra weight there, making them a bit too pendulous. She blushed, as she did her mental inventory sitting right there in front of him, and got to remembering some of his vital statistics.

Ronan sensed the change in mood, and leaned

across to kiss her. "Finished your drink?" The peaty notes of Scotch whispered across her cheek. She nodded and took him by the hand into her bedroom. There was none of the scuffling and urgency of twenty-something lovemaking in their languorous exploration of each other's bodies. Ronan's hands played over her body, his lips kissed every inch of forbidden flesh, and Alison let out her captive breath and surrendered to the easy familiarity of his body.

They left the curtains open to the stars, their brightness undiminished by the gentle orange glow of Galway reaching into the sky.

Lisa called to say that April was home. "Alison, when you walk in the front door, it's so amazing! It's not just the smell of a baby, which is so beautiful, isn't it? But her *presence* in the house – you can feel it. In every room, not just the nursery, with all the baby bits and pieces in it . . ."

Alison laughed. "Happy to have her home, then?"

"Do you know what? I'm almost glad she came when she did. I will never take her for granted. She's so precious; I just have to keep stopping myself from grabbing her and cuddling her all the time. She's *so* beautiful. When are you coming home to see her?"

Alison's promise to come home every month was already broken. Her mother seemed to be quite self-contained, her life having shrunk even smaller without the daily chores of caring for her husband. She kept telling Alison to make the most of her time away, not to worry about her. Promising that maybe she would come in the summer for a visit. But it was nearly the end of June and she didn't seem to have made any plans for a trip.

"I'm not sure, Lisa. It's really busy here now. What about you coming over here? You'd love it! You could take April for walks and . . ."

"I don't think Michael would be happy for me to take her away just yet. She's still so tiny, and we're just getting used to having her at home. He'd miss her too much."

"OK, I understand. I'll look at my diary and ring you back later with a date. But I have news too!"

"Is it Ronan-related by any chance??"

Alison smiled. She wouldn't tell Lisa everything at once. "It's lovely. I feel like we've gone back ten years, even though we're in Galway instead of London. It's a bit surreal, I have to confess, and it's moving very quickly. It feels so *right* though. Ronan is so much more in his element here – he was always a bit on edge in London, and maybe that's why I never thought he'd stick around. Now, he seems really rooted, and comfortable, and it adds to the charm."

"You mean lust!"

"Well . . ."

"You're sleeping with him, aren't you?"

"It's fantastic! I can't believe after all this time that I've found him again, and he still likes me, and –"

"So it's true love, is it?"

"I told you, didn't I? I knew I wouldn't be able to resist. I had no idea how much I was missing being with someone. I feel complete, in a scary, lovely kind of way."

"Why scary, for heaven's sake?"

"You've forgotten what it's like at the beginning, haven't you? You've been with Michael so long, you and he are just a part of each other. I feel like Ronan fills a gap in me, but I'm scared that if it doesn't work out, it will be even harder to be on my own again."

"It sounds like you and he are meant to be together – it will all work out, I'm sure. I can see it now: you won't want to come back to London and we'll see even less of you." Lisa couldn't help it – she was a bit jealous of Alison's new love. Michael was great, and really supportive with baby April, but it felt like they were engaged in the task of parenthood together, rather than having the sublime experience that she had thought it would be. Lack of sleep and the worry of the last few months pushed it all out of proportion, she knew, but it didn't make her feel any better.

"Don't be ridiculous. It's early days, Lisa. I still can't believe that it's happening, even though we see each other most days, and he still makes me laugh, and he is so horny! I think I've lost a few pounds just from bonking!"

"Chance would be a fine thing," said Lisa, and then regretted it. She shouldn't take the edge off Alison's happiness.

"Lisa, you need a break. Tell Michael to come too. We have loads of room. Just for a long weekend?"

"*We?*" Lisa spluttered. "Alison, are you holding back on me?"

Alison laughed. "Ronan is kind of a semi-permanent fixture here . . ."

Ronan had practically moved in after that first night together. She wasn't sure how that had happened. Somehow one side of the wardrobe seemed to have become filled with his trendy suits and he had insinuated his underwear into one of the drawers in her bedroom. Two pairs of his shoes peeked out from under the bed, and his 'spare' toiletry bag had acquired a permanent look on the glass shelf in the bathroom.

"Do you make a habit of sleeping with people and then moving in, or only with me?" she had joked after another lazy weekend together.

He feigned surprise. "Moving in?"

"Well, I don't know how many more suits I could fit in the wardrobe, and there's the golf bag . . ." She turned over and tickled his stomach.

He grabbed her. "Would you rather if I kept all the stuff at my own place?" He kissed her nipples in turn, licking them into erectness.

"No, it's just that it seems to be happening by osmosis rather than by design," she said, finding it difficult not to gasp between words.

"Who says I haven't got designs on you?" he said, and proceeded to lick her all over.

She stretched out, surrendering to his kisses. She was completely unselfconscious now about her body. He knew every inch of it, and gradually, she had relaxed about walking around the bedroom naked, rather than grabbing her kimono to conceal her cellulite. "You don't need to worry about losing weight – you're beautiful, just as you are," he had reassured her, when she had insisted on going for her evening run one time when he

325

had 'popped around' after work. "It helps me to unwind, and I love the sea air," she had said, pulling on her trainers. "Help yourself to a drink. I'll be about an hour."

It was while she had been jogging along, looking at other couples, some with buggies, some just holding hands for a Friday evening stroll, that she had realised with a jolt that she was part of a couple now. She and Ronan did things together more often than alone, they had shared jokes, they made plans for weekends, they had even been invited to Seán's for dinner the following Saturday, and he had made a point of saying it was social, not work.

They met with Seán formally once a week to review the budget and the spending on the holiday village, and they had tried to keep up the pretence in front of him that theirs was a purely professional relationship. He wasn't stupid, and repeatedly winked lewdly at Alison across the table, as if to ask if Ronan was giving satisfaction. She ignored him. There was nothing worse than a spurned male. Still, Seán was proving very creative, and the ideas for the village were really exciting. It would be unique in Ireland, although she had seen some of the design features in Mediterranean holiday villages. Alison would have major kudos back at the office, especially since Dave's Dubrovnic development had come up against some major hurdles. He was struggling with the local planning people. They were probably only doing what the Galway authorities hadn't done, and enforcing the rules about coastal development. But that was Dave's hard luck, and in the meantime, Alison was lucky to have Seán and Ronan on the ground – people who seemed to know how to make the system work. Two or three other projects were simmering along nicely, and Alison was starting to relax about how to get things done in Ireland. As the Guinness adverts said, there was a pace to things that couldn't be hurried, and it was only a waste of energy to get stressed about it. The secret was to have enough prospective work on the back burner, so that when one project started to move ahead, there were others always waiting. The holiday village should be completed in about eight months, just in time for the spring season next year, and she was full of ideas about how to promote it. The key would be strong advance sales. Her commission was based on cash into the business, not on promises or plans – she couldn't relax until all the units were sold.

Sophie and Liam were coming around for dinner, and Alison was looking forward to playing hostess. It had been a long time. Back in London, she had got out of the habit of entertaining. This evening, she was planning to have a crabmeat mousse wrapped in smoked salmon, followed by sea bass and baby new potatoes. Pavlova for dessert, but she had cheated with a bought one. Three bottles of Chablis were chilling in the fridge, and she had olives and nuts to nibble beforehand. She polished the glass table and laid out her newly purchased Galway crystal goblets and Celtic-patterned tablemats. Ronan hadn't met Sophie and Liam yet, and she just knew they would get on really well. He was so sociable and confident he could talk about anything to anyone. Alison had warned him about Sophie's cancer, so that he wouldn't put his foot in it.

She had started her chemotherapy. Her hair was thinning, and her skin was pallid. She was still the same cheerful Sophie, seemingly taking it all in her stride, but Alison wondered how much of it was an act. Sophie had to wake up every morning and pretend to the kids that everything was fine. She sometimes sounded as if she even believed it herself, which was probably a good coping strategy. At her next check-up, they would decide if the chemo was working, or if she needed to have surgery. Sophie was very anxious about it, and Alison had decided a night out would do her and Liam good. She had picked Sophie's favourite food and wine for the menu. A sixties compilation CD set a suitably up-beat tone as she lit the candles on the dinner table.

Ronan came in, kissed her briefly on the cheek and hurried into the bathroom. "Just going to have a quick shower," he shouted out through the door.

Alison sighed. The others were due in about five minutes and she knew Ronan would leave the bathroom in a mess. That was something that his ex-wife hadn't managed to change about him. She checked the oven, and opened the first bottle of wine.

The doorbell chimed exactly on time, and she kissed Sophie, giving her an extra little hug but not wanting to say anything to spoil the mood.

Sophie acknowledged it with her eyes then smiled brightly. "Wow, lovely smells!"

Liam shook her hand. That was something Alison still found bizarre about Ireland. People often shook

hands in social situations where the English or the
French would kiss on two cheeks. Alison liked the
handshake. It seemed more genuine, especially when
you didn't know somebody very well.

"So, where have you hidden him?" Sophie whispered,
seeing at a glance that Ronan was not in the open-plan
living and kitchen space.

"Having a quick shower," Alison said, rolling her
eyes to heaven. Sophie laughed. They had compared
notes on the bathroom habits of their men, and Alison
had been relieved to hear that a happy marriage could
survive wet towels on the bathroom floor, and toilet
seats left up.

Liam was standing with a beer in his hand, looking
at the sea view. "It is lovely here, isn't it?" he said, a bit
enviously.

"Ronan said he'll take us all out on his boat later in
the summer. The kids as well, if you'd let them. He has
life-jackets the right size."

"I'm sure he has," said Liam, giving Alison a knowing
wink. Separations and divorces were still not quite as
taken for granted in Ireland as they were at home, Alison
had noticed.

Sophie felt the need to intervene. "That would be
lovely. Michelle and Oisín would get a great kick out of
that."

Alison opened the balcony windows and they
stepped out, holding their drinks. There was still a
slight chill in the evening air even at the end of June but
she loved the smell of fresh river water swirling into the
sea beneath the window. Ronan joined them, bringing a

cloud of aftershave and soap. He kissed Sophie on the two cheeks, and shook Liam's hand.

"Welcome," he said, and Alison loved him for acting as a host, even though he'd only been living in the apartment for a few weeks.

Liam was being very reticent tonight, Alison thought later, as they finished the main course.

Sophie enthused about the food. "I love it when someone else cooks for me. It's such a novelty!"

Liam looked a bit shamefaced. "I'd cook for you, but you never let me into the kitchen."

"I know, because by the time I've cleared up after you, I might as well have cooked it myself," she said, putting her hand on his cheek to soften the comment. "He does a very nice Spaghetti Bolognese," she told everyone.

"The classic male dish," said Ronan. "I can cook that too."

Wondering if he had ever cooked it for his family crossed everyone's mind, and remained unspoken. The pavlova went down well, and it was while they were having coffee that Sophie suddenly looked exhausted. She was uncharacteristically quiet, and Alison leaned over and said that she wouldn't be offended if they wanted to go home early.

Sophie nodded. "I'm going to bed at about this time, these days. It's the only way to survive and be any way civil to the children in the morning."

Everyone discreetly gulped down their coffee, and Liam stood up. "Thanks, Alison, it's been a lovely evening. Your cooking is fantastic." He kissed her and she guessed that she had crossed some hurdle in his books. He had hardly acknowledged Ronan at all, which she thought was a bit strange. They didn't seem to have much to talk about after all.

Liam wondered whether he should say anything to Sophie, as they drove home.

She let her eyes close, leaning against the headrest. "I hate being this tired."

"It was a nice evening though. I really like Alison. I wasn't sure in the beginning. She seemed a bit 'la di da'. But she's quite down to earth, isn't she?"

Liam had a bit of a hang-up about 'nice' English accents, having had some unpleasant experiences in London with people working in City firms where he was doing refurbishment work. The accent played to his social inadequacy, and he felt as if they were talking down to him. Sophie had often reminded him that he was a graduate, and some of these people had probably left school at eighteen and gone to work in offices, with hardly any qualifications. He had no reason to feel inferior.

"But they're rich. They come from a certain stock, went to certain schools, and they walk around as if they own the planet," he had said crossly.

"So what? Let them get on with it. You're running your own business – you have no need to worry what anyone else thinks of you."

She hadn't realised that Liam still felt this way, and was surprised that Alison, of all people, had had that effect on him. She was quite insecure herself, and certainly didn't lord it over anybody. Wasn't it strange, how people reacted? Sophie was still musing about the whole thing, when she realised Liam was talking to her.

"Sorry, love, what did you say?"

"You didn't tell me that Ronan was Ronan Murray."

"What do you mean?" But the vague familiarity of his name was nagging at her again.

"He's the guy that was in the news, last year. He was the partner of Barry O'Sullivan, the business man who swindled all those people out of their investments."

"Of course!" Sophie kicked herself. "I knew his name was familiar! He comes from Ballina, so I just thought I remembered it from secondary school or something. What are we going to tell Alison?"

"Maybe she knows already."

"No way, she would have said. She was a bit wary of getting involved with him anyway, with his family lurking in the background, and her planning to go back to London at the end of the year."

"Barry O' Sullivan got ten years in jail, you know."

"Yes." It was all coming back to her now. The controversy about Ronan getting off scot-free, when the other guy claimed Ronan was equally responsible. They had worked as a double act, he said. But Ronan had managed to convince the jury that he had been misled by his associate, and had been involved in the financing deals in good faith. "We'll have to tell her."

"Surely she couldn't have got this far, with him living in her place by the looks of things, without realising what kind of guy he is?" Liam thought swindlers were the worst kind of criminals, luring people into situations and trapping them, taking all their life savings, and then smooth-talking their way out of the whole thing.

"Maybe he was innocent?" Sophie said hopefully.

"I seem to recall that O' Sullivan's appeal was based on proving Ronan was more than fifty per cent responsible."

"But he lost the appeal, didn't he?"

"Yes, but there's no smoke without a fire."

They drove the rest of the way home in silence.

Sophie couldn't sleep that night, and every time she turned over, or opened her eyes, Liam was there, looking at her like a parent waiting for a toddler to nod off. "Go to sleep, Liam," she said, irritated with him. She knew she was being unfair. He was just loving her, and was looking after her. She wished he hadn't said anything about Ronan. Now that she knew, she had to tell Alison. Ignorance was definitely bliss. She had gone about her life as normal, even while that lump was growing silently and malevolently inside her. Now, the chemotherapy was poisoning the rest of her body, spoiling her quality of life, and it wasn't even guaranteed to work. Those cells could still be growing away, eating up her breast. She imagined a black worm inside a rotting potato, tunnelling through, making caves to curl up and build its energy, ready for the next onslaught. Was Ronan the same, living like a parasite off Alison who was oblivious of his power to destroy her? If the holiday village turned out to be another scam, Alison's career would be finished. And could Ronan be trusted not to walk out on her as he had on his family? The whole reason for Alison coming to Ireland was to build her career. Finding her old sweetheart was an added bonus. She was trying so hard to reinvent herself. In just a few months, Alison was already less obsessed with turning forty. By her own benchmarks of success, things were looking good. Ronan could sweep it all away, leaving her with nothing.

Sophie couldn't let him do that to her.

"I'm supposed to be meeting the kids tomorrow," Alison said a few days later, as they walked on the prom for their weekly chat.

Sophie sighed. Should she wait for a while, or tell Alison now?

"That will be nice," she said. "I'm surprised he hasn't introduced them to you before now. They must know about you, surely, if he's seeing them every week?"

"Funny you should say that," said Alison. "I worked out the other day that he hasn't seen them for at least a month. I was thinking back over the nice things we've done at weekends, and how much exploring I'm doing now that he's around, like Ashford Castle, and Kylemore, and Clifden. We've had some lovely days out, but then I started feeling guilty because maybe I'm hijacking him at the weekends when he should be having the children."

"Did you say anything to him?"

"Yes, and he said he was feeling guilty, and he'd have to make it up to them in the summer holidays, maybe take them away somewhere."

This was the moment. "Alison, Liam reminded me where I had heard Ronan's name before . . ."

Alison laughed. "Ronan knew you would say something, after the other night. As soon as you left, and I asked him if he'd had a nice evening, he told me everything. He knew that was why Liam didn't really talk to him. He felt like he was measuring him up, deciding whether to trust him."

"So you're OK with it all then?" Sophie was surprised, but relieved.

"He says that Barry was the ultimate conman, and the whole thing was his responsibility, but he wanted to drag Ronan down with him, so he wouldn't look like the complete baddy."

"So what was Ronan's involvement then?" Sophie couldn't help asking.

"He was the accountant. O'Sullivan had kept a double set of books, and Ronan only ever saw the legitimate ones. He had no idea that those pensioners were being screwed."

Sophie wondered if Alison was being naïve. If O'Sullivan needed an accountant to keep the 'straight' books, then how did he manage to keep another set of accounts without any help? But she had done her bit, by sharing what she knew. It was Alison's business what she did about it. She just hoped Alison wouldn't get hurt. "Sorry, I hope you didn't mind me bringing it up – it's only that I'd hate for . . ."

"Sophie, for my own peace of mind, I did a check. I felt so guilty for doubting him but I needed to know. I did some research, and I used one of my guys from the

UK to run a detailed check – he confirmed what Ronan had said."

Sophie smiled. Alison hadn't got to where she was without having an instinctive business brain. Even love didn't dull her sense of focus when it came to work. "Thank God for that! You two are great together." She heaved a sigh of relief. "So, what are you going to do with the kids?"

"They're taking me out on the boat. I had no idea they had named her Gráinne Uaile after a woman pirate. I love that idea. And she was from Galway."

"Have you ever sailed before?"

"No, and it's one of the things I've promised myself to learn while I'm here. So if I like it, I'm going to book myself on a sailing course. I'm really excited about it."

"I'm sure you'll love it. Sounds like it's a good place to see the children for the first time too, because everyone will be doing their own thing on the boat, and you don't have to sit across a dinner table, trying to make conversation."

"My thoughts exactly," said Alison, grinning.

After the walk, they went for their ritual cup of tea.

"When is your check-up?" Alison asked. The pace of the walk had been noticeably slower than usual, and Sophie looked like she needed the rest.

"Monday. They'll do a full scan and blood tests and everything. If it's grown, or not receded, they'll recommend surgery."

"How do you feel about that?" Alison put her hand on Sophie's.

"Terrible. I've had some counselling sessions, and

Liam has come to a few as well. I'm really worried that I won't be the same person, with a big chunk of me missing. What if he doesn't fancy me any more?"

Alison patted her hand. "Sophie, you'll still be the same wonderful person you are now. Liam loves you. It's so obvious. He adores you. Why would that change, because you lose a breast?"

"You haven't seen the documentaries, and the pictures they show you. It's hard to imagine, but your whole body changes. There's a big scar, down your chest – like a white line, where your breast should be . . ." She couldn't talk any more.

"Don't they give you a false one?" Alison asked, not sure if it was the right thing to say.

"Of course, but you know all those jokes, about silicon breasts? They feel completely different. I might look like I have a nice perky breast under my T-shirt. But I'll know. And Liam will know."

Alison let her cry, thinking she probably didn't let go often enough. She worried too much about upsetting the kids or Liam.

"It might not even come to that," Alison said, after a while. "One step at a time."

"That's the name of a book someone at Mass recommended me to read. It's about a woman who lost her sister to breast cancer, and had it herself. *'The race is won, one step at a time'*."

"That's true about most things, isn't it?" Alison said, thinking that was how she should treat tomorrow. Meeting Ronan's family was a huge hurdle for her. Tomorrow might determine the future of their whole relationship. If she didn't hit it off with them, Ronan might walk away. And what if she hated them, and wanted to walk away, herself? She would take her own advice, and play it by ear.

They hugged, and Alison wished her friend luck. "Call me, if you want to talk."

Sophie waved and walked back to her car. She was already focussed on collecting the children and what she would cook for tea.

Ronan was uncharacteristically edgy, and Alison didn't probe him. They ate scrambled eggs and smoked salmon on toast for an early breakfast, and he left to drive to Athlone. They should be back by ten, he estimated, and wondered if Alison could make a picnic lunch to have on board? She went to the market and bought fresh, warm walnut bread, baked ham and some cheese and grapes. He hadn't thought to tell her what the children liked to eat, but she guessed that she couldn't go far wrong if she had crisps and chocolate and some cans of Coke too. It was a kind of celebration, after all. There would be plenty of time later for sensible, balanced menus. The familiar knot of anxiety tied itself around her upper vertebrae, as she spread butter on the bread, and wrapped up the food. It had been a while since work had caused this tension in her neck. Starting to get fit had probably helped over the last few months, too. Now the knot was back, like an old but irritating friend. She flexed her neck and hummed to Rod Stewart's 'Baby Jane' on the stereo . . .

even though you're moving in high society, he was telling her, don't forget I know secrets about you . . .

It was funny how she reverted to playing her oldest CD's when she was feeling unsure about herself – that gravelly voice brought back the confidence of her twenties – she had felt invincible then. Sometimes it felt like a long time ago. She had tried to put her doubts about Ronan's history firmly behind her, but there was still something unresolved in her mind. Could his simple moment of realisation that 'being average was not good enough' be a fantasy? Had his wife thrown him out when he was under suspicion of serious fraud? It was too much of a coincidence that he had moved out just when the court case was going on. Alison had searched the internet for references to the case, trying to completely dispel her suspicions. Only when she found the news articles did she make the connection on the timing of Ronan's departure from home. She was surprised that a woman who had held Ronan to marrying her when she fell pregnant, then gone through a difficult few years with him until they were financially stable, would then kick him out, rather than stand by her man when he was falsely accused. Something didn't quite add up. She felt guilty for doubting him. But there wasn't just her heart to worry about. Her livelihood was at stake too. Her mother's words of warning echoed in her head, as she packed the picnic things, sticking in a couple of cold beers for herself and Ronan.

She felt almost sick with nausea when she saw Ronan's car pulling up outside the apartment block. She counted only three heads and wondered if one of the children was lying down, having a sleep or something. She picked up the cold-box, plonked her new peaked boating cap on her head, and locked up. She was halfway down the stairs, bumping the bulky box against her legs, when she met Ronan bounding up two steps at a time.

"Here, let me take that," he said.

She followed him down, resisting the urge to ask how the kids had taken the news about meeting her. She felt her muscles trying to form a smiley face that wouldn't look too false. Kids could slice through social artifice like a hot knife through butter.

There were definitely only two children in the car, and she looked enquiringly at Ronan. "Brian didn't want to come. He had something organised with his friends." Ronan's face was hidden as he lifted the boot to put in the food.

"Never mind, we can meet next time," she said brightly, and stood waiting for Ronan to decide how he would do the introductions.

"Are you getting in?" he asked, slightly tetchy.

She opened the front passenger door, and climbed in, leaving Ronan standing outside. "Hi, I'm Alison," she said, and two neutral faces stared back at her. There was no hostility, which was a relief, but there was very little warmth, either.

"Nancy, I like your dress," Alison said, hoping that little-girl vanity would win over social uncertainty.

"Thanks." She got the glimmer of a smile.

"Dara, you're a lot taller than I imagined." Her

attempt at male-ego massage fell flat. "How do you know, when I'm sitting down?" was his sullen reply.

"I can tell by those long legs."

Dara muttered something non-committal and Alison wondered what Ronan was doing. He seemed to be taking forever.

He finally got into the driver's seat and twisted around. "So, we've all met, have we?" he said and the children nodded. Dara looked out the window.

"Off we go, then," he said, and drove the three miles to the marina where the *Gráinne Uaile* was moored.

"That's a lovely boat," said Alison when Ronan pointed it out.

"She. Boats are called 'she,'" said Nancy. Alison could see a route to getting the little girl on her side. She would play dumb and let Nancy tell her all.

Dara looked as if he would be a more difficult proposition, and although Alison had been disappointed at first not to meet Brian, it would probably work out for the best. She could really put the effort into getting to know these two today, and then concentrate on him another time. It was hardly surprising that a lad of his age would opt out of the excursion, but she was most curious about him. In an odd way, she felt linked to him. Had Alison conceived that month instead of Sinéad, what chromosomal combination would have resulted? What kind of child would she and Ronan have had? It was hard to imagine herself the mother of a nine-year-old, but Ronan had told her that Sinéad was the same age as her. Alison wondered if Sinéad's thirty-ninth year was as full of self-doubt and resolutions as her own. Perhaps she was fulfilled by having had three children. Perhaps she felt like a failure, having lost Ronan. Or perhaps she was relieved to be rid of him, and was getting on with her own life.

"Come on," said Ronan, and she realised the car had stopped and the children were standing on the pier, impatiently jiggling up and down. They weren't allowed to go on board without an adult. As soon as Ronan swung himself up on deck, they followed, agile as monkeys and went straight to the locker with the life-jackets. Seconds later they were transformed into mini-mariners. Alison followed and allowed Nancy to demonstrate how to tie the strings on her life-jacket. Dara wasn't impressed by her lack of knowledge, and didn't return her conspiratorial smile.

Ronan waved at a hatch. "That's the galley, down there. Why don't you explore a bit while we make her ready?"

Alison stepped down into the narrow space, and was impressed at the compactness of everything. Crockery and glassware were stacked on special racks, and the tiny cooker was mounted on a gimbal which allowed it to swing forward and back with the motion of the waves. Alison enjoyed unpacking the hamper and finding places for everything. She felt she was laying claim to a new territory, albeit one that she hoped wouldn't be exclusively her domain. She went forward to the main cabin and opened wardrobe doors. She found a shower cubicle and toilet behind one, and lots of Ronan's clothes on shelves behind another. Sports kit, paper files, a Walkman, and a jumbled miscellany of objects filled several boxes in another cupboard. Forward again was a tiny cabin with two bunk-beds and she assumed this would be the children's space. Back to the living area, and she discovered the secret of the folding-out bunks. It was a very attractive little craft.

"This is great," she said, coming up through the hatch and feeling movement as they slid away from the mooring.

Dara jumped across to board again, having untied the ropes from the bollards on the pier. He was grinning, but when Alison tried to return the smile, his face closed over again.

"Brian usually does that job. It's Dara's first time," Ronan explained. "Well done, good boy," he said, and Dara smiled again with his father's greeny-blue eyes. Dara had freckles across his nose and his hair was a brown thatch in contrast to Ronan's black one. He looked more Irish than his father, Alison thought, without being able to put her finger on why.

Nancy was singing away, tying a pink ribbon onto a Barbie doll that had been kitted out in sailing gear, even down to the life-jacket. The little girl's hair was long and straight, a dirty blonde that would make her want to have highlights as soon as she was old enough. Her eyebrows arched in a deep forehead that was wrinkled in concentration, and she had a pert mouth and bright blue eyes. Alison imagined she must look like her mother.

"Who wants a chocolate bar?" Alison asked, waving the unashamed bribe of Crunchies. The gold packaging glinted in the sun.

"No, thank you," Dara said politely but firmly.

Nancy looked at him and she wavered. She succumbed to his glare, and refused the chocolate in a subdued tone. She licked her lips subconsciously as Alison started back down to put it in a cool place.

"Maybe later," Ronan said, and for the next twenty minutes he barked instructions to his crew, as they manoeuvred out of the marina and into the bay.

Alison could feel the reflected heat of the sun off the water, and put on some more sun-cream. "Have you guys got sun-cream on?" she asked the children, and they shook their heads. Alison looked at Ronan. She wasn't going to interfere, but the July sun was hot, and they were quite exposed.

"Put some on the back of your neck, and your face, at least," Ronan said, and the captain's orders were followed. Nancy found a bottle of factor thirty-five green sun spray in the aft storage seat, and struggled to get the lid off. She refused Alison's help, and only gave in when she realised she didn't have enough hands to hold her hair up and spray and rub. Alison held up the long sleek ponytail and gently smeared the cream onto the downy blonde hairs of the little girl's narrow neck.

"Thanks," Nancy said, and handed the bottle to her brother, who made a cursory effort and then put the bottle down beside him, determined not to make eye contact with Alison. Maybe Brian had set some kind of challenge to his siblings, determined even in his absence that nobody would make friends with her.

Alison's mother had advised her last night on the phone to take it very easy with the children. "Don't make too much effort. They'll come to you in their own time."

Ronan had hardly said a word to her since they came on board, and now he was consulting navigation charts and seemed to be ignoring her efforts to be friendly to the children. Still, it must be difficult for him too, and he wouldn't want the children to think he was lavishing attention on her at their expense. Alison went as far forward as she could, in her bare feet, and sat cross-legged, her arms braced on the deck behind to support her. She took off her hat and let her hair flow out behind, lifting her face to the sun. Let them all think their own thoughts. She was not going to try and push her way into someone else's family. As long as they could all be civil to each other when they were together, that was fine. Ronan could see the children on his own, if that was what everyone wanted. The sea breeze was cool, and she enjoyed the undulating sensation of the indigo waves as they sped through the water. After half an hour, she felt Ronan's hand on her shoulder.

"What do you think?" he asked, slipping down to sit beside her.

"Who's steering the boat?" she asked in a panic, looking back. Dara was at the tiller. She envied his casual confidence. He looked like his dad just in that moment.

"There's not much he can do wrong, out here," Ronan said. "I'm running her on the engine today because I'd need Brian if we were to use the sails. He's the only one who knows what he's doing."

"I'm going to take a sailing course this summer," said Alison. "So I can be a more helpful crew member in future, hopefully."

Ronan grinned and kissed her. "How do you fancy

rustling something up for lunch? We're going to the Aran Islands. See those misty shapes on the horizon that look a hundred miles away? They're closer than they look, but we won't be there for an hour or more. I'm starving."

Alison pulled her hair into a bunch and inched her way aft. It wasn't complicated, taking ham and bread out of a cool box. Why was it her job? But she hadn't been useful in any other way, so it was probably fair enough. She brought the food up, and Ronan pulled out a clever folding table from the side of one of the seats.

Dara refused to eat anything, and Alison was starting to think he was being very perverse when Nancy explained. "He's allergict to nuts, and gloo-ten."

"What about some ham?" Alison suggested, holding up a rolled piece.

"I'm vegetarian," Dara said, looking away.

"Since when?" Ronan asked, laughing.

Alison didn't think it was funny. Apart from the cheese, there was nothing else for the child to eat except chocolate and crisps.

"Since ages," said Nancy, munching a ham sandwich and alternating mouthfuls with sips of Coke.

"Are you allowed Coke, Nancy?" Ronan asked, and she nodded, sipping through a multi-coloured straw that Alison had thought would set a festive tone.

"She is not," muttered Dara.

Ronan shrugged his shoulders and raised his eyes to heaven, expecting Alison to join in the joke.

But it wasn't funny. She felt awful that she hadn't known about Dara's allergy, and now she was discovering they shouldn't be drinking Coke. Though Sophie was her benchmark and she was sure that Sophie occasionally gave Coke to her kids as a treat.

"Perhaps you should just have half a can then?" Alison said tentatively, and Nancy shot her such a look of venom that she backed off. "I'll know better for next time," she said, holding up her fingers to make a list. "No bread or meat, but maybe rice cakes and juicy tomatoes for Dara, and sugar-free Ribena for Nancy. What does Brian like?" She was looking at Nancy, who seemed the most likely to be lured into conversation, now that her claim on the Coke was uncontested.

Nancy shook her head sadly. "Brian said he's never coming on the boat again."

"Did he now?" said Ronan. He knew better than to probe the reason, in case Alison's feelings were hurt.

The outline of the islands was clearer now. "They say if you can see the Aran Islands, it's going to rain, and if you can't see them, it's raining already," Ronan said, and Alison laughed politely. She wondered how many people had told her that joke since her arrival. There hadn't even been that much rain since she had moved here.

She offered Dara a packet of crisps.

"I need my two hands," he said, making a big deal of showing her the position of his hands on the tiller. "Maybe in a few minutes," he conceded, and she nodded, leaving the packet on the bench beside him. She didn't want to end up like a tourist in Cairo Zoo, offering food bribes for the brief illusion of friendship with starved wild animals. Why hadn't she packed satsumas and bananas and mini-boxes of raisins? They were the kinds of things Sophie seemed to produce out of her rucksack like a magician out of a hat, whenever there was a crisis. Alison had watched her often enough. She just needed a bit more practice, that was all . . .

After an hour and a half, with very little conversation, they were bobbing on the waves outside the harbour at Inis Mor, and Ronan took the tiller.

"Thanks, Dara, you did a great job," he said.

Dara glowed with pride.

"Can I have a turn on the way back?" Nancy asked, in the universal whinge of a child whose sibling is in the limelight.

"Of course you can, love. I might need to help you a little bit, because it's heavier than you think," her dad replied, kissing her on the nose in the way that Alison had thought was exclusively for her, but somehow it added to the charm.

She climbed down onto the pier and offered Nancy her hand while she swung her leg over the rail. Dara deftly wound the mooring ropes and tied them securely.

"Can we have an ice cream?" Nancy asked Alison.

More bribery. What the hell.

"Yes. Dara, can you have an ice-lolly – is that safe?" He nodded. Poor kid must be starving, she thought. "Should we get Dara a bite to eat? A baked potato or something?" she asked Ronan in a whisper.

"He hardly eats a pick. I wouldn't worry about it," said Ronan distractedly. "Let's go up here to the pub and we can sit in the garden and have a drink. He can have another bag of Taytos if he's hungry."

No wonder the kids loved spending time with their dad, Alison thought. They sat in the beer garden overlooking the harbour, which was busy with the arrival of tourist boats. Work-worn fishing boats bobbed on their moorings and people milled around aimlessly. Dara and Nancy played darts inside the gloomy pub, half watching the large-screen television. Hardly quality time with their father, Alison thought, but she kept it to herself. Was this the measure of his fantastic new approach to fatherhood?

Suddenly there was a kerfuffle and shouting inside, and Ronan stood up. "I'll just check on them," he said, striding to the door.

Then she heard his shout. "Alison!" She ran to follow him.

"Dara's eaten a peanut," he said urgently. She could see he was controlling his panic. "Can you get his Epi-Pen? It's on board, in the galley, the drawer beside the sink." He was holding Dara on his lap. The boy was hyperventilating, and before their eyes his throat seemed to be swelling. She hesitated, wondering if she should take Nancy away with her.

"Go!" Ronan shouted savagely, and she ran down the hill, ignoring the sharp stab of a stitch in her side. She swung her leg up and pulled herself on board, wrenching her shoulder in the effort. Thankfully the galley hatch was left open. She had thought Ronan very trusting to leave the boat unsecured, but now she was glad of the extra seconds. The EpiPen was in a black case in the drawer, and she grabbed it and was back on the steep path in seconds. She shouted at a bunch of people crowded around the

door. "Get out of my way!" They were too surprised to hesitate, and stepped aside. She was across the pub lounge in two bounds, opening the case as she went. Ronan grabbed it, pulled up Dara's shorts and stabbed it deep into his thigh in one movement. Nancy was sobbing, kneeling at her father's feet, clinging onto his ankles. Dara was lying across his lap, his top buttons open, his eyes dilated with fear and the challenge of breathing. Ronan's soothing voice addressed them both, and they seemed cocooned in their own world, unaware of the stares of the people standing around. Within seconds, Dara's breathing eased, and Alison could feel her own shallow, panicky breaths deepening. Dara sat up and Ronan stroked his head. Freckles stood like brown blotches on his linen-white skin. The crowd drifted off, and Nancy's arms fell to her side but she still sat with her cheek against Ronan's shin, needing to keep a physical connection with him and unable to claim his lap.

Alison stood helpless, feeling like a voyeur in an art gallery, looking in on an intimate family pageant.

"Thanks, love," Ronan said, looking up, and she was overwhelmed by the gratitude she felt for his understanding of her isolation.

Alison was glad the day was over. She wasn't sure if the whole experience had put her off sailing, but she wouldn't go out on the *Gráinne Uaile* again in a hurry. Sophie's theory that the distraction of the sailing was a perfect foil to the tension of family introductions had been completely wrong. Sailing home with a huge sky above her, red and pink and grey in a magnificent sunset, and the depth of the dark blue ocean beneath her, Alison had never felt so claustrophobic in all her life. Nancy wouldn't leave her father's side, following him and waiting outside the cubicle even when he went to the toilet. Dara lay on one of the bunks reading a comic, lethargic with shock and the physical distress of his experience. Ronan was quiet and reflective. He didn't even say much to Alison when he dropped her off before leaving with the children.

"I'll be late, so don't wait up for me."

At midnight, Alison closed the blinds in the bedroom, not wanting to see the dark infinity of the stars. She needed the security of her own four walls and the comfort of her duvet. She felt completely out of control. What had happened to her? Had she just dropped all the barriers of self-protection that had been carefully nurtured over the last ten years? She felt completely exposed now to emotions that had never troubled her in single life. She had seen another side of Ronan today, and her reaction had shocked her.

Lisa was besotted with April, which was understandable, considering the circumstances of her birth, and how long Lisa and Michael had waited for her. What had really surprised Alison was that in that moment in the pub, before Ronan looked up, she might not have existed. The intensity of his love for his children had risen like an aura from him. He might feed them with politically incorrect food, and he might let them play darts in a grotty pub, but in that moment of danger his children were his complete world, just as April was to Lisa.

Chapter Twenty-two

It was time to bite the bullet, Liam thought as he pulled into the carpark. Her car was there again. He had left messages on her home phone over the last few weeks, saying that they needed to talk but she obviously had decided they would meet on her terms.

It seemed strange to see her sitting on the visitor's chair.

"There you are," she said, as if he was late for an appointment. She stood up. The bump was getting obvious now, if you knew what to look for. She was going to have his baby. Robbie, the foreman, was behind her old desk, stabbing the keyboard in frustrated jabbing motions, tut-tutting when the screen ignored his instructions. "Sorry, boss, I can't get the effing thing to work for me."

Liam had the feeling that he was really trying hard. Theresa must have been sitting there watching him and not helping.

"Don't worry. Thanks, Robbie. I'm in for the rest of the day. We can do it later."

Robbie picked up on Liam's tone, grabbed his yellow hard hat from the desk and clumped out, his caterpillar boots leaving a trail of dried mud on the blue carpet tiles.

The door closed behind him, and Liam turned to Theresa. "We need to talk, don't we?" He had to admit that the pregnancy suited her. She had that radiant look that Sophie had when she was carrying Michelle.

"I came to tell you that I'm going to take you to an employment tribunal for unfair dismissal related to my pregnancy. I thought it was better to tell you face to face, than for you to get a letter."

Liam had been fully intending to diplomatically broach the subject of money, and maintenance for the child. Theresa had cut to the quick and he felt cheapened, the conversation he had planned reduced to a mere financial transaction. "How much?" he asked, wearily.

"Oh, it's not a matter of money," she said sweetly. "I'm going for reinstatement. I will have an extra mouth to feed, and I will have to support myself and my dependant. This is a good job. I can work for another few months, as long as you don't ask me to carry any heavy weights or anything. Then I'll take my maternity leave, and come back to work afterwards." She paused. "Maybe part-time."

Shit, he thought. It has to be money she's after. I'm no good at playing these word games. Why doesn't she just come out with it and tell me the damage, so I can figure out how the hell to pay her off? He had debated about telling her about Sophie's illness, partly to get the sympathy vote he admitted to himself, and to get her to understand that she had to leave and not come back into his life.

"I see you haven't recruited a replacement yet," she said, into the silence. "Judging by Robbie's office skills, or lack of them, you'll need someone pretty soon, or you'll find yourself spiralling out of control."

He would spiral out of control all right, he thought angrily. How could a woman inspire such hatred in him, when he had been making love to her only weeks ago? He had to be hard on her, for Sophie's sake. There was no room for softness. Theresa had to leave, and not come back.

"There's no job for you here. Take me to a tribunal." She had to be bluffing. In a few days she would come back and name her price, and somehow he would find the money and buy her off.

"There's no need to be rude." She bent down to pick up her handbag from the chair. "My solicitor will be in touch," she said over her shoulder, and swept past him, leaving a hint of perfume that reminded him suddenly of the time he had shagged her on that very desk.

"Theresa, come back!"

She turned around, and his heart twisted when he saw the hope on her face. Tears brimmed in her eyes and he saw it suddenly. She had been bluffing, but it wasn't money she was after. It was him she wanted. A father for her child. He felt completely humbled. She stepped towards him, reaching out to embrace him. He had to stop her.

He shook his head. "Theresa, love," he said tenderly. She stood in front of him, uncertain but still hopeful. "Sophie has breast cancer. She might die on me."

Shock blanched her face and her mouth opened in horror. She sat down suddenly on the visitor's chair and Liam regretted blurting it out like that. She was pregnant, after all, and shouldn't be having shocks. He was useless at this kind of thing.

"I can't leave her and the kids. Is there somewhere you could go to live and I could send you some money, to help you out with the baby? Maybe to Cork?"

Theresa shook her head. "I have no family there any more, since Mam passed away last year. I've no reason to go back." Suddenly she sat up straight. "Anyway, you've made it clear that's not your problem. I'll just have a little drink of water and then I'll go." She went to the water dispenser, brushing away Liam's offer to get the drink. She stood with her back to him as she gulped down the ice-cold water, then she brushed her fingertips across her eyes, and took a deep breath. "Give Sophie my best wishes."

She strode to the door again in a *déjà vu* moment and was gone, leaving Liam staring at the pile of paperwork on his desk.

Father O'Leary made a point of coming up to her after Mass, instead of staying in his usual spot to shake everyone's hand on the way out. He touched Sophie's arm. "I just wanted to say you're in my prayers, and I'll be thinking about you tomorrow," he said.

"Thanks, Father," she smiled.

He wasn't self-interested all the time. He couldn't be, and he such a lovely priest. Why did that old lady want him to go out to Inverin every week, instead of taking Holy Communion from the local parish priest? Because she had known him for years and trusted him. He cared about her. The new young priests saw their vocation differently. Father O'Leary was one of the older generation, and Sophie was glad of it.

"I'm still not really telling people, Father," she cautioned him, because that was something else about him. He meant well, in that he would be asking other people to pray for her, but she didn't want that. She would fight her own battle, and ask God for help but she didn't want to become a Parish Cause. That would be too mortifying. They would all be looking at her wondering if you could notice any difference with the false breast, what clothes she was wearing, imagining her going to bed with only one breast under her nightie. Wondering if she and Liam still . . .

"Let me know how you get on," he said, meaningfully but discreetly, as a few other people were within earshot.

"I will of course, Father," she said. "Thanks." Did he ever think of his parishioners in male and female terms? Would he have any idea in his head of what Sophie would look like with two breasts, never mind one? She shivered. It was a bit like imagining your parents having sex. They must have done, but it didn't bear thinking about really.

Her mother had been fantastic when she heard the news. She was upbeat, and encouraging, and seemed to know a lot about the whole thing. She said that with early detection there was a good chance of saving the breast, and not to be worrying about it. Sophie didn't tell her that this discovery did not constitute early detection. The lump was quite advanced, and like the tip of an iceberg, there was a lot more underneath. She didn't want her mother to worry. She had gone along with the platitudes, like a child whose mother is sticking on a plaster to fix a sore finger, both of them knowing that the plaster won't make any difference, but the act of putting it on will fix everything. The child wanting to be nurtured. The mother wanting to be needed.

Chapter Twenty-three

Alison looked at the toast crumbs Ronan had left on the table, and the mug with dregs of coffee. He had an early meeting in Dublin, so he had left while she was still asleep. She had woken at 7.30, and savoured the aroma of real coffee wafting from the kitchen. She liked the sense that the day had already started before she woke up. A wet footprint on the bathmat. The radio playing in another room. Alison had already forgotten the feeling of beginning and ending her days alone, each one like a sentence, ending in a full stop. She was in a shared continuum of days, overlapping into shared nights. Ronan had made enough coffee for her too. She sipped it, standing at the window. The sun was shining. It was a pity she wouldn't see him until Wednesday, because he was going straight to London from Dublin Airport tonight. They wouldn't get a chance to digest the day they had spent with the children, and discuss the next outing. She thought they might like the coral beach at Carraroe. This time she would make a child-friendly but healthy picnic. Bring a Frisbee, and maybe a kite. If they had lots of fun, maybe the two younger ones would persuade Brian that she wasn't a complete ogre, and he should come next time. Today was Sophie's check-up and Alison overcame her hesitation to intrude, and called her. She would just leave a message, so that Sophie knew she was in her thoughts. Liam answered.

"Oh, I thought you'd have left already," Alison stammered, thinking how stupid that sounded. Why would she be ringing, then?

Liam hesitated. "We're just on our way out the door."

"I won't delay you. Tell Sophie I wished her luck."

Alison couldn't settle down to work at all. She was supposed to be planning the opening event for the holiday village, with PR, local dignitaries invited, the usual stuff. She had no flair for this, and in London there was a whole event management team, who did all these things without even thinking. In Galway, Alison had no useful contacts, and no idea how much any of it should cost. Seán had been no help and she didn't want to admit to Ronan that she was struggling. Three sheets of A4 lists later, she was just muddled. The whole pot of coffee had disappeared which would explain the shakiness, she supposed. Eleven o'clock. Sophie would know by now. Should she call? What if it was bad news? Sophie would have a whole list of people to tell first – her mother, her sisters, and probably even the priest, before Alison could expect a call.

The doorbell rang and she wondered if it was the

new bed being delivered. Alison had convinced herself that if there was a proper bedroom, rather than a pull-out sofa in the spare room, her mother would come to stay. She opened the door wide, expecting to see a sweaty delivery man bending under the weight of a mattress.

Sophie was standing there. She looked so tiny and vulnerable. And happy.

"It's no bigger!"

Alison grabbed her and hugged her tight. "Oh, Sophie, I've been so worried! Where's Liam?"

"I told him to drop me off here and go back to work. I couldn't just go home. Do you want a walk?"

Alison grabbed her jacket and slammed the door. "I'm so full of caffeine I can't sit still. To hell with the bed delivery."

Sophie bounded down the stairs and Alison followed her. They were like teenagers running down a convent corridor on their last day at school.

"I know it's not the end. I'm not stupid enough to think I'm free of it. But I feel like I've been given another chance."

Alison took her arm and they strode towards the sea. The silent swans ignored them. Seagulls shrieked high above. "Thanks for coming to tell me."

"You were the first to know I had it, apart from Liam, so I thought you should be the first to know I'm beating it. For now, anyway."

"You are. You haven't really doubted for a minute that you'd beat it, have you?"

"When I started praying, it was from fear. I begged

God to not let me die. I asked Him to just let me raise my children. I even offered to work for the Vincent de Paul, like the bribes I used to offer Him when I was a child. 'I'll put ten pence in the poor box if you let me find my skipping rope'. But during the last few months I've started looking at everything differently. As if I've woken up after being in a sort of dream. It's a real cliché to say you take things for granted, but it's true. You take for granted that you're going to wake up this morning, and do pretty much what you did yesterday, and maybe say sorry if you had an argument, or ring somebody you've been meaning to talk to, or weed the front drive. From now on, I can't take anything for granted. The cancer can still get me. It's very early days. I've months of treatment ahead, and I'll have to go for check-ups for years and years. I'll have to feel my breasts every morning, grateful that they are still there, but wonder if they will betray me again. Or maybe it will come back somewhere else, where I don't even find it until it's too late."

Alison just listened. There was nothing to say. They walked the length of the prom, and kicked the end wall with the soles of their feet, joyously, bouncing to turn and walk into the face of the rising wind.

"As soon as Michelle starts school, I'm going to put Oisín into the crèche four days a week, and I'm going to get a job."

"Wow." Alison was surprised. She would have thought Sophie's new appreciation of her life would have involved spending as much time with the children as she could.

"The only problem is my skills are a bit rusty, and I'm not sure I want to do the translation work. I think I want to be with people more. It can be a bit lonely sitting in the house working on the computer all day. I want to get out."

"I have an idea." Alison was excited. She had a budget for the launch, which should stretch to paying a salary, if it was managed well.

"What?"

"You did such a fantastic job organising those viewings for me, and you told me you used to drum up business for Liam. Would you fancy organising a PR event for the holiday village launch? I could pay you."

Sophie felt uncomfortable about saying it, but she wasn't a charity case, needing to be rescued. "I was planning to look in the *Galway Advertiser*, to see if there were any jobs going, maybe in an office," she said.

Alison begged her. "Sophie, I need you. I'm so bad at these things. That's what I was doing this morning. Making endless lists of things, but I just got a headache thinking about it. You're brilliant at organising. It would be like a project, a way of finding out if it's the kind of work you enjoy. And the hours could be really flexible, to fit in with the children."

That swung it for Sophie. Her newfound determination to have a life outside the house wasn't just a selfish need for fulfilment. She had to set her children up, to make them independent, so that if the worst came to the worst, they would deal with it better. Oisín was too clingy, and once his sister went off to school, he would be lonely too. Crèche would be good for him in lots of ways. And if Sophie had a job that enabled her to pick the children up after school, so much the better.

"When does it start?" she asked.

"I've got a job," Sophie declared that evening, when Liam got in.

The children had run to hug him, gabbling about their day. His relationship with them had changed. He had become more involved, and not only in the practicalities of bath-time and bedtime. He knew more about their friends, and what they liked to eat, and he had even cooked pasta on Sunday night, with a very tasty cheese sauce. Michelle had declared it was better than Mammy's sauce and, to his delight, had asked if he could cook it every night.

"What?" Liam looked at her in amazement.

"Mammy's going to organise a big huge party, and I'm going to be a big boy in the crèche when Michelle is a big girl at school," Oisín declared.

Sophie was back in control and Liam liked it. He wasn't going to burst her balloon by getting annoyed that she had told the children before she had even consulted with him. The old Sophie was back. Queen of the household and ruler of his world, and that was fine with him.

"How did you manage to do that so quickly?" he asked. She still had to mind herself, and he was worried she would wear herself out. But he knew better than to say any of that to her.

"Alison needs a big event organised, and I'm going to do it. If it works out, I might market myself as a freelancer."

"When do you start?" He thought they should all go away for a nice summer holiday in the sun, and he had been planning to book it as a surprise. This might scupper his plans.

"Not until September, when Michelle is at school. I'll only work a few hours a day. It's perfect."

"Sounds like it," he said, kissing her. "It's good to have you back."

He could see the love in her smile. How had he ever betrayed her?

He had been so selfish, peeved that he wasn't getting enough attention, but instead of talking to her about it, or changing something in himself, he had just gone looking for attention somewhere else. His affair with Theresa had been all about his ego – reassuring himself that he was still sexy, and that someone found him interesting to talk to. What he had done was destroyed someone else's life, and nearly destroyed his own. He could see now that, for all her bravado and sex-kitten act, Theresa was in love with him, and she had really thought that having his baby would win him over, make him leave his other life behind to have one with her. He would never be sure if she had done it on purpose, but in some ways it didn't matter. There would be a child without a father, and it was his fault. He still hadn't figured out how to support Theresa while keeping her at a very long distance. He couldn't just walk away, as much as his first cowardly instinct had been to do that. Would Theresa still be taking him to tribunal?

He was preoccupied for the evening, and Sophie noticed it.

When they made love that night, Sophie had to ask him. Now that the spectre of losing her breast had been banished, at least temporarily, she needed to know if Liam had been afraid.

"Would you have still fancied me if I only had one breast?" she asked, feeling the weight of his hand where it lay on her left side, liberated to touch the area that had been taboo only the night before.

"Of course I would, darling. Your breasts are nice but they're only a part of you. I love the whole of you, and most of all, I love you for what's inside your head. You would still be my lovely Sophie."

That was the revelation he had had, as he looked at Theresa that last time in the office. Beautiful as she was, he hardly knew her as a person, because that wasn't what the relationship was about, for him. It had been purely to satisfy his selfish need for reassurance, and for the sex. Sadly, Theresa had thought it was more.

"So if it's all in the mind, I'd better not get Alzheimer's then," Sophie giggled.

"If we are given a chance to grow old together, you can get whatever you like," he said, kissing her.

Alison's mother had finally agreed to come for a visit, and Alison was excited. Ronan was less than enthusiastic and Alison could understand. He considered the apartment as home now. They were spending so much time together, and for a couple of weeks now she had been expecting an influx of his possessions from his own place. There was plenty of storage space, but she didn't want his stuff to arrive while her mother was there, making it obvious that he was moving in. It was much better to leave it vague. Ronan was doing a lot of travelling and he was taking the children away for the last week of July, so his time in the apartment would hardly overlap with her mother's. Alison wouldn't have to explicitly tell her mother that they were living together.

"When are you going to move your things in?" Alison asked him one evening over a leisurely supper.

"What do you mean?" he asked, surprised. There wasn't any more stuff. He had a few bits and pieces on the boat. The *Gráinne Uaile* had been his home for almost six months before he met Alison. There was no way he could afford to pay rent as well as the exorbitant maintenance payments he handed over to Sinéad every month.

Alison had a moment of panic. Was she pushing too hard? "Well, we haven't really talked about it, but we're kind of living together, here, aren't we?"

"Yes, and it's considerably more comfortable than if we had moved into the boat together!" he laughed.

"You're not telling me that was where you lived before?"

"It certainly was. And for one person it was fine, although sometimes I did yearn for solid ground under my feet."

Alison suddenly felt naïve, and a little bit used. She had somehow got the idea that he had an apartment on the other side of town – it was a natural assumption to make when he referred to his 'place' or said he was 'going home'. They had never gone there, and she had never questioned that. Now they were living together here, but there was no evidence of his presence, apart from his clothes and his golf clubs. Her apartment, without any of his personal marks of occupation, could just be another hotel room for him, with the added bonus of a woman laid on for his convenience. Where did he stay when he was up in Dublin, or over in London? She had suggested once that he could stay in her house in London, to save money on a hotel bill, but he had dismissed it, saying there were three other people meeting at the same hotel, and it was much more convenient to stay there. With his mobile phone he could be anywhere, she supposed, when he called her to say goodnight, or she called him to make plans for the weekend. Were they actually living together, or was she just his girl in Galway? The wine tasted acidic now, and she threw the rest of it down the kitchen sink. He seemed oblivious to her change of mood.

"I'm just going to catch the news headlines," he said, and sank almost horizontal on the sofa, flicking channels with the remote control. His long elegant frame, draped across the soft chocolate-brown leather, was still the same horny body she loved. But who was he? And who did he think she was? Alison refused to ask the predictable question – "But where do I stand?" Deep down she knew exactly where she stood. The only decision she had to make was if it was somewhere she wanted to be.

Her mother looked a bit frail, walking through the arrivals door at Galway Airport. Alison waved and smiled, feeling like a child, excited after being away from home. She took her mother's small case, and linked arms with her.

"We're only twenty minutes away from the apartment," she said brightly. "How was the journey?"

"I found Heathrow a bit intimidating, I must admit," her mother said. "But I was quite pleased with myself. I managed to check in and find my way around without asking anybody. Your dad always took charge in these situations, and it felt a bit strange to be on my own, but I did it."

Alison couldn't think of her father being so adventurous if the situation were reversed. "You did so well. You know I would have travelled with you, if you'd wanted me to?"

"Yes, thank you. But I need to start being a bit more independent, and this was the first step. There's a bit of life in me yet!" Her mother smiled tentatively as if she was tempting fate by making such a declaration. Alison had just a tiny inkling of the loneliness her mother must feel after a lifetime of shared days and nights.

They drove towards town, and Alison found herself gabbling about all the things they could do together. "I'm really my own boss, here, and the projects I'm working on are going so well that I think I can take some time off, while you're here. There's so much to see. The weather will be fine, hopefully, and you'll see Galway at its best."

Her mother had a new outfit on, which Alison thought looked rather dashing, with nautical navy and white stripes. "I like the new clothes," she said.

Her mother smiled shyly. "I got them in the new Primark on the high street. It's so reasonable. I felt like a little change, but I wasn't too extravagant."

She could afford to splash out a little bit, with the payment she had received on the life assurance policy, Alison thought, but the habits of a lifetime were hard to break.

"Let's have lunch first, and then we can go back to the apartment. You must be starving."

"Will I meet Ronan this evening?" Her mother sounded nervous.

"No, he's away on business until the end of the week, so I have you to myself." She could see her mother visibly relaxing in the passenger seat, and taking more of an active interest in the scenery as they went out the coast road towards Furbo.

"There's a lot of building going on."

"That's why I'm here, because the whole industry is booming. We'll pass one of my developments in a few minutes."

"How nice," her mother said absently. "They're very close to the sea, some of those houses. I wonder if it's chilly in the winter, with the wind coming off the water?"

"Probably. My holiday village will be quite seasonal,

I should think. People will buy the chalets as an investment, and rent them out, or maybe use them for a couple of weeks of the year for themselves."

"It would be nice to be that rich, wouldn't it?"

"It sure would," said Alison, not ready to share her secret. She was planning to invest in one herself, but she hadn't even told Ronan yet. She would wait until the time was right.

Alison waved towards a turning on the left. "My friend Sophie lives down there," she said.

"Oh, yes, how is she? Wasn't she the one with cancer?"

"The chemotherapy seems to be working, so fingers crossed. But you never know with these things."

"No, indeed." Her mother was quiet until they passed the building site for the holiday village.

"That's the one I'm working on," Alison said proudly.

The sea was a navy-blue and purple swell just beyond the outline of a stationary JCB digger. The foundations were in, and the landscaping had already started, so that when the building work was finished, there wouldn't be months and months of waiting before some greenery softened the new white walls.

Seán had been difficult to persuade on that point, saying, "People are investing for the long term. They won't be worried that the grass isn't up yet."

"That's not the point," Alison had argued. "We want to be different, to make this village unique and exclusive. You can't do that if it just looks like a building site. We need to get the first season off to a flying start. People should feel like they're on the Mediterranean coast. We need azaleas, and rhododendrons. Hardy plants with bright colours. The bamboo along the roadside of the site will give privacy too, until the trees are more mature."

Seán and Ronan had looked at each other and sneered. She was not to be dissuaded, and had simply commissioned the landscapers to start working. Seán and Ronan were money-men, not marketers. She knew what would make the chalets sell. It was her job, after all.

"It's hard to imagine what it will be like when it's finished, but the location is lovely," her mother said.

They had a leisurely lunch in the Mill Café, then Alison thought her mother looked a bit tired. "Let's go back and get you settled in and I can quickly check my emails," she said.

After an hour or so, Alison came out of the office to find her mother busy in the kitchen.

"I thought I'd just tidy up a bit," she said, not sure if Alison would be annoyed.

"I didn't expect that you'd be able to sit still for long," her daughter declared, putting on the kettle. "Shall we have a cup of tea and then a stroll?"

"Lovely."

Alison enjoyed showing her mother the sights. Sarah was quietly excited by this adventure, and enjoyed standing for ten minutes listening to a street musician, even tapping her toes and discreetly clapping. She bought a multi-coloured scarf in one shop, and some silver Celtic earrings in another.

"You're turning into a shopaholic!" Alison teased.

"I haven't been on a holiday like this for a long time. I'm going to make the most of it."

They went back home and sat in the bay window watching the changing shades of the evening sky. Alison had a gin and tonic while her mother sipped a sherry. Later Alison grilled lamb chops and served them with floury jacket potatoes and minted peas.

Sarah surprised Alison with her insight.

"The people are very different here, and the pace. How are you finding it?"

Alison had to admit that, having adjusted, she would find it difficult to go back to the London kind of rat race.

"It's just as competitive here, and you have to be completely on your toes, but it doesn't seem quite so all-consuming. People have real lives as well as their jobs, and they are happy to switch off when they leave the office. Here, a phone call can wait until the morning. In London, you don't relax until you've made the phone call, even if it's eight o'clock at night."

Her mother glanced at the clock. "Yes, it would seem strange to call someone about work at this time of the night."

The phone rang, and they laughed. "It's probably Ronan. Excuse me." Alison took the receiver into the bedroom, kicking the door discreetly closed behind her, and throwing herself on the bed, ready for a chat about the day. She felt exuberant.

It took her a moment to realise it was Lisa on the line.

"I can't believe it, Alison. Michael's been having an affair!" her friend sobbed.

"Oh, Lisa!" Alison couldn't believe it either. "Are you sure?"

"He's just admitted it. Said he couldn't keep the secret any longer. It was eating him up. He says it's over, but how do I know it is? How do I know he wouldn't do it again?"

Alison wished she was sitting with Lisa on her sofa, hugging her and drying her tears. It was so difficult over the phone.

"Why did he have to tell you now?"

It was a rhetorical question, to fill the silence from her end, but Lisa launched into a speech about how selfish men are, and that he obviously decided he couldn't keep the secret, so he just told her, said sorry, and now she was supposed to just get over it, and pretend it never happened.

"We're a little family, now," she sobbed. "April's only been home for a month, and already her mummy and daddy have had a massive row. What if we split up? How can he do this to us?"

"Lisa, where is he now?"

"I told him to get out. He's going to stay with his friend Andrew for a couple of nights. Unless of course he goes off to have a shag with the nearest girl he can get his hands on."

"Did he tell you who the woman was?"

"A new clerk at the chambers. She's left now. Gone to Manchester. So I will never know if their sordid little fling finished because of that, or because, as he claims, he realised the error of his ways."

Alison was silent.

"Ali, could I come over, with April, like you suggested? I need some space to think. I can't kick him out of his own home but at the moment I can't bear to be in the same room as him. I keep imagining I can smell someone else's perfume."

"Of course. Mum is here until next Tuesday, but as soon as she's gone you can have the room for as long as you want."

"Thanks."

"Are you sure it's the right thing to do? Leaving with April, I mean. Shouldn't you try to talk things through?"

"Yes, of course we should. But not yet. I need some head-space."

"And you want to punish him a little bit too?" Alison knew Lisa.

"Mmmn. Maybe a bit of that too. Is that so wrong?"

Alison managed to give a non-committal response. Lisa said she would investigate flights, and let her know when to expect the invasion.

"It'll be great. I can get to know April, and you two can just chill out while I'm working."

Her mother had been dozing on the sofa, and she opened her eyes when she heard Alison coming back. "How is he?"

"It was Lisa. She's really upset. Michael has just told her he's had an affair." Alison burst into tears, the effort of being strong for Lisa finally taking its toll. She flopped down beside her mother, and leaned on her shoulder, sniffing and blowing her nose.

"Why do people do these things? It seems to take a disaster like getting cancer for people to realise what they have. Michael is lovely, earns loads of money, has the most amazing wife in Lisa, and now their dream of a baby has finally come true. But he has to go and sleep with someone else. Why can't he be happy with what he has?"

"Your expectations are much higher, these days. You're all used to getting everything you want."

"But you and Dad were happy, for all those years together. Why can't people seem to make that kind of commitment any more?" She was asking for herself as much as for Lisa.

"Darling," the word seemed strangely exotic coming from her mother's lips, "your father and I weren't happy for all those years. That's what I mean about expectations. We didn't *expect* to be happy every minute of every day. Or even every month of every year. There were times when I was tempted to walk out on him. And no doubt he had those thoughts too. But walk out to where? Sometimes you have to settle for what you have. There's a kind of happiness in that too."

Alison found it very difficult to believe. What was the point of living, if that was your idea of the pinnacle of happiness? "I'd rather be on my own, if that's what it came to."

Her mother nodded. "You were like that as a child too. I used to worry that you wouldn't make friends, because sometimes friendship is a compromise, and you could be very stubborn."

"I've got loads of friends." Alison knew she was sounding defensive.

"Of course, you have. Some lovely ones too, like Lisa. It's important to be there for them when they need you, and you always have been. That's a nice quality you have."

Her mother's arm was around her shoulders now, and Alison couldn't remember ever feeling so close to her.

"You've changed, even in the last year. You have so much to give, but don't get taken for granted, that's all."

Suddenly, her mother seemed to become uncomfortably aware of the intimacy, and she offered to make a cup of tea. Alison let her bustle around, laying out on a plate shortbread biscuits they wouldn't eat, but needing the ritual of movement, while the kettle boiled.

It was as she was dozing off in bed later that Alison realised she hadn't heard from Ronan. Maybe he was expecting her to call him? She checked the clock. Too late to ring him now, she thought, and rolled over onto his side of the bed, inhaling the lingering scent of his aftershave and his maleness.

Chapter Twenty-four

There was a light breeze on the Prom, and Alison and Sophie were ambling at their new-found pace.

"Would you like to come to our Community Mass?" Sophie asked Alison, expecting laughter.

Alison had been listening for weeks to all her gripes about the hassle of organising it, and how nobody else seemed to volunteer for any of the jobs.

"As long as you don't ask me to do anything," she replied. "I was completely intimidated by that Mass you took me to when I first arrived. All that standing and kneeling and sitting. I didn't know which end of me was up!"

"It will be a bit different this time, since we'll be on the beach. No pews. It will be much less formal."

"True. It sounds lovely. I hope you get nice weather for it."

"We have a contingency plan of going up to the church if we have to."

"So you didn't surrender and offer your living-room, then?"

"Certainly not. I have enough on my plate."

"How are you feeling, these days?

"A bit better, thank God. I have some of my appetite back and a little bit more energy. Every day still feels like a fight, though. Sometimes when I'm making the bed in the morning, I look at it and think I can't wait to get back into it. "

"When is the Mass?" Alison couldn't believe that Sophie was still lumbered with organising it. She should give her some moral support by turning up.

"In two weeks' time. The fifteenth of August, the Feast of the Assumption. I keep looking at the long-range forecast, but I think it's a bit pointless. The weathermen can't even predict from day to day, so it's a bit optimistic to think they can do a fortnight."

Alison wondered if she would still have Lisa and April staying by then. It had already been a couple of weeks and, as much as she loved her friend, the strain was showing. Ronan had hardly shown his face recently, and Alison had started to feel like a Bed and Breakfast landlady. He kept saying that July was a busy time, with everyone sorting things out before their holidays, and that things would calm down in August, when business was slow. Last night, she had confronted him.

"We hardly see each other these days," she had opened with a fairly neutral gambit, as she removed her make-up at the dressing-table.

He had nodded distractedly, looking up from some

work papers. The bed used to be exclusively for wild sex and deliciously deep post-coital sleep. How had it so quickly become just another place for work to intrude?

"It's been really busy, love. You know it has. The final phase of any project is always hectic. Seán is very demanding, and I have another guy like him up in Dublin, expecting me to drop everything for him, whenever he calls. There's a lot of balls to juggle."

He put the papers on the floor and tried to melt her with his sexy smile, but this had been building up for some time now, and Alison had to get it off her chest.

"I've only seen the kids a few times, and they're on their school holidays now so I thought we'd be seeing a lot more of them. Is there something you're not telling me?" She was convinced that they had taken a dislike to her, despite her best efforts. She needed to know.

Ronan shook his head. "It was never going to be easy, introducing them to someone new. They're only just getting used to the idea that I'm not with their mother. We have to take it slowly."

She recognised the tone of voice he used to pacify Seán when things at work were not going smoothly.

"That presumably means seeing them infrequently, rather than not at all." Alison knew she was sounding frosty, but she was determined not to be treated as some recalcitrant client. This was their future they were talking about.

Ronan sighed with exasperation. "Well, if you must know, Brian is refusing to see you. Sinéad has met someone else, so when I have the kids, she wants me to have all of them, so she can shag him to her heart's content without being interrupted. Frankly, I don't want to fight with my kids when I see them, so I am taking the easy option."

"It might be the easy option in the short term, Ronan, but it is not sustainable in the longer term. If we're going to be together, they will just have to get used to me. They don't have to like me. I know I've got my work cut out to show them that I'm not taking you away from them. But I'm not afraid of the challenge."

Ronan went silent and she wondered if she had touched a nerve. .

"It's really difficult for me, Alison. I want to be there for the children. I don't want to just take the selfish option and spend all my time with you, and then find they've grown up and I've missed it. I want to be part of their lives."

"So do I," said Alison, "but only if you want me to be a bigger part of your life too. At the moment I feel like a convenient stopover when you're working here 'down west', and fairly low on the list of priorities when you're away. That would have to change, if our relationship is going to work."

Ronan was surprised by this new assertiveness. The Alison who came to Ireland in the spring had seemed happy to drift along, letting things happen at their own pace, which was great. When they had been together in London, Ronan had felt she was eager to move the relationship on to the next stage all the time. He hated that kind of pressure. She had always been the go-getting career girl, and he was the drifter. In Ireland, she had let her hair down a bit, and was much more relaxed and confident. He enjoyed every minute he spent with her, and she was trying really hard with the kids, which he loved her for. Now the pressure seemed to be building again.

"You've changed, since you've been over here," he said, and Alison wasn't sure from his tone if it was a change for the better as far as he was concerned.

"I don't think I have. Inside, I'm still the same . . . but I suppose I'm more sure about what makes me happy."

"Are you unhappy with me then?"

"I need more, Ronan. Not straightaway, of course. I don't want to rush things, but sometimes I'm not sure of where I fit in your life, and you've become a really big part of mine."

She couldn't believe she'd said it out loud, and imagined Lisa clapping her hands silently in the other room. Lisa had been coaching her on how to put her feelings to Ronan, without it turning into a row. That was ironic, considering she wasn't talking to Michael and was showing very little inclination to take April home again. But they had been together for ten years with hardly any arguments, so Lisa was an expert, as far as Alison was concerned. Alison had never managed to express her needs before, without seeming critical or pushy. Maybe she was still pushing Ronan too hard now, but there was the psychological pressure of knowing she wasn't going to be in Ireland forever . . . unless there was a reason to stay.

Her worry, that she was repeating the same mistake with Ronan and chasing him away, had been dispelled by Lisa. "You're at a different stage in life. You both know what you want out of a relationship, and if Ronan isn't giving you what you need, you should tell him and give him a chance to do something about it." Alison knew she was right, but felt selfish. Shouldn't she just sit tight and wait for him to show that he felt the same way as she did about the future?

Lisa had shrugged. "Of course you could. But Ronan strikes me as someone who needs to have things spelt out to him. You're a grown woman. Tell him straight. You've got nothing to lose. The relationship isn't what you want, so either it has to change, or it has to end, and you're the one who has to take the first step, because frankly, life is very comfortable for him at the moment, and he'll be happy with the status quo."

Alison was sitting on the edge of the bed now. Ronan had been quiet for a long time, not looking at her.

"What do you want me to do?"

Finally she felt like she had his full attention rather than his just humouring her.

"If we are going to be together, we need to get a bigger place," she said, "where the children can come and visit, and have their own space so they can get used to me being around, in a more normal environment. Meeting at Leisureland or in a restaurant is not going to build any bonds. We're always short of time and frankly, it's not very enjoyable for any of us."

"That is a big commitment," Ronan said. He enjoyed the freedom of travelling away, staying in hotels, catching up with friends in various places during the week, and then spending his weekends either with Alison or with the children. Mixing them would be stressful.

"Well, I think we're both grown up enough to decide if it's the kind of commitment we want to make, or not. I've told you what I'm prepared to do, so it's over to you."

Alison went into the living area and stood at the full-length window, looking at the dark waves. She was always soothed by the quiet power of the sea, even when it was tamed by the harbour walls. She could hear Lisa singing a lullaby to April and felt a deep ache inside her.

He was asleep when she slid into bed. She wasn't surprised. Ronan was quite reflective, for all his extrovert tendencies, and he would want time to think things over.

In the morning, Alison was up first, and went to make coffee. It didn't take Ronan long to pack and she wondered if he had always foreseen this outcome, and had travelled lightly into her life. He stood behind her and she could feel his breath on the back of her neck. She wouldn't turn because the tears might come and then she might relent. He put his hand on her shoulder and she reached up and placed hers on top. They stood there for a moment, swaying slightly in unconscious harmony with the waves, and then he slid his hand away and she heard his keys dropping on the wooden table and the gentle click of the closing door.

Lisa found her standing in the same place, her arms folded across her body.

She hugged her tight. "He might come back."

"He didn't leave anything to come back for."

"That's good."

Alison looked at her, shocked at her matter-of-fact tone.

"So if he comes back, it's only for you."

Alison summoned a wry smile. "So it's just us girls, then. Is April asleep?"

"She's been up since five, and has just gone back for a snooze. She's making up for the lack of cuddles early on in her life, and she'll only fall asleep if she's being rocked in my arms. Michael's mother told me I was making a rod for my own back, and I said if I have to rock her to sleep until she's five, I don't care."

"Let's have a coffee, then. I suddenly feel a bit shaky."

They sat at the table, not needing words.

Sophie was sympathetic when Alison rang her later in the morning.

"I thought you should know, since it will only be me for dinner on Saturday," she said.

"Need a walk?" Sophie was already grabbing the car keys. "Meet at the usual place?"

Alison was relieved to be doing something. Inspired by Alison's courage, Lisa was going to ring Michael this morning for a long chat, and if it went well, she would probably be packing up soon too, leaving Alison to her solitary space. She had got used to having all the other people around recently, and it would be difficult to go back to the radio as her only companion in the empty rooms.

The breeze was gentle as they walked along the prom, the giggles of children digging and paddling with their mothers in rolled-up jeans rising from the beach below.

"We're off to Turkey just after the Mass," said Sophie. "Liam organised it. One of those club holidays I have always dreamed about. The children are entertained in the mornings, and then we can have little outings, or go to the pool in the afternoon. Liam always said they were too expensive, but it's a special treat."

"That sounds great. And then Michelle starts school?"

"I can't believe my baby is starting school! I'm really excited about the job too. I can't wait to get my teeth into it."

"You certainly have a busy few months lined up."

"And I plan to enjoy every minute."

"Good for you. But don't overdo it."

"I won't. But tell me, how are you feeling about Ronan? Was he really the man for you?"

"I thought he was. In some ways, the fact that he's putting the children first makes me love him even more. But I've also realised that unless I can have more of him, I won't be happy with just a little bit of Ronan. I don't even mean more of his time, because life is busy, and that's just how it is. I mean more of his thoughts, and his attention. Even when he's somewhere else, I would like him to be thinking about me, and sometimes even putting me first."

"Maybe when he's not seeing you at all, he'll realise that too."

"I don't want to hold out too much hope of that,

either. If it's meant to be, it will be, and if not, I have to just get on with my life. You've been a real inspiration to me." She looked at her friend. "And I wouldn't dream of comparing my situation to yours. But I would like to have the same attitude as you. I want to live for the moment, and look forward to the future, but not take anything for granted."

"How's Lisa doing?" Sophie had met her, and they had clicked immediately.

Alison had felt a little bit excluded from the baby talk but they had been sensitive enough not to keep that going for too long.

"She's calling Michael now. They'll work things out. They're such a great couple. Michael wrote her a long letter, and I won't tell you everything in it, but he did say that he felt excluded by Lisa when April arrived. Lisa spent every spare minute at the hospital, and then when the baby came home, she was obsessed with making sure April was OK. He was jealous of all that attention, and of course they weren't getting any sleep, and he was going off to work completely exhausted. The girl at work flirted with him and gave him lots of attention and he fell for it. Classic scenario."

Sophie nodded. "So do you think she'll forgive Michael?"

"She already has, but she's worried that if she makes it too easy for him, he might be tempted to do it again. Aren't we women terrible? She's staying away to punish him, but actually what she really wants is to be with him, playing happy families. She could have gone to stay with her mum, but then Michael would have turned up and sweet-talked her into coming home. She has no willpower when it comes to her man, so she had to come all the way over here to make sure she resisted the temptation."

Sophie laughed. "All the way over here makes it sound like we're in the Burmese jungle or something."

"There are times when it feels as different from London as being in the Burmese jungle," said Alison. "In the nicest possible way, of course."

"Of course!" Sophie laughed. "So, is the invitation to come to your cool pad in London for a weekend still on offer?"

"Most certainly. I was just waiting for the word."

"Why don't we do it in December? I'll be off the chemo by then, please God. I can do my Christmas shopping in London, and we can celebrate our birthdays."

"I was kind of hoping to ignore mine," said Alison.

"Let's ignore them together then!" said Sophie.

"I've already extracted a solemn vow from Lisa that she won't organise a surprise party. Will you promise the same?" Alison looked expectantly at Sophie.

"Of course. We can just go out for a nice quiet dinner and the theatre. How does that sound?"

"Sounds good to me." Alison sighed with relief.

"It's nice to have something to look forward to," Sophie said.

Alison wondered how scared she must have been only a short while ago, not knowing how far forward she could look at all. Sophie was so brave.

"Have you told your mum about Ronan yet?" Sophie asked.

"Not yet. She won't be surprised though. For the first time in my adult life, she ventured an opinion about what I should do. I must have been such a cow when I was a teenager that she gave up trying to advise me about anything years ago. I resented both of my parents for never taking any interest, but actually they were probably too intimidated to tell me what they thought."

"What did she suggest you should do?"

"She told me not to be taken for granted. I think Ronan was onto an easy number, staying with me when it suited him or he felt a bit horny, but without any kind of commitment. She was worried that he was using me."

"Do you think he was using you?"

"I don't think he was consciously doing it, but I suspect it's part of who he is. He's used to being popular, and sexy and having money, and I guess that means women fall at his feet a bit. I did too. He's had two or three girl friends since he broke up with Sinéad. But I want more from the relationship than some casual arrangement that might turn into something else. He's already got a failed marriage behind him – I'm not expecting him to walk me up the aisle, but it has to be going somewhere, for the children as much as for us. It's not fair on them if they keep being introduced to women who seem important, and then disappear out of their lives."

"There wouldn't be a long queue of women lining up to take on three children, that's for sure," said Sophie.

"I'd happily be a lot more involved with them, if Ronan wanted that."

"You really love him, warts and all, don't you?"

"That's what love is, isn't it? All or nothing."

When the phone rang at 11.30, Alison was surprised. Ronan's number came up on the display. She forced herself not to answer, her heart pounding. She had to be strong. She wasn't ready to talk to him yet.

His voice on the answering machine sounded metallic, remote. "Hi, it's me. I just want you to know that I understand where you're coming from. I need to think about what you've said. It's a lot to take in, and I don't want to treat it lightly. I love you. You know that, don't you?"

He hung up, and Alison let the tears come. Why did being in love have to hurt so much? Had she been unfair, and not given him a chance to put his point of view? Was she chasing him away, instead of accepting that there was a pace to any relationship, and this one just needed more time? She needed to talk to her mother and, unthinking, she dialled the number.

Her mother's voice was muffled. "Hello?"

"Oh, Mum, I'm so sorry, did I wake you?"

"Hello, darling. No, not quite. Are you all right?"

"Ronan's left me." Alison managed to get the words out without sobbing.

"Oh, love, I am sorry. Did you talk about it? Do you know why?" Alison could hear her mother sitting upright in bed, and imagined her pulling on the crocheted bed jacket she wore when she sat up reading.

"It was my own fault, really. I told him I wasn't

happy unless there was more to the relationship. I sometimes felt like a stop-over rather than a really important part of his life."

"Keep strong, love. If he understands what you meant, and is willing to change, he'll come back. If he doesn't understand, then you would just be storing up the pain for later. It wouldn't work out in the long term. It's better to know now."

"It sounds ridiculous, but I want to be part of the children's lives too, because I've realised that they're all intertwined. They are a part of who he is, and Ronan wasn't really sharing that part with me."

"That must be difficult for him, too. His loyalties are split."

"I know, and I want to help. I don't want to be their mother. I just want them to accept me for who I am."

"Sometimes that's the most difficult part."

Alison sighed. "Sorry for waking you. I just had to talk to someone."

"I'm glad it was me. I'll give you a ring in the morning. Try and get some sleep."

Chapter Twenty-five

Liam watched the two women laughing together in
the kitchen and envied Sophie's ability to make such
close friends. John had given him the cold shoulder a bit,
since that time when he had seen Theresa in the golf club.
He disapproved, though he would never say anything
to Liam, and he had withdrawn from the friendship,
unable to reconcile what he knew with his high regard
for Sophie. Then the breast cancer had loomed and taken
over everything else, and Liam hadn't made the time to
see John and put him straight about finishing with
Theresa. There just never seemed to be a good moment.
Watching Maeve coming in and kissing Sophie's cheek,
and then hugging Alison made him wonder how men and
women could be so different. He could see that Maeve
was consoling her for the break-up with Ronan. To his
knowledge, Maeve had only met Alison once before,
but there was some kind of bond that connected
women even when they didn't know each other. They

told each other stuff when they hardly knew each other, and didn't seem to mind. Alison had been looking a bit wan for the last couple of weeks, when she had come out to see Sophie. They had spent hours at the kitchen table, with Alison in tears, wondering if she had done the right thing. He wondered if Theresa was doing the same at someone else's table, or if she was coping with everything by herself. He had written her a long letter, explaining how sorry he was, and telling her the details of the bank account he had set up for the baby. There had been no answer, but he wasn't expecting one. The cautious side of him would never have put anything on paper – Theresa might use it against him, to make some kind of claim, or cause him trouble. But the last time they had met, Liam had seen in her face that her tactics were all bravado, to hide how much she was hurting. He had to trust her, and to do the right thing by her. Deep down, he also admitted that if she did turn the letter against him, he deserved it, and he would have to face up to the consequences. But, for Sophie's sake, he hoped that would not happen. There was a great air of optimism as the women packed up picnic hampers with the food that everyone would share after the Mass. He was a bit nervous about his reading, never having been a great one for being the centre of attention. At the height of Sophie's stress, he had offered to do one of the readings, to save her having to go and ask someone else. Michelle was running up and down the stairs singing the children's hymn. Oisín was playing quietly for a change, constructing a very tall Meccano tower in the playroom. There would be tears when it collapsed, but for now, his endeavours were being rewarded. He had the same habit as Liam, of sticking his tongue out when he was concentrating, and his father stood and watched him from the doorway, feeling oddly removed from the fever of activity all around him. The doorbell rang again, and it was Father O'Leary, a bit breathless having had to walk a few hundred yards past parked cars all along the road.

"It's fierce busy in here," he gasped.

Liam offered him a drink and they slipped into the lounge, where Liam poured each of them a large whiskey.

"To steady the nerves," he said, holding the amber liquid up to the light.

"Indeed, indeed," said the priest, sipping appreciatively. Now was probably not the moment to be bringing this up, but there was never a good time, in his view. He looked discreetly across the room and saw through the double doors that Sophie was busy with the food. The babble of female voices would ensure that he wasn't overheard.

"I had a message from someone who asked me to let you know that you are expecting a son."

Father O'Leary had debated with himself what form of words would best convey this news, and had almost said 'another son' but decided against it.

Liam gulped down the rest of the drink and spluttered. Theresa must have had her twenty-week scan. Of all the people for her to tell! She could have just rung him, or written to him – but maybe she was worried about somebody seeing the letter.

"You needn't worry. The party concerned divulged

the news in the confessional and therefore placed me under an obligation not to reveal it to anyone else. But I was asked to let you know that until the child is eighteen, his paternity will not be revealed, and you are not expected to take any responsibility for him *whatsoever*." The emphasis on the last word could only have come from Theresa. "The mother has decided to emigrate to Canada, where she has some family connections, and have the baby and start a new life out there."

Liam couldn't believe it. He would have another son, and he wouldn't even know what he looked like, or what his favourite games were, and maybe he might never meet him in his whole life. The enormity of what he had done struck him like a blow in the stomach.

"I would suggest," said the priest, clearing his throat, and Liam thought, here it comes, the killer punch, "that you have got away lightly on this matter, and that it would be incumbent upon you to count your blessings." He paused and nodded significantly towards the kitchen. A bubble of laughter floated out followed by the women moving towards the front door, laden with boxes and cool bags.

Liam nodded and only after the priest had followed the women into the hall, did he realise he hadn't spoken a word during the whole exchange.

"Come on kids. We're ready to go!" he shouted, to get Michelle's attention.

"Can I leave the tower up?" Oisín asked, standing up carefully so that he wouldn't knock it over.

"That is a very special tower, and you can leave it there. We can do some more work on it when we come back." He locked the front door, after checking that he had the crumpled piece of paper with his reading in his jacket pocket, and he walked with his children, one holding each hand, following the trail of people who were coming out of their doors and gateways, and meandering down the road towards the beach.

The blackberries on the hedges by the roadside were bursting with juice and the reed buntings were flitting optimistically among the bushes. The tufts of grass in the middle of the lane when they turned towards the sea were soft underfoot, and Michelle and Oisín skipped alongside him, singing snatches of the hymn. The tide was out, and the huge rock they had nominated as an altar stood proudly dark against the pale blue sky. No clouds threatened rain. Father O'Leary's chasuble flapped in the breeze as he stood behind the altar, making the final preparations. Rugs and blankets, some deckchairs and even a wooden bench had been arranged facing the sea, and neighbours who were familiar, and some less familiar, were sitting and standing around chatting. A cormorant stood sentinel like a lookout from the Penal Days, staring out to sea. Seagulls bickered above, waiting for their spoils from the picnic. The children sat obediently at the front, overawed by the novelty of the situation, and on their best behaviour. Liam watched Sophie chatting to everyone, double-checking that they had their prayers and readings, and that the offertory gifts were laid out. Waves lapped gently, obligingly retreating rather than advancing. Father O'Leary had mixed up the tide tables and had a panic the night before, until Sophie reassured him that all would be well. He hadn't been completely convinced of nature's adherence to the rules until he had seen it for himself. He cleared his throat, and wished he hadn't had that whiskey with Liam. His vocal chords felt a bit constricted.

"Welcome everyone, to this Community Mass, and thanks be to God, the weather has held for us, and the tide is going in the right direction!"

He felt suddenly filled with vigour, as he looked at the faces of his parishioners, some of whom had been cynical about his efforts to create more of a community feel about this precious Sacrament of the Mass.

"Sometimes we slip into a bit of a routine, and Mass is just the place we go to on a Sunday, to catch up with God like we catch up with our friends, fitting Him in to our busy schedules. I thought that having our Community Mass here, in a place where we come for recreation and relaxation, a place where we can see the majesty of God's creation all around us, might help us to view Him in a different light. It might help us to talk to Him as someone at the centre of our lives, rather than just a chore to fit in with everything else. Our prayers to Him today are about thanksgiving, and praise for the wonders of His world, and the joy He gives us in our lives."

Alison let most of the ceremony wash over her, its rituals as unfamiliar to her as the location was to everyone else. But when Liam stood up, she paid attention, knowing how nervous he was and wanting him to feel her support.

Sophie had her hands clasped tightly together, and she was willing him to succeed, to speak confidently and clearly. She had heard him rehearse the reading several times, and he still stumbled over parts of it, although the words were familiar.

"The first reading is from St Paul's letter to the Corinthians." Liam looked across at Sophie, and recited the first lines without reading from the page. *"Love is patient and kind; it is not jealous or conceited or proud. Love is not ill-mannered or selfish or irritable. Love does not keep a record of wrongs; love is not happy with evil, but is happy with the truth. Love never gives up, and its faith, hope and patience never fail . . ."*

Alison was embarrassed to feel tears welling up. She hadn't brought a tissue and missed the next few sentences, while she scrabbled in her handbag trying to find one.

"Now that I have grown up I have no need for childish ways. What we see now is like a dim image in a mirror; then we shall see face to face. What I know now is only partial; then it will be complete, as complete as God's knowledge of me. Meanwhile, these three remain: faith, hope and love – and the greatest of these is love."

Liam sat down, relieved to be finished, forgetting to say, *"This is the word of the Lord."*

The priest said the words, and wondered was it his imagination that the congregation's response, "Thanks be to God," had a bit more resonance here on the beach, than he usually heard on a Sunday morning?

Sophie reached out and touched Liam's arm, as he took a deep breath. "Thanks," she said.

"No problem," he replied, his chest swelling. Life was good. Only when he had been reading the words out loud had it sunk in that Theresa had gone away because she loved him. He didn't deserve that kind of love, after what he had done to her, and nearly done to his family. He had no way of making it up to Theresa now, but despite her message, he would leave the bank account in place for the boy. He might need it when he grew up. But it wasn't about money at all. He made a vow to really live by the words he had just read out to Sophie, and to appreciate how close he had been to losing the love of the most important people to him in the world.

"Are you OK?" Sophie asked, seeing his eyes tightly shut.

"Just saying a little prayer," he said, and smiled at her.

Chapter Twenty-six

"I can't believe it's nearly a year since we met," Sophie said as they lounged by the pool, after a sauna and a very cold plunge. There was only a very slight hum of traffic from outside, coming in through the skylights in the high domed white ceiling. Women wandered around in white fluffy robes and slippers, and although it was much busier than the spa in Connemara, everyone had the same air of calm relaxation. Outside, instead of skylarks and waving grasses, there was the buzz of Long Acre, full of Christmas shoppers and tourists wandering around Covent Garden. They were fitting in a half-day session at the Sanctuary to wind down before their birthday dinner at the Savoy.

"Just the two of us," Alison had said. "I feel like I'll be celebrating for most of this month, with the work do, and Mum organising a family party, and Lisa's booked a meal for a few friends next week. Tonight is just for us."

"Liam has a surprise for me, when I get back, he said," Sophie smiled. "I can't believe he's looking after the children for three days without me. Ger was a bit upset at being usurped, I think, because she was originally going to have them when I was due to come at Easter."

"Oh yes, of course. So Liam is quite happy to take charge?"

"Delighted. I think he wants to prove to me that he has really changed. The kids had big plans to keep him busy!"

"So what's been your favourite part of the weekend?"

"Feeling better than I have done for months. It's six weeks since I finished the chemo, and I'm starting to feel a bit more normal. Seeing London again has been great. I loved the London Eye. The views were incredible, and the fact that you're moving is so cool, compared to going up the Duomo in Florence, or the Eiffel Tower. I really want to take the kids up on that when they're a bit older. I don't miss the London lifestyle, though. A few years ago, I went through a phase of wondering what life would have been like if we'd stayed here. I thought maybe we'd taken the easy option by just going home to settle down. But I'm delighted that we did. London will always be here to visit, but I'm glad I'm not living here."

"Me too," said Alison, and Sophie sat up.

"You're not serious!"

"I told them today that I don't want to come back. Steve said they were ready to offer me a partnership next year, when I finish the projects I'm working on.

They want to send Maurice to Galway to take over from me, and continue the great work I started."

"That's just exactly what you wanted!" Sophie clapped her hands, and then realised that everyone was staring at them. "Sorry." She put her hand over her mouth.

"It *was* what I wanted. Not any more. Lisa will kill me when I tell her, but there isn't much for me to come back to. Mum says she'll come over really often to stay, and the flights are so cheap I can come and see friends for weekends whenever I want."

"That's great news! I wish we had a proper drink to toast with. Carrot juice doesn't really do it." Sophie held up her glass. "To new beginnings!"

"Thanks for being such a great friend over the last year. I couldn't have done it without you."

"Wait 'til you see the grand opening event. We are going to take them all by storm!"

They had facials and manicures, and emerged tingling onto the busy street as darkness fell and the lights came on.

"It's like a fairy land, isn't it?" Sophie said, as they passed garishly dressed shop windows and miniature Christmas trees garlanded with tiny white lights. The jingling of a bell startled Sophie, as she stepped off the pavement, in front of a bicycle wheel.

The rickshaw rider smiled as he swerved around her. "Sorry, love."

The women looked at each other. "These are a new phenomenon for me!" said Sophie. "Another import from China!"

"To Bankside, please," Alison said, and they climbed in, laughing.

Sophie leaned out to make sure she didn't miss anything as they trundled down the sidestreets behind the Strand, the rickshaw rider puffing with the effort, pinging his bell at careless shoppers who got in his way. Snatches of music drifted out of shops, and richly scented air wafted from salons as partygoers were made even more glamorous. They crossed the junction at Waterloo Bridge without mishap, despite Sophie's impression that cars, taxis and motorbikes were converging on them from all directions. She gasped as they crossed the bridge. Far around the curve of the river she could see the tops of the Parliament buildings, with Big Ben glowing benevolently on the city, faced by the purple and pink-lit capsules of the London Eye. A brightly spotted catamaran swept under the bridge as they passed, and a police launch left a busy white trail as it accelerated under the arches. The gloomy grey concrete of the Royal Festival Hall was unrecognisable in the darkness, with rotating holograms projected onto every flat surface. The loops of white lights strung between the lampposts along the embankment seemed to go on forever. They turned down a quiet street and followed the line of the river past Gabriel's Wharf and Coin Street, buzzing with late evening drinkers and gourmet pizza eaters. Sophie loved the cobbled yard outside Alison's quirky-looking house, and she stepped out of the rickshaw feeling like an anachronistic princess. Alison paid the driver and he turned slowly, his tyres slipping on the damp cobbles.

"G'night, ladies," he shouted, as he retraced his route.

"That was fantastic, thanks!" Sophie enthused as they went inside.

"I thought you'd enjoy that. They've only been around for a few years. Really expensive, but good fun."

They got dressed and cracked open a bottle of champagne. Sophie stood at the window looking down at the river. "You are going to keep this place, aren't you?" she asked, overawed by what it must have cost. Alison was a dark horse when it came to how much she earned, but it must be a lot.

"I'm not sure. I wouldn't want to rent it out, with all my things in it, and I'm not sure how much use I'll get out of it, just for weekend visits."

"You really mean it, don't you?" Sophie paused. "Even without the man in your life?" She wondered how much Alison was waiting and waiting for Ronan to reappear and make a lifelong commitment.

Alison nodded, sipping her champagne. "I'm sure. I've hit my target of a size 12 dress for the Christmas party. I feel so much healthier, and so much happier in Galway. Work is enjoyable rather than just a source of stress. A man would be a bonus, but Ronan made me realise that a man who is just in your bed isn't the whole answer, either. I wanted to share everything with him – the ups and downs of the kids, adventures exploring new countries together, talking about things that matter. That's what I thought we were aiming for. Maybe I was being naïve. It still hurts like mad that he just went, and didn't even want to talk about how things could be better. I thought after a few days he'd come back and we'd talk about it, but I haven't even had an email or a text. It feels just like the first time . . . unfinished business."

Sophie nodded, and wondered if Lisa's advice to Alison about being tough had been the best. Still, Alison had been on a couple of dates with guys from the Chamber of Commerce and, although she hadn't been struck by any of them, at least she had her confidence back.

"You're not tempted to get in touch with him? At least this time around you know where to find him."

"What would be the point? I've told him I love him, and I want to be with him for the long term, and I would love to get to know his children better. What else could I say?"

"You're right. If that's not what he wants, a conversation isn't going to change his mind."

The taxi Alison had booked turned up at eight, and they crossed the river again, riding on the euphoria of champagne bubbles. "The Savoy is the only place in London where you drive on the wrong side of the road," the cab driver said, as he dropped them off, having turned onto the right-hand side of the short road, so that they could climb out beside the hotel door. A doorman helped them out, and then gallantly swept his arm to guide them into the hotel. An army of white-jacketed waiters glided around the restaurant, their gold epaulettes shimmying as they walked. A maitre d' greeted them graciously and Sophie was delighted when they were shown to a window table with a riverside view. The tinkle of fine crystal and china and the refined laughter of other diners set the tone for a really special meal. As they perused the menus, the sommelier stepped up, clearing his throat to get their attention.

"If I may, ladies? He presented them with a bottle of Bollinger, and an underling appeared behind him with a silver tray and two glasses. "With the compliments of Mr Liam Hanrahan."

"Impressive," said Alison, whistling as the champagne was poured. "Ten points for initiative."

Sophie smiled. The new Liam was certainly a lot more attentive.

"Happy birthday!"

They were glad their friend the doorman was able to summon a taxi with a whistle and a click of his fingers as soon as they stepped outside. Otherwise they might have spoiled their sophisticated image by staggering to the Strand, giggling helplessly.

"Good night, girls?" the cabbie said, as he drove off.

"Most definitely," said Sophie, glad of their demotion from ladies to girls. Must be the giggling, she thought, unable to remember when she had last been this drunk. She didn't have to fly home until Monday morning so they could recover tomorrow.

"As birthday celer . . . celerbrations go, I think that

was pretty good," slurred Alison as they fell through the apartment door, kicking off their high heels.

"Me too. Bed now," said Sophie, downing a pint of water and two Paracetamol to try and fight off the hangover before it set in.

Breakfast at midday perched on a high stool by the window at the top of the Tate Modern seemed like heaven.

"I think you should keep your London pad. We have to do this more often," Sophie said, munching her second *pain au chocolat*.

"It does look particularly nice today," Alison admitted, as the sunlight reflected off the water far below. They watched muffled-up couples meandering along the riverside and crossing the Millennium Bridge. A guy on roller blades glided past, swerving like a snowboarder as he overtook the slower pedestrians.

After two cappuccinos Sophie was raring to go.

"Between breast-feeding and sleepless nights and then the worry of the last six months, my social life has been limited to say the least. I'm making a New Year's resolution to go out more."

"To get hangovers?" Alison wasn't feeling too bad.

"No, to live a little."

"Sophie, you live a lot. You are incredible – so strong and positive about everything. Your kids are fantastic, and that's down to you, in large part. I'd happily ditch the social life and have kids to read bedtime stories to, and to tell me about their day at school, and who they had a fight with in the playground."

"Maybe it's not too late," said Sophie, patting her knee. "Maeve's sister only met someone when she was forty. She's forty-three now, with two kids."

"Scary!" said Alison.

"Well, you just never know what's around the corner."

"As we've both discovered, this year."

"Fancy a walk along the river? We could see how far we get before lunch."

"We've just had breakfast."

"So, what? Diets are out the window this weekend."

"You're on. We don't even have to retrace our steps. When we're tired we can get a train back to London Bridge, or even a boat!"

When Sophie looked through the living-room window, she saw Liam on the floor with Oisín, and what looked very like a Lego Tower Bridge. Michelle was serving them with pink plastic cups of tea, oblivious to their preoccupation with the building task. She glanced up and saw Sophie's face at the window. "Mammy!" she screeched, and ran to the front door, just as Sophie opened it. She hurled herself into Sophie's arms.

"How's my best girl?" Sophie looked at her daughter, who looked as if she'd grown in just three days.

"Fine. And the boys are fine too. I minded them for you until you came back."

"Thanks a million. They look fine to me. I think you did a great job."

Sophie's welcome from the boys was equally rapturous, and she flopped on the sofa, not caring that it had acquired some new jam and chocolate stains or that the floor was completely strewn with toys.

"It's good to be home," she said.

"I like your nails," Michelle said. "They're really nice, now, like Alison's."

Liam said "It's good to have you home. Although we've had a great time, haven't we, guys?"

The children nodded, but they leaned against her, taking turns to kiss her and hug her, not even bickering. Just happy to be close to her.

"So how were the big city lights?"

"Still big. We should take the kids over soon. They'd love it."

"You weren't tempted by the glamorous life then?" Liam had been a bit worried that she would be unsettled by the weekend away.

"Not at all. And do you know what? Alison's going to stay in Galway! I don't know what the work situation will be, but she told them she's not going back."

"Wow, that's a big change for her," Liam said, but he was glad for Sophie. He sometimes wondered if she got on better with Alison than some of the friends she'd known for years.

"She said she might buy one of the chalets in the holiday village."

"She'd be mad. They're completely overpriced. She'd be lonely in the winter, too."

"It's only three miles out the road!" Sophie said.

"But it's only going to have people in it for a few months of the year. She might not feel safe, if she's the only one living there."

"I have a feeling there will be more than just her living there all the year round. The level of interest has been fantastic you know."

Sophie was really enjoying the job – she was organising the PR and marketing as well as the launch event. Michelle was settled at school now and, after the Christmas holidays, Sophie was looking forward to getting stuck back into finalising the launch. They were hoping to have the local TD cutting the ribbon, but the lady in question was being noncommittal about her diary until the New Year. Like any good politician, she was probably waiting to see if something better came along.

The children were giggling and Michelle had her fingers over her mouth to stop herself from speaking.

"What's all this?" Sophie said, looking at Liam.

Michelle took her by the hand and led her upstairs to the spare room. Oisín flung the door open. Sophie gasped. The room had been completely fitted out as a home office, with a new laptop sitting on a beech wood desk, and a little filing cabinet with a printer and set of filing trays.

"I thought you could set yourself up from home, to do the freelancing you were talking about," Liam said, and she hugged him. They were planning for a future again, and that felt so good, after feeling like life was on hold for nearly six months.

"Happy birthday!"

Michelle opened the drawer of the desk with a flourish, to reveal a cake, in the shape of the number forty. "Auntie Ger made it for you."

"Did she now?" said Sophie, and she couldn't stop smiling.

Chapter Twenty-seven

The weather forecast was good, but Alison knew from experience that in February there was little relationship between the forecast and the reality. Just as in the UK, the meteorologists seemed to focus on the South East, and forget that the Gulf Stream played puck with the weather along the west coast. She didn't care. Even if it rained, the launch would be a success. Sophie had done a fantastic job. She had lined up photographers from all the local papers. The TD who was cutting the ribbon had been involved in a financial scandal in November, and this was her first public event in her crusade to repair her tarnished image before the General Election predicted for the autumn. The photographers would have a field day. The catering was being provided by the hotel management college, with the final-year students managing it as a project that counted towards their exams. They would be trying really hard, and it was hardly costing Alison

411

anything. She could see chefs in gleaming whites scurrying around to prepare the buffet, which was going to have an ice sculpture designed around a maritime theme. Oysters and caviare were being served on silver platters. Waiters stood around with trays of champagne and Bucks Fizz. A huge gazebo had been erected over the central garden which could have been a prize-winning entry in the Chelsea flower show. Low-level planting in shades of white and grey, wild grasses and smooth sea stones were complemented by tiny purple-headed alpines and vivid pink spreading rock plants. There were even bougainvilleas and palm trees, although it might be a bit far north for them, Sophie had advised. Seán, who had completely scorned Alison's idea of landscaping, admitted that it looked stunning. Steve, her boss, had flown in last night to stay at a local hotel. He was due to arrive at any minute, and would no doubt make a speech that claimed most of the credit for the project even though he had never set foot in Galway before. Alison had already resigned herself to that. But she was staying and Steve would be flying back to London. Good luck to him. She was seriously thinking of launching out on her own, but first things first.

Three cars drove down the bamboo-lined laneway that gave complete privacy from the main road. A statuesque woman Alison recognised from the *News* emerged from the first car, the door held by her driver.

"Hello, how are you," Alison greeted her, and showed her to the marquee where Seán took over, delighted that he had the opportunity to shake the politician's hand. When it came to financial wheeling and dealing, she and Seán would get on like a house on fire.

Alison left them to it, going to check the show house to make sure everything was just right. She had bid for it, but was up against another buyer who had topped her offer so handsomely she couldn't compete. It would have been handy to just move in, with it furnished and decorated so nicely. Sophie had been involved in the interior design, and it was modern and stylish without any clutter. Just what Alison liked. Still, she was enjoying house-hunting, and it was giving her a good insight into the local competition among developers. She was aiming to have all her stuff moved over from London by the end of the month. The riverside house had sold for much more than she had expected. Alison had been so embarrassed by the amount that she had halved the number when she told her mother. The management of the Globe Theatre had bought it, and planned to extend the museum through the side wall of their current exhibition, maintaining the external appearance, and recreating a Shakespearian period home inside. It would take a couple of years, and Alison was looking forward to seeing what they would do. She had found it easier to let the house go, knowing that it was going to be put to such a use. Steve had told her she was mad to get out of the property market in London now because it would be impossible to come back in when she got tired of Ireland. He just didn't understand, and she hadn't bothered to try and explain.

The sandalwood pot-pourri scent in the hall of the

show house reminded her of the spa in Connemara, and she closed her eyes, going back over the year in her mind. The anticipation of turning forty had been much worse than the arrival. The anxiety and the stress that had been a part of her for years were now completely gone. She felt fitter and healthier, and she was drinking less red wine and coffee and more water. Her highlights had almost all grown out, and at the end of year party in London everyone had said how fantastic she looked. Glancing now in the living-room mirror, she agreed with them. Her waist was more accentuated, and her skin was clear and bright without its customary layers of make-up. She just wore mascara, lipstick and eyeliner, and the natural tones of her skin were brought out by the honey-coloured fine wool suit she had found in Brown Thomas. She stepped to the window, drawn as always to the sight of water, and saw Ronan's car parked behind the others. Seeing him was the only part of today she was dreading. He had avoided her since September, not turning up to the regular meetings with Seán and sending financial reports by email. She had found it easier that way too, and was grateful. But he had to show his face today and Alison hadn't quite decided how she should play it.

She saw Sophie scurrying across the glass-covered walkway and decided to intercept her, to confirm the order of the speeches. There was a protocol with politics and religion in Ireland that was beyond Alison, and Sophie seemed to have an instinct for it.

"Have you got a minute?"

She heard Ronan's voice behind her in the hallway.

He sounded nervous, which was most unlike him. For the first time, she hadn't felt his presence before seeing him, as if his aura had diminished in some way. She turned. "Hello, Ronan. I thought you'd come today." She managed to keep her voice neutral.

"How could I stay away? It looks fantastic. You and Sophie have done a great job." He came towards her and she wondered if he would go for the polite social kiss. She turned her cheek slightly and he obliged.

"Listen, I have something to tell you." He was holding onto both her arms and looking at her intensely.

She fought the urge to grab his face and kiss him. "I don't think there's time, really. Can it wait?" She waved towards the crowd gathering outside. "We need more than a snatched few seconds, don't we?"

"You've no plans for afterwards?"

Alison shook her head. Sophie had suggested that they go back to her house for a drink, for a debrief, but Alison wanted to take her out to lunch the next day as a treat, and they would talk about it then. Alison would be ready for a hot bath by the time they had finally dispatched the journos and dignitaries – they would all stay until the drink ran out, and there seemed to be plenty of that, judging by the bill she had signed off.

"Meet you back here, at about six?" he said. "It should be all over by then."

Alison nodded and hurried off to see Sophie.

While the politician was making her speech about regeneration in the West of Ireland, Alison stared across the crowd at Ronan, who seemed to be studiously avoiding eye contact with her. What was he going to tell her? There had been an urgency about him that was unlikely if he was just saying they were finished for good, but she wouldn't let herself hope. She hadn't even had a chance to tell Sophie, who was looking anxiously at her to make sure she was OK. The ribbon-cutting and social pleasantries washed over her in a blur, but Seán was going around giving her lots of credit, telling two of his cronies that she was the best thing that ever happened to his business. She smiled, her face aching with the effort.

Alison's feet were killing her as she hobbled along the path to the show house, and she was desperate for a drink. She had been carrying around a glass of water all afternoon, determined to keep it together. Sophie had just hugged her and congratulated her on a great success. The TD had got away lightly, with the journalists in a benevolent mood after their out-of-season 'freebie'. The politician had hinted to Alison that if there was anything she could do for her, in the future, just to let her know. Alison had smiled. Finally she was part of the back-scratching club that made the world of business in Ireland go around. The last vehicle had swept up the lane ten minutes ago, and she couldn't avoid the moment of truth with Ronan any longer. He had moved his car to the driveway outside the show house. Lazy thing.

"Hello," he said tentatively, opening the front door of the show house as she walked up.

"Hello. Making yourself comfortable, are you?" she

couldn't resist. He was being a bit cavalier, although the new owner had agreed for the show house to be open to the public today.

"Glass of wine?" He was holding one out to her. Where had he got that? She followed him into the living-room. "So, how have you been?"

She sat on the sofa facing the full-length window, and he stood in front of her, his tall frame in silhouette against the sky outside. An up-lighter glowed in one corner of the room. He had had the cheek to light a fire, too. The room was cosy and homely.

"I hope you're planning to clear up afterwards," she said.

"Of course I am. You've never really seen my housekeeping skills in action, have you?"

"No." She couldn't help laughing.

"I do have some hidden talents in that direction."

"I think you've got lots of hidden talents," Alison said, unable to stop grinning. It was so good to see him.

"I was wondering if we could give things another try." He sounded more like his old self, not nervous now that he had broken the ice with her. But did he think he only had to smile and raise his eyebrow and she would come running back?

"Has anything changed?"

"Well, I took your advice about space for the kids. I've bought a house."

"Have you? Where is it?"

"You're sitting in it." He grinned, enjoying the moment of shock.

"It was you!"

"Sorry. I wanted to surprise you."

"I nearly paid fifty thousand euro over the top to outbid you!"

"Seán would never have let you have it. He knew I wanted it."

Alison suppressed her anger at their complicity, and she was still confused about what Ronan was suggesting.

"I've really missed you. I've tried to live without you, and that's why I kept away from all the meetings as well. To see if I could survive by not seeing you at all. But I'm miserable. I love you like I've never loved anyone else. I knew I'd have to do something tangible for you to believe that. So I bought this place. But I'm making no assumptions."

"So you're not asking me to come and be your little woman, and keep it nice and clean for you?" she said sarcastically. Her heart was pounding. He could be so frustrating. Was he making a commitment, or not?

"No, I don't think we should rush into anything. We've made that mistake twice already! You should keep your own place too. I took on board what you said about the children, and I've had a long heart-to-heart with Brian. I said I'd buy a decent-sized place for them to come and stay, and sometimes you might be here, and other times they would have me to themselves. He said he was OK with that. Nancy admitted that she really likes you, and she would like to spend more time with you. Could we try again, starting at the beginning, with me taking nothing for granted, and take it one step at a time?"

"We'll have to agree some terms," she said mockingly, pretending to take out a notebook from her bag.

"I wouldn't expect anything less." He kissed her and sank down on the sofa beside her. They made love in front of the fire to the sound of the waves crashing on the black rocks outside, harbingers of a change in the weather.

THE END

If you enjoyed *More to Life*, don't miss
out on *Daddy's Girl*, also by
Sharon Mulrooney.

Here is a sneak preview of
Chapter one . . .

www.poolbeg.com

Daddy's Girl

SHARON MULROONEY

POOLBEG

Chapter One

They were already laughing when the condom fell off. Somehow, when it did, the wrinkled piece of soggy rubber seemed to be hilarious, and Maria giggled helplessly. She snuggled up to Joe and they fell asleep. They were woken at eleven o'clock by the strident ringing of the doorbell. They looked at each other in a half-awake state, curious about who was at the door, but not inclined to get up and answer it. Suddenly the letterbox flapped, and a voice yodelled, 'Yoohoo, Joe darling, are you not up yet?'

'Oh my God!' he shot upright in the bed. 'It's Mum! Quick, you've got to hide!'

Before Maria knew it, she was standing in the bath, hidden behind the shower curtain, her beautiful green velvet dress and sexy black underwear bundled in her arms, and her feet in a puddle of water.

Joe yelled, 'Just a minute, Mum!' and pulling on his

tracksuit bottoms he opened the front door of the flat.

'Hello, love.' His mother kissed his cheek and wrinkled her nose at the pungent garlic odour mixed with stale cigarette smoke and alcohol on his breath.

'You were out late last night, I gather,' she said with slight distaste, making her way into the kitchen.

'It was the Medical School Ball,' he muttered.

'Oh, was it any good? Any nice girls there?' she asked coyly.

'It was a great night, but I went with a gang of the lads.' He flicked the switch on the electric kettle, and avoided looking at her.

'Where's Mike this morning? I suppose he's already up and in the library, studying?' Mrs Shaw enquired. She liked Mike. He seemed like a nice lad, and a good influence on Joe.

'I haven't seen him this morning.' They had struck a deal that Mike would steer clear last night, and stay at Michelle's place.

His mother raided the breadbin, was disappointed with the sad crust of wholemeal bread, and then delved into one of her shopping bags.

'I brought some doughnuts. I'm down in Galway for the day with Rita Duffy. I said I'd help her to find an outfit for her daughter's wedding.'

'That's nice.' Joe scratched his head and tried to shake it clear.

'Then I thought I'd pop in here for elevenses with you.'

'Mmm.' He sipped his coffee gratefully.

'Although it looks more like breakfast for you.'

Joe sank his teeth into the jam doughnut, and his salivary glands leapt into action as the tart flavour of the raspberry jam hit his tongue. He stood up and filled a stolen Guinness pint-glass with water from the tap and drank it in one go.

'Did you have a lot to drink?' His mother looked up at him doubtfully. He was a bit pale. Was that a trace of a lipstick-mark on his neck?

'A fair bit. It is the big social event of the year, you know.'

'I'm not disapproving, Joe. You're a student. You have to have a social life. But at the same time, I'd hate if it affected your studying. The exams are coming up soon . . .'

'I know, Mum. Don't worry. I'll be fine,' he said absently. Why did she have to pick this morning, of all days, to 'pop in'?

She looked at her watch. 'I must use your loo, and then I'm off. I said I'd meet Rita for lunch'.

She missed Joe's look of alarm as she bustled off to the bathroom.

Maria heard the bathroom door opening, and froze. She had managed to manoeuvre herself into her underwear, but she needed help for the dress. Standing in a black Wonderbra, G-string and sheer black pull-ups, she wondered whether it would be better for Mrs. Shaw to swish back the curtain and discover her naked, rather than kitted out like a playgirl. Her face burned. She had to cross her legs when she heard the tinkling sound of pee, and she exhaled gratefully and took another deep breath concealed by the sound of the toilet flushing. She started to shiver uncontrollably and inched away from the shower curtain so that she wouldn't make it rustle. Joe's mother hummed as she washed her hands, touched up her lipstick and patted her hair.

The door closed and Maria nearly collapsed to her knees in the bath. The bottom of her dress was trailing in the pool of water and some bizarre capillary action in the fabric had made a dark stain soak right up the length of the dress. At last, she heard the front door opening again and had one leg over the side of the bath when she heard Mrs Shaw's parting comment.

'I'm glad you're not involved with anyone, Joe. You have a lot of work to do, and there's plenty of time for girls when you're qualified.'

Joe's murmured response was lost in the rustling of the shower curtain. Maria sat on the loo, her first doubts about Joe creeping into her mind.

Joe yelled, 'She's gone,' through the bathroom door. 'Do you want a coffee?'

'Yes, please,' she said, carrying the dress over her arm. It was soaking wet. 'Joe, can I borrow some clothes off you? My dress is soaked.'

'Sure, help yourself.'

She splashed her face with cold water and looked

closely at her bloodshot eyes. What a night! She had drunk three cocktails before the meal, then wine, champagne and had finished off with Baileys. She patted her face dry with loo-roll. She wouldn't touch the towels that were hanging on the back of the door. They looked like they hadn't been washed since the beginning of the term.

When Maria came into the kitchen in Joe's Gap khakis, cinched at the waist with his brown belt, and a big white shirt with the sleeves rolled up, he thought she had never looked so gorgeous.

'You should always wear guy's clothes – you look great.' He took her in his arms and kissed the top of her head.

'Thanks.' She smiled up at him. 'Where's that coffee?'

'Sorry about Mum coming.' Joe was gulping down another pint of water with two Solpadeine tablets.

'It's OK. How is she?' Maria didn't know why she asked. She had never met the woman, and was unlikely to, judging by what she had overheard.

'Fine. She's down shopping for the day.' He sounded a bit sheepish, but she couldn't be sure. Was he ashamed of her? Was she not good enough for his mother?

Joe looked across the table at Maria. He would have loved to tell his mother about her, but he couldn't face the interrogation. What did her father do? Where did she come from? What were her ambitions? For that, read, 'Would she distract him from his study? Would she appreciate what kind of family she would be marrying into? Would she be a good doctor's wife?' Maria would hate being questioned, and it was a bit too soon for all that anyway, so it was easier to pretend that Maria didn't exist.

Maria looked into his hazel eyes, then at his sandy tousled hair sticking up, full of wax from last night, a little blotch of red jam smeared on his cheek, and she thought, if I can find him attractive with bad breath, morning stubble and a hangover, this must be the real thing. She smiled at him, and he smiled back, relieved. She obviously hadn't heard his mother's comment.

Pauline laughed like mad when Maria told her the story.

'But wouldn't it bother you if your man didn't tell his mother that he was seeing you?' Maria asked, wringing out her hand-washing in the kitchen sink.

Pauline snorted. 'Chance would be a fine thing. I have to find a man first, and then I'll worry about whether he tells his mam. I wouldn't worry about it, seriously, Maria.'

'But it's been a year.' That was ages. More than long enough to know whether she met the mother's criteria. 'I love him, Pauline, and I can't imagine being with anyone else. What if I'm never going to be good enough for his mam?'

Pauline sighed, and Maria wanted to kick herself. She'd done it again. Pauline didn't even have a man, and here she was, wittering on about her insecurities.

'He's a lovely guy, Maria. The good ones are always real Mammy's boys. He'll introduce you when he's good and ready. Just live for the moment, as they say.'

'You're dead right. Did I tell you he gave me an orchid last night, as a buttonhole? It reminded me of our Debs. Do you remember that?'

'Yeah, I took Larry, who went off to be a priest. Trust me to pick that one! Do you remember the party back at Geraldine's house afterwards?'

Maria laughed. 'Her mam was on patrol, so me and Martin O'Dowd went out the back and had a good snog on the garden bench.'

'There was a queue for that bench, wasn't there? Even I got a snog that night!'

Pauline was always putting herself down, and sometimes Maria found that frustrating. Ever since school, Pauline had lacked the confidence to make herself look really nice. Maria was always lending her things and showing her hairstyles in magazines. If Pauline would only do something with her hair, and lose some weight, she would be really attractive. She had a great smile, huge eyes and fantastic skin. But Maria didn't want to push it too far and hurt Pauline's feelings. She sloshed her woollen jumpers and silky underwear into a bucket and nudged open the back door with her bum.

Pauline watched Maria hanging the clothes on the line and sighed. Maria had a great figure and even with a hangover and her hair all frizzy, she looked fantastic.

What other students hand-washed their clothes, not because they were too lazy to go down to the laundrette at the bottom of the hill, but because the clothes were wool and silk? Maria had always had style, since she was about nine years old. She had a feather-cut hairstyle and French polo necks long before anyone else in her class. Pauline buttered another piece of toast and sipped her tea. It didn't matter, she told herself. She was going to be a successful lawyer with no time to waste on men.